Li

Russell Lucas was born in Bombay and
moved to Britain when he was sixteen.
In 1952 he returned to India and
worked there for three years before
coming back to work in the motorcar
industry. In 1990, he published his first
collection of short stories, *Evenings at
Mongini's*. He is married and lives in
Bedfordshire.

Lip Service

An Oedipal Fable

RUSSELL LUCAS

Minerva

A Minerva Paperback
LIP SERVICE

First published in Great Britain 1991
by William Heinemann Ltd
This Minerva edition published 1992
by Mandarin Paperbacks
Michelin House, 81 Fulham Road, London SW3 6RB

Minerva is an imprint of the Octopus Publishing Group,
a division of Reed International Books Limited

The quotation on p. 284 is from *Night and Day*
by Tom Stoppard, and is reprinted by permission
of Faber & Faber Ltd.
The quotation on p. 307 is from 'Der Matrosen-Song'
by Bertolt Brecht, and is reprinted by permission
of Suhrkamp Verlag, Munich.

A CIP catalogue record for this title
is available from the British Library
ISBN 0 7493 9992 9

Printed and bound in Great Britain
by Cox and Wyman Limited, Reading, Berks

For Leslie, Julian and Pamela

Acknowledgements

I would like to thank Nadia Lawrence,
without whose friendship, constructive support and
creative insights this might not have flown.
Also Toby Eady my agent and Helena Petrovna,
who is fondly remembered.

Chapter 1

*It's a wise tin of milk
that knows its own cow.*

— Anon.

In 1957, Laszlo Horvath arrived in England with his beloved Moura. She was a chubby blonde with high Magyar cheekbones, deep-set blue eyes (Danube blue was how she described them), full petulant lips, large even teeth and a warm flirtatious smile. She was twenty-two years of age. Laszlo was just two months old, bald with wisps of chicken fluff beginning to appear above his ears and around the bulge of his substantial brachycephalic head. He had been baptised, circumcised and vaccinated against whooping cough before their departure for the West. Moura, proud of the amplitude of milk in her swollen mammaries, was unselfconscious of unbuttoning her blouse to reveal a plump segment of breast and the dark Mickey Mouse nose of a nipple she wiggled into Laszlo's rapacious pink maw for instant pacification. Moura's Mickey Mouse nose of a nipple journeyed (with its twin) through Budapest, Vienna, Frankfurt and Paris to London as she was consigned by officials in a serpentine route across Europe, dribbling sustenance into her cherubic Laszlo. Her lovers, for Moura had many, exulted about muscatels, dates, figs, black olives, prunes and even beetles; and their lyrical celebration of the shape, colour, texture and size of her dugs was something she had come to expect from the least imaginative of her partners. Oh, how they enjoyed plugging her Mickey Mouse noses into their eye-sockets, ears and nostrils, rolling them against velvet phalloi, biting, licking and chewing the last drop of pleasure from the voluptuous brown snouts.

Moura loved the sun, bead curtains, taking showers, ikons,

1

Matisse interiors, oranges, the smell of frying garlic, red wine, cheap jewellery, strong perfume, laughter, men with hard, flat stomachs, Art Nouveau prints, the work of Hector Guimard, the sound of counter-tenors, the face of Edwige Feuillère, Scriabin, white doves, Samoyed dogs, the female superior position, leather, silk knickers, the character of St Francis, Brazilian coffee, anisette, Jesus, flowering avocados, crème-de-menthe, chinoiserie, De Sica's *Bicycle Thieves*, walking barefoot, le Douanier Rousseau, images of tigers, the unaccompanied violin, making novenas, salted pistachios, Armenians, being kissed behind the ears, sleeping unclothed, her own feet, rain on window-panes, distant trains in the middle of the night, Hieronymus Bosch, the *Arabian Nights*, fields of poppies, yellow roses, circumcised penises, Turkish delight, cobblestones, the Stabat Mater, Aeolian harps, overstrung pianos, fresh prawns, the voice of Callas, glass menageries, coal-barges, goat-cheese, strong brown hands, burning sandalwood, sunflower seeds, street markets, friendships with homosexual men, pampas grass, singing children, ravens, crystallised ginger, fin-de-siècle post-cards, marbles, onyx bidets, lemon trees, the Tarot, accordions, marquetry, ice-frosted glasses, Célestins, the planchette, men with harelips, silver bells, cigar smoke, the Sermon on the Mount, feather boas, fat whores in tight dresses, Django Reinhardt, eucalyptus, snake-skin shoes, fur capes, bamboo screens, sponges, neon lights, lovebites, the smell of tar, playing bezique, freshly laundered sheets, the Latin Mass, coupling before a mirror, the silent films of Charlie Chaplin, aspidistras, striped awnings, oysters, sequinned dresses, pickled walnuts, Carmen Miranda, the sound of frogs, small velour hats, gypsies, sesame bread, family photograph albums, potted palms, duck pâté, the taste of semen, and butterflies. Moura had a butterfly tattooed on each cheek of her rounded arse.

Moura was afflicted by two strange dreams. In both these dreams she found herself naked and immobilised on a marble altar in the centre of a vaulted chamber. She heard what at first sounded like the whisper of distant seas, but as the intensity increased, the sound was transformed into the hissing of snakes and the squealing of bats. Now there were two doors, one on either side of her, that led to the chamber in which she lay. As the sounds of the snakes and bats grew louder, Moura heard the scrape of approaching footsteps and knew that a presence would emerge through one of the doors. Only a micro-moment before the door opened could she apprehend whether her visitor would be the welcome familiar or the undesirable one. The terror of uncertainty resided in that penultimate spasm of dreamtime. The benign phantom was a tiny fellow wearing a high spiked crown, swinging a censer of incense, who crooned as he approached. He had dark curls and a scrolled beard, reminding her of the Jack of Spades. He moved around her trembling body, nuzzling her harmlessly with what felt like the moist snout of a foraging pig, before gliding back through the door. A clairvoyant whom Moura consulted advised her that this was the spirit of Pepin, father of Charlemagne, master of the Holy Roman Empire. It was a sign of benediction. After a dream in which Pepin appeared, Moura never failed to go to mass and offer a novena of thanks, using her favourite saint Rita as an intercessionary. Pepin always presaged good fortune, a windfall, a happy meeting or a new lover.

The second visitor, who was undeniably sinister, was a tall, bald, snarling man with eyes like burning coals. He was lipless with serrated black teeth. He reminded her vaguely of Gurdjieff from a photograph she had once seen. This spirit, wearing a karakul cap at a rakish angle, also entered accompanied by snakes and bats, but when near, he sprang at her, his evil intention, which she intuitively divined, being to bite her nipples off. Moura always awoke when she felt his hot breath against her skin, shaking, soaked in sweat, screaming herself out of the nightmare. This spirit, she was assured, was Saladin the Saracen. He came to punish her for recent acts of bad faith or omission of charity. Moura responded to the appearance of the dreaded Mohammedan by placing, when unseen, small gifts in some passing stranger's shopping basket, like a piece of salami, a salted herring or a bag of sugared almonds. As a supplementary act of devotion, she refrained from tobacco, alcohol and sexual friction for at least seven days. This was usually sufficient to keep Saladin at bay for several months, but after a visit from the Saracen there was always something unpleasant ahead: a urinary infection, a loss of money or a romantic betrayal.

Moura, a friendly girl, had always enjoyed men. The first time, the time she remembered sentimentally as her official defloration, was with a sixteen-year-old butcher's assistant, although she had facilitated his ingress by removing her hymenal impediment with an experimental cucumber several weeks earlier. He was a thin, beaky youth with quick, dark eyes, the smudge of a moustache and a left cheek marked by a crimson nevus.

'It is,' she declared playfully, tracing a nail-bitten forefinger around the perimeter of the blemish, 'remarkably like a map of Australia.'

They coupled on a nest of straw-filled sacks occulted by a feathered curtain of gamey iridescence and a row of plucked capons. This initial conjunction gave her such immoderate pleasure that, even before she had tugged her white cotton drawers over her blossoming, thirteen-year-old rump, retrieved her satchel from the top of a barrel of pork offal and hooked it down the cobbled rear alley to school, she concluded that the experience was one that would sustain indefinite repetition.

There was also the grey-haired ex-soldier, a lean, leathery fellow with a tired face and watery grey eyes, who never quite made it. He did tattoos in a tiny room behind the cattle market. It was very much an unofficial piece of enterprise.

'How old are you?' he sniffed suspiciously, taking in her rounded figure and luminous young face in one quiet but sensual glance.

'Don't worry,' Moura laughed, 'it's not for public exhibition. Nobody who matters will even know about it.'

The tattooist licked his lips reflectively.

'Nobody?' he asked.

'Well,' Moura said, 'I may be too young for you to draw pictures on my skin, but I'm also too old for my myopic grandmother to notice the intended location of your artwork.'

4

'And where exactly will my needle be needed?' he enquired, rubbing his crotch vulgarly as his eyes held hers.

'On the cheeks of my arse,' she revealed without a blush.

He was silent for some time. Then, going to the door, he drew a bolt across it.

'You appear to have a tasty tail,' he whispered, walking round her.

He asked her to lift her skirt, which she did briefly.

'It's all there,' she assured him, 'exactly where one would expect an arse to be.'

'You'll have to remove your drawers,' he explained, sucking a tooth thoughtfully.

'All in good time.' She held him off as he tried to press against her. 'I want a butterfly on each cheek,' she said solemnly, escaping around the tattooing table, 'a Red Admiral on the left and a Purple Emperor on the right.'

'I'll have to check my reference book before I start, but I'd like to do a preliminary survey right away.'

Moura laughed at him.

'You only want to get your hands on my bottom.'

'I'll do the job for nothing,' he promised hoarsely, 'absolutely nothing, my little darling.'

He made a clicking noise with his mouth as his tongue adjusted his false teeth. Moura's eyes settled on the bulge in his trousers. She knew all about men's bulges when they came near her, and remembered one of her grandmother's sayings.

'Nothing is for nothing,' Moura observed. 'In other words, I quite understand what you're after.'

'You've the makings of a tart,' he sneered unpleasantly as Moura unlatched the door.

'Hold your tongue,' she warned. 'If I wasn't serious, I wouldn't be wasting your time and mine. Now, let's get down to brass tacks. Is putting your cock up me all you require in payment?'

The man nodded. His eyes danced with lubricity.

'The butterflies will feel sore for a week or so,' he predicted. He was suddenly avuncular.

'We'll have to wait a while then,' she decided.

'Give us a kiss before you leave,' he breathed, coming at her again.

'Don't be a mushy old fool,' she replied, running off.

'Hey, be sociable,' he called. 'Have a hot kromesky or a glass or two of bikaver.'

But she had gone.

When Moura returned on the arranged day, her friend Eva was with her.

'She's my chaperone,' Moura informed the man.

But despite being watched closely by her classmate, the old soldier allowed his fingers to wander occasionally. Eva shouted at him from time to time and the tattooist glared at her angrily.

'Shut your gob or I'll muck up this job,' he snarled.

'OK, but keep your fingers away from her pussy,' Eva snapped.

The man looked around fearfully.

'Keep your voice down,' he pleaded.

When completed, the result was magnificent. A work of art.

'I'll be back in a fortnight,' Moura promised.

He nodded quietly, uncertain whether he would ever see her again. It was a gamble he was willing to take. When the two weeks had passed, Moura turned up at the shop as she said she would. But he was irritated when he saw Eva standing beside her once again.

'What the hell is she doing here?' he demanded.

'Eva is extremely interested in how these things are done,' Moura informed him cheerfully.

'I can't do it with somebody standing over me. God, there's something sleazy about having an onlooker when one is involved in the act of love. Sexual union is a very private affair.'

'Well, that's the way it's got to be,' Moura insisted. 'I don't want you fiddling about with parts you're not using.'

The old tattooist was profoundly unhappy.

'You're a tricky young bitch; that's a fact.'

'We can both call each other nasty names,' Moura said. 'Anyhow, I'm quite prepared to keep my part of the bargain.'

'Can't your friend look the other way?' the man asked. 'Out of the window perhaps? We can manage our business behind that curtain.'

The girls were not persuaded.

'I intend to keep my eye on everything. Like a referee,' Eva declared. 'Moura is only thirteen and needs my protection from any mad excesses.' She held up a whistle that was dangling around her neck. 'One dirty move,' she threatened, 'and our boy-friends from the abattoir will be in here before you can slip your mouse back in its trap.'

The tattooist opened the door. His interest in having Moura had suddenly evaporated.

'I don't want to see either of you near this place again,' he warned.

'I told you he was too decrepit to get it up,' Moura giggled to Eva as they left.

'Go on, fuck off,' the man hissed, stepping back into the unobserved shadows of his shop to make a phallic fist at their backs.

Chapter 2

There was one matter that had occupied Moura's mind a great deal on her journey to London. It was resolved quite suddenly in a railway carriage north of Paris. She was holding Laszlo to her breast with one hand and flicking through the pages of a soggy copy of *Elle* that she'd found in the toilet, when she lingered at the celebration of a beautiful and famous compatriot. She studied the dreamy photographs. Ah, she sighed in her heart, ah. It was not that Moura was envious, but she was more than a little weary of her crumpled clothes that stank of sour milk, perspiration, body odour and stale cigarette smoke. She needed a little enchantment. A young soldier with a crewcut who got in at Beauvais helped her. He was instantly friendly, introducing himself as Patrick Golette, offering her a strip of chocolate and staring with interest at her slippery nipple as it plopped out of Laszlo's mouth. He waited for Moura to tuck it away before he asked her what she was called. She nibbled at the chocolate gratefully.

'Maya,' she smiled. 'It means illusion.'

It was a name she had always coveted. Her mind was still haunted by the misty photography and the diaphanous gowns she had just seen. Perhaps, she hoped, with a name like that she wouldn't smell all that rank to him. But smell didn't appear to be a problem for Corporal Golette. He seemed to be impressed with her anyway.

'It's a beautiful name,' he murmured, trying her with a Gitane.

He talked confidentially about the toughness of French military training, his shit-luck with the Baccalauréat (if only he hadn't cracked his skull at sixteen), of his family fortune, his knowledge of the pop scene and the best places to take a girl. He seemed pleased to hear that she was unattached (a widow) and had a good job with the Hungarian Trade Mission in Paris. He gave her some more chocolate, confessing that but for his skull injury he might have been a professional prizefighter, a chess champion or even a doctor of philosophy, but that it didn't affect his terrific ability in bed, apologising should she consider that admission unacceptably coarse. She told him that she found him sensitive and unbelievably modest. Furthermore, she would be pleased to go dancing with him when she returned to Paris. His eyes lit up and, taking out his note-book, he looked at her expectantly as he prepared to scribble her address.

'What's your full name?' he asked.

'Gabor,' she said, 'Maya Gabor. Write to me, care of the Hungarian Trade Mission.'

He got up to go. The train screeched into Abbeville. He turned back with hope in his eyes.

'Anytime,' she called, waving. 'Call me anytime.'

Later that night, as the train sped towards London, she kept repeating the name to get the feel of it. Maya Gabor. Maya Gabor. Why not? Maya Gabor it was going to be.

In London, Maya was allocated a council flat at Crystal Palace and attended English language classes run by a small Hungarian widow with red hair, facial eczema and milky blue eyes. Her name was Maria Toth. She disliked Maya and complained to her younger brother Gaspar, a dental mechanic, that Maya was duplicitous, having a greater knowledge of the English language than she admitted. She also alluded more than once to Maya's whorish tendencies. The insubstantial reason for this intemperate slander was that Maya had, within days, befriended all the male members of the class, who buzzed around her during coffee breaks like wasps on a treacle tart. Gaspar, who was a romantic, had dreamed all his life of meeting pretty, lascivious women and so was encouraged rather than deterred by his sister's poor assessment of Maya's character. Maria and Gaspar had lived in South London for twenty years, having arrived from Hungary when she was twelve and Gaspar two. Unlike many of the émigrés of 1957, Gaspar had an antipathy to what he suspected was lower-middle-class affectation and professed a breezy Brechtian affinity to street-walkers, petty criminals and other social subversives, whom he regarded as guerrillas in the class struggle. He alarmed his sister with confident predictions of the coming revolution, plastered his bedroom with anarchist posters, and joined picket lines on what he called authentic proletarian demonstrations with the same enthusiasm that other men went dancing or visited the cinema.

'This is not the Weimar Republic,' his sister declared bitterly.

'There are many similarities,' Gaspar replied stubbornly.

He had just finished *Resurrection* and saw Maya as a more accessible Maslova, a woman he was convinced would have been happy sharing his life at Crystal Palace.

'This Maya you keep talking about,' he said to his sister at breakfast. 'Why don't you invite her for Sunday lunch? It's the least we can do for a fellow countrywoman.'

Maria sniffed with disgust.

'That minx will eat you alive, Gaspar,' she predicted. 'She's had more lovers than you've had sliced salami. And then some.'

'How do you know that?' he demanded angrily. 'Were you sitting on the mattress when these guys were queuing up to mount her?'

'Don't be so foul-mouthed,' Maria reproved.

But Gaspar did not stop dreaming about Maya and made his plans accordingly. He had a confidential chat with his barber in Forest Hill about aftershave lotion and perfumed hair-oil. Then, in a fit of madness, he crept into one of the better shops in Bromley and bought three Van Heusen shirts, a pair of stylish brogues, a country cap and a Donegal jacket with hunting flaps. The class implications of this last purchase gave him a twinge of conscience and he hoped that Maria would not perceive his moral inconsistency when he wore it. It was, however, the aftershave that alarmed her.

'What's that dreadful stink?' she asked quickly as he staggered in with the shopping. 'I wouldn't go out of the house smelling like that if I were you,' she declared offensively.

He thought it prudent not to respond to the provocation.

Maria, he concluded, was unused to sexually stimulating odours. The following Saturday he surprised her again by trading in his pre-war Morris Eight for an almost new Ford Popular. She did not seem impressed after inspecting the new vehicle very carefully. The doors were slammed several times and the tyres given critical kicks.

'I really can't see the difference,' she remarked, 'and anyway, can we afford the extravagance?'

'It's more reliable should we want to scoot down to Brighton for the weekend,' he suggested.

'And what should poor people like us want with fancy weekends in Brighton?' she demanded.

'Don't be so bourgeois,' he snapped fiercely. It was Gaspar's ultimate insult.

He took to driving the Ford Popular to night school to pick up his sister. In due course he was introduced to Maya. He was astonished by her beauty and friendliness. Maslova wasn't in the same ball-park. Furthermore, she appeared to like him. And did not seem to have any reservations about his aftershave either. Gaspar could hardly believe his good fortune when Maya expressed a strong interest in visiting the tomb of Karl Marx. He in turn agreed to accompany her ice-skating, an activity that had for him resonances of Eisenstein's *Ivan the Terrible*. They went ice-skating two evenings a week, rarely returning before one in the morning. The weekend at Brighton was inevitable.

It was at an hotel that he could hardly afford. They had a late dinner that included Scampi Hongroise (its felicitous presence on the carte delighted them) and two specially ordered bottles of Ezerjo. Maya was the one who suggested bathing together when they got to their room at midnight. They were full of wine and laughter as they embraced each other's slippery bodies under the needle-sharp jets of the shower. Their ecstasy could not be contained. And it was simple rapture that occasioned the thrusting leverage of two lovers trying to couple in a confined space. The sink unit cracked, a glass screen splintered and pipes through which the water coursed with a malignant velocity, sundered. They slipped on their robes and rang room service. It

11

took many minutes for the men who arrived to stop the spouting water, and more than an hour to mop and drain their room. The plump Turkish night-manager, Mr Netaji, unshaven and crumpled, seemed supercilious and unpleasantly bitter. Gaspar suspected that he had been sleeping with one of the maids, probably the bespectacled girl with fat legs who kept looking at her watch while they were taking coffee. Mr Netaji informed them that the Golitsyn plafond (Ivan Golitsyn was known as the Rastrelli of the 1880s) had been seriously damaged in the famous Liane de Pougy Suite below them; the colours of a handpainted Korean wallpaper had bled; a gouache (attributed to W. Sickert, 1901) had been stained and the Otis lift-circuits would probably require extensive maintenance. It was nearly two o'clock in the morning before they were alone once more.

Maya giggled as Gaspar brooded wearily over the probable cost of his liability. But she made him forget, lowering her head and reviving his inert cock with the gentle molluscoid rhythms of a warm mouth. And in the end, the episode at the hotel ended well enough.

When he phoned her a couple of days later, Gaspar reflected that it would have been fascinating if he had been able to capture the moment of their coupling under the shower, with his Leica. Photography was one of his particular skills. She appeared puzzled.

'A time exposure,' he explained.

He informed her that he would like to do an erotic series with her as the model.

'What if they fell into the hands of a blackmailer when I'm rich and famous?' she laughed.

But Gaspar considered that she had a solemn responsibility to posterity. He was, he reminded her, speaking as an artist who was principally concerned with beauty and truth. And Maya, who approved of those sentiments, agreed. A session was arranged for the following afternoon when Maria would be taking Sunday School at the Pentecostal hall. Gaspar calculated that they could have at least three hours all to themselves. He confessed huskily over the phone that he was hot with anticipation. The prospect of pointing his wide-angled lens into her most delicious crannies made him throb with creative impatience.

'I'll pick you up if you like,' he suggested, speaking in no more than a whisper because of his sister's presence in the next room.

Maya answered him with a kissing noise down the phone and said that she would expect him at one, having arranged a baby-sitter for Laszlo at that time.

As he wallowed in the possibilities of audacious poses, he suddenly remembered that he had run out of film. A dozen rolls at least, he decided, slipping on his coat and hurrying out of the flat. He had to get to the chemist before they closed.

'Where are you going?' Maria called.

But her brother was out of earshot. Maria, whose life was now haunted by inaudible telephone conversations and Gaspar's sudden absences, had begun to fear the worst. And the painful discovery of a packet of French ticklers in the New Testament she had given him as a birthday present some years ago did little to palliate that fear.

Chapter 3

Little Laszlo was suffocated with love by Maya. She always took him into the shower with her, drying him on the rug before the gas-fire, rubbing him with a fluffy towel, kissing his body to delirious distraction, dusting him with a hyacinth-scented talcum powder and squeezing him almost breathless, again and again. In his turn, Laszlo rewarded her with his precocity. He demonstrated an aptitude for numeracy and literacy at an age when many infants were squirting their way through bowel-training, showed signs of elementary deductive logic when his contemporaries were articulating brutish screams of incompre-hension, and exhibiting an aesthetic sensitivity that astonished all who understood his prejudices.

At five, the age he was enrolled at the local primary school, Laszlo indicated his distaste for Dali, paper flowers, Bing Crosby, china wall-ducks and the David Shepherd painting of an advancing elephant. When Laszlo first saw this pachyderm on the wall of their neighbour, Ada Mulcahy, he screamed himself into a fit. Once Maya had established that Dali gave him migraine, the most modest display of paper flowers made him nauseous, Bing Crosby's warble produced abdominal cramps and even diarrhoea, and that china wall-ducks provoked asthma, she took great care to protect him from these hazardous triggers. She replaced the Dali with a reproduction Cézanne landscape that Laszlo chose, filled vases with real flowers when she could afford them and donated the Bing Crosby records and china wall-ducks to a Labour Party jumble sale. She also had a discreet word with Ada Mulcahy about Laszlo's antipathy to the work of David Shepherd.

When Laszlo started school, Maya got a job in a Catford jam factory. She arranged that Ada, who lived in the flat across the hallway, collected Laszlo from school each day. Ada and her husband, Des, had a child of their own, a mentally handicapped girl called Aurora who was three years older than Laszlo. Ada doted on Laszlo and supplemented Maya's kissing and cuddling. Every afternoon, she picked up Aurora from her special class before calling for Laszlo and hurrying him back to the flat before Maya returned from work. With the David Shepherd elephant turned to the wall, Aurora secured in a safety-pen, a Muddy Waters record, at that time Laszlo's favourite sound, on the turntable, Ada took the five-year-old into her bedroom for his daily caresses.

Laszlo loved the smell of peppermint dentifrice from her warm lips and the way her lazy right eye turned slightly inwards. The eye always rolled off centre when she removed her glasses and pressed her snub nose against his. This was always a prelude to the tummy tickling he especially enjoyed. Ada's fingers marched everywhere – well, almost everywhere – and it was the 'almost' aspect of their peregrinations that heightened Laszlo's excitement and undermined the presumed innocence of the play, which was irrevocably compromised when Ada Mulcahy whispered to him: 'And will you tell Maya what we really did today?'

Laszlo gave her a knowing grin.

'Of course not, Ada.'

He was always rewarded by a fierce hug and a wet raspberry just below his navel. Then, coming out of the bedroom, Laszlo played Huff and Puff or Bob Apple with Aurora, who was instantly pacified whenever Laszlo appeared. He recited nursery rhymes to her, enunciating the words in a slow, even voice that seemed to exorcise dark and unknown fears. Partially sighted, Aurora laid her flushed cheek against his palm. She stared at Laszlo, open-mouthed, her vacant eyes waiting desperately for a signal that would open a door that led into a garden of sunshine and flowers.

'He does wonders for Aurora,' Ada reported when Maya arrived to bear Laszlo away.

Maya ruffled the boy's hair approvingly.

'Laszlo's taught Aurora ''Bobby Shafto'', 'Ada whispered.

15

They waited expectantly for Aurora to perform, but all she did was to open and close her mouth, enjoying the sound only she could hear.

'Sing, Aurora,' Ada urged.

The girl turned away, burying her face in Ada's skirt.

'Time for our little splash,' Maya called to Laszlo.

It broke the spell. Maya had begun to sense a mild wave of irritation from Ada at these moments of appropriation and attributed it to her friend's growing possessiveness over Laszlo. It amused more than alarmed her. For being mischievous by nature, Maya secretly enjoyed Ada's resentment at being displaced.

After the bath, Maya dried Laszlo and herself. He sat on the bed watching her with owlish wonder. She sprayed perfume under her armpits and around the slight bulge between her navel and the inverted isosceles triangle. She stepped quickly into a pair of blue silk briefs and gave a ballerina twirl for his approval. Maya slipped on a lacy black bra and, rattling through the cupboard, withdrew a turquoise chiffon cocktail dress with sequinned pockets. It was something that Ada had made for her.

'Are you going out with Gaspar?' Laszlo asked.

'Who's Gaspar?' Maya pouted.

Laszlo's eyes gleamed with excitement. He started to giggle.

'You know Gaspar,' he shrieked.

Maya regarded him with mock sadness.

'Really, Laszlo. I haven't heard of anybody called Gaspar. Where did you dream up that strange name?'

Goodness. How that made Laszlo convulse with helpless body-aching laughter. At this point of his life, Gaspar had almost become his father. That's what made Maya's remarks so funny. Laszlo used to lie awake at night listening to the fatherly noises Gaspar made with Maya long after they thought that he was asleep. Creaking, moaning, low whispering, squelching, sighing, visiting the bathroom, resonant pissing, water gurgling, washing, lights being switched on and off, more creaking, moaning. It seemed as though they would never tire of their parental responsibilities. Once or twice, in the middle of a Sunday afternoon, he caught Gaspar with his hand up Maya's skirt. Laszlo enjoyed the way Gaspar leapt away from Maya, pretending to search for something in his jacket pocket. But the serious parental business rarely took place until after the television had been switched off for the night. Long after 'God Save the Queen'. The night-games were preceded by Maya coming to check whether Laszlo was asleep. Laszlo never failed to do what was expected of a dutiful son. Eyes shut, even breathing and, occasionally, a melodious, simulated snore. Then the door would be closed gently behind her. And hey presto, the Daddy and Mummy routine would begin again.

One evening, Maya came home with a man called Earl. He was a tall, swarthy fellow with frizzed hair, rubbery lips and a nose like a squashed aubergine. Laszlo was told that he was a boxer. Maya sent the child off to bed. He lay in his room waiting, wondering when Earl would buzz off and Gaspar arrive for his usual night-games. But Earl appeared to be a great talker. He talked and laughed and drank endless cups of coffee. Eventually, Laszlo fell asleep. When he rose for a pee at three in the morning, the flat was quiet. He flushed the cistern and made his way to bed. Then, as he closed his eyes, he heard those unmistakable Daddy and Mummy sounds. Needless to say, Laszlo was confused. Had Gaspar turned up at last? Laszlo listened. There was no mistake. Creaking, moaning, low whispering, squelching and sighing. He opened the door and went into Maya's bedroom. The noises were extremely loud. Laszlo was inventive enough to have prepared a strategy. Once inside the chamber of parental activity, he switched on the light, rubbed his eyes and announced in a tearful voice that he had severe stomach cramp.

It was inexplicable. Gaspar was not there. And not only were Maya and Earl quite naked, but they were lying in an unusual position. The wrong way round. Although Laszlo could not have sworn to it, believing the next morning that what he had witnessed was part of a dreadful nightmare, he had the impression that Maya had to remove a black tube from her mouth before she screamed at him. She had never screamed at him before. Laszlo was inconsolable. Maya tried to shake him out of

17

hysterics, but he refused to settle down until she agreed to spend what remained of the night in his bed. Earl had got dressed and gone home. Maya settled Laszlo on her shoulder as first light came through his bedroom curtain. He cuddled her silky warmth. Contented. And when he was certain that she was asleep, Laszlo tenderly kissed her brown Mickey Mouse noses.

Chapter 4

By Laszlo's tenth birthday, Maya decided that as he was evidently growing up far quicker than she would have wished, it would be imprudent for them to shower together. Laszlo, being a natural actor, made an enormous fuss, weeping far more copiously than his natural disappointment required. Maya made a concession.

'I will still kiss you after you have dried and powdered yourself.'

Laszlo sulked. 'All over?'

'Not quite all over,' she replied with a reluctant sigh.

Laszlo tried his cocker spaniel look.

'And you know why,' she declared, firmly outstaring him with saucer blue eyes.

Laszlo considered the new arrangements as he lathered himself with a cake of Pears soap before splashing happily under the tepid shower. Later, as he dried himself with a large towel, he examined his body carefully. He switched on the mirror light to make sure he didn't miss anything. It was true. He was becoming a man. He wondered why no men friends visited Maya at night any more. He deduced that the fatherly noises that had so enlivened his early years were being made elsewhere. In another flat perhaps, or even in the back of a motor-car. He was still thinking of Maya enjoying herself with men in unknown places when he hopped out of the bathroom. She eyed him warily.

'You've been very quick,' she accused.

Laszlo dusted himself exuberantly, making unpleasant noises as he hand-cupped his lean body, then threw himself on the bed and lay supine, waiting for Maya. She approached him with a smile.

'On your tummy,' she ordered.

'Maya,' he cried in dismay.

'Tummy,' she insisted.

Laszlo jumped gymnastically around, using the bed as a trampoline, before bouncing to rest, head in a pillow, sighing with breathy panache. She kissed him quickly down his downy vertebrae. Laszlo turned, tears in his eyes.

'Maya?'

She embraced him passionately, holding his body close to hers.

'Is this really the end?' he whispered.

'I'm thinking of you, my darling,' she answered, running her fingers through his soft yellow hair.

'Wouldn't it be wonderful,' he reflected, savouring the perfume of her breasts, 'if we could reinvent our lives?'

'It would, my dove,' she agreed.

Laszlo moved her adroitly into their secret game, asking her where they would head for in the make-believe existence. She suggested Nice, knowing that he was reading a library book on the Alpes-Maritimes. He approved of her choice of destination but insisted that the sun would have to be hot, the sky cloudless, and the sea a shimmering blue.

'Who would drive?' she asked, knowing the answer.

'Me of course,' he replied imperiously. 'You'll be dressed in frothy white lace and silk. I'll be wearing a red yachting cap.'

'Hot croissants with butter and café du grand crème for breakfast,' she murmured.

'Maybe a pastis or two later on,' Laszlo decided solemnly.

'My, a pastis,' she exclaimed. 'What do you know of pastis?'

He informed her that he would have preferred absinthe but it was now illegal since it was bad for the liver. When Maya pointed out that pastis was probably deleterious as well, he countered artfully by remarking that since it was a dream-pastis, they were dealing with dream-livers that were impervious to alcoholic corrosion. Laszlo often slid out of their game when particular conclusions did not entirely suit him. And he pouted when she suggested he would be driving a Rolls-Royce.

'Oh, Maya, you're hopeless,' he protested. 'Our car will be a yellow 1931 Hispano Suiza. The V12.'

There was a model of this Hispano Suiza on his bedroom table. Maya looked gloomy after making a rapid calculation on her fingers, observing that when he would be old enough to drive she'd be nearly forty. An old crow.

'Oh no,' Laszlo snapped, 'we'll both be twenty-five. And honeymooning at a deluxe hotel.'

'But what about my little Laszlo?' she proclaimed, embracing him.

'We could have a son, I suppose,' he mused, 'and a beautiful daughter like Aurora.'

'Poor Aurora,' Maya sighed.

'She'll be wonderful,' Laszlo promised. 'A ballerina perhaps.' He closed his eyes and touched Aurora's frozen mind with his dreams. 'And Ada will be your sister,' he decided.

'What strange and enchanted ideas you have,' declared Maya, wide-eyed with astonishment.

Laszlo was wondering how Ada's husband, Des, could be fitted into their plans. The best he could do for him was a job as a travelling mechanic. Laszlo considered that Des Mulcahy should be accommodated in a separate cage, fabricated at the rear of the Hispano Suiza just above the exhaust pipes. Here, Des would be compelled to crouch with his oil-can and tools, ready to service the vehicle whenever they stopped at a café for refreshment.

'It would be even nicer,' Laszlo reflected, 'if he were mute and tiny enough to travel in the battery container.'

'Who?' laughed Maya.

'Des,' Laszlo sneered.

Des Mulcahy and Laszlo did not like one another.

There was one cloud in Laszlo's relationship with Maya. It concerned the identity of his father. She once told him that his father was a revolutionary hero who had been executed by the Russians. It was Laszlo who chose to believe that the slightly old-fashioned photograph Maya kept in a silver frame, of a handsome young man in a poetic pose, eyes mistily ascendant, was indeed he. As he grew older, what had been at first childish speculation became an appropriation, and Laszlo used to tell school-friends who visited the flat that the photograph on

Maya's toilet-table was the radiant and heroic parent he had so tragically lost. For a long time, despite the extraordinary intimacy between Maya and him, it was a question that Laszlo found difficult to put to her. Perhaps he was not prepared to face the possibility that the man might not be his father. But one day, Laszlo grasped the nettle.

'Is that my father, Maya?' he asked.

'If you like,' she smiled.

'Tell me about him.'

'He was brilliant,' she reflected. 'A professor. Extremely brave. And a great patriot.'

'How long did you know him?'

'Not too long,' she admitted. 'He was much older than I.'

'You once told me that his name was George Gabor,' Laszlo reminded her.

'Well, it's a fine name,' Maya declared evasively.

Laszlo feared the worst. He had never known Maya be so slippery about what should have been a simple matter. He smelt a rat. Yet, despite his doubts, he hoped that what she had told him was indeed so.

Some months later, Laszlo found the identical photograph that Maya kept on her table, in a movie magazine. He sat with the magazine and the photograph of his putative father, making a long and careful comparison. There was no doubt. It was the same man. His name was Wolfgang Ferrari, a surname that he discovered was not Hungarian. Ferrari was known in the trade as the Pisan Ramon Navarro. Laszlo scanned gloomily across to the facing page, where under the caption 'Love Bites in the Sand' the dashing Ferrari could be seen again; this time in Legionnaire's garb. He was standing beside international producer Sham Shilverman with a chummy paw on the rounded arse of the alluring star of the film, Medusa O'Toole. The glittering trio were sipping vespertine martinis on location in Marrakesh during the shooting of a musical extravaganza about a Tuareg dancer who goes crazy when her French seducer does a runner.

Laszlo decided to keep the painful discovery to himself, suspecting that it was highly improbable that his father was a famous film-star. If he was, what were they doing living in a council flat at Crystal Palace? And why did Maya choose to hide a fact she should have proclaimed with pride? George Gabor indeed. Perhaps he was as much a figment of Maya's imagination as the vaunty Wolfgang. Yet he felt he was unable to confront Maya with a duplicity of that magnitude. And when Ada pointed to the photograph and said that he was growing up to be as handsome as his daddy, he managed a shy grin, accepting it overtly as the compliment it was intended to be, but in fact taking the comment with a large pinch of salt. Now Laszlo no longer told school-friends who the radiant man in the photograph was, fearful lest somebody recognised Wolfgang Ferrari. And when he happened upon a life-size cardboard replica of the swashbuckling Italian outside a cinema, posed with a rapier in one hand and a mocking smile on his lips, he hurried away in anguish, almost feeling the thrust of the swordsman's metal in his heart.

After Gaspar, there was a succession of men friends for Maya. Through the door passed many admirers. But Laszlo was not aware of any who spent the night in her room. It was Maya who helped to creak other beds in rooms he had never seen. Laszlo felt sad thinking about those other beds and other, unseen rooms. It was as though Maya had taken part of her life away from him, hidden it in unknown places and shared dreams with people he did not know. He pictured her dancing with strangers, being kissed by strangers and undressed by strangers. Laszlo's sleep was broken by visions of thick, nicotined fingers scuttling around the shadows of her compliant body like ugly spiders.

Chapter 5

Laszlo was now growing aware that although Maya often tired of her lovers, of late some of them appeared to be tiring of her. Occasionally, he found her weeping. A gift of flowers, he learnt, was as much a sign of early ecstasy as the token of a civilised dénouement. And once he heard Maya discussing abortion with Ada. He checked the word in the *Shorter Oxford*. Then he visited the public library to research the subject further. He discovered the day the abortion was to be performed and sat in class considering, with clinical detachment, the destruction of Maya's foetus, which he decided, being a sixteen-week embryo, would be the size of a mouse. So he drew a homunculus at the back of his geometry exercise book. Being a talented draughtsman, he made a good job of the mega-headed, sightless tadpole, its fishy womb-curled torso suspended in dark, cosmic sap, sensitively shaded to give the drawing depth. At the foot of the drawing, he inscribed: George Gabor Junior, alias Ferrari. His teacher, initially outraged by the inclusion of a biology illustration in her Euclidean pasture, became on reflection impressed by the quality of the sketch. She was, however, concerned at the psychic implications of the drawing and requested Mrs Gabor to call at the school.

Maya shook her head in disbelief.

'And what does this mean?' she asked Laszlo.

He stared at the floor and made no reply. Later, back home, she shouted at him, her voice cracked with the torment of her memories.

'And what does an eleven-year-old child know of the tragedy of a woman's body?' she sobbed.

She spoke sorrowfully of a woman's needs; of the subversive nature of unsolicited ejaculations; the insidious character of a man's seed, lurking shamefully in dark pleats of tissue; of the chaotic genesis of life; of ripping rodentine creatures from secret furrows. Flesh of one's flesh and blood of one's blood.

'Nature,' Maya cried, 'plays dirty tricks. She wraps the most terrible presents in beautiful boxes. After the pleasure there is, sometimes, pain.'

Laszlo was tempted to ask about Mr Ferrari's pleasure, but he held his tongue.

'Have you nothing to say to explain this dreadful humiliation of somebody you profess to love?' she screamed.

He remained sullenly silent.

'You have no heart,' she sniffed, 'Like another I know.'

He watched the mucus stream down from her nose. It was the point at which their relationship, although intense and close, began to change. He wanted to kiss her naked body and beg her forgiveness but knew it could never be. That night he dreamed an impure dream about her. It was the month before his twelfth birthday.

'Laszlo's a very well-developed boy for his age,' Des Mulcahy advised Ada. 'It's imprudent for you to have him on your lap and for you to stroke his thighs. As for kissing a big lad like that on the mouth, well, you're asking for trouble.'

Ada Mulcahy eyed her husband with scorn.

'Laszlo is like a son to me,' she proclaimed. 'Maya seems to have precious little time for the poor soul these days. He's a sensitive child and needs love and attention.'

Des was unimpressed by his wife's maternal motivation.

'Give Laszlo an inch, my girl, and he'll slip you six more. I bet he'll be corking a few bottles around the estate before he's out of short pants.'

He sniggered at his own bit of nonsense but Ada did not respond. He lit another Capstan Full Strength and lost himself for a few moments in wreaths of smoke.

'I'll tell you what, Ada,' he remarked, slitting his eyes. 'Laszlo is the most precocious young bastard I've ever encountered. He frightens me. I always suspect that he's three jumps ahead of us all.'

25

Ada clicked her tongue in disapproval.

'Laszlo is undeniably more advanced than most boys of his age. And he's not the sort to finish up as a gas-meter collection clerk for a start.'

Des gave a dry rattle of a cough, dropping ash all over his shirt, then struggled for a while to catch his breath.

'Last week,' he wheezed, 'when he went to the park, I stood beside the little bugger in the gents. I'll tell you what – that lad's got more than a navvy's handful there already.'

'I suppose that's a notch or two up on a pinch of slack skin,' she murmured pointedly, regarding him with contempt.

There was nothing to be salvaged from their ill-matched relationship.

'When I listen to your filthy drivel,' she sneered, 'I understand why you will never be more than a gas-meter collection clerk. It is you who are the child, and Laszlo the man. And you have a far more serious problem to concern your feather-brain with than Laszlo's early maturation. I suggest you give some thought to that dreadful cough of yours. Direct your attention to the blood you spit up when you're bad. It's time you visited the quack, my lad.'

'I'm fine,' Des replied, momentarily wild-eyed with apprehension.

Ada smiled inwardly. She could always shut him up by referring to his rotten cough. She knew that he imagined the worst about his pitiful lungs and was terrified of having those suspicions confirmed.

Shortly before Des went into the pulmonary unit for observation and tests, he ringed an account in the *Daily Mirror* about a Basingstoke housewife who had been given a three-year suspended sentence for sexually assaulting a neighbour's twelve-year-old son.

'Remember,' he said, squeezing Ada's hand, 'whatever you may think of me, we have always been a decent, law-abiding and clean-living family. We haven't had the best of luck in life. Aurora has been a burden as much as she has been a blessing. I

26

know that you've had a hard and largely unfulfilled life. You've deserved better than me. But when I go, don't allow yourself to be messed about.'

'What do you mean by "go"?' Ada laughed. 'It's just a few days at the pulmonary unit for tests.'

'God bless you, Ada,' he said in a haunted voice.

Des now sensed the final shadow moving over him. It was strange, Ada reflected, how those who do nothing with their lives often find the prospect of losing them most unendurable.

'And one thing, Ada,' he said. 'Don't bring Laszlo to the hospital at visiting time.'

'As you wish,' she said, kissing him on the cheek. 'You'll be right as rain, just you see, now you've given those old ciggies up.'

Des throttled down a rising cough with a convulsive spasm. Then, biting on his knuckles, he clenched his eyes and inwardly wept.

When Ada informed Laszlo that Des didn't want him at the hospital, he understood. And smiled. He knew that the grey, rat-faced man feared him as a rival, even hated him. Indeed, the knowledge of Des Mulcahy's resentment made him feel quite grown up and immoderately vain. Ada had confessed that the only reason she married Des was that he got her pregnant. It was on a darts outing to Baldock, a game at which he once excelled. He was good enough to make the *News of the World* semi in the year she met him. It happened on the rear seat of Brannigan's coach, just before they stopped for a pee at Welwyn. Everybody was paired off when they clambered aboard, but Des won the privilege of using the back seat in a three-dart contest before they left the pub. He got a hundred and forty. She often brooded about the combination of circumstances that had trapped her. If it hadn't been for his skill at darts, the fact that she was wearing courting knickers and a couple of nasty potholes the coach hit on the Great North Road, Des would probably not have managed to impregnate her. Neither of them had intended to go more than ninety per cent of the way. It was the drink, she reflected, and the bloody potholes.

27

'He was in and finished before I even knew it was happening,' Ada complained. 'Hardly had time to cough. And poor Aurora was in the oven.'

When Laszlo called around one morning, Ada told the boy that her husband was not long for this world. A clairvoyant had assured her that Des's next incarnation was impatient to come into the world. She was told that Des would be reborn somewhere in the Yangtze valley. In any event, quite some distance from Crystal Palace.

'Will he be a Chinaman?' Laszlo asked.

'Almost certainly,' Ada declared. 'There's a terrific demand for spare souls in China. We can hardly die quick enough to supply the need.'

She ran her hand affectionately up the boy's thighs.

'We mustn't be too loving in front of him,' she warned. 'It wouldn't be right to make his last days miserable.'

Ada kissed Laszlo on the lips, opening her mouth to take his tongue. Then she gave him hers in return. He enjoyed playing tongues with her before he went to school. She moved her hand to the place he liked best. Ada's hands seemed almost magical when they stroked his body. The pleasure was so exquisite that tears filled his eyes. He vibrated beneath her hardly bearable touch and, unbuttoning his flies, gifted Ada a hot tumescence.

'Who's a big boy then?' she breathed, caressing his mauve helmet with nibbles and wet kisses.

A spring deep in his scrotum was suddenly released. Milky sap spurted across Ada's face. A dull, inguinal ache informed him that it would be unwise to repeat the trick immediately. He sighed with fearful pride. Ada glowed with pleasure.

'I have,' she observed in a kind of sacramental awe, 'lip-reared you to manhood.'

Chapter 6

It was Ada who introduced Maya to Bunny Selveratnam, the tiny black clairvoyant who lived in the flat below them. The walls of his living-room were covered in photographs of relatives and holy men he particularly admired. In an alcove, arranged on speckled formica shelves before a smouldering chirag, were carved rosewood figures of Rama and Sita, a brass Nandi the sacred bull, a dancing Nataraja bronze, and a pink plaster bust of Yogi Govinda Popatsahib, the floater of Conjeeveram, wreathed in dried sunflowers.

Selveratnam missed Conjeeveram, the town in which he was born. Although he was becoming more confident of his spiritual mission in the West, seeing, hearing, tasting, feeling, smelling and evacuating substances nobody around him appeared able to do, there were times when he wanted nothing more than to laze in the shade of his widowed aunt's chunam wall, playing carroms with a friend, popping juicy jambools into his mouth and watching chickens scratching about the dusty compound around the wicked, milk-heavy buffalo tethered to a leafy peepul. But Selveratnam suspected that greatness was the ultimate sadness that awaited him. He knew he could not escape from the stranglehold of Destiny, being both blessed and cursed with a profusion of supernatural gifts.

He also worked as a waiter in a nearby vegetarian restaurant. This he considered a temporary arrangement, an unpleasant job, running in and out of a poky kitchen to plop thalis down before customers who did not recognise his spiritual worth. Sometimes, he wished he could float like his beloved Yogi Govinda Popatsahib, just to shock the gluttonous buggers out of their gross materiality. There were times when he felt that he was nearly making it, as he essayed tricky skips, springing out of the kitchen in the hope that he would take off, but Selveratnam only succeeded in spilling hot pepperwater in the tray or burning his fingers with the runny dhal that was the speciality of the house. For although he had at last mastered the conceptual essence of floating, Selveratnam hadn't quite cracked the awesome knack of actually defying gravity. Periodically, he received stern warnings and nasty threats about his messy service, which he endured with stoicism and saintlike sadness.

Ada and Maya made an appointment to see Selveratnam together. Maya, however, was an unwilling client, for although the supernatural did not alarm her, she was fearful of people trudging through the undergrowth of her subconscious, and as apprehensive about a past she did not want disinterred as about a future she imagined might be littered with unpleasant surprises.

'I don't think I want to get entangled in that sort of creepy stuff anymore,' she decided when Ada listed the little man's strange gifts.

'Don't be a silly goose, darling,' Ada said. 'It seems only good sense to be prepared for what's on the way. If it's bad, foreknowledge should give you time to arrange your affairs, and if it's good, what's wrong with starting the celebrations a little earlier than one normally would?'

But it was a reluctant Maya that accompanied Ada downstairs.

Selveratnam wore a saffron leotard and assumed the lotus position before he gave his mind to astral matters. Ada, who had been before, lit an agarbutty and placed it in a holder. Selveratnam, who was both absent-minded and poor-sighted, leaned forward, staring at them with a troubled look. Ada introduced herself and Maya once again.

'It's Mrs Gabor and Mrs Mulcahy,' she reminded him.

He picked up a marigold from a bowl, closed his eyes and twiddled the stem of the flower between his two fingers.

'He's trying to find the right wavelength,' Ada whispered in explanation.

Selveratnam opened his eyes and smiled. Maya was quite enchanted by his leporine front teeth. Her grandmother had once told her that a gap between the two upper middle incisors indicated the gift of prophecy. His lambent gaze fixed on her.

'The future,' he said, 'is not here or there but inside this.' He tapped his head to show them what he meant. 'Death, of course,' he smiled, 'is everywhere. There has been a time-blur. This is a displacement of our fourth dimension.'

'Is it serious?' Ada asked.

The Hindu mystic shrugged. 'It is not yet a case of time broken or time lapsed but of time smudged.'

'Smudged?' Maya murmured.

'Smudged,' he assured her with an enlightened wink. 'The universe is moving away from its ordained coordinates and so smudging time. Not only have Paris, London, New York and Conjeeveram moved, but even our organs have been slightly displaced. Now this is a fact.'

'Is there anything you wish to tell me?' Maya asked.

'I see you before the mirror of life,' he said. 'The question is, which one is you and which one is the reflection?'

Maya shivered.

'You are chained to deception, death and duality,' he intoned, 'but in your next incarnation I predict a great improvement. In the meanwhile, unless you submit yourself to the guidance of a master, all you can reasonably expect is the lust of men and the envy of women.'

He turned briefly to Ada, confirming that her husband would soon pass away and she would acquire a new lover. She appeared to be quite comforted by the news for, despite the morbid droop of her mouth, her eyes had an anticipatory twinkle.

'Think of death as a beginning,' Selveratnam remarked, flashing her an encouraging smile.

The Hindu regarded Maya with interest.

'You have the benediction of butterflies,' he murmured. 'Does that mean anything to you?'

Maya nodded, blushing as she met his soulful gaze.

'But I detect a dharmic wound,' he announced.

'Wound?' she enquired nervously.

'Nothing to fear,' he observed softly. 'Although this wound will open up again and again, causing great psychic damage, the pain will be submerged by sensations of pleasure and orgasmic excitements. Do you understand me?'

Maya looked at him wide-eyed, biting her lower lip.

'I think I do,' she said, frowning, wondering for a moment or two whether his intentions were entirely respectable.

'I allude of course to your wounded astral-vagina,' he explained brightly. 'Something beyond the skills of medical quacks. Only great gurus can heal astral-wounds, so it is a fortuitous karma that has brought you to me.'

Selveratnam exuded an optimism and confidence Maya found almost hypnotic, cracking his knuckles before he uncoiled himself with the energy of a released spring. The sitting was apparently over. Detecting that Maya appeared to be vaguely troubled by his allusion to her wound, he assured her that an astral-vagina was not the same sort of business as the real organ, being, in spiritually debased females, imprisoned within the physical one and thus occasionally bruised by the ingress and friction of foreign objects. It was, he informed her, the legacy not only of this but of previous incarnations. In an enlightened soul, however, the astral-vagina escaped through a woman's skull, hovering above her head like a golden-pink, mango-shaped aura, releasing the warm perfume of a ripe Alphonse, a phenomenon that could only be detected and enjoyed by clairvoyants like himself. He slipped on his white bath-robe and escorted them to the door.

'I would dearly like,' he confessed to Maya, 'to take you for a flight through the blur-lines of time.'

'Where?'

'To the source of the river of milk and honey. We can start our journey at the Thali of Boundless Light, where we can take a meal together.'

'The Thali of Boundless Light is the restaurant where Mr Selveratnam works,' explained Ada.

Maya looked puzzled.

'How will we travel?'

The tiny Tamilian's eyes lit up. He touched Maya lightly on the shoulder.

'Will you,' he asked, 'be my spaceship?'

And so started the most morally aware five years of Maya's life.

The flight that took off over a thali of potato curry, stuffed brinjals, puris, okra, limboo pickle, onion-rings in yoghurt, and spinach bhaji, touched down on Bunny Selveratnam's saggy bed, where he taught her a jolly mantra or two, for he believed that when a man and woman first lie together, the devotions celebrating the event should be filled with joy and laughter. Maya agreed. She introduced him to her butterflies, submitted herself to a spiritual inspection and giggled her way through a therapy of kisses, nibbles, sucks and remedial penetrations.

'I think I got to you in the nick of time,' he confided with a yawn as they listened to the dawn chorus, his head nestled on her rounded shoulder and a thin, hairy leg curled protectively across her pneumatic belly.

Things finally started to go well for Maya. She had been promoted to a staff job at the jam factory, learned to drive and acquired an elderly Hillman Minx. Since her conversion to vegetarianism by Bunny Selveratnam, she had subsisted on lentils, brown rice, grated carrots, nuts, fruit, curds and goat's milk. On Friday evenings after she finished work, she indulged herself with a packet of licorice allsorts. The curries Bunny had prescribed for her were light and not too strongly spiced. This, she was assured, was in accordance with the *Bhagavad Gita*. And as she could no longer bear the sight or smell of meat, she arranged for Laszlo to board with the Mulcahys.

Bunny instructed her in the seventy more important carnal positions, demonstrating how an experienced yogi could maintain coital conjunctions on his head or balanced on the toes of one foot. He informed her of an ingenious variation of the cock-posture, in which both participants were supported upon the male's palms, the female torso, positioned at right angles to the male trunk, suspended from his shoulders by a sisal harness, with the female's legs hinged around the male arse to effectively lever the lingam and yoni together and apart. In . . . Out . . . In . . . Out . . . Just like the Boat Race, he declared breezily. Bunny claimed that he had managed this on several occasions with a diminutive partner in Conjeeveram.

'Who was she?' Maya asked bleakly.

'The widow of my second cousin's brother-in-law,' he said. 'She was only twelve and agile as a wild goat. Of course, all this occurred in the dark days before my enlightenment. Shortly after I acquired wisdom at the feet of Yogi Govinda Popatsahib, I became a sunyasi, partially blurring my vow of chastity to save you. I regard our fucking as a kind of sacrament, being devotional, instructional and exclusive in nature.'

'Oh, Bunny,' she breathed reverently.

But Maya was disappointed that they could never quite achieve the Boat Race position, collapsing across the carpet at each attempt.

'It's basically a question of praxis, prana and pelvic thrust,' he advised her.

She looked glum.

'Also perseverance,' he smiled.

And so Maya began to practise yoga in a black leotard every morning. She built up a small library of books on oriental religion, the occult and parapsychology, plucked the sitar and took her holidays at an ashram near Berkhamsted. Over the period of those five years, she struggled to make the transition from hedonistic Magyar to contemplative Hindu. It was not easy. She had many relapses. Laszlo was dismissive about her spiritual quest and poked fun at Bunny behind his back. He was not persuaded that the Hindu was a person of any consequence. But Maya burned with the certainty of Bunny's importance. He told her that although the *Upanishads* were the start of human knowledge, his own disquisitions on the blurring of time would, when published, springboard mankind to a much higher plane of awareness. When he visited the Gabors, he always brought a pair of saffron swimming-trunks to wear, a deer-skin on which to sit and a few marigolds to twirl between his forefinger and thumb. However, Goulash, Maya's white Samoyed bitch, never approved of the mystic and snapped evilly if he settled down to meditate too near her sleeping-basket. Reincarnation was never far from Bunny's thoughts. One night, when squatting on his deer-skin and twirling a marigold, he confessed that he had been Buffalo Bill in his last life, that terrible existence being a karmic punishment for buggering the wife of a Tibetan shaman. The thought of Bunny slithering about in the blood and fat of dead buffaloes filled Maya with horror. Quite spontaneously, she threw herself before his deer-skin and kissed his feet.

Maya had often questioned him about her own previous incarnations. She had often imagined that she had been a beautiful temple-dancer and the wife of a great Brahmin prince. She pleaded with him for some confirmation of her suspicions.

'It will be necessary,' Bunny informed her, 'for me to know everything about your present incarnation first. There are often clues in one's current life.'

Maya looked thoughtful.

'I would prefer,' she said, 'not to disclose details of my relationships with other men. It was, after all, before I met you and started to tread the path of righteousness.' ·

'Think nothing of it,' cried Bunny. 'Do not omit the most trivial item. I am, after all, an enlightened being. Almost a messiah. To be honest, my beloved Maya, I wouldn't be too surprised if I was ninety per cent there already.'

'A ninety per cent messiah?' she whispered in awe.

He nodded modestly, offering her his feet to kiss once again.

Over the next few weeks, Maya rapidly filled ten exercise books in a florid script with as much biographical information as she could dredge from her memory. Bunny was astonished at her revelations. He had her manuscript typed and bound at an agency so it would be easier to read. And he read it several times. Maya was eager to learn what he had made of her literary endeavours.

'I must admit,' he confessed, 'that I find the account of your life unbearably erotic. Let me warn you. This book must never fall into the wrong hands. Lesser men could be driven mad.'

He contemplated her with sadness in his brown eyes.

'Even I defiled myself several times. For a man who is probably ninety per cent messiah, to stoop to such indignities is a tragedy of cosmic proportions.'

Maya drew his head to her breast.

'My poor little Bunny,' she sighed. 'Perhaps I dwelt overmuch on prurient minutiae.'

She undid her blouse, offering him her breasts. They didn't have time for much else as Laszlo was expected home in fifteen minutes. Bunny sucked her nipples gently. Maya smiled dreamily. He reminded her of the pet rabbit she had in Tatabanya when she was a little girl. It used to nuzzle her half-ripe plums with the same velvet tenderness.

'I was astonished to discover,' observed Bunny, 'that it is your twin sister who is the real Maya, that you were christened Moura and that Laszlo is not your son.'

'That particular confession gave me great pain. A dark and unpleasant secret. I haven't found the courage as yet to tell my Laszlo.'

'Do you ever hear from your sister?'

Maya shook her head.

'As you have no doubt read, my sister and I both conceived on the same day. She in Wolfgang's dressing-room before he went on for the matinée of *Die Dreigroschenoper*, and I later that evening at his lodgings. We played Lotte Lenya records and drank coarse red wine. He seemed hungrier for me than ever before, taking me bending over a chair with my knickers around my knees. I watched his dark and demonical face against my arched back in the mirror. Oh, how Wolfgang excited me. And my sister even more than me. She seemed to be captivated by the theatricality of his sex. Wolfgang made love with manic urgency as though nothing else in the world mattered. I remember he once took me while I was still wearing my fur hat and gloves; on another occasion, with a half-consumed sandwich in my hand; with one boot on and the other off; in the act of washing my hands; while I was conversing with a friend sitting at a pavement café below his window; and even while dancing, particularly when doing the tango. He would slide me into a dark corner and with great skill hook my leg up, aligning me for his crafty lunge. He treated lovemaking as a wonderful game that was filled with unexpected magic. Strangely enough, it was on the last occasion that we made love that I fell. I never saw him again after that night.'

'Your sister and you perpetrated an unforgivable charade on that poor man,' Bunny commented drily.

'I admit,' said Maya, 'that we shared Wolfgang in a most unusual way. As identical twins, we played what we imagined to be the ultimate sexual joke. It was all rather puerile, I suppose.'

Maya smiled at the memory of those times, but Bunny appeared unamused.

'I consider your deception quite disgraceful. Did he really believe he was making love to the same girl?'

Maya nodded, her eyes filled with merriment.

'It was incredible how he never discovered that the Polly to whom he made love every day, often twice a day, was really two girls. There was a difference, of course. My sister had a Purple Emperor tattooed on her left buttock and a Red Admiral on her right, while I had the two reversed. You see, when my sister saw the butterflies on my bottom she wanted some as well. I told her the story about the old tattooist and off she went. Naturally, the old boy wasn't going to get caught twice. He told her that she would have to do it first. Once for each butterfly. And he refused to consider a chaperone or any such nonsense. She had no choice. When she got back from her ordeal, with her arse still sore, I had a quick inspection and was amused to find that the butterflies were on different cheeks. The strange thing was that Wolfgang never noticed.'

'What a terrible thing to do.'

'Oh, he was hardly a victim,' protested Maya. 'It was my sister and I who became pregnant. My son George hardly survived twenty-four hours, but my sister's boy, Laszlo, made it. And shortly after we conceived, Wolfgang returned to Italy. He corresponded with my sister, who kept up the Polly subterfuge. She liked him rather more than I did. Sexual excitement is not the same thing as a serious attachment, and she had just that. She was also interested in the theatre, whereas I start to fidget ten minutes after the curtain goes up. Strangely enough, it was me that Wolfgang saw first. I won a ticket to the performance in a lottery. My sister, being the theatre buff, would have gone instead of me, but she had a rather horrid gumboil. So off I went to see *Die Dreigroschenoper*. I had almost fallen asleep when I noticed this dark, seductive fellow on the stage, giving me the eye. That woke me up. We flirted away through the performance and I positioned my legs so that he could enjoy an unimpeded view of my sky-blue drawers. After the second interval, an usher approached me and handed me a letter. It contained a stage-door pass and the most extraordinary note that I have ever received. It said that the performance ended at ten p.m. and Wolfgang Ferrari would be proud to couple with me before ten-fifteen.'

'What made you go?'

'I was crazy and hot for the guy that night,' Maya confessed. 'We made it with five minutes to spare.'

'I blush for you, Maya.'

'We had three glorious months playing an off-stage Polly Peachum. And while my sister maintained her involvement after he'd left Budapest, I had already found a new stimulation.'

'Your gynaecologist?'

'That's right. He had such sensual hands. Strong, but as smooth as satin.'

'And Wolfgang never knew that he was the father of a son — two sons.'

'My sister felt that information of that sort might alarm him. Subconsciously, I suppose, she had already decided to abandon her child if that was the price of a life in the theatre with Wolfgang. When my baby died, she gifted me her son. You can have Laszlo, she said, and I'll try for Wolfgang. We were both more than satisfied with the bargain. You see, although we were identical twins, temperamentally we were quite different. To put it bluntly, she was a cold fish while I was the opposite. After the uprising, I made it to London and she trekked to the Austrian border, where he was waiting for her in his red Lancia. I understand they were married in Como the following month. It was far too late to make disclosures about twin sisters and sexual deception. He had his Polly and that was that. On the other hand, I had my Laszlo and wanted nothing more.'

'Will you ever tell Laszlo?' Bunny asked.

'I've been on the verge of doing so for weeks. But I'm quite terrified, Bunny.'

'Truth,' Bunny observed piously, 'purifies the soul.'

'Are you sure?' she enquired anxiously.

'It's a damned fact,' he declared earnestly.

But Maya was dismayed by Bunny's news of her last visit to the planet.

'This, my dear Maya, is your first incarnation as a human being,' he disclosed.

'Oh my God, Bunny. And what was I in my last one?'

'You were a bitch,' he declared evenly; 'a pariah bitch, available to every dog in the village.'

'Are you sure?' she asked, with tears in her eyes.

'Would I lie to you?' he murmured, gently groping her. 'You were a shade smaller than Goulash, piebald with a springy ring-tail.'

Maya was profoundly alarmed when Bunny disclosed to her in confidence that the time-blur was getting worse. He explained that the aggregation of cinematic, televisual, literary and even religious experience had at last begun to effect subtle displacements in man's perceptions. Hordes of characters one had never met had immigrated to the heartlands of subconscious minds, using dreams to infiltrate the Collective Unconscious, which was becoming as overcrowded as a Bombay bazaar. He felt that the Collective Unconscious did not possess the psychic resources to deal with the problem. When Maya suggested that she did not think that the Collective Unconscious was a spatial concept, Bunny seemed irritated, reminding her a little waspishly that he was talking about metaphysical space.

'What's that?'

'The space between our souls.'

He told her that his unique spiritual talent was urgently required along the main time-fault, which he declared was located somewhere near Honkeyville, the capital of Terrastricken. Maya withdrew all her savings from the Post Office (five hundred and twenty-five pounds) and the little mystic prepared to fly westwards the following week. He kissed her goodbye and promised that he would return as soon as he had saved the world.

'Oh, Bunny,' she sobbed, 'mankind does not deserve you.'

She clung to him until the last possible moment. Then, before the final embrace, he asked her to be Mrs Selveratnam.

'When?' she asked, hollow-eyed with joy.

'In two years' time,' he declared, 'which, if the blurring is very serious, was about five years ago.'

'You mean to say,' asked Maya, 'that I could already be your wife?'

'All things are possible,' he declared.

Maya could scarcely believe her good fortune. She bought herself an engagement ring on hire purchase from Bravingtons and mooned around waiting for Bunny's first letter. It was a postcard of Old Prejudice Square, the heart of Honkeyville. Apart from the Gabor address and a snazzy signature, the text appeared to be in Tamil.

Chapter 7

The long-haired Laszlo's precocity, evidenced by his clandestine couplings with Ada Mulcahy, produced other minor vanities. He was given, during his early teenage years, to body-building pursuits, with the concomitant muscle-flexing conceits, apish grimaces and well-oiled poses for Mrs Mulcahy's delectation and cock-centred reveries.

'My little Laszlo has the conformation of an angel,' she'd enthuse, speaking about him in the third person as she exulted in the profanity of his glistening flesh.

There was also his modish preoccupation with what he called his 'Up West' clobber, like suede jackets, pearl-studded black shirts, genitalia-defining jeans, high-heeled boots, silver-buckled belts, chrome lanyards, bracelets, death's-head rings and spotted silk scarves, although he was uneasily aware that the flash was slightly diminished when paraded around the seedier trails of SE19.

A more significant obsession, however, surfaced in his fifteenth summer after a chance visit to the local cinema, and persisted in one form or another for the rest of his life. This was the cultivation of what he perceived to be the manners and speech of an English gentleman. Laszlo went posh. He became in that formative year mildly censorious of Maya's Hungarian pronunciation, coldly dismissive of Bunny's sing-song Tamilian articulation, and even endeavoured to repair the delinquencies of Ada's flat South London delivery. But she alone endured his corrective reproofs with tolerance, complimenting him on his own miraculously acquired phonemes.

'You talk like a proper toff, ducks,' she proclaimed, her slack mouth agape with admiration.

Bunny, on the other hand, considered the patrician drawl a tiresome joke, while Maya claimed that Laszlo sounded as though he had gravel in his mouth.

'Anything so unnatural cannot be good for you, my darling,' she murmured with a concerned frown.

He responded with a distant smile, in the style of his master, the great Leslie Howard. Laszlo had discovered *Escape to Happiness* on one of its periodic orbits around the secondary circuit. He was mesmerised by the flickering fantasy no less than sixteen times during his holidays. At first, the curious usherettes presumed that the tall, blond youth in a suede jacket and tight trousers making for the last row of the stalls was yet another afternoon loner dropping in for a surreptitious wank. But once their probing flashlights had established his innocence, they concluded that he was there for Joyce, a tubby young divorcée on whom he practised his whimsical smiles. ('Your Blondie's in again, Joyce.' 'Oh, I do fancy them shy and virginal.')

Little did the girls realise that this particular young male, despite his contrived self-effacement, was the consort of a married woman, and had probably risen from rumpled sheets before a recuperative shower and measured lope down to the Rialto. And although it was not true to say that the short, top-heavy Joyce's purple eye-shadow, false lashes, full, moist lips and lacquered raven hair had entirely escaped Laszlo's sly attention, his mind during the screening of *Escape to Happiness* was on higher things. He sat in the dark, enchanted by the chiaroscuro of Howard's civilised voice, shaded from hesitant modulations of exquisite sensitivity to the engaging assurance of quick and fluent disquisitions on transcendental themes like art and love, received with rapture by a misty-eyed Bergman.

Laszlo bought a record of *Intermezzo*, the honeyed violin theme of the film, subjecting it to such excessive appreciation that the gushy melody was soon submerged in a background of hissing erosion. Indeed, the sibilance of the decayed track became part of his sentimental memory of that time. He secreted photographs of Howard and Bergman in the drawer of his bedside table, but the contemplation of them, like listening to his record, was a furtive diversion.

There were those who declared that Maya had a touch of Bergman about her, although she was shorter and more rounded than the Swede. And it was Maya that Laszlo perceived when he stared at Bergman's face, the actress's features dissolving into those of his mother. Yet, strangely enough, he didn't possess a photograph of his beloved Maya, and despite vague promises that she would provide him with one, nothing ever came of her stated intention.

'I've more important things to do than be photographed,' she'd laugh when cornered, 'and anyway, I'm too old to be insulted by a camera.'

This was a private and oblique reference to the lascivious poses captured by Gaspar before the days of her enlightenment. She'd given Bunny those terrible photographs, along with the testament of her unworthy life, hopeful that they would be safer in the possession of somebody who was almost a messiah. Certainly, they would be out of the reach of Laszlo, who she suspected had taken to rooting around her room when she was absent.

Maya had frequently urged Bunny to burn the incriminating pictures. This he'd promised to do the moment they no longer gave him an erection, pointing out quite sensibly that their destruction would be a cowardly evasion of karmic responsibility, a minor aspect of which, he felt, was the ability of any man with spiritual pretensions to be able to examine erotic images with a calm mind and quiescent cock.

'How the hell can I ever become a pukka messiah,' he enquired miserably of her as they snuggled together in bed, 'if a few rectangles of paper give me a bloody horn?'

And being an aspiring Hindu, she resisted contentious references to the Christian saints, who she recalled tamed their turbulent flesh by throwing themselves into stinging nettles and diving into thorn bushes. These were not, perhaps, easily available alternatives in their neck of Crystal Palace, although the possibilities of broken milk bottles did cross her mind. There were plenty of those around the estate. She decided, however, that it would be uncharitable to encourage him in such excessive mortification, and pecked his snout tenderly as he dozed like a brown rabbit on her shoulder. Maya considered that sleeping with Bunny was a kind of sacrament, for although in many respects he was just like any other boy-friend, there was a metaphysical dimension to their relationship. None of her previous lovers had addressed their minds to prana control during coitus or sung sacred songs in between exquisitely organised fucks.

Laszlo longed to tell Maya that she was the most beautiful woman in the world and to kiss her hot and wet on the mouth, but at sixteen such practices were long past. He remembered the butterflies, hugging her strong thighs as they showered together, her slow, tickling nibbles down his vertebrae and the silken substantiality of those pendant, brown-nippled breasts when she kneeled over him. As he grew older, those images returned to haunt him. And when he was on top of Ada he used to close his eyes, invoking Maya in the most intimate moments, melting with the improbability of his projected desire and despondent at the reality of his situation. He was already discontented with Ada and sensed that they were in the terminal phase of their sexual association. He drifted towards manhood, a solitary, sardonic youth, slightly narcissistic, mildly bored by his peers and puerile group activities. He brooded about the father he had never known, being now of the opinion that his parent was alive and was neither a professor nor a patriot but some scoundrel who had abandoned his mother and himself. He resolved in vengeful moments to discover his identity, confront and punish him. Even kill him.

'Are you sure my father is dead, Maya?' he once asked suddenly as he lounged by the kitchen door, watching her slice a beetroot for the evening salad.

Despite Bunny's advice to tell Laszlo the truth, it was something she seemed unable to achieve. She looked at him blankly. It was the moment, had she possessed the resolution, when Maya could have set the record straight. She chose not to do so.

'Of course he's dead,' she replied simply.

'I'd like to see a real photograph of him,' he grunted.

44

'Photographs, photographs . . . Whatever is the matter with you? Why can't you allow the past to wither and die without poking about like a tramp in a trash can?'

'I suspect the blighter is still alive.'

'It will take more than your suspicion to resurrect him,' she mocked.

'So, he's really dead then?'

'Well, he won't be popping in to visit us at Crystal Palace, that's for sure.'

And that is how his exchanges with her usually ended. Trickling away like water into the sand. Their conversations about his father were always inconclusive.

There were minor triumphs. Joyce, the raven-haired usherette at the Rialto, now joined him in the rear stalls. At their second encounter, she left traces of lipstick on his underpants.

'You've got ever such a drooly voice,' she whispered as he zipped himself up in the dark. 'Like George Sanders.'

'Thank you,' he murmured with clipped elegance, a little miffed that she'd got it wrong.

'I'd love to do it with you,' she confided, 'but my place is impossible. I'm living with my brother and sister-in-law. They're Seventh-Day Adventists, like Alec, my ex, and secretly hope I'll go back to him!'

She tilted back in the seat to allow his fingers access between her well-fleshed thighs.

'I bet you'd be really tasty in bed,' he whispered, raking her glairy furrow with three probers.

She grunted and held his hand in position, pivoting at the edge of the seat. It was quick and intense until the final spasm and appreciative crushing of his fingers. He waited patiently for their release, surprised by a dig in the ribs as he clenched feeling back into his hand.

'Leslie Howard,' she breathed, her voice tremulous with the magic of realisation. 'Has anyone told you that you sound exactly like Leslie Howard?' Laszlo shook his head in surprise.

They arranged to visit a new Greek restaurant in Catford. It had, she enthused, a dance-floor and a live bazouki band. She spoke knowledgeably of tippling ouzo and dancing on tables. He smiled, and nodded agreeably. He did turn up for the date, catching sight of her just in time from the doorway of a toy-shop across the road. She was in a tight, pink dress, wearing a matching alice-band and carrying a diamanté-studded pouch that reminded him of Maya's shower-bag. Somehow, she looked different in daylight, lumpier and a little unsteady on high heels. It was quite unforgivable, but he turned and legged it in the opposite direction, a shitty move that put the Rialto out of bounds more or less indefinitely.

Selveratnam had flown westwards. The first Tamil cards had arrived. Maya was disconsolate. Goulash had developed kidney trouble. And Laszlo was into decisions. Not that he took decisions seriously. The careers master had asked what he would like to do with his life. Laszlo decided that the truth might have provoked derision. His ambition to become an English gentleman like Leslie Howard and acquire a woman as luminous as Maya, or even Miss Bergman, was at the heart of his unspoken needs. He had for some time concluded that the pursuit of wealth was the only concern worth a talented man's attention. OK, so he was a penniless Hungarian bastard living in a South London council flat. There were a few hurdles to jump. But Laszlo was convinced that, with resolution and low cunning, anything was possible. But he could hardly confess to this idiot of a schoolmaster that he aspired to be an English gentleman. He assumed a vacuous face for the impatient master, sensing that nothing much could come of this unnecessary meeting.

'What's on your mind?' the master, whom he perceived to be a red-faced lout, demanded. He could hardly have replied that he was haunted by the Gothic façade of a stately home in the autumn mist, his green Bentley parked along the gravelled drive, watchful thoroughbreds in a nearby paddock, and a rambling estate across which he could trudge, twelve-bore under one arm and a pair of spotted gun-dogs sniffing deferentially at his heels. A distant shout from the Crystal Palace estate of dumped cars, pools of sump-oil, burnt-out garages, walls scarred by graffiti, piss-damp lifts, smells of boiled cabbage along institutional-grey corridors and overflowing garbage bins.

'Well?' shouted the careers master.

Maya had recently introduced Laszlo to a boring accountant called Ben Drummond, whom she'd met at a management seminar in the hope that he could help her son. It provided Laszlo with an improbable idea.

'Something in the City, I expect,' he murmured amiably.

'A clerk?' the master sneered, limiting the horizons of this uppish young shit whom he'd always resented.

'A fairly junior one, perhaps,' Laszlo countered, a malicious glint in his eyes as he noticed the frayed cuffs of the teacher's shirt.

Laszlo had evolved into a not unattractive man. At seventeen, he was six foot tall, with broad shoulders and blond wavy hair. His deep blue eyes were perhaps set too close together, indicating, according to Bertoli's *Guide to Criminal, Lunatic and Schizophrenic Physiognomies* (Grossmann Press, Berne, 1870), basic dishonesty, shallowness of intellect and psychotic tendencies. Laszlo picked up the cockchafer-stained reference book for sixpence in a Brixton junk-shop. He examined the illustration of the archetype with close-set eyes carefully, noting that the villainous model was an Albanian terrorist who had been hanged for shooting a policeman in the throat. Bertoli's classic was sprinkled with lurid footnotes of this nature. It included an Austrian nun whose preternaturally pendulous lower lip denoted debauched, carnal proclivities. She was convicted in Wuppertal for procuring pubescent girls for acts of mutual cunnilingus. And an imbecilic Spaniard, with a forehead no larger than a crown piece, had been tucked away for indecently assaulting his master's pedigree Arab mare.

Laszlo pointed to the picture of the Albanian with close-set eyes. He asked Maya whether the man reminded her of anyone she knew. She screwed up her face in disgust, declaring it the most evil face she had ever seen.

'You don't think that looks like me?' Laszlo enquired anxiously.

47

She regarded him with horror.

'How in God's name could you look anything like that dreadful monster, darling? You're handsome. Like Michelangelo's *David*.'

'I have always suspected,' Laszlo confessed, 'that my eyes are too close together.'

'Nonsense,' she snapped, 'it's the other ones that are probably too far apart.'

But Bertoli's assessment of close-set eyes had struck a mark deep in Laszlo's psyche. For a while, he took to wearing sunglasses even long after dark. And while he felt he could live with Bertoli's classification of his mouth as 'weak', and his small ears as 'duplicitous', the reference to eyes recalled one of Bunny Selveratnam's remarks when they first met.

'You're a very lucky boy,' the clairvoyant had announced. 'You've got snake-eyes.'

'Snake-eyes?' Maya had intervened defensively.

'Snake-eyes are very good,' Bunny assured them. 'You will acquire great wealth, live like a prince and die in a woman's arms.'

Laszlo remembered that at the time of Bunny's observation, he could imagine no greater benediction than possessing the eyes of a snake. It was a felicitous thought for a twelve-year-old. But at seventeen, Bertoli's dismissive view of reptilian eyes in a human face did little to elevate his ego.

'Why do you creep around in those dark glasses at night?' Maya grumbled. 'One would think that you were a gangster.'

It was hardly an encouraging remark. And Laszlo decided gloomily that his affinity to Bertoli's nineteenth-century Albanian terrorist could not be easily evaded.

The body-building exercises were not forgotten. He fiddled around with a bullworker and indulged in spasmodic but manic spells of press-ups, astonishing his fellow-workers with feats of strength during his Saturday job at a Ravensbourne timber yard. Maya was proud of his physique and urged friends to feel his arms.

'Like steel,' she declared. 'He does two hundred press-ups a day.'

Laszlo smiled shyly as appreciative faces acknowledged the prodigy of his power.

'Jesus.'

'Feel his arms,' Maya invited proudly.

And 'feeling arms' was de rigueur when Laszlo was around.

To celebrate his final A-level paper, he dressed best, tucked forty-five pounds in his wallet and went up West, vaguely aware that he needed to do something discreetly disreputable. He met the actress after he'd taken a couple of halves in a Brewer Street pub. She spoke first and to his surprise joined him when he answered back. She was a small, nicely tanned and tubby blonde of about forty who told him that she'd been doing cabaret in Alicante. He was entranced by the experience of her husky voice and apparent familiarity with the great names of the theatre. She said that she adored the way he spoke and wondered why he'd never considered the stage himself. He removed his dark glasses and bought her a second gin and Italian.

'You've got lovely eyes,' she murmured after the fourth drink, suggesting her place.

She confided at the top of the narrow, unlit stairs over an Italian delicatessen that she needed thirty pounds to square the Maltese landlord who was trying to evict her. Laszlo only just made it, handing over the notes, which she held between her teeth as she fumbled with the door. He followed her into a small room smelling of cigarette-smoke, mildew and stale perfume. She drew the curtain that was around the bed and went into the bathroom. He undressed rapidly in the darkened room, sensing her surprise when she returned and eyed his nudity. She was in frilly black briefs and brassiere.

'In the altogether, are we?' she called, a tinge of asperity in her voice.

Then she fussed that it would have to be 'chop-chop', as she had an audition at the Shaftesbury in twenty minutes. He lay ostentatiously supine, his erect cock pointing to the mirror-tiles on the ceiling.

'Well, you can at least get the pig's snout in the air,' she conceded, scrambling astride.

She informed him that her knickers had a curtain, a theatrical touch which she thought he'd appreciate. She was heavier than he had imagined, somewhat clumsy with a low centre of gravity. He was sheathed with a congenial squish as she jockeyed into position, her resolute knees gripping his ribs. Reaching for her brassiere-shrouded breasts he discovered bared nipples protruding through lace mamilla windows and captured them between his forefingers and thumbs.

'Don't sod me about,' she warned when he attempted to gently milk her.

But there was hardly time for such depravity. She raced for the wire, riding him down the straight to an explosive sixty-five-second finish. At the door, she handed him a pink business card.

'Perhaps we could have a Chinese together sometime,' she suggested, 'and I might take you backstage to meet a few of the gang.'

Under a nearby street-light, he learned that he'd been entertained by Dolores Virgo, chanteuse, character-actress and novelty magician. It was, he reflected, a memorable end to a day that had started with a paper on Georgian lyric poetry.

In due course, Bunny Selveratnam did write Maya a postcard in English explaining why the three previous ones were in Tamil. The reasons, he informed her, were both occultic and aesthetic. The Tamil symbols resonated with a truth that came from his soul, and even if Maya couldn't understand them he was certain that she would derive great pleasure from looking at them in the way people looked at abstract pictures. His explanation so impressed her that she set up the postcards on the table every evening and wallowed in their astral vibrations for an hour or so. Sometimes Ada came in and wallowed a bit as well. It was Laszlo who broke the spell.

'Why don't you take them to the Thali of Boundless Light,' he suggested, 'and have them translated.'

Maya regarded him with horror.

'That would be cheating. If Bunny had meant them to be in English, he would have written them in English.'

'You could, of course, learn Tamil,' Laszlo said, driving his mother into a corner.

'It looks extremely difficult. Impossible even,' observed Ada, frowning at the curlicue script.

Maya looked troubled, but the idea of acquiring Bunny's mother-tongue had an underlying virtue that seemed to be in accord with her new Hindu disciplines. The following day she called at the restaurant and had a word with Mr Mudaliar, the proprietor. He was a tall, portly man, broad-nosed with heavy-lidded thyroidal eyes. He had strong white teeth and was very black. There was no more than a hint of condescension in his friendly baritone.

'Ah yes, little Krishna,' he recalled, that being Bunny's given name.

She informed him of her ambition. Mudaliar was entranced by the idea and took her hand in his.

'There's no problem, dear lady. Above my restaurant I have a quiet studio where I will be proud to teach you the rudiments of the Tamil language.'

'How much will it cost?'

'Nothing,' he replied instantly, washing dark, bulging eyes over her figure.

'Oh dear,' Maya murmured, biting her lower lip, uncertainty clouding her face for a flicker of time.

Mudaliar placed a fraternal hand around her shoulders, his confident fingers gentling her along.

'It will be my absolute pleasure, dear lady.'

He opened a door and switched on a light that illuminated an inner staircase. Then, stepping back with great civility, he invited Maya to precede him up the stairs. It was, to her surprise, a pleasant bedsitter, the white jalousie drawn, a trompe l'oeil in oils of mangoes, custard-apples and guavas on the far wall; a school-desk tucked away in a corner, two fabric armchairs, an aquatint of a mynah on a walnut table, a large terracotta pot with what looked like azealas threatening florescence, and a brass double-bed with an inviting blue and yellow guipure coverlet. Mudaliar watched Maya carefully. He smelled strongly of patchouli and what she suspected was methi ki bhaji, which after a tentative sniff or two Maya decided was not altogether unpleasant.

Chapter 8

Des Mulcahy died suddenly. He had, shortly before the end, begun to creep around the block, collect his morning paper, drop into the local for a jar of Guinness, maintain the living-room fire, help with the washing up, watch the sports programmes on the box and grumble constantly about his intention to return to work. His morbid pallor when he first escaped from hospital had prospered to a pinky grey, the stick had been discarded and he had started to gain a few pounds in weight. Then one afternoon when Ada flapped in from work she found him stiff in his favourite armchair. He had been dead for several hours. The racing page of the *Daily Mirror*, where he had ringed two fancied horses on the Ripon card, was on his lap. There was half a mug of cold tea and a nibbled square of shortbread on the table beside him. A coronary was the verdict. There was not a great deal of fuss, and few tears.

'Who would have thought his ticker would peg out,' Ada reflected when Maya arrived to pay her respects just as the ambulance men came to bear the corpse away.

'Had he any relatives?' Maya asked.

She didn't know much about her dead neighbour, despite Ada being a close friend. Des Mulcahy was a subject they rarely discussed. And he had never cared a great deal for Maya, suspecting that the vivacious Hungarian was not a suitable companion for his wife. A flighty piece of old turkey was the term he used to Ada. The kettle was put on and a few biscuits shaken out onto a plate. Ada trundled around the kitchen, setting down on the bar two of her best bone china cups and saucers, part of a set her mother had bought her as a wedding present. They hadn't been used for years. The rims were silver-grey with a pimpernel motif in charcoal and roses of coral pink. It was strange how she had never appreciated their elegance until now.

'He had an elderly aunt in Brisbane,' recalled Ada, pouring out. 'I'll drop her an airletter if I can find the address.'

It was the afternoon Laszlo had passed his driving-test. Maya had told him the news when he came in.

'I'd better go round,' he muttered.

'Do that,' Maya urged.

Ada opened the door. She had removed her spectacles. Her eyes were moist. Laszlo shrugged and made a gloomy face as he sidled in. She closed the door, taking him in her arms as she shucked off her shoes and locked one of his thighs between hers. She had often stood like this with him.

'I'll need you more than ever now,' she whispered, kissing him on the side of the neck.

He comforted her with several cursory pats on the back. Death was an embarrassment he had not encountered before. He chose not to talk about Des and hoped that she wouldn't either.

'I've passed my test,' he announced, gently attempting to liberate himself from her thighs.

Ada facilitated his escape by moving back for a moment to regard his face.

'Oh, Laszlo, how wonderful,' she breathed, capturing his head and drawing it down to take his lips with a sloppy kiss of felicitation.

'Is Maya expecting you back right away?' she enquired softly.

There was a raunchy edge to her voice that he instantly recognised. She searched his face anxiously for a response.

'Do you think I'm an absolute bitch wanting you on a day like this?'

'I'm sorry, Ada,' he murmured, edging away.

He stared at her dully, knowing that he could no longer pretend to feelings that did not exist.

'What's the matter?' she asked, apprehensive at his retreat.

There had been many occasions in the past when Ada suspected that this moment of rejection would come, yet now it had she could hardly catch her breath for the numbness across her chest. Although Ada's meditations on her Catholic obligations were sentimental and not inconveniently intrusive in her transactions with the boy she loved, she had feared that the corruption of Laszlo would keep her from a state of grace. As he grew older, she encouraged him to take the initiative in their encounters. It made her feel violated and less at risk.

'Do sinful things to me,' was an invariable plea.

But Laszlo, increasingly impatient with her aberrant requirements, often sneered that he did not believe in sin nor wish to involve himself with her minor masochistic obsessions.

'Bite me everywhere,' she'd pant. And, 'Suck me where you shouldn't.'

Given his collaboration, there were wild flickers of perdition in her squinting eyes and gasps of 'Mea Culpa' when he finally penetrated what they playfully called her dewy red hibiscus. Ah, dewy red hibiscus. The remembered phrase now brought tears to her eyes.

'But why, Laszlo? Why?' she asked hoarsely when he walked out of her flat.

It was a question that he did not choose to answer.

Shortly after Des Mulcahy was buried, Ada decided to place Aurora in the Sunshine Home for Christian Friends at Purley. Laszlo chauffeured Maya, Ada and Aurora down to the home. It was a tearful occasion, but weekly visits were promised, and they elected to take a rosy view of Ada's judgement as they returned to Crystal Palace.

'It's all for the best,' sighed Maya, squeezing Ada's hand.

'She became impossible,' sniffed Ada.

'Such a beautiful place,' reflected Maya, remembering the Jacobean flourish of the building at the end of an avenue of beeches.

'The rhododendrons and calceolaria outside the orangery were wonderful,' added Ada.

'All those plush emerald lawns for the patients to picnic upon,' enthused Maya. 'How Goulash would love to roll around there. She'd go quite mad with pleasure.'

'And never stop pissing,' said Laszlo.

54

He was nevertheless impressed by the establishment. It would, he reflected, make an ideal home for an English gentleman. The sort of place to which Leslie Howard would have been proud to bring a Bergman. He was not unaware that Miss Egremont, the moon-faced sister in whose charge Aurora had been placed, kept sneaking glances in his direction. On the third occasion he caught her, he responded with a foxy grin. A roseate tinge coloured her neck and cheeks. Miss Egremont was an unpainted, bespectacled woman, ovoid, with short brown hair and thick legs. She moved about with the suspicion of a clump (pes planus, perhaps), but her face was amiable, kind and sadly virginal, like the subject of an ikon, an obscure Armenian saint beyond the perturbations of the flesh. Yet she looked at him covertly and blushed. Laszlo was intrigued. And despite her plainness, he was flattered. How old was she? he wondered. Thirty? Thirty-five? He did manage to exchange a few words with her on the pretext of going back to give Aurora a bar of chocolate he bought at the refectory.

'I th-thought you'd gone,' Miss Egremont stammered in surprise.

'I forgot this,' Laszlo smiled, giving Aurora the chocolate.

He believed ladies were attracted to men with radiant smiles. He now flirted outrageously with shop-assistants, barmaids, women walking their dogs, waiting at bus-stops, even those in the company of other men. He paused for a moment before leaving the dormitory.

'My name's Laszlo,' he announced.

The sister smiled. There was confusion in her large grey eyes.

'I'm Cynthia,' she half whispered, evading his stare.

''Bye, Cynthia,' he called, trying out the sound of her name in a loud and confident voice.

He turned at the door and waited briefly, removing his dark glasses as a sign of growing assurance. She raised a hand in farewell, an unarticulated response forming on her lips.

There was, for Laszlo, an unexpected and positive consequence that flowed from Maya's transient relationship with Ben

Drummond. Some months after his introduction to the accountant – indeed, when they had almost forgotten him – Laszlo received a letter from a Mrs Froline Nablus of the First Nagasaki and Waikiki Trust advising him that he had been recommended for a place on the bank's training scheme by Mayhem and March. Laszlo later discovered that Mayhem and March, the firm of which Drummond was a senior partner, were the bank's taxation advisors. Maya was not impressed.

'That boring man,' she complained. 'My brain goes numb when I think of him.

She conceded, however, that there was no vice in phoning the Nablus woman. This Laszlo did, and was invited to present himself at the bank on a Monday three weeks hence. Maya made a few perfunctory noises of encouragement. But Mr Mudaliar of the Thali of Boundless Light had recently persuaded her that Laszlo's future lay in selling.

'He would make an excellent ice-cream salesman,' the restaurant proprietor had suggested. 'Besides, the money can be phenomenally good. If necessary, I'll assist him financially. A second-hand Bedford, a lick of paint, a reasonable freezer and he's trading.'

On balance, Laszlo liked the idea of running his own ice-cream business. True, it was not a gentleman's calling, but if he played his cards right he could have several dozen men tinkling around London for him in a few years. And Maya felt that her street-wise son could hardly do better than have a van emblazoned with brimming cones, Neapolitan pyramids and pennants with the legend *Laszlo's Lovely Ices* scrolled in scarlet and gilt above the enticements of the illustrations. Although she had once believed that Laszlo should be encouraged to consider a career in one of the professions, Mudaliar had changed her mind.

'Business, my dear. The boy can do no better than grip Destiny by the windpipe and manage his own enterprise.'

Even the careers master, whom Maya bumped into in the greengrocer's shop, seemed enthusiastic.

'That boy of yours will be a tycoon in next to no time,' he predicted.

The assessment was probably due more to the red-faced teacher's admiration for Mrs Gabor than to a belief in the detested Laszlo's potential, but his remark cheered Maya up.

'I'm sure he'll be delighted to hear your opinion,' she smiled.

He wasn't.

'Stupid bastard,' Laszlo grunted.

'But darling, he thinks the world of you,' Maya protested.

So the appointment at the First Nagasaki and Waikiki Trust, which would have been a prospect to celebrate just a few months earlier, was received with apathy. There was even surprise that Laszlo intended making the journey to the City.

'You're not obliged to take the job,' Maya observed gloomily as she pressed his grey flannel suit with a damp cloth while Laszlo buffed up his best black shoes.

Indeed, the mood in the Gabor household on the Sunday evening before Laszlo's interview with Mrs Nablus was one of sullen unease. They both seemed uncomfortably conscious that it would have been scandalously imprudent to have spurned what appeared to be a valuable career opportunity. Yet, on the whole, there was less evidence of unalloyed gratitude than unappreciative resentment at the Joker Fate appeared to have dealt young Laszlo.

Chapter 9

Every newborn is a messiah
– it's a pity he'll turn out
a common rascal.

– Imre Madách

On touching down in Terrastricken with the juicy news of a time-blurring crisis, Bunny Selveratnam found the media less than receptive. And the disclosure that he was almost a messiah received as much attention as would an admission that he generally shot indifferent pool or suffered from a mild form of eczema. So the mystic felt that he was more than fortunate in getting his first public engagement. He had been nudged on by police batons to the Eusapia Palladino Foundation in downtown Honkeyville when his money ran out. The secretary, whom Selveratnam had phoned before chancing the ten-mile schlep in leaky shoes, informed him that the organisation provided meals (nutburgers, ratatouille, oatcakes, thé de tilleul, etc.) for accredited guest speakers on metagnomic matters. It was also possible to arrange a bivouac bed with coarse blankets and a bean pillow in the cellar where they stored their fin-de-siècle memorabilia like planchettes, luminous trumpets, plaques, Tibetan prayer-wheels, a silver epergne that had once belonged to Madame Blavatsky, plaster busts of famous sensitives, and several hundred volumes of automatic writing in a number of as yet undeciphered languages. He could hardly put the phone down fast enough.

The stained-glass windows, onion-domed roof and pink ceramic façade were not hard to spot among the warehouses on Delahaye Boulevard. The construction was the work of Oscar Nepotist (1819–1901), a Pre-Raphaelite gazebo constructor who had anticipated Art Deco by half a century and was largely inspired by the old orangerie at Luton Hoo and the public latrines in Les Jardins Tropiques outside Grenouillet.

The afternoon slot, which Selveratnam had elected to fill, usually attracted no more than twenty or so geriatric beardniks in espadrilles and varicosed flossies wearing straw Iroquois headbands, rattling chains of dharma beads. But the really big card fell the South Indian's way. A lady in purple glasses and a Montez silk turban, hearing Selveratnam's unusual Tamilian articulation, slipped in and sat down at the rear of the hall. A sequoia bench was provided for casuals, travellers and latecomers. The lady was none other than Medusa O'Toole, whose work under the direction of Sham Shilverman had made her an ikon of Western subliminal perceptions. (See Zukertort's *History of World Cinema*, 1969). She had made the long psychic trek from explicit poses plastiques (open legs and sans culottes) in the Bourbon Ginery of Kleptomania, through the shuffling glories of a dozen Shilverman color-flix.

Miss O'Toole, who ran the Eusapia Palladino Foundation for spiritual and tax purposes, rarely made it to downtown Honkeyville. Her presence on this occasion was the result of a chance telephone conversation she had had with the negro janitor of the Foundation (a former blues singer called Husky Jem), who reported that he had discovered among the junk in the disused Persian Steam Room, the haunt of spiritualist sybarites before the Over There War, an authentic triple-lensed polyvisualette. She was minded to give this kooky example of the archaic period of cine-projection to Sham Shilverman as an unique eighty-eighth birthday gift. Shilverman, whose genius as a film-maker obscured his other attributes as a dancer (soft-shoe, taps, Hispanic American and strutting waltzes), sexual athlete (tailed the entire chorus of *Give My Regards to Irkutsk* – eighteen girls in fifty-two hours) and survivor (*Titanic*, 1912), had not only been Medusa O'Toole's principal lover for over fifty years, but was her closest friend. The tall, dark and handsome Shilverman, whose hawkish profile still juiced withered cunts all over the world, had given *Time* a run for its money.

Miss O'Toole had slid down from her eyrie, thirty or so blocks east, in a chauffeur-managed blue Bugatti Royale (the 1927, 12.762 cc, of course — a sentimental memento from the failed king, little Dave Windsor) to pick up the intended present. And while Husky Jem was sprouting hernias in his struggle to carry the one-hundred-and-sixty-pound polyvisualette up a spiral stairway with the assistance of Crippen the chauffeur and a couple of Mohave alkies who slept in the ventilator shaft, Miss O'Toole caught the last ten minutes of Bunny Selveratnam's act. She was enchanted. His phrasing was so unusual — she found his glottal stops lyrical — that she coveted him instantly. Before the secretary of the Eusapia Palladino Foundation had time to point the Indian mystic in the direction of the nutburgers (on Fridays they did a hummus dip as well), Miss O'Toole had appropriated him.

Bunny Selveratnam had survived an intemperate spring in Cheyenne Park, living on French fries, stale pasta and tapwater. But it was Maya's photographs that had really maintained his blood-heat. He tapped the precious prints, tucked in a body-belt under his T-shirt, and glanced apprehensively at the celebrated woman beside him. Her presence was overpowering. He settled his luggage (a red plastic Bigwood's Burgers bag) between his legs and, crouching in the shuttered intimacy of her air-conditioned Bugatti, turned his attention to the pink twinkle of the Concupiscent Complex through a rotating periscope in the glass roof. Miss O'Toole confessed that she had a special reason for capturing him. She desperately needed a holy man for a glittering reception she was giving that night in her mink-lined penthouse in Peacock Towers. He listened politely as she gabbled on about *Love Is the End*, a film Shilverman planned about the love affair between Gaia the Earth Mother and her son Uranus, who'd cut his father's cock off while he was on the job.

'His father's cock?' asked Selveratnam, aghast.

'Sure,' she nodded. 'Things were a shade more robust in the good old days.'

She told him that the film was particularly important to her because she was a high priestess of Gaia and was building an ashram to her in Provence. Miss O'Toole then pointed to a tower of light at the top of the Concupiscent Complex and told him that she lived as near as she could get to the Milky Way. Chester Concupiscent the architect had fixed it for her. She smiled to herself at the memory of the fixing. Selveratnam endured with stoicism her childlike delight with his person when she switched on a vanity strobe to have a better look at him. She prodded him gently with a curved vermilion talon.

'You're an incredibly tiny guy,' she breathed with admiration; 'a miniature Gandhi.'

'It's a disadvantage,' he sighed, remembering with horror the five times he'd been mugged in the last fortnight.

Miss O'Toole tapped the lump under his T-shirt.

'What's this?' she asked.

Selveratnam lifted his shirt, unbuckled his body-belt and fished out a photograph of Maya. It was a nude art-study that Gaspar had taken, one of a set Maya had given him when she decided to become a Hindu. She was posed a little self-consciously astride a Hoover, the suction nozzle holstered between her thighs.

'She's a very juicy piece of action,' Miss O'Toole conceded, 'not unlike I used to be a while back. I rather like the tattoos on her buttocks. What are they?'

'Butterflies.'

'Is she a hooker?'

'She's my fiancée,' Selveratnam murmured profoundly.

Miss O'Toole examined Gaspar's picture of Maya with interest. She smiled at Selveratnam kindly.

'She seems an unusual sort of lady to have taken up with a holy man, if you understand what I mean.'

'She's a Hindu,' he murmured.

'No shit.'

'I love her,' he confessed.

She gave him a big, wet smile.

'I need you to concentrate on tonight. You're going to meet a lot of very smart, influential and sweet people. Contacts are so important at this stage of your career.'

'What career?'

'Everybody has a career, sweetheart. Don't tell me you've never dreamed of being a Sham Shilverman, Wolfgang Ferrari or even a Sunburn Spillano?'

'Who are they?'

Medusa O'Toole laughed with delight.

'It would be terrific,' she reflected, 'if you could put on a bit of a show for my guests. A kind of taster before the dancing.'

'Taster?'

'Yeah. You know, chewing glass, swallowing prussic acid, an Indian rope-trick. Perhaps a bed-of-nails routine?'

Selveratnam sat up with a start.

'I'm not that kind of yogi.'

She seemed disappointed.

'Can't you do anything?'

'I can talk about the blurring of time, but basically I'm a clairvoyant.'

'That's a start,' she murmured with a frown.

'I'm also an adept at regurgitation,' he said. 'You know, live goldfish, marbles, pickled onions, golf balls, bananas even . . .'

This impressed Miss O'Toole.

'You can regurgitate bananas?'

Selveratnam nodded happily, pleased that he could be of some use, and grinned when she took his brown hand in hers.

'I'm sure I could even manage a couple of bicycle inner tubes if pressed.'

He was being slightly cocky, but she clapped her hands with joy.

'Now that is really splendido.' She was thoughtful for a moment. 'And what about sharp stuff, like diamonds?'

'If they were put in a bag first,' he suggested.

'Of course, of course,' she said. 'I happen to know a man in the precious-stones transportation business who would be very interested in your talent. You see, life has opened up for you already.'

Selveratnam moved back into a corner of the car. Miss O'Toole's perfume made him dizzy and he found the wet sheen of her generous lips intimidating. Her studio had once boasted that she had the largest mouth in Vanity Springs. She used to autograph her books (three illustrated editions with bubbles, entitled *Medusa Speaks*, *Medusa Speaks Again*, and *The Silent Medusa*) with huge, red kiss marks. They were now collector's items and retailed on the grey market at five thousand dollars a throw.

'I need a bath,' Selveratnam apologised, aware of his own gaminess.

She pushed her face nearer to him and sniffed him critically.

'You smell like a real person. Sweat, semen, goulash, cigarette smoke, a hint of urine, some smegma maybe; cosy corporeal odours. A lot of very worthwhile people have smelled that way. Prophets, saints, holy joes.'

'You don't,' Selveratnam ventured, darting a coy Chaplinesque smile at her. It was more than a little flirty.

She crushed his hand.

'I smell like a movie-star, sweetheart. A heavy, whorey smell. A hokum smell. Unreality is big business in the dream factories of Vanity Springs. But there's another me, which I'm sure you, being into clairvoyance and all that motherjazz, must have recognised. You see, deep down I'm a simple girl. An authentic godnik, a prophetess of Gaia. At my ashram at L'Amauresque – that's my place in Provence – I allow myself to flower. There, I'm free to smell like damp loam, yeast, warm truffles, goat-cheese. A woman moist with the sap of love.'

She moved closer, pinning him in the corner.

'Have you seen any of my movies?'

He shook his head glumly. The perfume made his eyes water.

'I've made twelve. They're all quite marvellous. Sham Shilverman once told me that I only ever made masterpieces, and he was right. Perhaps we can run through them together. If we didn't sleep, eat or visit the john, it would take about thirty hours.'

'A challenge to any true yogi,' he said gallantly.

'I could tell you the story behind the story.'

'Stories are dreams,' Selveratnam observed, 'and in every

dream there's a universe of other dreams, and in each dream in that universe is yet another universe of dreams. When we find ourselves in the wrong dream, our awareness is blurred. It is important that we dream the right dream.'

Miss O'Toole moved her purple spectacles closer to his face.

'We could go places with you given the right script,' she murmured. 'You do spout the most delicious whimwham I've ever heard.'

He informed her that he was only capable of truth, as he was basically an 'almost messiah' who had come to Honkeyville to save the world.

'What do you know,' she said, taking off her glasses for the first time. 'You've broken out of our shooting script. A genuine Hindu messiah.'

'An almost one,' he corrected.

He told her about the problem he was having subduing his erections when he looked at Maya's photographs. He was waiting for the benediction of detumescence.

'Never buck your balls, boy,' she advised. 'That's where the Life Force hangs out.'

Miss O'Toole informed him that they were using a Nicaraguan as a messiah in the film *Love Is the End*.

'We've stuck a turban on his head and renamed him Rama Ringaroo for political reasons, but his real handle is Pablo Fecundo de Laprida. He's tall, broad-shouldered and well-hung. Plenty of giblets, as they say, although Sham had him circumcised before he was put on contract. It makes a prettier close shot.'

Selveratnam was thinking about the messiah's giblets when he caught sight of her eyes. He flinched. They were a faded blue, pale beyond belief. They seemed too tired and old to be set in such a strongly constructed face.

'I'm waiting for my new eyes. A transplant,' she confided. 'I've ordered young ones. Azure eyes to match my copper hair. I'd like Irish eyes, smiling eyes from the West Coast, Galway perhaps – a virgin's eyes, but they're difficult to find.'

She placed a palm on his shoulder.

'How would you like to be my personal yogi?'

'What will that involve?'

'Well, I'd like to have you sitting cross-legged on a cushion in the corner of the room when I'm entertaining my guests.'

'Is that all?'

'I'd expect you to toss them the odd enigmatic line, read a palm or two and escort them back to a spare bedroom for a psychic massage if I give you the nod. You'll have everything you need if you play things my way.'

'Your way?'

'I've always hankered after leading my own yogi around Vanity Springs on a solid gold collar and chain.'

'Like a dog?'

'Don't get sniffy, kiddo,' she rebuked. 'Remember who I am.'

Selveratnam gazed at her in owlish bewilderment. She was not pleased at his lack of enthusiasm.

'Humility never hurt anyone, sweetheart, especially "almost messiahs".'

There was a sudden and alarming touch of coldness in her voice.

The Concupiscent Complex was a galaxy of light above them as the Bugatti swooped through a churrigueresque archway embellished with silver peacocks dancing on a tamarind tree illuminated by a transit of electric fireflies. It was an ingenious piece of circuitry. They swished down to an underground piazza and into a large lift. They hummed up to the hundredth floor and stepped out into a long gallery.

'There you are,' Miss O'Toole announced grandly, pointing to a row of posters. 'All twelve of my great movies. Arguably the greatest pictures ever made.'

As he walked beside her in the gallery, hurrying to keep pace with her swishing progress, Selveratnam realised that her one step was much longer than two of his. She looked down at him after they'd seen all the pictures.

'If you're really serious about taking a bath, I'd like to bathe

65

you myself. I would regard that as a supreme act of self-abasement. There's something deeply spiritual about bathing a holy man. Hell, how I'd love to have got my hands on Buddha or Mohammed. Even a practising pope would be delicious.'

The little mystic looked at her helplessly. He scuttled behind her into the ninety-foot, mink-lined lounge. He gazed at the mink-covered furniture. It seemed as terrifying as a polar landscape. Selveratnam sneezed. Again and again.

'I'm allergic to fur,' he apologised, his eyes and nose streaming. 'Is all the house like this?'

'All except the bathrooms.' She frowned. 'I'll have to fix you up with a bed in one of those.'

She rushed the sneezing Selveratnam through several doors into a purple temple furnished with marble statuary, urns, several sunken baths, gold fittings, murals from the *Satyricon*, and ceiling mirrors. Inset in the wall was a ten-foot tele-screen and several strategically placed lenses which Selveratnam suspected were the snouts of voyeur cameras. He felt vulnerable. She started to run one of the baths.

'Now, is there anything you need for this act of yours – apart from the live goldfish, golfballs, bananas and bicycle tubes, that is?' she asked.

'I'd appreciate a pair of saffron swimming-trunks, a genuine doe-skin and a bowl of marigolds.'

Miss O'Toole nodded.

'We've got a theatrical retailer called Nirvanarama that specialises in Hindu artefacts. It was started by a local elephant farmer called Sabu.'

The water was now fizzing quite fiercely.

'Don't let that frighten you. We use concentrated seltzer in the filtration unit. Get your duds off and dive in. I think the sandalwood smear that I'm going to use on you will drive you crazy. It has a multi-dimensional tingle.'

Selveratnam dropped his grubby jeans, took off his Mowgli T-shirt and finally pulled down his briefs. Then with a self-conscious shiver he stepped in, sliding down modestly to his neck. Miss O'Toole was having trouble with her glasses. They were all steamed up. She rubbed them with the back of her wrists, then reached down into the water to fish him up. He sensed that he was being rapidly dehumanised as Miss O'Toole soaped him with impersonal vigour. He was unhappy. The multi-dimensional tingle seemed to blur his normally acute perception. Dazed with shame, he clenched his sphincter defensively when her fingers slid crazily between his hams. He was aware of a whirring from somewhere in the ceiling.

'We video all the action in the house,' she explained in response to his questing head movements.

She turned to snatch a hand-towel to use on her glasses, then came at him again with the sandalwood dispenser.

'I can't see a fucking thing,' she bitched angrily.

It was the first time he had heard her use what he considered to be incontestably debased language.

Chapter 10

Miss O'Toole had considered that it would be prudent if Selveratnam, in view of his socially inconvenient allergy, remained in the bathroom. He sat cross-legged on a massage table furnished with a nylon okapi skin (the best Nirvanarama could manage), wearing a pair of xanthin Man Mountain Dean autographed wrestling shorts, miserable with the plastic marigolds in the pewter vaselet before him.

Selveratnam had devoured a mound of cucumber sandwiches, a rampion and whortleberry salad, some turnip cake and a tub of passion-fruit yogurt. He sipped his iced buttermilk, trying to imagine what his Maya was doing. Sleeping, possibly. Hopefully alone.

He now felt the first bewildering ache of separation. How he wished he was at that moment tucked up in bed beside her under the duvet with the cornflower cover he knew so well. He thought wistfully of her silken fair hair tossed across the radiant congruence of her features and felt a silly tear start at the corner of his eye. Oh shit, why had he left her on the other side of the ocean? Perhaps Miss O'Toole would loan him the money to fly back. He looked up at the telescreen, watching the guests standing around in little groups, holding glasses, laughing, buzzing in the mink-lined hive about matters he did not want to understand. Part of the party sound was Bimbo Braganza's languorous chords. She was a thin and toothy lady with sleepy dromedary's eyes, and prematurely white hair (she was hardly thirty) that went well with her Brazilian tan. Bimbo had a nervously attractive manner of twitching her head, a piano player's tic, every dozen bars or so. It was her trademark and set her apart from the other soloists who specialised in drawing-room cabaret. She only worked for the cream of Honkeyville society and was acquainted with almost everybody on the cocktail circuit. Her husband, an ex-wrestler called El (short for Elmo) Catrash, was demonically jealous of her. He hung around for hours in his pink stretched Cadillac, waiting to carry her home after every engagement. Bimbo on the other hand, despite her terror of Mr Catrash, was not averse to being invested by any gentleman who took her fancy. And most gentlemen who said hello to her, did. Bimbo had to slot in these extramarital flips in the fifteen-minute or so eating breaks that she as an artiste was allowed between sessions of seamless playing. The problem with this arrangement was that she hardly had time to grab the odd piroshki.

'I tort dose bums fed yuh,' Mr Catrash would grumble when Bimbo asked to be sped to an all-night café to pick up a hamburger with French fries and a side salad.

'Eet was just garbage, El,' she complained, 'prawn canapés, smoked salmon, leetle birds on steeks, lobster mousse, caviar. Oh, how I hater that sheet.'

'No hamburgers?' Mr Catrash would enquire solicitously.

'You must be keeding,' Bimbo would sneer, checking her face and neck carefully in the mirror for the stigmata of passion. Nine o'clock shadows were her principal barbes noires.

Miss O'Toole, like many other thoughtful hostesses, was mindful of Bimbo's sex breaks.

'You may use the second guest bedroom, Bimbo darling,' she'd say, handing over a key, when the pianist arrived.

Down below, by the trash-can area, in a pink stretched Caddy, Mr Catrash worked his way through a pile of Dick Tracy comics and consumed a dozen or so cans of diet Coke. When the need arose, he would get out of the limousine and piss ostentatiously into a two-gallon gasoline can he carried around for such a purpose. And nobody ever protested. But apart from everything else, Bimbo Braganza was a great performer who could pick up between five and seven thousand dollars for an evening's work. On the piano, that is.

Selveratnam was scheduled to give interested guests a ten-minute private reading. He was to follow the face-to-face with his regurgitation act, which Medusa felt sure would be the high spot of the night. Then it was dancing until cock-crow. It was an old O'Toole tradition to keep the guests around until the mixed-grill and chilled egg-flip breakfast.

Medusa O'Toole appeared on shot. Her celebrated face, still wearing the purple glasses, filled the screen. She knew exactly what to do. The legendary Sham Shilverman had once assured her that her talent lay in the way she used her unique mouth. And she never forgot his observation.

'Darling,' he said, 'that's the most potent kissing organ the world has ever seen.'

She had her detractors, of course. The pinko critic Gore Meagain (1930–1967), a fruity troublemaker if ever there was one, vulgarly libelled the O'Toole asset as 'something stitched together from recycled fallopian tubes'. It cost his paper, the *Terrastricken Monitor*, three million dollars out of court, and ultimately Mr Meagain his shallow life. A Latvian admirer of the actress, one Albert Nyrlandis, standing in the next stall of a public pissoir to her defamer, blasted him through his right ear with a forty-five as the sonofabitch, oblivious of danger, shook the final droplet from his cock. Nyrlandis, who pleaded diminished responsibility, drew a suspended sentence on a lesser charge of aggravated assault and became, until his death in a road accident, the Chief Security Officer at Sham Shilverman's Silver Peacock Studios at Vanity Springs.

Selveratnam watched Miss O'Toole with fascination. Her expressive lips teased the camera, the red pout flowered, moist and predatory, evoking the viscous magic of a stomatopod approaching its prey.

'Are you ready, honey?' she called out to the Tamilian. 'It's lift-off time.'

Selveratnam's show went well – probably because he hardly used his prescience at all. It was almost like a vaudeville act. This seemed to satisfy most of the tipsy guests who sat at his feet in the purple bathroom, listening with amusement to his enlightened observations on their business, love and family prospects. Where he suspected imminent death (in four out of twenty-seven cases), the horror was sidestepped with alacrity. But what had once been a clairvoyant certainty had now regressed into a blurred instinct. It was fortunate that the cigar-smoking gentlemen in tuxedos and the ladies in haute couture robes, beaming stupidly with the benediction of booze, did not want to become intimately acquainted with the cancerous worms lurking in their bowels, or small-talk about the haemoglobic sewage that would shortly inhibit the peaceful gush of life coursing through their arteries. So he joked and generalised, sipping his buttermilk while theatrically twirling a plastic marigold between his nose-picking finger and thumb.

'Take care,' he pleaded, 'when travelling in excessively fast automobiles, sleeping with your best friend's partner, walking alone up dark alleys, cheating vengeful people, shooting shit into your veins, being confronted with the handguns of drunken lovers, chatting up good-looking boys in public latrines or going shark-fishing in rubber dinghies.'

He went on and on, but knew that nothing could avert the inexorable karmic tide that was about to extinguish their present incarnations.

Sometimes he played the game in reverse, telling apocalyptic lies to make moral points. When a greying Episcopalian minister who looked like Abraham Massey asked Selveratnam if he would escape detection were he to slip an overdose of Nembutal into his paraplegic spouse's hot chocolate, the shocked Tamilian instantly predicted disgrace, conviction and a thirty-year haul in the penitentiary. However, something in his water told him that the pious murderer would not only evade the law, but would continue ecstatically humping his sixteen-year-old step-daughter, eventually leaving the district to live with this young woman, twenty-five years his junior, in unsequestered fornication on the victim's legatary dosh. And Selveratnam saw no remorse in their souls, only a vibrant happiness that mocked the moral justice he had always believed powered the universe. Perhaps their nemesis lurked in the next incarnation. It was a hopeful thought. But that vista was clouded and beyond his rapidly decaying long-term focus. The blurring had indeed become worse. He had even begun to have reservations about his ability to save the world. The doubts had started during the weeks he had spent dossing on a bench in Cheyenne Park. Perhaps it was the knocks on the head he'd suffered at the hands of muggers. His spiritual life, he felt, would never be quite the same again. Every time he attempted to meditate, he was diverted by the image of Maya's cherry furrow on that last afternoon they'd made love in his room. The memory of her moist and palpitant flesh consumed his consciousness, a salutary rebuke to his feckless flight away from the comfort of her encircling thighs. Oh shit. What had he done? And he sensed that the clouds had grown darker since his arrival at the O'Toole penthouse. His occultic potency was leaking away down some astral black hole. He felt that he was in a garden of beautiful but poisonous plants. Miss O'Toole and her friends had sorrow in their smiles and violence in their brittle laughter. The smell of a grave, damp earth and rotting wood, filled his nostrils. He had long suspected that Maya and he would not have long together. And now, he began to see only one thing. The dark tunnel from which there is no return. He feared death because of his attachment to Maya. Why had he left her? Who was he to save the world when he could not save his own love? He tried to still his mind before he began the regurgitation act. What was the bloody use of these silly tricks? He closed his eyes, aware of Medusa O'Toole's presence. He tried to struggle down the path to blissful nothingness, but she stood before him, an impediment to his peace.

'Om.'

'What are you omming about?'

'I'm trying to meditate.'

'Are you unhappy?' she enquired softly.

'Yes.'

'Dark night of the lower bowel. Try some bicarbonate of soda, darling.'

She made a move to remove her purple glasses.

'Don't,' he pleaded, knowing that the pale laser stare would diminish him even more.

'You're afraid of my poor old eyes,' she pouted sadly.

'Yes,' he whispered, whimpering inaudibly to himself.

'World saver indeed,' she mocked. 'That's a vocation for the priestess of Gaia. The Earth is not safe in the hands of rapists, defilers and polluters of women. If you want to play the messiah, be guided by me.'

'Messiahs don't take orders,' he protested weakly.

'My messiahs do, darling. Why won't you be my yogi pogy? Why won't you be Medusa's pet?'

He shook his head fearfully. Her wet mouth was unbearably close. Selveratnam confronted the labial menace with trepidation. A rustling appeared to come to him from within his own skull. It was a voice. A possession. And he knew who it was.

'Women,' Gaia murmured, 'have two pairs of lips and so are a celestial suck or two ahead of men.'

He remembered screaming as Medusa locked him in her arms and ravaged his mouth with hers, forcing her tongue between his teeth. He struggled into unconsciousness. When he recovered, he found himself sitting in a pool of water, propped up against the jacuzzi, its tepid fountain spraying over his bare shoulders. Over the speakers came the sound of an unusual voice. Bimbo Braganza, who rarely obliged with a vocal, was accompanying herself as she abrasively lisped to a 3–3–2 Havanatine rhythm. The bitter song was about unrequited lust.

Chapter 11

Medusa's interest in Selveratnam diminished significantly after his eccentric behaviour in the bathroom. Indeed, it evaporated. He was, she concluded, an unchivalrous turd. Abandoning the insensible mystic by the jacuzzi, she returned to her guests, flitting among them like a giant moth in her shimmering silver gown, nodding, smiling and accepting their compliments with the graciousness people had come to expect from her. Medusa's ears buzzed with murmurs of 'Wonderful', 'Terrific', 'Stupendous', 'Fantastic' and 'Wow'. And she herself was not unskilled at simulating sincerity, capable of a convincing 'I'm feeling like a million bucks' when tormented by fears of a disintegrating genito-urinary system; or a gushy 'But honey, you're looking utterly divine' to shadows her deficient eyes were unable to adequately define. She charmed Sham out of his invalid chair for what sounded vaguely like a bossa nova, resting her head on his shoulder as they bent their knees to the beat.

'You mad at something, honey?' he asked.

'I'm fine.'

'Sunburn can't stop talking about your tiny banana-swallower.'

'Anybody could do that sort of shit with practice, I suppose,' she grunted.

'Not me, honey,' Sham coughed, 'not me.'

They danced cleverly, hardly rocking more than half a pace backwards or forwards.

'I'm flying to L'Amauresque next week,' she announced gloomily.

'That soon?' he asked huskily, holding her closer.

Medusa felt bleak. She could not recall being rejected before. Ever since she was a little girl tap-dancing with the Pretty Pussies, the world had overwhelmed her with love and appreciation. Men had always wanted to kiss her. When she was barely twelve, a charming Southern colonel had gifted her a beautiful quarter-bred piebald and a Spanish saddle with a silver pommel for the privilege of being allowed to brush his grey moustache against her lightly fledged mons veneris. And her agent, Clay McHutchinson, educated her in the subtler proprieties of the smoke-filled gentlemen's clubs where her theatrical career had started. He fiercely protected her from those who tried to compromise her reputation with loutish language and dreary smut. And although Clay could be jesuitical in his estimation of the degrees of carnal complicity, he was pragmatic about the severely restricted options available to a working girl.

'There's no vice in guys looking at it,' Clay declared. 'You're not going to catch a dose or find yourself with a lump in your sump as the result of a respectable leer.'

He modified this rule to exploit the possibilities of the market as she matured to a nubile thirteen, permitting a chaste kiss (no tongues) on any part of her body for a hundred dollars a throw. Medusa was amused by the number of gentlemen who chose the same spot, and remembered how boring it was lying on red silk cushions, posed provocatively for a succession of elderly lechers. The kissing tickled her and made her giggle, but at an average of five hundred dollars a day Clay thought it was an inconvenience she should endure. When defloration did come, she was nearly fourteen and the occasion was meticulously stage-managed. Clay, a sentimental dog at heart, had arranged for a group of Paraguayan serenaders in the garden under the bedroom balcony, a white Pekinese puppy as a penetration gift, and the discreet presence of an old duenna in an adjoining chamber, should Medusa need her intervention. At the time, the negotiated ten thousand dollars in escrow, payable after a preliminary medical examination, hardly concerned her. After commission and expenses, it was discounted to about six thousand – still a significant sum, which she promptly invested in General Motors stock.

The evening started with her favourite card game of Pounce. Leon, the señor concerned, introduced her to tequila and blue Maresky cigarettes. Then he insisted on reciting poetry:

'La blanca palomica,
Al Arca con el vamose ha tornado
Y ya la tortolica
Al socio deseado
En las riberas verdes ha hallado.'

She asked him to stop after a few minutes as the verse made her dizzy, but Leon claimed it was the blue Maresky. Their yenidje leaves, he told her, had been dried between trays of cocaine crystals. At first, she imagined him to be a little effeminate, guided by his light voice, large doe eyes, and the nervous way he drew at his cigarette by placing it gently against, rather than between, his lips. Even when he disrobed, she was uncertain what she should look for, and watched him shower with child-like wonder. He appeared to be unaware of her scepticism as he soaped his hairy body, singing happily to her in an alien tongue. It looked, she recalled, quite contracted, wrinkled and innocuous, unlike anything she had been led to expect – until, that is, he asked her to towel him dry, at which point it inflated with astonishing speed. Everything turned out to be as uncomplicated as Clay had predicted. The moment the light was dowsed, the Paraguayans lowered their voices to a melodious hush, Leon lifted her shantung nightgown and she was astonished to discover that he had entered her without any obvious resistance, this being, she later realised, a positive consequence of the blue Maresky's narcotic effect. She tried to look at his face to ascertain whether things were going well, but it was too dark to see anything. After a while she began to enter into the spirit of the adventure.

'Am I doing OK?' she demanded as he panted away above her.

'Si,' he whispered, groaning and chewing the pillow beside her ear.

She learned in a frank post-ejaculatory exchange that gratuitous comment disturbed his concentration. He employed,

76

he confessed, the mental recapitulation of poetry as a counter-erethistic strategy, and he extolled in particular the anaesthetic virtues of St John of the Cross. At the time of their first coupling, however, she was ignorant of his aversion to conversation.

'Leon?' she called anxiously, suspecting something was amiss as he subsided onto her shoulder.

He lay across her, damp, drained and inert, at a time when she would have much preferred increased activity. She was alarmed. His eyes were closed, his respiration uneven and his face felt uncommonly cold. So she was relieved when he eventually raised himself, blew his nose on her discarded nightgown and dismounted from the saddle of her parted thighs. It was, she discovered as he struck a match and lit another blue Maresky, the end of Act 1. She switched on the light. From the garden came a round of polite applause from the Paraguayans. She and Leon enjoyed a kind of reflective intermission as they reclined together in the well of the bed, puffing away, sipping tequila and listening to a sad song about a poor hunchback who dived from the bell-tower after being denied the favours of a young negress. When Leon nibbled her ear and suggested it was time for Act 2, she responded with enthusiasm. Out went the light, the Paraguayans lowered their voices, and before first light they had managed Acts 3, 4 and 5.

'It was duck soup,' she boasted to Clay, making short work of a grapefruit and a slab of peanut-buttered seedcake in the warm morning sun. She would never forget the monkey flowers moist with dew and the soaring excitement of being a woman at last.

'It's much more than the breaching of a membrane, isn't it, Clay?' she murmured.

He shot her a cat-like and covert look, nodding slowly.

'I suppose it is,' he replied uncertainly.

Oh, the mystery of a man's dream, investing a strip of her skin with such importance. It was at that point that she first contemplated with sleepy contentment the white Pekinese puppy curled up in a hat-box. There was also, she remembered, her General Motors stock.

The Paraguayans scuttled off in their wheezing Hotchkiss, and Leon scorched away through a cloud of red dust in his snarling blue Hispano. It was strange Medusa never saw him again, the high-class young man who had occupied her body with such artistry and style. He died many years later, fighting for the Falangists, leaving as his epitaph a slim volume of romantic verse published at his own expense at Valladolid.

She sat with Clay by the swimming-pool over the debris of breakfast, sipping orange juice and listening to a record he felt she might like. Medusa thought it dreary. It was, she recalled, 'La Vie en Rose', a song she had always detested, repulsed by the nasal sentimentality of the chanteuse. She sensed after a while that his promotion of this tacky music had an ulterior purpose. He was making dog's eyes at her. His eyes were bark-brown and watery. He pointed out that the honeymoon villa had been rented until the following morning.

'You?' She laughed with incredulity. 'You?'

She had always seen him in his subordinate, administrative role.

'Why not?' he whispered, looking as lugubrious as a Labrador waiting for its biscuit. He tickled the inside of her thigh under the table.

'Don't,' she protested, knocking his hand away in disgust.

Of course, it was a ghastly mistake to mix business with pleasure. Their association rapidly regressed into a celebration of Clay's priapism. He was immensely proud of his veined truncheon, oiling it so it looked even bigger. On more than one occasion, she caught him standing naked before a mirror, smiling madly to himself. He became quite impossible and began to treat her like a wife or, even worse, a girl-friend, examining her breasts and thighs for evidential bites and scratches. Which made his continued poncing off her body all the more inexplicable. True, Clay only set up super clients for her like hot-shot industrialists, international gangsters, film-stars, religious leaders, state governors and Uncle Moose. That liaison had ended in a ballooning belly and Medusa's first enforced stay at the Nabrosky State Clinic.

After two years of misery, she was obliged to make the most of her opportunity to elope with a billiard-table manufacturer called Monty, a bearded bear-like man who smoked monster-sized cigars, wore fur coats and travelled around in a chauffeur-driven Dusenberg. They submitted to a marriage ceremony on her sixteenth birthday at a crumbling seventeenth-century church in Conception, providing the priest with fictitious names and addresses.

'Do you realise that we're only married in the eyes of the Almighty?' Monty laughed roguishly as they escaped in a shower of confetti, small silver coins and goat-droppings thrown by a band of beggars he had hired to play the part of wedding-guests. It was an ingenious move. Although they suspected that their marital lapses would probably aggravate God, they felt comforted that they would not be inconvenienced by administrative complications like divorce or alimony should one partner decide to legally enforce the vows. Monty, an older man (he was sixty-three), was quite the opposite of the offensively proprietorial Clay. Medusa's infidelity was never questioned as long as she was discreet. She admired Monty's tolerance and would have remained with him until he was carried off from the toxic effects of an elderly elk-pie thirty years later, had she not fallen crazily in love with Sham Shilverman.

Sham, who now found it painful to stand for more than periods of five minutes, liked to use that time to demonstrate he could still dance, particularly if the photographer's popping flash-bulbs caught him on the floor with a pretty girl in his arms. Nothing elevated his morale more than a smiling picture (he preferred them to use the 1929 print) of a lean, handsome heartbreaker in the *Movie Maker*, above a caption headline, 'Sham Shilverman cutting a rug at a Vanity Springs shindig'. Over the last seventy years, there had been hundreds of such pictures. Girls all over the world cut them out and pasted them on their bedroom walls – pictures of Shilverman enjoying himself, sharp as a hound's tooth and full of pep. He was known for his pep. Letters from prospective mothers begging for sperm donations arrived in his mail every day. They beat on his front door and ambushed him in the street. He became a victim of that 'pep' publicity. He was tempted into affairs more fortunate men would have avoided. And when an unscrupulous vibrator manufacturer marketed a giant 'Big Sham' model (it sold a million), his problems multiplied. In every 'in-depth' interview, Shilverman declared that what he was searching for was 'lerv'. It eluded him for many years. No sooner had he made a solemn resolve to 'lerv' one woman, when he found another he really preferred. Three marriages on, he was still overwhelmed by the difficulty of making up his mind. It took a Viennese psychiatrist to advise Sham that what he was really looking for was a woman with a big juicy mouth and long legs. But however hard he tried, the mouths were never quite big enough and the legs were always an inch or two shorter than he would have wished. He began to despair that he would ever discover both these qualities in the same person. And then he saw Medusa O'Toole. Divine intervention was the only way he could explain the miracle. He offered her the starring role in *The Waltzing Werewolves* seconds after they were introduced, indicating that she would have to return to Vanity Springs with him that night.

Monty saw them off, looking impressive in his ash mink coat and ermine cap. They stood at the door of Shilverman's private Pullman. He asked Sham to look after his wife and begged Medusa to hurry back to him as soon as possible. Kisses were blown to each other. Medusa wiped away a tear, a native prevision informing her that her happy life with Monty could be drawing to a close. It was a dull evening, scented by burning pine-twigs and whiffs of raw brandy from a nearby distillery. Snow had started to fleck through the air as the train pulled away from the almost deserted platform. Lights twinkled. From somewhere over the gorse-banked culvert came the muted jangle of a phonograph playing Cow Cow Davenport's 'Chimes Blues'. They waved to the bearded man in his ash mink coat. Monty waved back. Then he could no longer be seen. The moment he disappeared from view, Medusa forgot him. That precious gift of selective amnesia often protected her from psychic hurt.

When they returned to Shilverman's stateroom, Medusa asked Sham what he wanted her to do.

'Take your clothes off for a start,' he suggested, loosening his spotted silk cravat.

She felt vulnerable, compliant and excited all at the same time, her heightened perceptions inducing a sort of pulsing dizziness. They splashed together in the blue porphyry tub (he chivalrously on the faucet side) as they rattled past the scabby gas-stations, austere bars, clapboard chapels and wintry bleakness of the goodlands.

Jee-ho-vah . . .
Jee-ho-vah . . .
Jee-ho-vah . . .

went the train, rattling westwards at ninety miles an hour. Their unofficial chaperone, a jovial, wheat-coloured Puerto Rican scrub-lady and back-scratcher, pleasured their epidermises with a variety of abrasive tools and saponic sponges as she crooned to them. A profusion of bath-salts, shampoos and perfumed emollients. Steam everywhere. Medusa, who had until then enjoyed the intimate friendship of a number of well-endowed gentlemen, was nevertheless captivated by Shilverman's pythonic equipment. And Sham, despite his considerable experience, was immoderately stimulated by the well-fleshed ruby lips he glimpsed below Medusa's auburn thatch whenever she lifted a slender leg to be hammamed by the musical Hispanic. Brandy and sheegars were taken (Medusa had acquired the silly habit from Monty) in Sham's walnut-panelled boudoir. They reclined in their shorty dressing-gowns on a capacious bed, propped up by ptarmigan-down Dutch wives, silk-sheathed, tasselled and cool, reflected in the blue-mirrored ceiling. Shilverman had found that the smoking of a twenty-minute sheegar in contemplation of the act of 'lerv' produced in both partners the meditative calm necessary before any excessively ecstatic engagement.

Jee-ho-vah . . .
Jee-ho-vah . . .
Jee-ho-vah . . .

They savoured each other at a distance of three feet or so, their reined and snaffled desires expressed by the wriggling of bare toes and the fidgety friction of soles against insteps. They talked quietly of mundane matters, conscious that their ardour, almost unbearable when the rocking of the train moved them together, could not reasonably be restrained much longer. Medusa gave him a recipe for Benedictine-marinated cannabis cake, reminisced about her first childhood visit to London's celebrated Paedophile Club and admitted her addiction to Whit Waltman. Sham chatted about breeding German Rollers when he was a boy, the time he rode in a six-day bicycle race and of a poker game he got into in Paris with Doc Kearns, Battling Siki and Mistinguett. It was Medusa who rather suggestively killed her sheegar when there was more than a puff or two left. Shilverman, finding that invitation insufferably provocative, jetted two inches of Royal Perique through the shutters into the prairie night. They exchanged raunchy smiles. He parted her dressing-gown and went hungrily down in search of labial honey.

'Oh, Sham,' she panted, gripping his head between her muscled thighs, her eyes goggling at the ceiling-mirror.

Jee-ho-vah . . .
Jee-ho-vah . . .
Jee-ho-vah . . .

And the boudoir light stayed on until the train raced through eleven tunnels into the morning sunshine. But what they had really celebrated that winter night was the start of a brilliant partnership and twelve wonderful O'Toole musicals.

'I will never share you with another woman,' Medusa warned when they got to Vanity Springs two days later. It was, for her, an uncharacteristic piece of girlish nonsense.

'Will that be reciprocal?' asked Sham.

'Sure,' Medusa laughed prettily.

But Sham soon learned that Medusa found it difficult to keep her word. He realised in time that cheating boosted her oestrogen level, and the stimulation of clandestine affairs kept her young. Deprived of sexual variety, she became morose and suicidal, thinking little of slicing her wrists open if she didn't get the multi-orgasmic jigger-jag she felt she deserved. And so, although Medusa never returned to Monty, she did not ever move in with Sham, content to be referred to by the intrusive tabloids as his 'girl-friend'. However, passing traffic was central to her sanity. Sham had often driven down to her place at night, nursing a raving beat, only to find a strange car parked in her drive. And if he did get dispirited by the chance discovery of an unfamiliar pair of men's slippers on the tiger-skin rug by her bed or confused by her eccentric telephone conversations with unlikely tradesmen ('Not at present . . . Yes . . . Oh, yes . . . Later, perhaps . . . No . . . It's difficult at present . . . Ciao . . .') he knew that it was not a simple matter of infidelity. His Medusa was guided by Gaia. Indeed, Sham, and even Mord Freebee the Consultant Psychiatrist of the Vanity Springs Mental Hygiene Clinic, secretly believed that she was probably an incarnation of the Earth Mother herself, from whose wonder-cleft all rivers of desire flowed. It was quite a thought.

The band began to play a tango. Maybe it was because it was 'Despedida', an old favourite of Sham's, that he attempted an imprudently adventurous glissade while his eyes were shut and his brain struggled to remember Skinny Suzy, a Carib dancer from Dominica. It was her tune on those faraway, steamy evenings at Chantal's Bar in Roseau. A thin, sad girl, whose damp copper skin smelled of rose-petals and freshly dug earth. His right knee locked without warning. The discomfort was difficult to bear. He stumbled from the floor helped by Medusa, his face contorted with pain. A boyish-looking paparazzo popped several flashes at an old man struggling towards his invalid-chair.

'Fuck you,' Sham gasped, reaching wildly for the Pentax.

Medusa O'Toole fell upon the young photographer, using both hands to squeeze his throat.

'This is a private party,' she hissed.

Shilverman signalled to two swarthy men in tight dark suits. The response was electric. They ran forward to pinion and half-nelson the troublemaker to the bathroom, where a bewildered Selveratnam watched them smash and grind the camera on the floor-tiles. They dunked the photographer's head in a bidet filled with cold water before dragging their victim savagely into the hall. Selveratnam followed them to the front door. He shaped his forefingers and thumbs together in a benedictory O as he transmitted positive and pacific vibes.

'Om,' he hummed.

One of the men in a tight dark suit sprang tigerishly at the Hindu and banged him against the furry wall.

'What did you say, turdhead?' he snarled, drawing a clenched and heavily ringed fist back to ear level.

Selveratnam sneezed in his assailant's face. He was released instantly. The man ducked as Selveratnam sneezed again and again. The second man, having stepped behind the cloakroom door, screwed a silencer onto the muzzle of his revolver. The first man retreated a few paces from the sneezing Indian, using his handkerchief to wipe away flecks of phlegm from his face, hands and suit. The second man, moving out of cover, raised the revolver in his right hand, resting it on his left forearm as he aimed at the little sneezer's head.

'Total the turdhead,' the first man urged.

A finger had already been curled around the trigger when Medusa O'Toole arrived. She was probably just in time.

'There's no need for that, Vittorio,' she called. 'He's a sorta guest.'

Medusa smiled her legendary wet smile at Selveratnam when the men had vamoosed.

'We can't be too careful,' she explained ruefully, leading the sneezing mystic back into the bathroom. 'That shitbesmitten paparazzo was trying to humiliate poor Sham.'

Chapter 12

Medusa O'Toole had arranged for Selveratnam's transportation to the Spillano Garbage Corporation's offices in her blue Bugatti Royale as a result of interest expressed by Sunburn Spillano, the son of the President of the company.

'Our people can probably do business with this guy,' he had said to Medusa after watching the Tamilian's regurgitation act.

'There,' she said to the diminutive mystic as he spooned away at his mess of semolina and warm milk at breakfast, 'you're on your way to the stars. Submit yourself to Sunburn's genius and you could have a glittering future.'

'A commercial career is hardly what I'd imagined for myself,' Selveratnam reflected glumly. 'I'd hoped that Mr Shilverman would have given me some exposure in his new film. Getting started as a messiah is a difficult business.'

She regarded him thoughtfully.

'The world has more need of garbage-disposal technicians than it has for "almost messiahs". And in my professional opinion, sweetheart, you're more a run-of-the-mill chorus yogi than a top-of-the-bill messiah. Now Pablo Fecundo de Laprida, alias Rama Ringaroo, my Nicaraguan boy, can splash a very fancy crawl, scream Tarzan calls and swing from trees.'

'What kind of messiah is that?' Selveratnam asked petulantly.

'A box-office messiah, honey. The sort that sells tickets. A credible specimen needs to be at least six foot two and weigh a hundred and eighty pounds. He should have a melodious voice, good teeth, acceptable muscle structure, and head-and-shoulders symmetry that is not unbalanced by a modest-sized halo. And let's not forget the photogenic giblets.'

Selveratnam looked pensive. They'd discussed the grotesque doctrine of messianic giblets on several occasions. Miss O'Toole held a sort of neo-Blakean view that nakedness had important

Edenic resonances. Her messiah was essentially a 'before the Fall' character who eschewed fig-leaves. When Selveratnam pointed out that Hindus never had a fall, she laughed derisively, declaring that the concept was implicit in the fact of human imperfection.

'And that's revealed truth, sweetheart,' she snapped when he opened his mouth to protest, 'straight from Gaia's mouth. OK?'

She helped him into the silver lamé matador jacket she'd dug out of a basket of old theatre costumes (it was the only one that fitted), slipping it over his laundered Mowgli T-shirt. She pointed to the hat on the chair.

'You can have the tricorne as well if you want,' she smiled.

He shook his head. Then, looking up, he saw that Crippen had arrived to collect him.

'Give me a buzzo when you've got your sandals under the table,' she suggested gently.

At that moment the phone rang, and she was into a high-spirited business palaver with somebody of obvious importance. She didn't hear his polite goodbye.

'Sham,' she giggled girlishly. 'I've decided to mammy up for Gaia. Uh huh . . . Blackface.'

Sunburn Spillano, who facially bore a remarkable resemblance to the Italian philosopher and man of action Benito Bandito, was a smallish man. He was just four foot nine inches in his socks, although with a bit of clever leverage from ingeniously designed footwear he could pass for around five-three. There were slight traces of dwarfism in his stubby hands, rolling gait and relatively large head, but he was not, contrary to malicious stories, sensitive about his size, for he rarely made silly jokes against himself, which sort of over-compensation, it is said, often points to feelings of inadequacy.

Selveratnam found Spillano's office decorated with bright Lichtenstein originals and a phosphorescent SHAZAM on his sky-blue desk, well-lit and pleasant. Woven into the white carpet were the black words with twelve-inch-high letters reading

SPLAT . . . POW . . . BLAT . . . AH . . . EE . . . OW . . . SPLA . . .
AARGH . . . KER . . . RUNCH . . . and SWISH.

Spillano's success, for he was barely thirty-five, was attributed to a photographic memory when it worked. For he was also intermittently amnesiac. He claimed to remember the interior fabric of his mother's womb, in which location he had devoted the final three months of gestation to independently devising a system of square-root classification that, although not entirely original (Trachtenberg had arrived at similar conclusions some years earlier), demonstrated an unusual level of numeracy. He showed little interest in the written word and did not have any books in his office. He confessed that his brain absorbed information so rapidly that he had no serious need to use books for reference or reprise. The advantage his prodigiosity gave him over other persons made him at times impatient, but to his credit he endeavoured not to let frustration sap his equanimity when, in his own words, dealing with less-gifted bananas. He collected cigarette packets, marbles, ceremonial kites, and sink-stoppers. He enjoyed solving simple chess problems and colouring his Superman book with crayons. He lunched each day, at about eleven, on Risotto di Peoci or perhaps some grilled Pesce Spada, accompanied by a glass or two of Marsala. The meal was prepared for him at a Sicilian restaurant in nearby Vendetta Street and delivered by the proprietor himself in a silver Volpi Serenissima coupé. He always ate alone.

Spillano looked up at Selveratnam. He smiled.

'I'm glad you came,' he said, 'and I'd like you to know how much I enjoyed your show.'

'Thank you.'

'What would you say,' Spillano asked thoughtfully, 'if our organisation were to offer you what is sometimes referred to in the racier business journals as a promising career? It would mean money – a commodity, according to Miss O'Toole, you do not appear to possess in embarrassing abundance. I'm talking of the kind of money that would enable you to tipple French fizz, dine in fancy chop-joints, wear sharp jackets, travel in flash limos and enjoy the company of well-constructed ladies who would not be excessively offended if you interfered with the more interesting parts of their bodies.'

Selveratnam nodded politely.

'What would I have to do?' he asked.

Spillano wagged an instructive finger.

'You would be a sort of executive courier. A familiar big-wheel at international airports, carrying a smart, monogrammed bison-skin case in which there'll be the usual boring commercial documents.'

'Is that all?'

Spillano's eyes slitted.

'There will, of course, be another bag.'

'Another bag?'

'Something like the bicycle tube you slid down that cultivated gullet of yours at Miss O'Toole's party.'

'And what would I be carrying in that?'

'It would only confuse you to get involved with mind-sapping details. And we never intentionally confuse our staff. The unions wouldn't approve. So leave the microscopic print to the technicians. OK?'

Selveratnam appeared doubtful.

'Do you mean that I wouldn't know what I was transporting in my own body?'

Spillano nodded his head.

'That's exactly what I mean. We call it ignorance insurance. The information we inflict on our employees can be summarised under three heads: instructional data, unequivocal commands, and terminal warnings. We don't horseshit around with management opinions, company propaganda, public relations studies, sales graphs, flow-charts and toothy pictures of our employees in quasi-social contexts. We are not in the friendship, self-deception or fantasy business. The Spillano Garbage Corporation is dedicated to the high-speed generation of profit and not much else.'

Sunburn Spillano showed his white even teeth. There was a long, uncomfortable silence.

'Basically, Mr Spillano,' Selveratnam said, 'I'm a spiritual type. I feel I have a messianic role.'

'Is that so? Well, right now, Mr Selveratnam, we wouldn't even have a slot for J.C. himself. However, we'll work on it. Who knows? In a couple of years, messiahs could be the flavour of the month. Tell me, can you walk on water, levitate, raise the dead and all that sort of motherloving jazz?'

Selveratnam looked perplexed.

'I've never really tried walking on water,' he admitted, 'which anyhow would be a rather hazardous enterprise, since I can't swim. As for raising the dead, one would, I suppose, need regular access to fresh corpses to get the hang of it. A job in the morgue would probably provide the appropriate opportunities for training, something I would find unbearably repugnant and which would be against the strict obligations of my caste. However, I thoroughly comprehend the principles of floating, although I haven't as yet attained the accepted astral standard, which is ten seconds with one's toes off the ground. Naturally, free falls from aeroplanes, being fired from cannons and other artificial aids don't count.'

'Naturally,' grunted Spillano.

'Of course,' Selveratnam declared proudly, 'my guru, Yogi Govinda Popatsahib of Conjeeveram, is a genuine floater. He frequently hovers for half a minute or so. Like a hawk.'

'It's strange,' Spillano observed, 'how all the juicier miracles seem to be in other places or in other times. But speaking commercially, resurrection has very lively possibilities in the Western world. It would beat the steaming shit out of life assurance. And Spillano Garbage is always prepared to market miracles.'

Selveratnam shrugged.

'I suspect that you're taking too narrow a view of a messiah's responsibilities,' he complained. 'You see, Mr Spillano, I'm an authority on the blurring of time.'

'Blurring of time, eh? That's hardly going to contribute to a sexy bottom line, Mr Selveratnam. Now, we feel that you and the Spillano Garbage Corporation are on track for an innovative and mutually lucrative relationship. Think of it as a pre-messianic assignment. Miss O'Toole informs me that you're contemplating family responsibilities. A fiancée in London is what she hinted at.'

'That's correct.' Selveratnam frowned.

'So what you need right now is security,' Spillano urged.

Selveratnam closed his eyes and meditated for a cool three minutes. Spillano made his flesh creep. He had trained himself never to be seduced by first impressions, but he sensed that his estimation of Spillano would not be significantly improved by the passage of time.

'I'll have to think it over,' he finally decided.

Spillano swivelled his chair, clicking down a notch.

'You have already thought it over,' he said cheerfully. 'Which means that when you leave here, you will either chassé out of the premises as a pensionable employee of the Spillano Garbage Corporation, or be offered a swift and silent suck down the waste disposal tube.'

Selveratnam rose. He was trembling.

'Are you threatening me?' he demanded indignantly.

Spillano met his eyes with an unblinking stare.

'Our latest garbage impacter,' he murmured reflectively, 'could crunch a messiah of your marque into a shoe-box in fifteen seconds flat, and we could probably accommodate your lady friend in London in the same container as yourself. For company, you understand.'

Selveratnam wished for a miserable moment or two that he was still a waiter at the Thali of Boundless Light, haunted by the suspicion that he had tried to rise too far above his ordained station. His native deference surfaced. So when Spillano extended his hand, he realised that it would be inadvisable not to grasp it in unequivocal affirmation of his contract of employment.

Chapter 13

There was an effervescent sense of *déjà vu* at the Vanity Springs ranch of Sham Shilverman. Now aged eighty-eight, he had been persuaded to disinter an original if contentious screen-play from the 'Pending' bin stacked on the cobwebbed cellar mezzanine over his dusty racks of claret. The apocalyptic project, based on an amorphous Medusa O'Toole concept, was one he had first planned in 1926 as *Uranus Hits the Dirt*. Shelved because of technical difficulties and the demise of the great Sorrentino (star of *Le Chic*), it resurfaced in 1941 as *The Final Conjunction*, when it again had to be abandoned because of the unacceptable gloominess of the theme at a time when the industry was committed to febrile laughter and the happy perchow of gunfire across bomb-torn sets. In 1948, he nearly made it as *Goodbye, Gaia,* but political pressure and a tedious campaign mounted by the Armageddon Society, who felt that the treatment usurped Jehovah's role as the authentic destroyer of the human race, sidelined it until 1950, when Shilverman considered tacking it together in Rome as *Ciao Ciao, Chronus*. The Vatican took a bleak, unhelpful view. His Italian bankers ducked out and the masterpiece went back to the mezzanine. Now Medusa had dug it up again.

The updated title, *Love Is the End*, Medusa felt had commercial resonances. She had therefore sent out a one-page synopsis to the bankers, with herself tentatively pencilled in as Gaia the Earth Mother and Wolfgang Ferrari playing Uranus, her heavenly lover and son. The terminal love scene or Final Conjunction was envisaged as a thermonuclear orgasm that reduced the world to steaming clinker. A spectacular to end all spectaculars. It was described in the publicity handouts as a religious meditation, a gripping tale about the resurrection and sex lives of the patriarchs and the arrival of a cock-happy messiah.

Pushkin, Sham's barley-brown mulatto valet, to whom the task of unearthing the original script had been delegated, spent three peevish hours sorting through mouldering papers, wheezing unhappily as insidious fungal debris tickled his bronchi. Having sneezed several dozen times and coughed strings of jelly-like sputum over the Château Latour '61, he emerged with red-rimmed eyes and a modest folder (just six closely typed pages in a black three-ring binder) onto the verandah where his master reclined in a rattan rocker, sipping Irish and Donegal spring-water, talking gentle nonsense to Tiresias, the soporific red macaw.

The guests were gathered around the bar, one or two of them joshing Nesta, the beige-coloured cocktail waitress, who rattled the ice stylishly over her hennaed head. Apart from Medusa O'Toole, it was a gathering of money men. The Spillanos, Sheik Yusuf Hamami of Ethical Friction, Sam Yamaha of the First Nagasaki and Waikiki Trust, and Hengist Dunkelbaum. Dunkelbaum, the bronzed, grey-haired proprietor of L'Amauresque, the property in the hills near St Tropez leased by Medusa for her ashram, had his eye on Nesta. The tall, buzzard-faced Dunkelbaum was an inveterate womaniser who had already tentatively fixed up the bubbly receptionist at the Pokerdice Plaza, the hotel where he was staying, a lugubrious Mexican room-maid with acne from the same establishment, and even the tiny Korean matron who ran the Lao-Tze Tea-rooms, where he took his afternoon pot of ginseng infusion when in Vanity Springs. The wealthy Dunkelbaum liked nothing better than a new woman. He tried everyone, everywhere. What his passionate but humourless insistence could not achieve, his substantial billfold often did.

'Five hundred dollars, darling, and who's to know? I'm in. I'm out. We don't need problems, I'm just a simple family man. OK? Come on. Seven hundred and fifty. I'm not joking. Here. Feel the money. Who cares? Leave your door ajar and I'll be there. No funny business. Straight sex. You needn't do anything against your conscience. Would a Catholic lie? Just conventional inter-course, darling. Ten minutes. Maybe twenty. Less time than it takes to sip a martini. Seven hundred and fifty. Why so much? Because suddenly I love you. I need you. No, I'm not mad. Only madly hopeful. Two o'clock? I'll be there.'

Hengist Dunkelbaum operated around the world in this way. The line hardly varied. Quiet, a little humble, insistent and crudely gracious. When he revisited a hotel, he would enquire politely as he undressed his partner:

'Have we coupled before, darling? No? Good. Basically, I'm a straight guy. Nothing to which your priest could take serious exception. However, I do side-deals for slow suckeroos. A hundred extra? OK, forget I said that. I got swept away. It was that first sight of you stripped down to the tasty bits. Those pubies of yours. So nice and bushy. Like a beaver. You got Latin blood? I thought so. Very pretty, curly stuff. I love the tinge of auburn. Let me give you some good advice. If you ever need a really hot stud, consider three things. First, the nose. It should be big, strong and hooked like mine. Second, the forehead. Look for plenty of bulge. And the hands must be broad with thick fingers. The thicker the better. Like bananas. These are good signs. Never go for creeps with snubby snouts and fairy fingers. You're giving yourself trouble. Small pricks, quick comers and, what is worse, deviates. They want to look, sniff, suck, pull . . . but when it comes to performance, they're bad news. Remember – a hooked nose, a bulgy forehead and banana fingers. You can't go wrong. Find a guy who looks like me and you're on a winner. Fancy a little buggery? No offence. Some very ritzy ladies prefer it that way. Another hundred if you're game. Don't imagine I'm crowding you. I'm a natural lover, sweetheart. And you're a honey. What's your name again?'

Apart from his proposed direct funding, the importance of the Dunkelbaum connection was that he had some years previously leased the film's proposed location, L'Amauresque, to the Eusapia Palladino Foundation, one of Medusa O'Toole's charities, which was precluded from using its assets for anything but religious purposes, so pocketing significant tax advantages. It was now argued that the devotional nature of the film could bring it within the ambit of that legal prescription. The private consideration for this revenue avoidance shuffle was an un-written arrangement whereby Dunkelbaum had what was euphemistically referred to as primary introduction rights over Ferrari in respect of actresses being auditioned who did not have a speaking part or hold an Equity card. Sham's adjudication was invoked when Hengist discovered that the enterprising Wolfgang had actually mounted some applicants before he had even shaken their hands. He threatened to slam an injunction on the continued use of L'Amauresque until he was accorded what his Lebanese lawyer playfully called 'full friendship rights'. Sham acted with expedition. The two spoilsports who complained to Equity were paid off and Hengist was supplied with a rota of non-union whores, who he imagined were actresses.

It was Hengist Dunkelbaum, too, who suggested they use a Hindu messiah, as Sunburn Spillano had pointed out that the raunchy messiah storyline could invoke death threats from Jewish, Moslem and Christian extremists. (Hengist had long advocated that an illustrated copy of the *Kama Sutra* should be placed in every hotel bedroom alongside the Gideon Bible, claiming that in many cases the Hindu classic would be of greater practical value than the Scriptures.) Medusa had been ecstatic. Hindus were so civilised about carnality. She had always been a sort of Irish-Hindu at heart and had once wanted to play Arjuna in a musical of the *Bhagavad Gita*, but Sham thought that the purists among the O'Toole fans might be confused at her appearance as a butch charioteer. He suggested that her ampli-tude of what he called her female 'add-ons' could never be occulted.

'Even you couldn't act away those God-given attributes, honey.'

But the idea of a Hindu messiah persisted and became central to the revised treatment.

Shilverman was not expected from the verandah until sunset. He insisted on watching this phenomenon every day, although Medusa was unhappy at its morbid implications.

'I don't want to miss any more of these than I can help,' he'd mutter, squinting sadly at the orange disc sliding swiftly between the grey teeth of the bare sierras. 'It reminds me of Americky, Pushkin.'

'Americky, sir?'

'A dream country, Pushkin, where people walk tall. Where the black, brown yellow and pink races work, play and love together. A country where men and women can pray and fuck together in freedom.'

'Like Terrastricken, sir?'

'No, no, damn you. It's nobler than Terrastricken. God help us. Don't you ever have wonderful dreams?'

'No, sir. I never had a decent education, sir. I just learned to dream about all the ugly places God in his infinite wisdom had forgotten.'

Sham Shilverman examined the folder Pushkin had handed him. Then he allowed the servant to lead him in, clutching the folder in his right hand and giving that arm to the valet. Sham scraped a hickory stick before him with his left. He was certain that everybody would turn towards him when he appeared at the door, to greet him with expressions of affection. They did. He looked around, using his neck like an ancient turtle. He noticed that Wolfgang Ferrari, his leading man, wasn't present and wondered whether he was in bed with Steffi, Hengist Dunkelbaum's wife. It gave Sham a malicious buzz to think that Hengist's wife was being screwed by somebody else. There was a kind of moral equilibrium in Steffi's adultery.

'Where's Wolfgang, Hengist?' he asked mischievously.

Hengist shrugged and carried on talking to Nesta, competing for her attention with a short, squarely built Japanese, whom Sham recognised as Sam Yamaha, the director of Non-Standard Funding at the First Nagasaki and Waikiki Trust. He nodded at Sheik Yusuf Hamami's raised hand of salutation and noticed Sunburn Spillano's back. The little man was standing by the window, catching the last of the sunset. Joe Spillano, his father, didn't appear to be in the room. Sham sensed it was too much to hope that Joe had snuffed it, and his fears were confirmed when he heard the older Spillano's inimitable croak from the hallway. Well, all the money men had arrived to slice the cake between themselves before they threw him his crumb. I'll be lucky, he brooded miserably, if I break even on this fucking trick.

'Shammy?'

Sham glared fiercely. No bastard called him Shammy. The bloody Arab was probably trying to be friendly.

'Wolfgang's in Paris, Shammy,' the Sheik called, grinning like some prick who'd slipped his straitjacket.

Sham shuffled away. A defensive move. He couldn't endure any more of Sheik Yusuf's current obsession, which centred around a Wally Wazir (the Hashemite Hokusai) portrait which the Sheik was trying to fiddle into the National Gallery in London.

Wazir's egregious allegorisation of the bearded, apprehensive and middle-aged Sheik showed a clean-shaven, pop-eyed adolescent posed between a pair of sphinx-like beasts (whose faces resembled youthful and dewy-eyed Omar Sharifs), before the crimson snout of a white Rolls-Royce, grey minarets, blue date-palms and sand-pink dunes. Medusa had questioned the Sheik about the animals' extraordinary resemblance to the celebrated Egyptian film-star. The Sheik shook his head happily, then exposed his wonderful teeth. He appeared to be transfused by joy when discussing the art of his protégé. He explained that the creatures were zhivagos, found only between the Tigris and Euphrates, very near the location of the Garden of Allah. Of course, they were now extremely rare. There was a legend that they had been excluded from the Ark by that Zionist trouble-maker, Noah. It was blatant bisexual discrimination, zhivagos being perfect hermaphrodites and a threat to Noah's pedantic biological assumptions.

'And they survived the Flood?' Medusa enquired drily.

'A mating pair floated around on their backs for forty days and nights, sister,' the Sheik exulted, smoothing his beard.

Medusa learned that zhivagos are male during the day and female during the night, so mating is only possible at dawn and sunset, during the ten seconds or so when their sexual ambiguity enables them adequately to perform either function.

The work of art had been donated to the National Gallery a

year earlier and had lain in their storeroom, the British public being deprived of its display because of some reservations about the anachronistic nature of what one picky expert called 'Wazir's Japanese-renaissance pastiche'. The delicate matter was still under negotiation, three earlier financial inducements to purchase wall-space outside the Ladies' Toilet being firmly declined. Sheik Yusuf hoped that Spillano Garbage, lately retained as publicists, would succeed where he had failed. But even Sunburn had found that Wazir's effective promotion was difficult as the painter was some sort of recluse who lived in a secret oasis.

'He's intensely shy,' the Sheik explained, 'and is only happy in the company of zhivagos, racing camels and intimate friends like myself. Besides, there's a grave danger that he might be executed by extremists. For blasphemy.'

Conscious that he couldn't face the toothy, burnous-clad Hamami without several more slugs of McGills down his gullet, Shilverman made for the verandah again.

'Sham.'

He scraped slowly around in the direction of the voice. It was the phlegmy sound of Joe Spillano, who'd wandered in from the hall. Somebody he was never pleased to see. A former 'Blue Wave' director (private circulation only), in the good old Rat-a-tat era, he had been the masseur of Al Volpone. After a short spell on the Rock (a minor complicity rap when Al Volpone went down), Joe had moved to Havana, where he put together seventy-three 'C' or Climax movies for well-shod wrist-benders. Over the years, most of them had been impounded and destroyed by zealous enforcement agencies. However, percipient semiologists of the Sixties had recognised a neglected talent and had taken him up, celebrating the twelve surviving examples of his oeuvre at a festival in Copenhagen. They awarded Joe a silver cock (such humourless symbolism) as a tribute to his contribution to fringe cinema. Now the bastard was President of the Spillano Garbage Corporation. Money leaked out of his arsehole.

'Sham,' Joe Spillano called again. It sounded like a curse.

'Sonofabitch,' Shilverman responded.

'I've been to the john,' Joe explained, wiggling a little finger.

'You incontinent?'

'Bastard.'

They clenched hands emotionally and swayed like two decaying elms in a high wind. Sham was pleased to find that Joe, eight years his junior, was crumbling. Spillano's ovoid body had for many years cast a shadow across Shilverman's life. He concealed his repugnance for the broad, pulpy face and mocking, spittle-flecked lips. The weary grey eyes in those fleshy pouches were as furtive as they had always been. Joe seemed shakier than the last time they'd met and his grip was cold and feeble. Sham could have broken those stiff old fingers like dry twigs with just one good squeeze. Joe moved away. Even in the Thirties, Joe had the pelvic wobble and pale, spongy skin of a subterranean creature.

Sham would have given a million bucks to know the whole truth about Joe and Medusa during the summer of 1932, when Sham was in Europe for a couple of weeks. There had been dirty whispers – no more than that. By Christmas that year, things had moved on. After Medusa's miscarriage and her short spell at the clinic, the sun shone again. Joe had got hitched up for the second time and everything was going well between Medusa and him. And now, forty-nine years later, it had started to burn him up again. Sham knew that Medusa had cheated a lot. But as long as he couldn't put a face on her partners, it didn't matter too much. They were generally 'nothing' guys – drifters, hotel waiters and broad-shouldered college kids. But the thought of Joe Spillano as Medusa's lover was something he found almost unendurable to contemplate. He had once made it his business to take a peek at Joe when they were showering at the Dutch Schultz Gymnasium (1934, perhaps after he'd whacked Spillano at squash). He'd sneaked a critical look at the thin, tripe-white cock that dangled like an albino elver between Joe's androgynous thighs. How could any woman, he wondered, accept that dreadful piece of pasta inside her body? And now, even the former flash of Spillano's auburn Bohemian-length hair was no more than argental wisps, exposing patches of stippled ivory skull. Sham hated him. He was fucking unnatural. Spillano never admitted to balling anyone – not even a whore. It was his goddam secrecy that hurt. Perhaps if he'd come out with it like a real man, 'Sure, Sham, I gave Medusa one all right,' he might have survived the shock. But not knowing nearly fifty years on – that hurt as bad as an abscessed tooth.

Sunburn Spillano of the Spillano Garbage Corporation approached Sham and declared that the corporation would insist on nominating the director. This particular demand dismayed Shilverman, who had been straining his leaky colon to hire the great Marlon D. de Mille.

'He's kaput,' Sunburn informed him with a cruel laugh.

'What?'

'De Mille is not on the agenda anymore.'

Shilverman, who had been thwarted by an unobtainable whine from de Mille's ex-directory number all morning, looking genuinely bewildered.

'When did this happen?' Sham's amnesiac lapses were becoming more frequent.

'Last year, Sham. I was there when they toasted the stiff.'

'Shit.'

'Don't worry. I've got somebody even sexier.'

'Who?'

'My old man.'

'Joe? But he only made pornos, Sunburn.'

Sunburn frowned, feigning disappointment at Shilverman's cavalier assessment of his parent.

'They were very arty bits of merchandise.' He winked, making an indelicate gesture with his middle finger.

Sham looked across the room at Medusa. She was chatting to Joe. It began to smell like a set-up. He was suddenly suspicious about the earlier handmushing and alligator smiles. He edged his way towards them.

'Sunburn suggests we use Joe as director,' he ventured, watching Medusa intently.

Joe flashed his ceramic teeth. They were symmetrical, refrigerator white and painfully phoney.

'I don't mind doing this for you, Sham,' he said generously.

Wild grinning all round. Sham waited for Medusa to save him. She didn't. It was going to be a shitty evening after all.

'I have no problem with Joe,' she gushed traitorously, damping Spillano's sepulchral face with her mouth.

For an unreasonable moment, the sight of those red lips against Joe's flabby jowl induced a kind of madness. Whorecunt, he seethed to himself in anguish, dazed with venom, but repented almost instantly as his normal feelings of squelchy affection for the woman ebbed back.

'I would, of course, require a veto on ideas, concepts, casting, camerawork and final script,' Sham warned.

Joe Spillano shrugged cheerfully.

'You can have what you want, Sham, so long as my name goes on the credits.'

Sham felt an uncomfortable twinge across his chest. If it wasn't for the Spillano money, Joe wouldn't have got near his picture. The job, he felt, was no more than an easy path to Medusa. Sham wished Joe Spillano dead. That awful grin again. He swallowed an Irish and turned away, evading Sheik Yusuf's eye. Why had he got himself involved with all these vultures? For Medusa. Making movies made her feel like a young girl again. He lit a Castro de luxe, enveloping himself in a blue fog. There was, he reflected, little love lost between these bastards. Dunkelbaum distrusted the Spillanos, whom he suspected of coveting his L'Amauresque property; the Spillanos had their deadly sights on Dunkelbaum; and although involved in a number of deals with the Sheik, they were conscious that he too was a rival who was probably trying to fix a private bargain on L'Amauresque with Hengist's wife, Steffi. Sheik Yusuf was convinced of everybody's treachery, which was why he smiled a great deal, quoted proverbs about Allah being the friend of honest businessmen and addressed those he particularly feared as 'brother'. Sam Yamaha nodded his head and listened a great deal. Being a good listener was part of his quiet charm. But the capricious Yamaha, for whom corruption was a way of life, was not above switching affiliations for personal advantage.

Sham joined Medusa. Everybody had gravitated to her. She turned to the beaming Sheik.

'They were much appreciated, Yusuf,' she glowed.

'I'm overjoyed that you approved of them, sister,' the swarthy Arab replied.

The Sheik had presented Medusa with a blow-up effigy of Sham. And Sham had been given one of Medusa. Secretly, they were both more than a mite flattered by the conformations of their pneumatic surrogates.

'They were OK,' Sham acknowledged with a grunt.

'I was hoping,' the Sheik twittered, 'that the legendary Mr Shilverman would assist me in my battle with the philistines of the British art establishment. A personal note enlisting the support of the President of Terrastricken, perhaps?'

Sham was conscious of teeth everywhere, waiting for his response. He grunted again, a little more affably this time. Sunburn handed him a publicity release. Sham screwed up his eyes and held the paper to the light. It was headed, 'WALLY WAZIR . . . THE CARAVAGGIO OF THE CARAVANSERAI.'

'I thought your boy was the Hashemite Hokusai,' Sham growled sourly.

'Would you believe it, brother,' Sheik Yusuf laughed, 'he is that as well. Two artists for the price of one.'

There was a glint of triumph in Hamami's dark and limpid eyes. Sunburn announced that Spillano Garbage were sponsoring a Wazir retrospective in Honkeyville, where a petition endorsing the painter's genius would be launched. Sheik Yusuf disclosed that he hoped that Wally Wazir would be joining the board of Ethical Friction as Artistic Director, another reason why it was important that Shilverman Productions use the services of his company for *Love Is the End*. Ethical Friction were, he declared, the acknowledged market leaders in raunchy rubberware. Yamaha intervened, pointing out that inflatables could cut the bill for the orgy sequences by significant sums. The Japanese had privately admitted to Sham that he was a collector of Ethical Friction's 'Sleep With a Celebrity' range, enjoying, particularly, frisky threesomes with Queen Victoria and Mae West. Yamaha was partial to short, well-padded females.

'We can provide beautiful couples in a hundred erotic positions,' the Sheik enthused.

'Aesthetically speaking,' Joe Spillano observed, 'we will need quite a few unbeautiful pneumatics as well.'

'Even repellent ones,' Medusa said.

The Sheik nodded.

'Of course,' he assured them. 'Ethical Friction will provide sagging buttocks, fleshy hips, pendant paunches, withered breasts and wrinkled cocks.'

Medusa shot Sham a covert look of approval.

'We can do anything to promote the illusion of reality,' the Sheik boasted, 'even chancres, desert sores and venereal warts.'

This snippet of technical bravura was received in thoughtful and appreciative silence.

Chapter 14

The London office of the First Nagasaki and Waikiki Trust, or the First Nag and Waik as it was known in the trade, was a square Palladian construction of Dorset stone. It had been built after the Great War by a Bavarian bank that had since transferred to taller and glossier City premises more suited to the greenery of a sub-tropical habitat which many bankers appear to prefer. The original Bauhaus feel of the interior persisted, sustained by a preponderance of chrome, leather and brutalist furnishings. The well-lit foyer was reminiscent of the entrance to a smart speishaus on the Kurfürstendamm, seemingly designed to exor-cise the neuroses of clients scuttling in from their twilit hyper-inflationary nightmares to the luminous and cigar-scented opulence of a less vulnerable funk-hole.

Laszlo was directed to the second floor, where he was greeted by a green-eyed young woman with bobbed red hair whose face and milk-white arms were mottled with freckles.

'Mr Gobar?' she smiled.

'Gabor.'

She pouted amiably, shaking her head in easy self-reproof as though she was inured to making mistakes with foreign names. He was led along the perimeter of a foreign-exchange dealing-room, filled with Reuter screens, monitors, personal computers, ringing phones and noisy young people working at the top of their voices. A short girl with wild black hair and dark shining eyes stepped from behind a vending machine, a plastic cup of coffee held precariously between her thumb and middle finger. She stared at him, licking her full red lips with lively interest.

'Hi,' she called.

'Hi,' Laszlo replied, returning her stare and allowing her more than a chivalrous amount of space in passing.

He turned back instinctively before he followed his guide

around the corner towards Mrs Nablus's office. The girl with the wild black hair and dark shining eyes was waiting for his retrospective peek. She wiggled the fingers of her right hand and smiled. Laszlo flapped his hand in response, making a mental note of where she sat. He was still thinking about her when they arrived at Mrs Nablus's office. If the girl with the wild black hair and dark shining eyes looked adventurous, the bespectacled Mrs Froline Nablus had a dramatic presence that humbled him. She could have been a character from Racine, a Phèdre or a Bérénice. The gentle swing of her tendrils of frizzed hair had for Laszlo a mesmeric quality. A timeless profile. She reminded him of the embossed Demeter on Maya's pewter biscuit-barrel. He imagined sheaves of corn, poppies and snakes around her head. They shook hands, Laszlo stimulated by the satin softness of her palm. She turned to Laszlo's guide.

'Thank you, Alice,' she murmured in a sing-song voice with just the trace of a lisp.

The green-eyed young woman with bobbed red hair went out. Mrs Nablus explained to him that Trainee Induction was not her usual responsibility but that she was sitting in for Mr Tanazaki, who was on a special assignment in Frankfurt. She had a wide-eyed, bewildered look as she sorted through his papers. Laszlo suspected that she was not bewildered at all, and wondered whether she had been embarrassed by his tight trousers when he came in or was merely trying to put him at his ease. He gave her the benefit of the doubt without a moment's hesitation. There were not many, far more experienced men who would have taken a contrary view.

Froline Nablus, recently promoted, now had significant additional responsibilities for European Commercial Paper. She was much admired by the treasurers of many of the greatest corporations for her sharp professional skills, pleasant manner and vibrant physical qualities. On her desk was a large portrait of her husband, Joe. He was a plump, white-haired man of unmistakable charm, and, it was reputed, considerable wealth. A biochemist of international repute, his work on the intestinal endopeptidases was deemed by many to have been worth a

Nobel Prize. Joe Nablus spent most of his working year in Tripoli, joining his beautiful wife Froline each summer on the family yacht, *Shin Shinaki*, for a four-week Aegean cruise. He was forty-five years older than Froline; they had been married for five, investing their annual honeymoons with an ecstatic intensity that instantly subdued sceptical and loutish onlookers. They wined, dined, danced, swam and happily enjoyed each other to the exclusion of everybody else. Sadly, pregnancy eluded Froline. There was nothing she wanted more than to become a mother. Joe, a frequent visitor to the Voronoff Clinic in Alexandria, had significantly enriched his sperm count. Indeed, in clinical trials he had inseminated three Somali nurses and an Iraqi physiotherapist, but Froline bore no fruit. Responding to the hypothesis that Froline's sterility was due to the seating at work, the clinic had provided her with fertility rings woven from the manes of she-camels in season. Froline always carried a spare ring in her crocodile document-case on outside visits, provoking the suspicion among corporate clients and many of the fashionable City restaurants that she was afflicted by an obscure form of haemorrhoids.

Froline was besieged by suitors, but she appeared to resist all solicitations with dignity and resolution. Each night, usually just before eleven, she took a ten-minute call from Tripoli. As they were certain that MI5 tapped the line, Joe and Froline restricted themselves to matters of honeyed intimacy, scrupulously avoiding all tendentious references to the weather, the US Bond Rate, or even the prospects for Third World debt. And to make life more entertaining for the British Secret Service, they slurred away in Nabi, a very private patois invented by the Nablus family at the turn of the century and now understood by only three people in the world.

'There are two simple tests you will have to take in order to be enrolled as a trainee,' Mrs Nablus advised Laszlo after giving him a brief account of the bank's activities.

'May I take them right away?' he asked softly, dreaming of nuzzling the faint down on her upper lip with his nose.

'That's the general idea.'

Laszlo contrived a humble and attentive look as she outlined the nature of the proposed aptitude and personality tests, but she did not appear to be wholly persuaded of his serious intentions. As he nodded, distracted briefly by her tiny, ruby-studded ears or diverted by a mole at the base of her throat, he became aware too late that she had noticed his lapses into étourderie and now regarded him with a gaze of chilled reproof.

'Is anything the matter?'

'No,' he replied innocently.

A shadow passed over Joe Nablus's portrait posed before a sun-dappled background of yacht-mast and rigging. The Assistant Treasurer — European Commercial Paper distanced herself from the flashy young man in a tight suit who appeared to be more concerned with her appearance than he was with the First Nagasaki and Waikiki Trust's induction arrangements. She pursed her full lips. A vengeful look. Remote. Byzantine. Buttons were pressed on her desk-console as she addressed him. His bowels curdled and he suspected that all was lost. The red-haired Alice came cruising through the dealing-room, her springy hair bouncing rhythmically with each loping stride.

'Miss Bebbington-Smith will escort you to the Training Department,' Mrs Nablus announced.

The tone was affable enough. But Bebbington-Smith? Did she mean Alice? She did. And why had she forgotten to smile? It was as though the warmth of their first few minutes had been sucked away through the overhead air-exchange ducts.

'Will I know the result today?' he enquired submissively.

'We'll write to you before the end of the week,' she promised, dismissing him with a downward movement of her head to the papers before her.

The door opened. Alice gave him a diffident smile.

'It's on the next floor,' she whispered.

Laszlo wanted to hold Froline Nablus's hand again. It was not offered. Perhaps Mrs Nablus was more important than he suspected. He glanced back briefly to check whether he could see her knees under the table. He could not.

'Cheerio,' he piped in her direction, sensing as he uttered the word that it was an inappropriate farewell.

There was no response. His Demeter, a phone-receiver in her small brown hand, did not appear to hear him.

The tests seemed ridiculously simple. Laszlo slouched out of the building thoughtfully. The idea of working for the First Nagasaki and Waikiki Trust suddenly appealed to him. More. He wanted the job enormously. Bitterness with himself at his remembered lascivious glances engulfed him. What an idiot he'd been. Of course, he had not uttered a word that could have counted against him, but the lubricity in his eyes had been unmistakable. He suspected that he had made Mrs Nablus feel threatened. Insulted, even. What an insufferable prick he'd been. He considered phoning her to explain his behaviour. But what explanation could he invent? It was my medication for hayfever that made me heavy-lidded and horny, Mrs Nablus. Nothing more than drowsiness, Mrs Nablus, not lust. I have an eidetic problem. A rare susceptibility to artificial light unless adequately protected, Mrs Nablus. I'd have been OK, but I forgot to use my tinted clip-ons, Mrs Nablus. Shit, he thought. Shit. Laszlo stopped to light a cigarette, noticing his reflection in a shop-window. Jesus – as he'd feared, the grey suit was far too tight. Everything bulged. Especially his cock. He brushed his fingers over the lump pensively, certain that he'd offended Mrs Nablus with what she must have imagined was an erection. Laszlo was gloomy. Phoning Mrs Nablus, he decided, would only compound the offence. And by the time he'd reached Moorgate Tube Station, he'd persuaded himself that he might have to settle for a career in the ice-cream business.

Chapter 15

To Laszlo's surprise, his acceptance by the First Nagasaki and Waikiki Trust arrived the following morning. He noted that he had been assigned to Non-Standard Funding, the department headed by Sam Yamaha.

Initially, he worked with a small and spiky red-haired lady called Zelda Hashamoto, the American widow of a former executive of the bank. The late Mr Hashamoto, a reputed genius at Foreign Exchange, had dived one night into an unobserved net of conger eels. His partially eaten body was only discovered as the fishermen beached their catch at cockcrow just outside Kerkira. It was Mrs Hashamoto's third marriage and, at fifty-two, she'd more or less settled for the life of a single girl in the spacious Edwardian villa she'd inherited at Belsize Park and partly sublet to an unobtrusive New England family. She had on her desk a framed and autographed photograph of a lovely young woman, who Laszlo later learned was Sylvia Plath.

On Laszlo's first day, Mrs Hashamoto covered his desk with a pile of unorthodox funding applications that included a company prospecting for gold in the Arctic, a syndicate promoting Thai boxing on the Centre Court at Wimbledon, a python farmer in Tower Hamlets, a girlie magazine produced in Braille, the organisation of a national polo league, and a specialist hostess agency called Brighter Bedrooms of Beckenham. Mrs Hashamoto informed him that she required a sensitive evaluation, no more than a two-thousand-word précis, on each of the six applications by the end of the week. He regarded her with incredulity.

'But I'm only a trainee,' he protested.

'Self-deprecation is not our house style,' she warned, returning to her work with a disappointed frown.

Laszlo picked up the first folder. By lunchtime, he'd drafted a thousand words on permafrost and started an illuminating paragraph on the polar bear hazard. Mrs Hashamoto rarely spoke. But before she departed at five o'clock on the evening of the first day, she addressed him as she fiddled on her Lincoln green, feathered velour hat.

'Has anybody told you that you sound like Leslie Howard?'

Laszlo shook his head.

'You should try giving poetry readings,' she mused. 'I rather like that nicely shaded delivery of yours.'

Somehow, spooked by Mrs Hashamoto's unspoken but vaguely implied expectations, Laszlo felt obliged to work late, taking the phone off the hook and knocking off his first two evaluations by nine. He loped out of the building a little wearily and headed for The Golden Balls across the road. The saloon bar was almost empty. He ordered a pint of lager. But before the glass touched his lips, there came a warning shout from a large, pale man with a broad Calmuck face, soulful brown eyes and wet, sensual lips. He had thinning hair and clumps of ginger moss along his pudgy chops and chin that just about passed for an undistinguished half-set.

'Australian muck,' the stranger called, pointing to Laszlo's lager. 'If you do me the courtesy of pouring that antipodean poison down the sink, I'll treat you to a jug of fairly respectable ale.'

Laszlo smiled. The stranger had obviously been drinking for some time. He set his lager on the counter. It was replaced by the barman with a pint of Abbot. And that was how Laszlo met Bevan Chancer.

During the first ten minutes of their acquaintance, Laszlo learned that Chancer had a First in Mathematics from Aberystwyth, was a virtuoso on keyboards, could recite the Gettysburg Address in Welsh, was celebrated among his friends for his Fettucine and Prawns and believed that his beautiful wife was at that moment servicing the needs of a long-distance lorry-driver.

'I'm sorry,' murmured Laszlo.

'Oh, that's all right,' Chancer boomed. 'The most excellent

mystery is just about buggered anyway. She's doing her own thing and I'm being rather immature about the whole business. It's all terribly silly. That poor old lorry-driver man won't be able to keep the girl in knickers.'

He explained how his wife enjoyed having expensive lingerie ripped off her body during love-making.

'Wild silk, Habutai preferably, and hand-loomed lace,' Chancer brooded. 'Nothing else will quite do.'

The Welshman confided that he was the Manager of Corporate Banking at the First Nag and Waik. Laszlo told him that he was there as well. Chancer narrowed his eyes as he swayed, trying to place the younger man.

'I started today,' Laszlo said, 'in Sam Yamaha's department.'

Chancer belched thoughtfully.

'Ah,' he reflected. 'Ah.'

He did not appear to be vastly impressed at the mention of Yamaha's name.

'I'm with Mrs Hashamoto,' said Laszlo.

They tippled in silence for a while. Apart from the moon-faced Irish barman, they were the only customers on the premises. The silence of the City night almost bruised Laszlo's mind. Then Chancer spoke. He informed Laszlo in an unsteady and sepulchral voice that Mrs Hashamoto was a sort of a poet who ran a poetry circle in the Barbican. He predicted that she would capture Laszlo as a reader before the month was out.

'I do her Dylan Thomas,' Chancer murmured, 'but take particular care to have one or two before I shuffle on, of course.'

'Of course,' Laszlo nodded.

He suspected that he was a little stupid with the unaccustomed strong bitter. Chancer rose, leered pleasantly and wagged an enigmatic finger at him before making crabwise for the gents. The Welshman had not returned by the time the Irish barman had called 'Time'. Laszlo ventured into a cold and drizzling night, wondering for a few confused moments in which direction Moorgate lay.

At the end of the week, Laszlo had come to some breezy conclusions about the funding applications that Mrs Hashamoto had placed on his desk. He informed her that the Braille girlie magazine and the Beckenham hostess agency were the only projects worthy of further consideration. She gave him an approving nod as she finished scanning his reports, advising him that he would be required for a trainee assignment with Mr Harada in the near future.

'Mr Harada?'

'Toshiro Harada,' she said, 'the European President of the bank.'

And once again she waited until she'd fitted her Robin Hood hat on and was primed to slip through the door before she tried a private question.

'Tell me, Mr Gabor, would you care to read a little Gerard Manley Hopkins for me next Friday evening?'

He shrugged his shoulders.

'Why not?' he smiled.

Bevan Chancer was slowly drowning in deep emotional waters. He sat in his glass box of an office, seething with resentment at the perfidy of his wife, Thelma. Flanked by spotted flowering maple and luxuriant Chinese evergreens, he brooded. He found it difficult to forgive her for starting her affair several months before she actually confessed, and was disconsolate at the reflection that he'd been sharing her tube with a long-distance lorry-driver called Mr Bricuse. He'd established that the long-distance lorry-driver was slipping it to her sometime between seven-thirty and nine-thirty on Tuesday nights, this being her Conversational Portuguese slot, and recalled with bitterness how unresponsive she'd been on those nights.

'Don't you love me?' he'd enquire, biting a nipple and attempting to grope her into a more co-operative mood.

To Thelma's credit, she invariably conceded his conjugal rights if he was sufficiently magisterial, but occasionally demonstrated her resentment by declining to open her mouth to accept his probing tongue.

'Kiss me properly,' he'd curse as she jerked her head away.

At these times, Thelma lay sullenly beneath him, lips clenched and eyes closed as he harvested her rebellious flesh. He suspected that these must have been the nights when he'd been preceded by Mr Bricuse. It was not a pleasant thought. But Chancer, a romantic type, was quite prepared, given Thelma's compliant nod, to happily resume the conjugal knicker-ripping that had once been the glory of their matrimonial intimacy.

Since she'd gone her own way, he rarely drank less than six pints of Abbot a day, supplementing this with a beaker or two of Courvoisier. Thelma had once suggested to him that the yellow nodules around his eyes and the deep fatigue of which he continually complained were indications of cirrhosis of the liver. She joked about his premature ejaculations, although he suspected that was to frighten him into a more moderate pattern of drinking. However, whenever he visited the Executive Washroom he never failed to examine the spider blood-vessels on his cheeks. He sometimes imagined that he was having difficulty in passing water and wondered bleakly whether he had prostate trouble. He was conscious, standing at the urinal, that he had to shake his cock more vigorously than ever before.

Returning to his office, Chancer found all three phones ringing. Picking them up, he replaced them immediately. They started to ring again. Chancer disconnected the phones once more, waiting a moment or two before he put them back on their rests. They started to ring again. He lifted the receivers and laid them on his desk. He listened to the anguished buzz of voices trying to reach him and trembled, wondering whether he should try Thelma at work. Reaching into the filing cabinet, he found a bottle of Courvoisier behind 'Leveraged Leases', and trickled two inches into a coffee-cup. He replaced the first phone. When it rang, he picked it up. It was his mother.

'Bevan?'

'Mother?'

'I want you to drop in this weekend. I'd like you to run your eye over my tax-return.'

'We're a bit stretched at present, Mother. They've lumbered me with some extra assignments.'

'Don't talk such absolute tosh, Bevan. Remember who you're speaking to. Bring Thelma along. I can run to the debris of a Towey salmon poached by our sporty vicar, salade niçoise, a nesselrode pudding, fresh figs, dolcelatte and two or three bottles of Sancerre.'

'I'll let you know, Mother.'

'I shall expect you both, Bevan.'

Chancer replaced the receiver. It rang again. He regarded the instrument bleakly for a moment or two as he drained his coffee-cup. Then he lifted it to his ear, announcing himself with a depressed yawn. This time it was the Director of Corporate Business, who'd been trying to reach him for half an hour. Chancer was a little miffed to find that the great man sounded unusually testy.

In contrast to Bevan Chancer's apparent regression, Laszlo Gabor's star was in the ascendant. Supported by Mrs Hashamoto and Sam Yamaha, Laszlo was entrusted with and diligently discharged more complex responsibilities each succeeding month. The poetry readings at the Barbican led to new friendships. Working dinners at Yamaha's Knightsbridge flat became regular events. He was soon on first-name terms with Zelda Hashamoto, Froline Nablus and Sam Yamaha himself, even finding time for discreet affairs with a corporate treasurer from Maxibank and a very busy vice-president of a stockbroking firm who slotted him in between five and five-thirty on Tuesday mornings before her sauna, squash and breakfast conference at London Wall. Laszlo was careful not to spend too much time with the chablis-tippling Young Turks who clustered in The Golden Balls at lunchtime. If he did duck in there for a quick sandwich and an iced Perrier, there was usually a woman involved. But whether it was the leaky secretary of a flashy director from a merchant bank or the garrulous girl-friend of somebody who was close to a key player in a takeover bid, it was always pleasant when he could combine flirtation with the opportunity to make a little money. The City was full of whispers, although few were worth excessive attention. And if insider trading was an ideal to which none but the incorrigibly rapacious aspired, it was professional recommendation, incontestably arm's-length, but often hallowed by Divine guidance, that generally provided the bespoke battalions with an odd splash of bubbly or a down-payment on the Ferrari.

It was during this particularly heady phase of his career that Laszlo concluded that it might be to his short-term advantage to collect what appeared to be a valuable scalp. Fortunately the assault was tolerantly received. It got no further than an ambitious hand halfway up Mrs Hashamoto's reedy thigh. She informed him amiably that she had never been a girl for fornication and, at rising fifty-four, had chucked the idea of further copulation, deciding that the aesthetic demerits of employing her cranky body to couple, significantly outweighed any marginal satisfaction she could imagine.

'I'm as dry as a stick of kindling timber,' she laughed, patting him on the head. 'Besides, I've begun to find intensity rather amusing.'

Then one morning, hardly two years into his career, Sam Yamaha informed Laszlo that Toshiro Harada had decided to appropriate him.

'This could·be your big chance,' Zelda Hashamoto enthused, with an enigmatic flicker in her viridescent eyes.

Chapter 16

Laszlo still drove Ada Mulcahy to the Sunshine Home for Christian Friends most Sundays unless she had a weekend shift at the laundry where she worked, on which occasions he went down by himself, taking packets of confectionery for Aurora and her friend Tom, a partially-sighted and partly paralysed young man who brayed and beat one hand against her knee most of the time. Tom's physical handicap was starkly hemispheric. The right side of his head and body seemed to be of relatively normal proportions, although the sighted eye he possessed was acutely myopic and he only had a thumb and two fingers on that hand. His left side, however, was as grotesquely twisted as a Bacon painting, a white, sightless eye in a misshapen sector of face, an undeveloped shoulder with a short, dangling appendage ending in a pink baby claw, a concave chest and a withered leg no more than a foot long. Laszlo always took a bag of peppermint creams for Aurora and chocolates for Tom. Aurora preferred Laszlo coming on his own, for he allowed her to pack her mouth with several peppermint creams at a time. She couldn't get away with such behaviour when her mother was there.

'Aurora, don't be a pig,' Ada would reprove, fishing about in her daughter's mouth for the wodge of creams and dropping them into a handkerchief.

When Laszlo was on his own, he only advised her to be careful lest she choke. She understood this and nodded happily when he spoke, cramming yet another piece into her bulging mouth to urgently replace the mush sliding down her gullet. Aurora saw off the peppermint creams in minutes.

'All gone,' Laszlo would say glumly, kissing the beautiful, auburn-haired young woman on her freckled forehead.

'All gone,' she would repeat forlornly.

Aurora loved to push Tom's chair along the polished corridors, and when the weather was fine they went around the perimeter path of the garden, again and again. They were inseparable. Every morning when Aurora got up, she asked Cynthia Egremont whether it was Sunday. On the day the reply was in the affirmative, she waited in the recreation room for Laszlo. The moment she glimpsed his blond head above the silvery-grey perowskia that bordered the car-park, she trundled the braying Tom out into the garden to meet him. Laszlo would embrace Aurora and, dipping into his carrier bag, give her the peppermint creams. Aurora's excitement was transmitted to Tom, who snorted noisily and jerked up and down in his chair as he heard the crinkly silver paper around his chocolate being unwrapped by Laszlo. He put his fair head to one side and opened his slobbery maw to receive the chocolate. It was obviously appreciated. Laszlo popped a cube in whenever Tom stuck out his tongue, a sign that he had consumed the previous piece.

Laszlo's affinity with Aurora and Tom contrasted strangely with the plushier companions he was beginning to acquire in the City. And if his devotion to Cynthia Egremont's two flawed charges inspired her admiration, he suspected that he needed them as much as they did him, for although his infirmity was less apparent than theirs, Aurora and Tom were fellow travellers. Laszlo, who had never found it difficult to initiate quick and casual relationships, remained significantly less gifted at sustaining liaisons that encompassed the intimacy many people proclaimed they enjoyed with one another. But nowhere was Laszlo's loneliness more evident than in his transactions with the shadows whose beds he shared. He was diverted like a child by the meretricious glitter of evening's promise, only to be subdued by the ashes of morning's light. He reached out in his mind for Maya, trying to rediscover her incandescence in other smiles, other sighs and in the pliancy of other bodies, provoked in the fearful night by the uneasy conviction that he would always lie with strangers and never escape his solitary fate.

He had at one time invested his broken dreams in Cynthia Egremont, and remembered the first occasion he visited the Sunshine Home on his own. Cynthia had watched him playing with Aurora and Tom from an upper window. He waved cheerfully. She waved back. He organised a game of Huff and Puff with them. They squawked and screamed. There was much noisy delight. It was just before midday when Cynthia came out. She appeared genuinely pleased to see Laszlo. He surprised her with a gift. It was a modestly sized box of caramel liqueurs. She had seemed embarrassed and questioned the present with her eyes, an uncertain smile and playful movements of her shoulders. It was a young and gauche gesture.

'For me?' she asked softly.

He nodded. 'That's right. I thought you might like them.'

'I really can't accept this,' she protested, blushing as she had done when he first caught her looking at him.

He sat on the stonework of a raised parterre of hyacinths, swinging his legs.

'There's just twelve liqueurs in there,' he smiled. 'Hand them around to your friends and, before you know where you are, there won't be a problem.' He didn't intend to make an issue of a trifling gift.

'It's extremely kind of you,' she whispered.

Laszlo placed another bit of chocolate on Tom's tongue. He had dribbled a little as he waited to be served. Laszlo wiped Tom's jaw with his handkerchief. He had always got on well with mentally disadvantaged people. A facility for communicating with them was something that came naturally to him. Tom stopped braying and beating his knee. He clung to Laszlo's fingers and swung them happily as he attempted several new sounds.

'You've made a hit with Thomas,' Cynthia observed.

'Lah lah,' mumbled Tom, placing his head against Laszlo's side.

'My God,' she exclaimed, 'I do believe he's speaking your name.'

Laszlo grinned. There were times when he had been alone with Aurora that he felt certain he had opened a door nobody else ever had. When he sensed that she was withdrawing under a carapace of incomprehension, the right gesture or phrase to entice her out again invariably suggested itself to him. Their transactions evolved into a complex and secret language that had subtleties strangers would never have suspected. Being with Aurora gave him an inner peace he experienced with nobody else. And he knew that Aurora had for him an instinctive love that was part of the rhythm of her life. It was as natural as breathing.

He gently scratched Tom's rugby-ball-shaped skull with his fingers.

'Lah lah,' came a deep catarrhal gurgle.

Aurora appropriated Laszlo's other arm, squeezing him with rapture. Using the deformed but functional hand, Tom rubbed Laszlo's forefinger against his cheek. Cynthia beamed as Tom responded to Laszlo's initiatives.

'Has he got any relatives?' Laszlo asked.

'He's quite alone in the world. He was abandoned. Found in a Tesco shopping-bag outside the gate. He was named Thomas because he was discovered on the 7th of March, the feast day of St Thomas Aquinas. His other name is Flute. That's because there was a flute of French bread in the bag with him. We were going to call him Thomas Tesco Flute but thought better of it.'

'What an extraordinary coincidence,' murmured Laszlo in a faraway voice.

She regarded him with interest.

'The 7th of March is my birthday,' he announced. 'We are fellow Pisceans. Perhaps Tom and I can celebrate our next birthdays together. I'll get Ada to make a cherry cake and we'll all drink raspberry fizz, the kind that leaves you with blood-red lips and a demon moustache.'

Laszlo smiled at Tom, positioning his lips at what he judged to be the correct focal length from the sighted eye. He caressed the blond down on Tom's flushed cheekbone with the heel of his palm. The gentle comfort of Laszlo's hand calmed Tom. He remained motionless for some time, seemingly stilled by an inner music. He breathed noisily, his respiration troubled by the congestion of mucus crackling in his nose, eyeing Laszlo vacantly. Then a haunted smile emerged on the broken contours of his face.

'He's actually smiling,' she whispered.

'Tom and I are getting to be good friends,' Laszlo boasted lightly.

Cynthia was undeniably impressed. Laszlo was elevated by her obvious excitement at the demonstration of his power. He could not subdue a glow of conceit at Tom's unusual tranquillity, enjoying the revelation of a sorcery that lay somewhere between snake-charming and spiritual healing. Laszlo looked at Cynthia Egremont and tried to read the signals. Was it morbid fascination, he wondered, or a more personal admiration? He was not quite sure with this woman. Something did not quite fall into place.

'Perhaps,' she suggested brightly, 'if you're in not too much of a hurry, you may hazard a little lunch with us and later see our golden orioles.'

'I'd like that very much,' he said, contriving a shy but not unknowing grin.

Laszlo received an answer to the question he had asked himself about Cynthia Egremont, a few months later. He lunched her one summer's day at Osculata's, a restaurant near Sevenoaks. They sat by a Venetian garden with bridges, a lily-pond, fountains and a dovecote. In a tranquil corner, sheltered by potted stephanotis, yucca and palms, they were served poached gulls' eggs, brown baps, coriander butter, sweetbreads floraline and some gâteau gavache. They tippled a youngish Brouilly, and he watched intently the unusual sparkle in her bespectacled cinnamon eyes that seemed to have caught the broken sunlight through the trees. But the serenity of that obscure Armenian saint glowed from her serious face. After lunch, he had walked her slowly to the car behind a towering screen of horse-chestnut. They stopped and he drew Cynthia's awkward body to his, kissing her lightly on the mouth. She was unresponsive and solemn. Inside the car, he had reached for her hand. It had a strength and roughness that surprised him, reminding him unexpectedly of Ada Mulcahy's.

'Well?' he murmured.

It was then that she told him about Miss Proby, the matron. Laszlo recalled a dark, regal woman with large breasts, black arched eyebrows and a petulant lower lip that seemed to be on the verge of shaping an inconvenient question. There was a long silence as Laszlo considered her response.

'Haven't you ever? With a man, I mean?'

'Only my father,' she whispered in a low, numbed voice.

'Jesus.'

'I'm perfectly content with my life as it is. At least, I think so. Iris is a wonderful mate. We've been very happy together for the last six years. And I do love her dearly.'

He couldn't think of anything appropriate to say. Nothing more than sanitised phrases that would not in any way address what he imagined to be a great hurt. He asked about her father. She smiled, perceiving instantly that he was looking for simple explanations.

'Oh, he was as much a victim as I was, I suppose,' she sighed. 'We were locked into an unreal situation after my mother died. I was just thirteen and knew instinctively that something would happen. The greatest fear, terror even, was waiting for the first time. And after that, it was no more than a very unpleasant family secret. I even imagined for a while that I was fulfilling my mother's role. It was one step on from making the beds, doing the washing-up and cooking the Sunday dinners. He was a con-venient scapegoat, I suppose, when I reflected on my later development. But I suspect I wouldn't have been any different, at least not in regard to my feelings for Iris, if he hadn't fiddled about with me. I might have come to the truth after an unsuccessful marriage perhaps, or never at all. A hell of a lot of people plod through life without ever suspecting who or what they really are. Iris has been my life-saver.'

It all ended fairly amicably, taking coffee in Iris Proby's office, Laszlo meeting the matron formally for the first time, a woman with luxuriant black hair pinned up around a face that had the power of an eagle. Miss Proby gleamed happily as she watched him, faintly but not unkindly amused at his interest in Cynthia. But despite her friendliness and charm, he felt like a fox that had been cornered in the chicken-run with feathers around his wet chops.

Toshiro Harada, the European President of the First Nagasaki and Waikiki Trust, sat behind a mahogany desk inlaid with lapis lazuli and cochineal replications of the Tarot along its front and sides. These cabalistic images were repeated in vermilion and black hide on the working surface protected by smoked Bohemian glass, scrolled prettily around the perimeter. The desk was a rare example of the work of Franz Frankenstein, a cabinet-maker who flourished in fin-de-siècle Prague and whose work had only recently been gathered together for a belated and well-deserved retrospective at the modest Sachs-Sardo gallery in Brignoles. On one corner of the desk stood a table-lamp (Danzig, 1926). Had it been marginally more restrained, it might have passed for a pleasant piece of Tiffany Art Deco ostentation. Its fluted, electro-plated vertical standard rose from a block of cream onyx, around which was fitted a collar of green enamelled figurines of vamps and red ones of gigolos; a tableau of clinking glasses, raised by marcelled and brilliantined smilers, demented at the prospect of eternal cocktails. The asparagus-coloured faience shade was a large, dimpled globe with crystal pendants suspended from the base. Their coruscating refractions when the lamp was lit invested the ambience with a kind of visual laughter. On the wall behind Harada hung two immense Heinrich Dossers (1885–1930), abstract expressionist works in red, pink and white. A number of muddy water-colours by the Norwegian painter Birgit Toft (1934–?) were arranged around the room. Harada had been stealthily collecting Tofts for years. All the pictures depicted dead hedgehogs in dappled sunlight, this being, of course, the only subject Toft elected to paint. To the right of the desk was an early Dali of a young man playing a French horn, and a Gwen John pencil sketch of an engorged penis, which Harada liked to imagine had been posed by Auguste Rodin himself. There was also a chunky wall-clock with a block face, its Arabic numerals italic and slightly offset, and a glass bookcase filled with banking yearbooks and technical trash. On the polished parquet floor lay a pair of cerulean Kirghizi skimmers.

The pleasure Harada derived from his office was partly diminished by the fact that his only window included part of the Nat West Tower in its perspective, a disadvantage he mitigated by partly drawing the hyacinthine persienne to occult the offence. Harada, a smallish man of about fifty, was dressed in a feuille-morte three-piece and wore a satin tie the colour of chopped liver. He looked pensive.

Laszlo entered Harada's office and was waved to the green leather armchair before the European President's desk. Harada offered him a Chesterfield then, taking one himself, lit both cigarettes. The Japanese filled his little lungs with smoke twice before speaking.

'My dear Gabor,' he said, 'I have a regular requirement for small-breasted and depilated Caucasian girls of not more than 1.47 metres in height and forty-four kilos in weight. Since prudence dictates that these females must be above the age of consent, some creative simulation of prepubescence will be necessary.'

Laszlo puffed at his cigarette and gave a deferential nod.

'Have you heard,' Harada drawled discreetly, 'of Brighter Bedrooms of Beckenham?'

Chapter 17

*The most charming characteristic of the City
is its subtle fragrance of greed.*

Oswald Mosley.

Laszlo's appointment at the age of twenty as Manager of Special Off Balance Sheet Strategies or SOBS, after scarcely two years at the First Nag and Waik, did not astonish either Sam Yamaha or Zelda Hashamoto. They were both, of course, unhealthily perceptive people. Zelda had recognised quite early on that Laszlo, unlike many of his peers, had been unimpaired by a university education or deformed by bourgeois, Procrustean breeding. Nor was he betrayed by a superior intellect. He possessed instead the flashy facility that was so crucial in the City, and a cheerful amorality which, she predicted, when properly matured, would enable him to beguile his way into a board-room or two. He was, she suspected, capable of almost anything, an attribute of significance in anyone with vaulting aspirations in the financial jungle. The sort of creature, she felt, who would in time acquire the statutory Roller, snarling Ferrari, reproduction Tudor manor, prettily accented wife and golden offspring capering their ponies around the paddock.

'What a pity,' she remarked wistfully to Yamaha, 'that we don't have more young men of his calibre.'

Laszlo's new responsibilities encompassed the drafting of confidential memoranda, the management of Harada's sensitive correspondence, the monitoring of his diary, the appraisal of abnormal funding needs, and the procurement of lollypop-sucking young females for the European President's private entertainment. The Knightsbridge apartment that went with the assignment, across the square from Yamaha's, had a nursery-

123

bedroom supplied with toys and equipment devised for the subtlest fantasies. This was reserved for Harada's exclusive use. The activities were fairly unobtrusive. A scribbled instruction that read 'Mallory Towers, number 34, Tuesday after 20.00 hours' was sufficient to ensure that the companion identified would be waiting in the nursery for Harada's arrival at the specified time. The Mallory Towers file contained the photographs, descriptions and proclivities of wide-eyed, melancholic gamines in skimpy uniforms, laddered black tights and pigtails. Other desirable attributes were inky fingers and the ability to effectively simulate fear and distress. Harada, however, did not approve of vulgarities like screaming, shouting or coarse language.

'It would not be seemly,' he warned Laszlo, 'to allow your neighbours to suppose that this was a place where excessive coercion is used or where the young guests are subjected to unacceptable depravities.'

But Harada was crazy for barely audible sobbing and an abundance of tears. There was nothing the Japanese enjoyed more than the passionate lapping of warm lachrymatory salts from the eye-sockets of his schoolgirl visitors.

Laszlo's promotion was marked by a modest celebratory evening at Yamaha's place. Harada, who had always been acutely sensitive about social visibility, declined. He was content, however, to authorise the expense of providing food, drink, two serving maids, and a decorous fille de joie that he thoughtfully asked Laszlo to lay on for Sam. He suggested somebody short, dark and pneumatic.

'A poulet,' Harada murmured drily, 'that Sam could mistake for a rubber inflatable when the lights were out.'

The guest list was small if not particularly select – Laszlo, Yamaha and Chancer being joined by Froline Nablus, Zelda Hashamoto and Sam's awaited gift from Brighter Bedrooms of Beckenham. Among other significations, the evening marked the termination of Laszlo's persistent but discreet interest in Mrs Nablus. Froline, politely pleasant, even affable, had done nothing to encourage him, having perceived from their first meeting that the tigerish young Gabor was a woman-eater. Invitations to dinner, theatres and concerts were ingeniously evaded, although she was not averse to the occasional business lunch, preferably chaperoned by clients in whom they had a mutual investment. If he chose to remain sceptical about her attachment to an elderly husband whom she rarely saw apart from their annual yachting trips around the Aegean, there was no evidence to suggest alternative attachments. Laszlo believed that she had less regard for him than previously because of his reputed private services for Harada. But it was more than that. He only apprehended the depth of her indifference when she unexpectedly betrayed him by a whimsical disclosure to the guests that he'd attempted to impress her on the first interview by turning up in indecently tight trousers. Everybody laughed long enough for it to have hurt. Laszlo smiled. And that was the end.

They were being entertained by Froline's racy observations on the philistinism of her Islamic inheritance and the grotesque improbability of females being able to express themselves as musicians, poets and painters. She joked about the caveat in the Hadith that required artists to provide souls for their depictions on the Judgement Day. And at this point of blasphemous hilarity, a rangy blonde arrived. She was happily apologetic about being late. Laszlo frowned. He'd ordered a short brunette called Jenny (Catalogue number BR/18). There had been solemn assurances about chubbiness. Now this. Attired in a floating Pre-Raphaelite gown under a black, glittery jacket, the blonde jangled silver jewellery and flashed red painted toe-nails through her flat sandals. She had cropped yellow hair, blue eyes and the cheerful vulnerability of a lost courier. She made for Yamaha, ducking several inches to allow her obvious date to peck a cheek and provide an opportunity to whisper her name. Yamaha carried off the deception fairly well, sliding off her twinkling bolero before advancing with her and the announcement that this was Roswitha. She neglected, of course, to provide her catalogue number, which he half heard as a mumbled BL/18 something. An obvious computer cock-up. Elegant fingers were fluttered, a chablis lifted from the offered tray and Roswitha gushed that she was a ski-instructress hot in from Klosters.

'But you don't look tanned enough to be a ski-instructrice,' Mrs Nablus observed archly.

Her use of the archaic form of the word was slyly deprecatory, Yamaha having inadvertently let the cat out of the bag when he informed the ladies earlier in the evening that he was expecting an old friend called Jenny. Roswitha understood the intent of Froline's scepticism but deflected the mockery with a good-natured shrug, explaining that she'd been in the clinic for twelve weeks with a fractured pelvis following an accident on the piste. Then Zelda Hashamoto, being slightly contemptuous of the house practice of charging expensive whores to the bank's bloated entertainment account, joined in the fun.

'Oh, merciful God,' she exclaimed, 'I hope it hasn't compromised your ability to produce bambinos.' The contrived horror was wickedly overdone.

'Everything is OK now,' Roswitha assured her, patting her quim.

Laszlo grinned at the anatomical confusion. But Bevan Chancer was swollen with solicitude. He appeared to be the only person present who was unaware of Roswitha's real profession. The Welshman edged closer, appropriating the space around her.

'Bevan is our great musician,' the Japanese teased. 'He used to play in a famous jazz-band. You know, like Count Basie.'

'Not like Count Basie,' Chancer murmured unhappily.

Yamaha winked, a signal Roswitha interpreted as permission from the patron to socialise with the tall Welshman.

'I love jazz,' she ventured, devoting herself to Chancer with a gushy smile.

Laszlo, not unaware of Chancer's growing interest in Roswitha, cleared matters with Yamaha.

'She's on expenses,' he said, nodding towards the girl. 'Fifty quid for the hostess bit and another two hundred and fifty to stay the night. Do you want her?'

Yamaha shook his head, advising Laszlo that she was far too thin and tall for his tastes.

'Take her home yourself,' he suggested graciously.

Laszlo considered the slender blonde from Brighter Bedrooms.

Her hand was now being massaged by a moist-eyed Chancer. It would, he concluded, have been ungentlemanly to intrude on what appeared to be evolving into a mutually satisfactory arrangement for the evening. He decided to take a raincheck on Roswitha but felt that this was definitely not his night.

'Would you care to slip back to my place for coffee?' Chancer enquired anxiously as everybody milled around preparing to depart.

Roswitha looked across at Yamaha for instructions. She managed the quick eye movement that asked the question. He returned a half-smile, nodding approval before turning to Laszlo. The girl sailed out on Bevan Chancer's arm. But there was a sniggering exchange between Zelda and Froline after the couple had left. Something was amiss. Chancer was clearly not entitled to benefits of this kind. He didn't even rate an air-conditioned Mazda.

'You should have snapped her up,' Yamaha complained, clicking his tongue in reproof.

'I'm much too soft-hearted,' Laszlo replied gloomily.

'Ah well,' Yamaha sighed, 'at least I've got Queen Victoria pumped up for tonight.'

Over the next three years, Harada's confidence in Laszlo Gabor increased to the extent that the European President admitted to alarming reservations about Sam Yamaha's integrity.

'Matters might have already gone too far,' brooded Harada.

Laszlo was entrusted with an investigation of Yamaha's principal accounts. Harada stressed that it was important that neither Mrs Hashamoto or Sam Yamaha should suspect the nature of his assignment.

So Laszlo got down to business at his personal computer in the Knightsbridge apartment. He chased down references to the Spillano Garbage Corporation, which with Sham Shilverman Movie Productions and Sheik Yusuf Hamami's Ethical Friction covered the major part of Yamaha's responsibilities. Sam had once told Laszlo that there were more than six thousand cross-contractual agreements between those three corporations alone, written under eighteen legal protocols in twenty-seven countries and subject to nine taxation systems. The Spillano Garbage Corporation was reputed to have racy underworld connections, but nothing had ever been proved. Their entrepreneurial skill in exporting dangerous and contaminated rubbish to the Third World was well documented. This ingenious enterprise had provided sensational copy in the subversive press for many years. But the well-wishers of the corporation dealt with these trouble-making rags with exemplary pizzazz. Although a repertoire of fire-bombs, acid-sprays and even fairly innocuous tooth-chippings of mouthy liberal journalists was often unfairly associated with the company, Spillano Garbage's proud record of non-conviction stood respectable comparison with the greatest multi-nationals in the free world. A radio commentator who had been accidentally shot in the groin by a passing motor-cyclist was insensitive enough to attribute this unfortunate act to his campaign against the corporation's advertising slogan, 'What's good for Spillano Garbage is Terrific for Terrastricken'. Miss Natalie Tolstoy, a spokesperson for the corporation, when interviewed on a visit to the stricken journalist with a bunch of betonies in one hand and a fifth of Hot Pussy (a matured honey-sweet rye) in the other, said, 'There's a lot of fair-minded people in this country who will always root for the greatest corporation in the world.'

As he tracked his way through the accounts of the Spillano Garbage Corporation, Laszlo became enmeshed in the concept of Sunburn Spillano's financial sterility. According to a Yamaha footnote, Sunburn Spillano because of intermittent amnesia (an old head injury) had been registered as a mentally incompetent person. He was also a Financially Sterile Entity. The Yamaha note read: 'An FSE is not the same as a destitute individual as FSEs subsist on funds vested in other parties. Necessaries are provided by agencies in which FSEs, have no direct or indirect control or interest; nor do FSEs possess powers of attorney in their support agencies. FSEs do not possess personal investments, bank accounts, credit-cards or loose change, nor can they manage assets belonging to third parties. Technically speaking, FSEs have no tax liability, but this is a view that is deemed provocative by hostile revenue authorities.'

Laszlo shivered. The First Nagasaki and Waikiki Trust appeared to be in hock to an FSE. He left a message on Toshiro Harada's residential answer-phone. Then he poured himself a stiffish malt.

Chapter 18

Selveratnam found the job with the Spillano Garbage Corporation much more exacting then he imagined it would be. The first month took him to São Paulo, Lisbon, Nairobi, Marseilles, Sydney, Reykjavik, Caracas and Mombasa. There were also many internal shuttle flights from Honkeyville to Lynchburg, Capone City, Scarface Falls, Rape River, New Prejudice and Capitalist Creek. Although the money was astonishingly good and he had the opportunity of visiting places he would never have paid to see, Selveratnam often forgot where he was. He spent most of his life in the air and began to believe that he was in the same plane with the same passengers and crew on each occasion. Often, several of his journeys merged into an isochronous nightmare. Now and again, he forgot his own name and kept staring into mirrors to check his identity. Some days he imagined that he was a giant Dutchman, and on others that he was a Peruvian boy who had lost his parents. On really bad days, he even failed to recognise his own reflection. Although he travelled Dream Class, pampered by angelic hostesses and befriended by high-class riders (invitations to golf, booze, dine, swim, ski, sail, fish, shoot and screw with the nicest people around choked the memory of his pocket computer), Maya was always in his thoughts. During the first couple of years, he phoned her from airports, scribbled postcards (English and Tamil) in the busy lounges of luxury hotels and from the candle-lit tables of the exclusive restaurants he was forced to use between flights. Tasty young men offered him mescalin chewing-gum in airport washrooms, and wobbly young women with smudged mascara and condoms held discreetly under their watch-straps asked him for lights in airport bars. Temptation was everywhere, yet in the first four years or so little Selveratnam was only compromised once. And if we except that unsolicited hand-job from a bell-hop in Cairo who was supposed to be valeting his trousers while he was still wearing them, his nose was fairly clean. Even his later encounters with whores were relatively innocuous, inspired more by spiritual enquiry than vicious lechery.

The most rewarding aspect of his job as an executive courier was that he was invariably welcome at his destinations. And the precious packages he carried were usually transferred in exotically comfortable locations to recipients who radiated a sinister but not unpleasant mystique. Once, however, in Toulon, he was trapped by a tenacious young tart he had found difficult to elude all day, having committed the strategic error of buying her a croque-madame and a large pistachiou sundae. And try as he would, she seemed unable to comprehend that he had no interest in her caramel-brown, anguine body.

'You think my tits are too small?' she demanded, hooking her arm through his.

'Big, small – they mean nothing to me,' Selveratnam had advised her quietly.

'I'm very, very tight,' she assured him earnestly, making a popping noise with a finger in her mouth that sounded like a cork being pulled from a bottle.

It was no use. She had appropriated his arm. And then he was unaccountably approached by his contact in the hotel foyer (one hour prematurely due to a cock-up of time-zones) while the girl was pressed against him on a lover's lounger partly occulted by exotic flora.

'Lisez-vous Robbe-Grillet?' the monocled stranger, who looked vaguely like S. J. Perelman, whispered from behind a branch of potted magnolias.

'Seulement les derniers romans,' Selveratnam replied, slowly enunciating the aide-mémoire he had inked across his palm.

'Quel dommage,' the man sighed.

The package was passed with melodramatic stealth, and the monocled stranger, recognising the girl and sensing something was amiss, rushed out of the entrance into the bright evening sunlight. Normally, the transactions were more leisurely. An invitation to dinner was not uncommon; sometimes a trip to a cabaret or a swish around the city in an air-conditioned limo. Occasionally, Selveratnam met the contact's family and engaged in simple pleasures, like patting the children on the head, joining them in a game of royal ludo or reading everybody's palms before he returned to his hotel. But on this occasion the intrusive young hooker had buggered up even those harmless diversions. He found it difficult to restrain a disappointed scowl as he contemplated the girl. And she appeared to be unhappy at what she had witnessed.

'You were using a code,' the whore snarled nastily. 'I suspected that you were a criminal right from the start.'

Selveratnam tried to excuse himself, but the girl clung to his arm.

'I have a brother in the Légion Etrangère,' she threatened, 'and his lover is a senior police officer. It's five thousand francs or else.'

'Else?'

'They'll have your black arse behind bars quicker than you can fart.'

'As to the blackness of arses,' Selveratnam protested, 'there's probably not much to choose between mine and yours.'

'Shut your gob,' came a venomous cry that reverberated through the Calanques Bar.

Selveratnam sprang to his feet and bolted. He just made the lift before her, crashing the door behind him and creaking upwards to the seventh floor. Jogging along the sound-proofed corridor, he fancied that his drumming heart had slid into his lower bowel. It would be expedient, he decided, to check out of the hotel as soon as possible. But by the time he had packed his bison-skin luggage and edged the door ajar to peer out, the girl was standing there, glaring balefully in his direction. He was overwhelmed by the need to shit.

'Bastard,' she hissed.

Selveratnam ducked back into the room. Perhaps, he reflected, it might be easier to slip out of town later that night. He undressed rapidly and ran the shower, coming to the unpleasant conclusion, as he soaped himself, that she was working with the management. He could hear her shouting abuse through the keyhole. No casual whore could have been so ridiculously audacious. He had hardly dried himself when the impassioned banging started. Again and again. Fearing that she'd splinter the wooden panels, he tried Room Service. It was a forlorn gesture. The male receptionist's French was incomprehensible. It was obviously a shakedown. Buying the young lady off appeared to be the only solution. Folding himself into a towelled wrap, he unlatched the door. She was not alone. Beside her was an immense, bearded man in a crumpled grey uniform. He wore a black kepi. The man informed Selveratnam that the girl was his little sister and that she had alleged that the Indian had violated her in his room earlier that afternoon.

'He chewed my nipples raw,' she sobbed, brushing Selveratnam aside.

She rushed into the room and tossed herself on the bed. The bearded man in a kepi sauntered in after her. Selveratnam knew the jig was up when she disrobed with professional speed.

'Look,' accused the man in the kepi, pointing to a plaster over her left nipple with a silver-tipped walking-stick, 'another snap of your evil jaws and she'd have been mutilated for life.'

'How much do you want?' Selveratnam enquired miserably.

The man considered that two thousand dollars would be reasonable compensation for his baby sister's dishonour. They finally settled for eight hundred francs in cash, five hundred in traveller's cheques and his gold Hanuman ring.

'You can fuck me for another two hundred,' she suggested sweetly as they prepared to leave. 'I'm very, very tight. Honest.'

Selveratnam shook his head.

'I'll take all the coke you've got,' the man confided at the door. 'We pay the keenest international street-prices. You won't get a straighter deal anywhere along the French coast.'

After the unfortunate Toulon experience, Selveratnam assiduously averted his eyes when women smiled at him. He even broke his vow of veracity when a Garboesque skinhead in a boiler suit and outsize sneakers followed him into a men's toilet in Stockholm.

'Don't be fright, darling,' the skinhead implored him huskily. 'I'm really a cunt.'

'And I'm gay,' Selveratnam countered desperately.

He felt the pain of the lie in his solar plexus. The six-footer looked crestfallen.

'You no wanna cunt?' she croaked plaintively.

'Not at present,' he assured her, diving below the menace of her outstretched hands and darting for the exit.

That night in his Swedish hotel he went through his usual ritual of laying Maya's art photographs out on his bed. For the first time in four years, the display didn't provoke even a trace of an erection. Selveratnam was dazed by the spiritual implications of his flaccidity. Could he, he wondered, have made the big time? Was he a twenty-four-carat messiah at last? For the next hour he tried to induce a hint of starch into his limp tool. He pulled, rubbed, flicked and tickled it in an effort to produce a response. Nothing. Selveratnam was as soft as a snail. Charged with the exaltation of this significant experience, he could hardly endure the frustration of not sharing his wonderful news with another human being who could apprehend the importance of the event. Annunciation follows in the footsteps of revealed truth. It was now midnight. He dialled Crystal Palace. He allowed the phone to ring two hundred and twenty-eight times, this being a propitious figure and the number of Yogi Govinda Popatsahib's bungalow in Conjeeveram's Rolling Temple Gully. But there was no reply. Where was his Maya? he wondered bleakly. After the elation came a dark night of his soul. He was tormented by a sudden frenzy of coughing. And for the first time he coughed blood. What could it mean? He dredged his mind for appropriate symbols. Was it a sign from the Universal Consciousness? More blood. He tried Maya again. Once more, he hung on until the phone rang two hundred and twenty-eight times. At one-thirty in the morning, his fiancée did not appear to be taking calls. Was she ill? On holiday? Visiting a sick friend? Other explanations depressed him. In desperation, he rang Medusa O'Toole in

Honkeyville. It was, he calculated, only eight-thirty in the evening there. The maid answered and redirected him to the ashram at L'Amauresque. But it was another hour before he managed to reach her.

'I think,' he announced portentously (at three-thirty a.m. L'Amauresque time), 'that I am now a real messiah.'

'Who the shit is this?' demanded a voice thick with sleep.

'Bunny Selveratnam,' he said brightly.

'Who?'

He spent five minutes trying to explain who he was. She said that she was unable to place him. The name, she yawned, wasn't even vaguely familiar.

'You fixed me up with the Spillano Garbage Corporation four years ago.'

'I did?' She sounded doubtful. But there was more than a hint of barbiturates in her uncertain slur.

'This is bloody ridiculous,' Selveratnam shouted, losing control of himself.

The phone went dead. He coughed some more blood. The L'Amauresque number remained unobtainable. The little messiah was going out of his mind. At four-fifteen a.m. Stockholm time, he called a taxi and asked to be driven to the nearest sex establishment. There was an important question that had to be answered. He was just in time. It was nearly five and the girls were going to bed. A buxom platinum blonde in black-rimmed glasses reluctantly agreed to do the business for five hundred krona.

'I have no intention of penetrating you,' he assured her. 'This visit is merely to confirm my lack of erectability. Or otherwise, of course.'

She didn't seem at all surprised at his comments, just nodded coldly and extended her palm.

'It's still five hundred,' she sighed, taking and counting the notes before allowing him through the front door.

He was led up the stairs to a small bedroom on the first floor. It was a cosy place. Black and gold flock wallpaper, folkweave rugs on a polished pine floor, blue mirrors, two Lautrec posters and a blown cane vase (raspberry and cream stripes) filled with a vigorous spray of helianthus. In one corner was a lemon wash-stand and bidet behind matching bead curtains. He traced the pleasant odour of oranges to some fresh peel in the ash-tray on the window-sill. But it was the chunky brass bedstead with its red and white chequered cover that warmed his heart. It evoked happier times with Maya.

She slithered out of her short yellow dress and unzipped his flies, then switched on a strobe at the foot of the bed, posing with her plump thighs apart. The blonde removed her rings, creamed her hands and reached for his genitals. She could, he thought, contemplating her handsome and intelligent face, have been a Professor of Philosophy or the wife of an ambassador to an important country.

'You're a little softy, aren't you?' she murmured as she got to work. 'But don't worry, things will improve.'

They did not speak as she laboured diligently with experienced fingers. In the distance a dog barked. From somewhere in the house a clock chimed the half-hour. The signs of impatience became evident after a few minutes.

'Perhaps you'd like to kiss me there,' she frowned, indicating the location with a long, silver-painted index-nail.

'I'd rather not,' the little mystic replied stiffly.

'Move closer to me,' she insisted, releasing his cock for a moment and drawing his head between her knees. It was a petulant move and unexpectedly fierce. Selveratnam coughed. A plume of blood bespattered her flaxen pubes, salmon-pink furrow and white, arched thighs. He coughed again, clamping his hand over his mouth. It was too late. There was blood every-where.

'You unspeakable beast,' she cried, springing out of bed and crashing through the bead curtains to the bidet. Whimpering and wailing, she crouched over the spray.

'It was just an accident,' he explained, dabbing himself with a handkerchief.

But nothing he said or did could stop her sobs of revulsion as she sluiced the blood away. Her anguish echoed through the night. Doors opened. Several whores came in. One or two seemed outraged. Some giggled. At first glance, the bed looked like the scene of a brutal murder. An indignant whore felt obliged to slap Selveratnam's face. Another tugged at his hair and tweaked his ear.

'Piss off,' the bespectacled blonde screamed as he escaped down the stairs, 'or I'll have you minced up. Mother of God. What have I done to deserve this fucking nightmare?'

Selveratnam had to wait until Singapore before he could try again. The pretty Eurasian whore did not take long in coming to a conclusion.

'I regret, dear sir,' she lisped, after spending half an hour trying to inflate him with her voluptuous mouth, 'that you appear to be one hundred per cent impotent. Of course,' she added sympathetically, 'in most cases the problem is temporary, the invariable cause being psychological. Many travelling gentlemen like your honoured self exhibit these symptoms. They're usually caused by excessive anxiety about a wife or a girl-friend. Concern that the object of their affection is being poked by somebody else can make the best of men go limp.'

'Psychology,' scoffed Selveratnam, 'is not a system in which I have abundant faith. In my case, the cause is undoubtedly spiritual. You see,' he observed as he adjusted his candy-striped Y-fronts, 'I'm probably a messiah.'

The pretty Eurasian whore seemed unimpressed. She started to brush her hair before the mirror. It frizzed out like a crinkly brown fan.

'Are all impotent men messiahs?' she enquired in a little-girl voice, smiling at his reflection.

It was the sort of silly question, he decided, that did not deserve a considered reply.

But the pretty Eurasian whore proved to be flukily correct about the ephemeral nature of his condition. The moment he heard Maya's voice on the telephone (a London–Bangkok call), his organ inflated miraculously. For some strange reason, the realisation that he was still some way short of full messianic status did not unduly depress him, as he had feared it would. Indeed, the recovery of his potency made him pulse with excitement. In the four years he'd spent away from Maya, Selveratnam had pleasured himself as he fantasised over her naked images. He suddenly perceived that masturbation, far from being the symbol of insufficiency, had probably been his salvation. The secret and sweet sacrament of those lonely nights in strange hotel bedrooms around the world. He wondered bleakly whether he would ever be able to accept the limitations of another body's demands after years of private ecstasy. But it was not a reservation he chose to share with Maya, at least not while they remained apart. He surrendered uneasily to the recognition of the duplicity, apprehending that his spiritual prospects had diminished but taking comfort in the glorious restitution of a stiffened cock.

'I thought I'd made it,' he told Maya over the phone, investing his voice with the holy quaver that had once induced her to kiss his feet.

'Being an "almost messiah" is more than most people can achieve,' she mocked playfully.

Her light-hearted tone slightly depressed him, and he was sceptical about the gravity of an enquiry about his levitation, quickly conceding a significant lack of progress in that area. He tried to elicit whether she was practising, with an appropriate Hindu diligence, the vows of chastity they had made on the night before his departure.

'What?'

'Are you being faithful to me?' he asked impatiently.

Maya tittered. It was, he suspected, an evasive strategy.

'What's so funny about that?' he demanded irritably.

'When are you coming home?' she enquired gaily, changing the subject. 'Ada keeps asking about you.'

'Soon,' he promised.

He rubbed his crotch discreetly, conscious of his visibility in the telephone booth at Bangkok Post Office.

'That's what you said four years ago,' she laughed.

And her inexplicable giggling had not stopped when he finally put the receiver down.

The practice of swallowing and regurgitating large objects several times a day at last began to cause him problems. His pharynx, oesophagus and stomach were not, he believed, what these organs should have been. He felt as though his mouth had been forcibly kept open during a particularly nasty harmattan. Soreness, occasional pain and the dramatic gouting of blood had begun to alarm him. He sneaked in to see a doctor in Kowloon.

'What the hell have you been doing with your pipes?' the physician demanded.

'I'm a professional regurgitator,' Selveratnam explained.

'What exactly have you been swallowing?'

Selveratnam shot him a gloomy look.

'That's an extremely confidential matter. Even I'm not supposed to know. And should my employers suspect that I had made an unauthorised disclosure, even the recipient of such data would be in the gravest danger.'

The physician looked anxious.

'As a medical man, Mr McGinty' – a pseudonym Selveratnam used in the East – 'anything I hear in this consulting-room is privileged information. Naturally, it would be in both our interests to ensure that anything you say goes no further.'

Selveratnam cracked his knuckles and regarded the Chinaman unhappily.

'It's my luminous sperm that concerns me as much as my throat. You see, doctor, I have ambitions to get married and raise a family.'

The Chinaman went across to the sink and washed his hands. Selveratnam suspected that the gesture was invested with more than a hint of symbolism.

'I need help,' the Tamilian pleaded.

'You're not a well man, Mr McGinty. These employers whom you seek to protect have not really played the yellow man with you.'

Selveratnam's shoulders dropped. He dabbed his eyes with a handkerchief.

'I'm on my way to the ash-tip then?' he enquired plaintively.

'That's hardly the way I would put it.'

'I have no complaints about the salary, pension scheme, share-option packages, transportation and hotel arrangements.'

The doctor nodded.

'Well,' Selveratnam confessed reluctantly, 'among other things, I swallow and regurgitate rare gem-stones, miniature cameras, platinum ingots, hallucinatory substances, microfilm, alarm inhibitors, strongbox keys, and capsules that glow in the dark.' He decided that it would be inappropriate to inform the Chinaman about standard paperwork like hot bonds, security information, hit-lists, exotic letters of transit, ransom demands, bank vault codes, and urban guerrilla strategies for a number of freedom-fighting organisations.

'Listen, Mr McGinty,' the Chinaman warned, 'if you don't chuck this job immediately, you'll be chewing the proverbial spare-ribs with your ancestors much sooner than planned.'

'It's my living.'

'Death more likely. To be frank, Mr McGinty, you're seriously ill. Report to your company physician as soon as you can. You need urgent help and prolonged medication.'

'May I carry on masturbating?'

The doctor shrugged.

'Sure. But no more regurgitating, Mr McGinty,' he warned, wagging an admonitory finger at the Tamilian as he showed him to the door.

The Chinese physician followed the progress of the diminutive mystic down the stairs, fascinated by the epaulettes of blue light that were clearly visible on either side of Selveratnam's scrawny neck.

When Selveratnam got back to Honkeyville, he made an appointment to see Hank Moroni, the company physician. Moroni went over the Hindu very carefully, taking blood, semen and sputum samples.

'I wouldn't let the luminous sperm concern you overmuch,' he smiled, shaking a test-tube of mauve spunk and holding it to the light.

'No?'

'No.'

'And my throat?'

'I'll scribble out a certificate excusing you regurgitation duties for a month.'

'Is it that bad?'

'Shucks, no. You're festering a bit in the wrong places, but apart from a modest fissure you're in great shape.'

'I'd love to return to London for a spell,' Selveratnam murmured wistfully. 'It's been more than four years.'

'I don't see why not,' Dr Moroni mused. 'But first I'll have to get your certificate okayed by Miss Natalie Tolstoy. Miss Tolstoy signs everything, of course, Mr Spillano being a Financially Sterile Entity. It should be a formality. A month back home should do you good.'

But it wasn't that simple. Spillano rang for Moroni, favouring him with a shark-like smile as he came in. The doctor sat uneasily through Spillano's ruminations on the little Tamilian's indispensability.

'Hell, Moroni, I'd just chewed a nice piece of Pesce Spada; the bits are still in my teeth. I was feeling radiant. The day was sunny and beautiful. And then this paper.'

He fluttered the medical certificate irritably between two fingers, then gave the doctor an unblinking stare that lasted for almost a minute.

'Didn't you know that Selveratnam couldn't be excused duties? His contract specifically excludes that sort of shit.'

Moroni looked glum.

'Allow me to explain, Mr Spillano, ' he said.

'Explain? Explain? What are we, all of a sudden? Fucking philosophers? Explanations are for children, Moroni. Spillano Garbage deals in solutions. One-line shots. Shazamos.'

141

Spillano buzzed for Miss Tolstoy.

'Is that all, Mr Spillano?' Moroni enquired nervously.

'Shazam,' Spillano shouted.

The doctor scooted away, grey-faced and contrite. Miss Tolstoy came in and sat down.

'Natalie darling,' Spillano said, 'we've got this Indian guy who's developed a frisky throat.'

She nodded.

'You know this fink?'

'He read my palm in the cafeteria a month or two ago.'

Spillano blinked like a lizard in sunlight. The idea that the corporation had allowed the Tamilian enough home-base time to read palms offended him. Palm-readers, like poets, whistlers and staff who visited the john more than twice a day on company time, made him very jumpy.

'I want this putz in my office ten minutes ago,' he snarled as pleasantly as possible.

Miss Tolstoy got up and ran out. Spillano picked thoughtfully at the shreds of Pesce Spada between his teeth. He had already anticipated the wear and tear of Selveratnam's tubes and discussed the question of their eventual refurbishing with a Dr Zeiss in Geneva. Zeiss had some reservations about whether Selveratnam would be as effective with a transplanted system. Spillano had suggested using anaconda tissue (there had been some interesting work in Haiti with anacondas), but Zeiss was defensive about rejection. He had promised to speed up his research into suitable relining material. That was ten days ago. Spillano had hoped that Selveratnam would last five years at least and felt betrayed by the Tamilian's signs of premature wear and tear. Four years and the guy was falling to bits.

Miss Tolstoy returned with Selveratnam. He did not look a million dollars. Spillano waved him to a chair, then shot him a cautious smile.

'You're looking just terrific,' Spillano said in a slow, even voice.

'I've got a badly lacerated throat, sir,' the Tamilian whispered sadly.

'Nothing that a peyote swab and a saline gargle won't fix,' Spillano enthused.

'I'm dying, sir.'

Spillano panned his steely gaze from Miss Tolstoy to Selveratnam and back again.

'We don't allow our executive staff to die, do we, Natalie?'

'No, Mr Spillano,' she proclaimed. It was an upbeat vote of affirmation.

'Listen,' Spillano murmured, leaning towards Selveratnam, 'you're a very lucky boy. As you know, you've got a five-year holiday-exclusion clause in your contract.'

Selveratnam nodded miserably.

'We're considering liberalising that arrangement as we approach the four-and-a-half-year point. In the meantime, I've hired this specialist in Geneva who's going to reline your gullet with anaconda material.'

'Anaconda?' croaked the Tamilian in horror. 'That's a snake.'

'Anacondas are in the swallowing business as well,' Spillano pointed out. 'Nor are they averse to an occasional spot of regurgitation. But first we've got an assignment for you in the one place you've been crazy to get to. London.'

'London, England?'

Spillano nodded. He didn't consider it politic at that point to mention that the trip would entail several preliminary loops lasting about nine months, around Tahiti, Honolulu, Riyadh, Lagos, Rio, Madrid, Mecca and Funchal. Being human, he first wanted to savour the tears of joy welling up in Selveratnam's expressive eyes and coursing down his brown cheeks.

A sick and demoralised Selveratnam found Natalie Tolstoy a sympathetic confidante. During his infrequent visits to the office, he never failed to seek her out. 'Where's Miss Tolstoy?' he'd ask if he did not find her at her desk. He had been known to hang around the car-park in a snowstorm waiting for her red Buick to return after lunch-break, and even to make a number of anxious passes along the corridor outside the Ladies' Washroom if he had been told that was where she was. His tired eyes would light up the moment he caught sight of her, and she could always be expected to be genial whenever they met. Sometimes, when Sunburn Spillano was out of town and his tight flight schedules permitted, Selveratnam would get quite cosy with Natalie Tolstoy. He used to persuade her to peek down his throat, feel the distension around his sternum and jiggle his creaky xiphoid. Once, she even invited him to her apartment. He was taken by the deep, pink rugs, bean-bags, giant plush rabbits, chrome and crystal dining-area and a collection of two hundred tennis-racquets glued to the walls. He suspected a Spillano influence when he saw her triptych of Superman paintings, each six by four and dominant over a fireplace constructed of ceramic baked-bean tins.

'I have always been infatuated,' she confessed, 'with the romance of scrap metal. From my bedroom window, I have a fantastic view of the largest fully automated metal-crushing complex on the East Coast. Mountains of tins, automobiles, motor-bikes, iron bedsteads and really out-of-this-world junk. The crushers wake me at five every morning. I stand at the window watching the scoops chomping into metal and dropping chunks of this wonderful stuff into the crusher. It never fails to excite me.'

Selveratnam nodded politely, trying to understand. He sniffed the air anxiously. Miss Tolstoy had fixed him a meal. He feared the worst. She had cooked an aubergine, peach and spaghetti curry as a special treat. It had, she said, been prepared in accordance with a recipe given to her by her girl-friend, Marigold Nieszawa, whose mother was one-quarter Sikh.

'It's a Sino-Benares cuisine concept,' she informed him proudly, ladling the pungent slosh into imitation Rhages bowls.

He was apologetic, making do with a spoonful or two of rice and half a baked potato.

'It's impossible for me to take even a mouthful of curry without an unbearable sensation of burning. It feels like molten lava. What was once for me a joy and my birthright is now culinary torture. My inner passages, Miss Tolstoy, are not what they used to be.'

At the end of the meal she spoiled him with a generous helping of a coconut and huckleberry sorbet.

'Good for your throat,' she winked.

'You're very kind,' he acknowledged, his eyes rheumy with gratitude.

He chattered about Maya, lisping eulogies to her beauty and intelligence. Her manuscript, now stained, torn in places and dog-eared, was produced.

'It would make a wonderful film,' he reflected. 'A moral tale about a woman's path to realisation.'

But Miss Tolstoy was particularly interested in the photograph of the naked Maya posed with the extension nozzle of a vacuum-cleaner between her shapely thighs.

'Did you take this picture?' she enquired.

Selveratnam shook his head.

'Not me. You see, Miss Tolstoy, before my Maya was converted to Hinduism, she had many men. It was her karma. In her last incarnation, my beloved fiancee was a ring-tailed pariah bitch. She was available to every dog in the village. They queued to mount her. On they jumped. One after another. Alas, the subconscious memory of that terrible life remained, resulting in a serious dharmic wound. "Isn't it obvious," I asked Maya, "where that wound is located?" The poor girl regarded me with dismay. "My God," she whispered, "do you mean my vagina?" I smiled. "You are very perceptive," I said. "But I'm alluding to your astral-vagina, the psychic damage to which may be submerged by sensations of pleasure and orgasmic excitements. The spiritual risks of mindless promiscuity are far-reaching." She understood immediately. Enlightenment followed. "It is preferable," I instructed her, "to cleave to one highly principled mate. Allow me to become your exclusive lover and guru." So we became engaged.'

Selveratnam managed a triumphant smile.

'What a truly inspirational story,' Miss Tolstoy murmured. 'Would you care for another scoop of sorbet?'

Chapter 19

While Bunny Selveratnam was dozing over an early Medusa O'Toole movie in the Dream Class on the flight to Dar es Salaam, Natalie Tolstoy and Sunburn Spillano discussed Maya's extraordinary memoirs (photocopied when Selveratnam was out of the office) and examined with morbid interest the picture of her jokey use of a vacuum-cleaner nozzle. They agreed that it would be impossible to distinguish Maya from her twin, Polly. Now, apart from Polly Ferrari being the wife of the celebrated Wolfgang, who also happened to be Sunburn's cousin, the son of Joe Spillano's errant sister Sylvana (deceased) and an unknown father, she had her own celebrity, being a one-time script-editor for Pasolini and, in Italy, an instantly recognisable ikon associated with the promotion of Ciccolini's Chocolates. But from Sunburn's perspective, the importance of Polly resided in the fact that she was an undercover associate of the Spillano Garbage Corporation, a relationship of which her husband Wolfgang was ignorant. If Polly's subterfuge in respect of her link with his company was advantageous to Sunburn, the suddenly acquired knowledge that she had a twin sister, and that Wolfgang and she were the parents of a son called Laszlo, had, he reflected, even more succulent possibilities.

Spillano Garbage had been secretly endeavouring to purchase L'Amauresque with the intention of returning the property to its former use as a businessmen's country club. It had been planned that Polly Ferrari would front the new enterprise, picking up ten per cent of the equity as a not-insignificant inducement. They had ambitious plans for recruiting the most desirable hostesses in Europe, creating a matchless gaming environment, reviving the once wildly popular nude dancing sessions, providing round-the-clock screenings of Joe Spillano erotica and furnishing every chalet with a selection of Sheik Yusuf's inflatables. The Medusa

O'Toole lease was a secondary inconvenience Sunburn was certain he could resolve once he had purchased the site. Medusa's obsession that she was the priestess of Gaia was her own eccentric business. But the construction of an ashram on a valuable parcel of realty was something he was not about to accept with equanimity.

While there was every chance, given the juiciness of a pre-emptive price, that Hengist Dunkelbaum would sell to a phantom partnership of Sam Yamaha, an imagined friend, and Polly Ferrari, a woman he had lusted after for many years, his probable reluctance to proceed with the transaction once he suspected that it was the Spillano Garbage Corporation that coveted the estate was predictable. Hengist Dunkelbaum regarded Spillano Garbage as a monster with an insatiable appetite. Polly had confirmed Hengist's hatred of the Spillanos. 'They are unscrupulous vampires,' he once disclosed to her. 'I will do everything possible to impede their progress.' His malign observations were conscientiously conveyed to Sunburn and meticulously recorded for future reference. Under Unacceptable Abuse.

'Be nice to the guy,' Sunburn had advised Polly. 'If he wants to send you flowers and amorous cards, so what? He's just an old-fashioned philanderer. The bastard has always cheated on his wife. But don't surrender prematurely. Remember what we're after. Take it easy. An occasional café à deux; maybe a discreet but chaste dinner together. Drive him mad. When you're ready, let the schmucko snatch a kiss or get away with a fumble. But we don't want to be compromised until he's done the business. I'll leave it to your discretion, OK? In the final resort, it's your play.'

But the information that Natalie Tolstoy had laid before him had irresistibly tightened his grip on Polly. The play was now incontestably his. He buzzed her with the alarming news that a blackmailer had tried to enlist the services of the Spillano Garbage Collection Agency (their financial company) to extort money from a Signora Polly Ferrari. He quickly detailed the data he had in his possession.

'Your deception,' he declared, 'invokes certain obligations for

147

me, for not only is Wolfgang my cousin but this guy Laszlo is his son and my kin. Spillano blood is involved. In normal circumstances, I'd have convened a family council. However, you may be surprised to learn that I have decided to protect you, although it is my clear duty to do otherwise.'

Sunburn's magnanimous subordination of the Spillano blood interests to her welfare moved Polly to tears.

'Thank you, Sunburn,' she whispered. 'I'm in your debt.'

She asked him who the blackmailer was and what were his damage-limitation plans. Sunburn replied that the limitation had been fairly comprehensive, the person having already been enclosed in a concrete slab earmarked for use as a mosque cornerstone; something that a subsidiary was erecting in Kuwait. It was a spontaneous and inventive response. Natalie Tolstoy smiled. Sunburn raised a self-congratulatory thumb and winked at her. He informed Polly that he did not propose for obvious reasons to identify the blackmailer. Polly shivered. She suspected that they wouldn't have shed Laszlo's blood, for he was one-quarter Spillano. Could the victim, she wondered, have been her sister Moura? Suddenly, she felt guilty that she had always been haunted by Moura's possible reappearance. The question had to be asked. Sunburn assured her that the person was neither her sister nor her son. Molten with relief, Polly was speechless for a while. Sunburn, familiar with the complexities of the human heart, enjoyed the hiatus, grinning at Miss Tolstoy until Polly's sobs abated at the other end of the line. It was comforting for him to know that Polly Ferrari was his creature at last.

From that point on, she diligently reported every nuance in her campaign of persuasion. Natalie Tolstoy was the intermediary. Dunkelbaum's first kiss was relayed within an hour of the act. She reported that Hengist had used his tongue and that the venture had taken place aboard the *Voracité* outside her cabin. A fortuitous swell provoked by a modest mistral in the harbour of St Tropez had thrown them together. He had held her face between his palms and insinuated his mouth on hers. A crude Frenchy. She had pushed him away, managing to escape to the saloon, where Wolfgang was taking drinks with Steffi

Dunkelbaum. Hengist's lugubrious eyes, dog-moist with longing, had rested on her for the rest of the afternoon. He smouldered and hovered, but she denied him another opportunity to strike before Steffi dragged him off home.

Although news of Polly's elegantly managed cock-teases elevated Sunburn, it had an unsettling effect on Miss Tolstoy. The petite twenty-five-year-old brunette, disguised by dark glasses and an auburn wig, began to make the one-hundred-mile round trip to an exclusive singles bar more often. She was still relatively virginal (only a single undistinguished penetration in the back of her Pentacostal deacon's De Soto grocery waggon) and found that an hour or so of very close dancing accompanied by some discreet frotteurism in the dark was as much as her troubled libido could take.

Sunburn was lunching with Basin Sorel at the Socrates Club when he was called to the phone. He had been expecting a call from Bunny Selveratnam's Dar es Salaam contact. The caller was not who he thought he might be.

'It's Yusuf, brother. Sheik Yusuf from Damascus.'

The Sheik appeared breathless and excited.

'Listen, Sunburn, there's been a serious robbery at the Kulhanian Institute of Decorative Arts in Lisbon. The bastards have lifted the Twinkle of Fatima. As you know, brother, I've been negotiating its sale to the Iranian government. There are those who would regard the blue stone as a holy artefact.'

Sunburn grunted.

'The implications of its theft could be dangerous for many people. It could be held that its disappearance is not unconnected with its imminent transfer to Iran.'

'What are you trying to say?' Sunburn growled.

'That the robbers are dead men,' the Sheik declared. 'Listen, Sunburn. I can arrange an unofficial reward for hard news of the stone's whereabouts. Perhaps a million pounds. Or even more. I'm receptive to any approach.'

'I thought that the stone belonged to the Institute.'

'A mere technicality. They want its return. I'm bidding for proof of its location. There's a serious difference, brother.'

'I'll keep my ears open, Yusuf.'

'Remember, brother. Everything is negotiable. Everything.'

Sunburn Spillano ambled thoughtfully back to his table. The string orchestra was playing 'Make Believe'. He looked down at Basin.

'Wanna dance, baby?'

Basin Sorel smiled apologetically.

'I've been rather overdoing the bourride,' he murmured, fanning the offence away from his mouth.

Sunburn held out his hands.

'So why should a little garlic come between us? Eh?'

Chapter 20

Medusa astonished Joe Spillano when she casually disclosed that filming of *Love Is the End* had already started.

'But we're not due to take off for another six months at least,' he protested.

Medusa gave him an O'Toole special. Her big, wet-mouth smile.

'We've been doing snippets from way back,' she laughed.

'Am I the director or am I the director?' he bitched, limping in pursuit of her.

They strolled around the statuary in Shilverman's garden. She appropriated his arm, squeezing it gently to placate him.

'I've had a few hand-held jobs operating ever since that business meeting at Sham's,' she grinned. 'Intimate footage of little me. You won't be disappointed.'

'Migod, Medusa. Are we talking about the same meeting? Four years ago?'

'Sure thing.'

Joe Spillano looked confused. He turned to Sham for support.

'What the hell gives, Sham?'

Shilverman almost smiled.

'I'm comfortable with an unstructured approach, Joe. The script calls for a swirling time-concept. You've got to remember that we've been horsing around with this since 1926. An awful lot of shadows. In that time there's been cameras everywhere.'

Although there were still problems with the funding, agreement had at last been reached to start work at L'Amauresque as soon as Wolfgang Ferrari could be released from his current commitments. Joe Spillano, however, was still unhappy with Basin Sorel's script, which was using clips of players who had been dead for more than forty years. But Medusa was happy. Her habañera from *Carmen* (1927), her rhumba with Sorrentino

(1928), were classics that had never been publicly exhibited. Basin Sorel agreed that inserts of such quality could only enhance the film.

'What do we want with banjo picks?' Joe snarled.

Banjo picks, indeed. The film had so stimulated Medusa that she had stitched the mise-en-scène of *Love Is the End* to the shadows of her own life, moving seamlessly between them with an assured facility, neglecting to look out for those occulted lenses in even her most private moments. Joe Spillano, whose celebrity rested on the dewy flap-shot rather than the free-fall vérité in which Shilverman Productions had entangled him, was uneasily aware that he had probably got control problems.

'Just how many cameras are out there, Medusa?' he asked anxiously as Nesta fixed the drinks on Sham's moonlit verandah.

Medusa posed elegantly by the stephanotis, tilting her better side to the light as she squinted across the valley to the blue and yellow fluorescence of Vanity Springs' monster night-signs.

'Only accountants care about numbers, Joe,' she murmured huskily. 'I'm just overwhelmed by the immensity of the truth-rocket we've launched into space.'

'And what the shit does that mean?' he demanded testily.

She looked at his trembling lips and warned that he would have to get more involved in the picture that would carry his name on the credits. It was time he attended to minor details like rushes, cutting, continuity and costs.

'My commitment,' she assured him solemnly, 'is conceptual and, of course, psychic.'

That night, as Medusa and Sham lay in bed together, she disclosed that the film was making a real human being of her at last. She had acquired both humility and tolerance.

'I now believe in a girl called God and, what is more important, I believe in me.'

Sham squeezed his hand between Medusa's thighs. She raised her left leg a smidgen to let him in, tensing at the feel of his cold fingers but reaching down to warm his exploring hand. Sham grumbled that he hadn't seen a plugged nickel from their so-called backers. Sunburn Spillano kept talking about a bigger slice, Yamaha suspected that the First Nagasaki and Waikiki Trust probably needed more collateral, Dunkelbaum thought they ought to have another concept-conference, preferably in St Tropez, and Sheik Yusuf complained that, apart from Spillano Garbage, none of his business associates appeared to care about the way he'd been humiliated by the British art establishment. Apparently Spillano Garbage had distributed a million giveaway shopping-bags throughout Europe, carrying the Wazir reproduction of Yusuf and his charismatic zhivagos on one side and the name, address, telephone and telex numbers of Ethical Friction on the other. Also a line or two from Omar Khayyám.

'Suddenly, not only do the galleries queue up to exhibit the original painting,' snarled Sham, 'but the shopping-bags have become fucking cult objects.'

'Sunburn's a genius,' Medusa laughed. 'Spillano Garbage plan to sell the next million bags at ten bucks apiece.'

'And did I tell you,' brooded Sham, 'that the Arab considers that we should roll the credits over the poxy Wazir picture? I told the guy that *Love Is the End* has nothing to do with an adolescent Bedouin and his dubious companions.'

'What did he say to that?' she asked.

'He thought my conclusion was narrow, covertly racist and probably anti-Islamic.'

'Wow.'

'So what the fuck? I suppose a couple of pepsodented zhivagos are as good as a mangy metrocat.'

Sham snuggled closer to Medusa.

'Do you think I'm too old to put another monster epic together, Medusa?'

'Ninety-two is no age for a superman.'

He lay silent beside her for a while, listening for sounds from the past.

'What are you thinking about now?' she sighed.

'It's Gertrude's birthday next week,' he whispered.

'I know, I know.' She shivered, clinging to his dry body in the dark, willing herself to escape evil memories.

She had never mentioned the other one to anyone – not even her beloved Sham. But was there another one? Was there? She always felt exhausted when she strained her mind to recall those times, and in the end preferred to believe that the shadows were hauntings from half-forgotten dreams. There was the elderly man she knew as Uncle Moose, a thick-set fellow with a walrus moustache, gold spectacles and a white stetson, whom Clay had arranged for her to receive on Sunday mornings. Church-bells time. He was strong cigars, sweet-smelling pomade and creaky leather, heavy and wheezy across her young body in the curtained room. Quick and businesslike was Uncle Moose as he strutted in and out. It was a hot lavender tub, then feathering all around with scented talc after he had cantered away. And presents to enjoy. Peppermint creams, sets of silk lingerie from Paris with lace inserts in the most daring places, and one hundred silver dollars chinking in a canvas bag.

Uncle Moose, Clay had warned her, was a very important hombre. His face could be seen in every newspaper in the world. It would be prudent, she was told, never to disclose to anybody that he was her friend, for Uncle Moose had many foreign enemies who might use even the most innocent information against him. Bearded anarchists, scheming Chinks, mad Mexies and bloody Bolshevists. The kind of scum who would as soon toss a fizzing bomb under the bed on which poor Uncle Moose was humping her than pick their noses or scratch their malodorous arses.

When she fell, everything was arranged. She was sent to a farm in upstate Nabrosky to rid herself of the basketball-sized swelling.

'It's Uncle Moose's brat,' she told Clay as he rocked sleepily on the honeysuckled porch watching yet another sunset, listening to the ululation of timber-wolves.

'How in tarnation's name can you tell that?' he demanded irritably, stopping his half-hearted wood-whittling and giving her a reproving stare.

'Because I'm a very sensitive person,' she explained. 'I knew the exact micro-moment of conception. I felt the throb of Souza music in my tubes and the tingle of new life in my blood. Flags unfurled in my body and I sensed distant puffs of celebratory gunfire from over the horizon of consciousness.'

'Chickenshit,' Clay snarled. 'Hallucinatory chickenshit.'

She was certain that her misguided insistence that Uncle Moose was the daddy decided her infant's fate. She barely managed a tired look at the red, crinkled, black-haired girl that slithered out of her before it was swaddled in warm towels and hurried squawking out of the room. Through the window she watched the green coach and four that had come for her child. Two greys, a roan and a flashy chestnut, lather wet and streaked with ochre dust. She only saw the shadows of the people. Heard voices. Subdued. Foreign. Two men and two women perhaps. But within the hour the carriage had clattered away. Later, she asked Clay about the identities of the callers. The reply caused her first madness.

'They are,' he said, 'the Estrelitas, circus performers from Europe. World-renowned acrobats.'

Acrobats. The thought of acrobats tossing her baby around a circus-ring made her dizzy with horror. A red-raw ball of flesh. She could not stop screaming and had to be sedated before being rattled off in a brougham to the clinic. It was late at night. She was unsure whether it was all a memory, a bad dream or just something else. She must have been ill, dazed from the pills they gave her, sobbing when she got a glimpse of Uncle Moose at the head of an Independence Day parade.

'There's Tusker Ruseveldt,' a woman crazy with excitement yelled. 'There. The fat guy with a walrus moustache, gold spectacles and a white stetson. He's the ex-President of Terrastricken.'

At that point, everything slowed down in her mind. Then stopped. It was an avuncular, silver-haired doctor who appeared to know everything that sorted her out, explaining that it was something she'd seen in one of those new-fangled movies. There were a lot of silly movies in those early days.

'Gertrude would have been forty-nine,' Sham sighed.

'I feel antique,' she murmured. 'Could have been a grandma. Or a great-grandma if she'd fallen young.'

'She'd have been a real beauty. A dancer like you most probably.'

'And you kept her safe all these years. I'll always love you for that, Sham.'

'I bought her a diamond ring,' he murmured.

'Another diamond ring?'

'It's always been diamonds for Gertrude. Forty-nine diamond rings shimmering like stars in her spirit-jar. You ought to see those twinkling rocks, Medusa. Just once.'

'You know I can't. They warned me at the clinic that it would unsettle me to even take a peek.'

'She's a sweet thing. No bigger than a rainbow trout.'

'That's a terrible comparison. A smelly old fish. Poor Gertrude. She was well-developed for her age, wasn't she, Sham?'

'Just one hundred and sixty days, honey. If only she'd waited a mite longer to be born. Impetuous, like her mama.'

'Sham, do you think I killed her? Was it me?'

'Goddam no. It was the fucking lawyers that killed her. Fucking legal men. That fucking contract with those fucking financial clauses about you finishing the movie.'

'It was only money, Sham. I could have given up the picture.'

'Too late now,' he murmured, struggling with his breathing.

'That's the most terrible phrase in the language,' she sighed. 'Too late now.'

Sham dozed off. He surfaced for short snatches, reflecting how many times they'd had similar conversations about Gertrude. Uneasy disquiet as he recalled the many secret enquiries he'd placed with Spermtrek about former seeding arrangements. There had been no positive responses. So he lived in a ferment, anxious about what a positive Spermtrek response might disclose. The nightmare vision of a flabby arse quivering between parted thighs. A tripe-white elver voiding grey spawn into a shrimp-pink cavity. Sonofabitch. But there were happy dreams about murder. He dreamed of killing Joe Spillano many times. Sham smiled grimly to himself when he remembered how he'd once tried to run Joe Spillano down in his silver Cord, aiming for that dangling elver, but had missed, crumpling the car into an arizonica. Nobody ever suspected a thing. Not even Joe, who called in at the hospital the next evening, grinning like a demented beast, bearing nectarines, soft nougat and a fistful of purple petunias. The bastard made solicitous noises about Sham's cracked femur and stitched skull. Sham had regarded him with venom but managed a polite display of teeth.

Now, he pressed against Medusa, licking her eyelids, conscious that he had the makings of a spongy erection.

'Honey?'

Medusa didn't answer. Her profound respiration had evolved into a sibilant snore.

Chapter 21

Laszlo Gabor's relationship with Bevan Chancer had steadily deteriorated. The trouble probably started when Laszlo, indulging a puerile caprice, transposed the last two letters of Chancer's name on a widely circulated memorandum. It was a minor mischief, but Chancer was not a forgiving man. Laszlo, who had been at the bank for about five years, was, at twenty-three, ten years younger than the Welshman. While Chancer unhappily conceded that the arse-licking Gabor's progress had been obscenely impressive, the rumour that the Hungarian was earning four times as much as he was filled him with dismay. And the fact of the apartment in Knightsbridge and the use of an air-conditioned Mazda, benefits usually only accorded to the President and heads of international departments, seemed beyond any rational explanation. Chancer considered that he was far better qualified than Gabor and worked, or so he imagined, just as hard. Yet nothing he did produced the sort of rewards Gabor enjoyed. Nor was Chancer encouraged by hardly credible reports that Gabor was in the business of procuring tiny Caucasian girls with smallish breasts and depilated pubes for Harada's entertainment. The information emanated from Gabor's cleaner, who had since been dismissed. Chancer did try an anonymous letter to the police, but nothing came of it.

Matters came to a head at a party given to mark Froline Nablus's appointment as Vice-President. It started as an acrimonious but complex technical discussion relating to the function of Gabor's (SOBS) department. It regressed to a rhetorical nadir when Chancer, buoyant with drink, playfully implied that young Gabor was a pimp. At which point Laszlo quite distinctly called him a turd. And that before at least a dozen of Chancer's minions. Everybody in the room appeared to have heard Gabor's insult. He had called the Manager of Corporate

Banking a turd. Chancer remembered the several seconds of meditative silence followed by a few evil sniggers and his nauseous feeling as he wondered what people were saying in that polyphonous blur of resumed small-talk.

Apart from the fact that Gabor, despite his title, was hardly much more than a clerk, there remained the deeper question of honour. Chancer was, after all, a Welshman. In Mountain Ash, such a provocation would not have been allowed to pass unpunished. Yet the blow he aimed at Laszlo Gabor was very much an afterthought. He had profoundly regretted since then that it had not been more maliciously delivered. He had employed a not-too-resolutely clenched left fist, the right being occupied in preserving a goblet of Rémy Martin. The grappling was minimal. Chancer had fallen across a dish of quail bouchées and damaged the ramparts of a strawberry mousse. His adversary had stumbled awkwardly into a waitress bearing a tray of glasses charged with Pol Roger. He had tried to detain Gabor, who demonstrated reptilian agility by slithering adroitly out of the embrace, severely damaging Chancer's nose with a brutish forehead. Blood. Somebody screamed. Glasses were shattered. But in the end nobody was much alarmed. And Chancer often reflected that it was his restraint that saved Gabor from significant damage.

At the time, Chancer had not quite abandoned hope that Thelma might be induced to return. They had even managed a trial reunion. He ripped off her silk underwear with rekindled enthusiasm. But it lasted barely six weeks. He then discovered that his wife had not just one but two other lovers. His life went haywire. Despite Thelma's emotional assurance, and that while clutching rosary beads blessed at Lisieux, that he was the only man in her life, he learned that she was still parting her elegant legs for Bricuse the long-distance lorry-driver on Conversational Portuguese nights. That was not all. She was also being humped on Origami evenings by the chinless shit for whom she worked. It was hardly bearable. And when her Liberal Party diary, interleaved with polaroid photo page-marks of hideously inflated penises, with scribbled data on their backs relating to the

frequency and duration of sexual encounters, had been discovered in her lingerie drawer beside a knobbly vibrator, his
world crumbled. He even contemplated writing to David Steel
(Thelma had been a candidate for Balham District Council), but
Froline Nablus persuaded him not to carry bitterness too far. But
the sense of gloom remained.

Despite Laszlo Gabor's remarkable advancement, he too was
beginning to feel disenchanted with the path his life was taking.
Not only was the continuity of his career threatened by the
shadows that seemed to be falling across the First Nag and Waik,
but he had begun to have unhappy reservations about the nature
of the service he was required to provide for Harada. It was, he
reflected, ungentlemanly. He now saw Maya only on Saturdays,
for he spent his working week in Knightsbridge, and she her
Sundays at the Thali of Boundless Light. He could hardly invite
her to the apartment, for which he was little more than a
caretaker. There was scarcely an evening when Harada was not
in the nursery with one of his friends from Brighter Bedrooms.
Laszlo would have liked, given the resources, to have been able
to purchase a house in the country for Maya and himself. But not
only did his duties with the bank involve a constant presence in
town; Maya, he suspected, would probably have been reluctant
to leave Crystal Palace, away from her friend Mr Mudaliar and
the Thali of Boundless Light. He saw no immediate solution. And
he was disquieted by the feeling that Toshiro Harada's power
would soon be eroded now the ownership of the bank had passed
to a person who was controlled by a Financially Sterile Entity.

Passing along the lower floor on his way to Harada's suite,
Laszlo noticed a tall, bearded Arab, splendidly attired in billowing
desert robes, being greeted by Froline Nablus outside her office.
He waited until the unknown Arab and Froline disappeared into
her room before approaching the secretary.

'Who's that?' he murmured to the girl.

'Sheik Yusuf Hamami of Ethical Friction,' she whispered,
bestowing a hungry smile on Laszlo.

160

Laszlo could see through the glass panels that the Arab and Froline had settled themselves, heads lowered over the table. They appeared to be talking quickly and with great intensity. It would not, however, have availed the curious Laszlo much to have overheard the conversation. They were speaking Nabi.

An astonishing transition of the First Nag and Waik's investor base had taken place without any significant publicity. In 1974, the bank had three hundred and fifty thousand shareholders. A year later, the figure was scarcely two hundred thousand. In 1976, they had a shade over a hundred thousand on the register, which by 1977 had declined again by about thirty per cent. The subsequent annual tally was twenty-six thousand, and in the last year was down to two hundred. Laszlo had raised the matter with Harada, who just shrugged his shoulders.

'Do you realise,' observed the European President with a frown, 'that one hundred and ninety-nine of our stockholders are females resident in the Kabikicho district of Tokyo?'

'What does it all mean?' Laszlo asked.

Harada's eyes glittered.

'If I disclosed to you that these females are all gainfully employed prostitutes, what would you say to that, huh?'

Laszlo gave the matter some thought.

'Would these females,' he suggested, 'be the nominees of a more commercially credible group?'

The Japanese nodded. He seemed pleased by Laszlo's perception.

'Correct first time. The ladies are, in fact, employees of the Yoshiwara Little Heartaches Syndicate,who retain their signed share transfer certificates, which the syndicate, as agents, have leased to the Spillano Garbage Corporation for ten-year periods with terminal options for renewals vested in the lessee in perpetuity. Simple, huh?'

'And what is the consideration?' Laszlo enquired with incredulity.

'Sixty million pounds per annum.'

Laszlo made a scratch calculation with a biro on the back of his hand.

'That's about forty per cent of our taxable profits,' he declared.

'I've simplified all the loops,' Harada said, 'and it means that the Spillano Garbage Corporation is the de facto proprietor of the bank. To be specific, control is now exercised by a Miss Natalie Tolstoy.'

'Tolstoy? Tolstoy?'

'She's the secretary who sits in the office adjacent to Sunburn Spillano, who, as you know, is a Financially Sterile Entity.'

'The whole deal appears to be illegal,' Laszlo concluded dismissively.

'Possibly,' Harada conceded, 'and the Yoshiwara Little Heartaches Syndicate will shortly pass into the hands of the Receiver as there have been defaults on every one of the twenty-five separate bond issues, whose proceeds were used to purchase our equity. I suppose the Japanese Central Bank may institute an investigation, but a public scandal could precipitate a run by depositors, which may be politically inexpedient at present and may have wider implications for the credibility of Japanese banking.'

'Who,' Laszlo enquired, 'is the owner of the other share? The two-hundredth?' He was scratching around with what appeared to be an idle question.

'Joseph Spillano, the film director.'

'What,' Laszlo asked, 'does this all mean for us?'

Harada tapped his fingers on the table gloomily and did not venture a reply. He offered Laszlo a Chesterfield, then referred to his desk-diary. Unlocking a drawer, he extracted the 'Mallory Towers' file.

'I'd like Kirsty to have lunch with me tomorrow. At your place, of course. I think she's on page fourteen.'

Laszlo remembered the red-haired Scots girl with a limp.

'If there's any difficulty about travelling in the costume, ask her to bring an overnight bag. She can change in the nursery when she arrives. Drive her yourself if necessary. Door to door. No taxis or company chauffeurs. OK?'

Laszlo nodded uneasily. For the first time in five years, his mind was filled with negative thoughts of resignation. He sensed that Harada was as pessimistic about the future as he was. Perhaps the involvement of Spillano Garbage meant that Yamaha would emerge as the new force at the First Nag and Waik.

'Take care now,' Harada muttered half to himself as Laszlo left.

The European President escaped into a reverie that centred around Kirsty and the prospect of her visit. She always whimpered when set difficult sums. Quadratic equations usually started Kirsty off. Troubled blue eyes filled with apprehension. Tears. Whimpering. 'Don't be afraid, Kirsty,' he murmured, rehearsing the pleasures to come. He sensed a presence. He looked up with a start to see Miss Carvalho before him. A tall, bespectacled woman with bushy black hair. She disguised her solidity in a charcoal costume. Her pale, puffy face seemed remote and unfriendly. A sad illusion due to a defect in the articulation of her lower jaw. There was a canine scepticism in the grey eyes. Harada and Miss Carvalho glared at one another. It would be uncharitable, he knew, to encourage a smile. Smiling betrayed her ugliness. Miss Carvalho was middle-aged, efficient and loyal. She was also almost indispensable.

'I'll take my coffee now, Maxine,' he said, acknowledging her scowl. The scowl was her best face by far.

He ruminated on his latest acquisition, an unusual and erotic Wally Wazir that Froline Nablus had induced Sheik Yusuf to sell to him for a paltry thirty thousand pounds. It now hung above the toy-cupboard in the nursery of the Knightsbridge apartment where he entertained his young companions. The Wazir pastel was a joy. A tender evocation of innocence. It revealed an unclothed Arab girl, lightly fledged, legs casually parted, asleep on a carpet at the entrance of a tent.

'The child looks a little like you,' he told Mrs Nablus.

Harada neglected to mention that it was Gabor who first drew the resemblance to his attention, appropriating the observation as his own. He was pleased to detect that the remark made the usually self-contained Froline blush.

He did not like to think of certain private matters when Miss Maxine Carvalho was present. He feared that she had the power to rummage through the untidy bedrooms of his mind, sniffing around the thin white bodies of his partners like a disapproving mastiff. So he waited until she had left the room before he contemplated private joys like the remembrance of the naughty girls that had played in his playroom. Riding the cock-horse; lying below him in the great cot; the ones that tossed their heads from side to side; those that jumped about a great deal; the tremblers, lip-biters, thumb-suckers, gigglers and whisperers of wicked words. But Kirsty's whimperings gave him an exquisite pain. He dreamed of little Kirstys trapped beneath the rubble of broken buildings. Survivors who needed comforting. Whimpering. Endless whimpering in the night of rushing winds. Those terrible winds in the darkness of a final desolation. Nagasakis upon Nagasakis, and he, Harada, wandering alone in a silent world, listening intently for the last whimper.

Chapter 22

At approximately one o'clock on Sunday afternoon, a small Indian in a crumpled three-piece suit (chalk stripes and blue worsted) and a jaunty fedora that did little to improve his appearance arrived at Maya Gabor's front door. He was carrying a bison-skin executive case and looked ostentatiously unwell. At the point of death even. Bunny Selveratnam had returned. He could not have chosen a less opportune time to surprise his fiancée. Maya's doorbell was depressed intermittently for at least fifteen minutes. There was no reply.

Across the hallway, in the Mulcahy apartment, Ada, her turgent feet propped on a cushion, scanned the *News of the World*. The quack had been niggling her for some time with suggestions that it would be expedient for her to lose a stone, take more exercise and moderate her smoking. Des would have been much amused at the thought of her as a smoker. But the really heavy fagging had started after he'd passed away and Laszlo had packed her in. It used to be one or two a week, special occasions and sometimes a drag at Laszlo's when they'd made love. Now, it was rarely less than forty a day.

Ada Mulcahy loved sitting beside Laszlo in the air-conditioned Mazda on the occasions he drove her to the Sunshine Home to see Aurora, even though he generally didn't have much to say for himself. He was rather secretive with her these days, never giving much away. Several times, unknown to him, she'd cased his place at Knightsbridge from across the square, watching the lights of his apartment go on after dark and, much later, off again. Once she'd sneaked up in the lift and listened outside the oak front door. A white business card with *L. Gabor* in italic script was slotted into a brass holder. She remembered that the carpeted landing smelled of furniture polish, honeysuckle, fresh melons and eucalyptus, and she wondered wistfully about the girls that he must have taken through that door. There had to be girls, of course. Laszlo was not the sort of man to go short.

Sometimes, when they were alone in the car, she longed to ask him to do it with her again. Just once. But the words never came out. It was strange, but she'd never felt like trying it with anybody else. Ridiculous still to hope for that sort of resumption after five years. Well, she didn't really hope. Dreamed, maybe. Her teeth had gone home a bit. They'd have to be fixed. A bridge to replace the awful clicking denture. Then her hair rinsed and fluffed into a more cheerful style. Not to forget the avoirdupois. No potatoes, sugar or sweet sherry for three months at least. An iron resolution was needed. And if he didn't relish doing a straight job with her, perhaps he'd go along with a suck-off. It was a proposition that she'd have to put to him when they were on their own in the car. No equivocation. She rehearsed the request in her mind, again and again, but knew she would probably be incapable of articulating the words.

'All I'm asking for is the opportunity to gobble you off. That's all I want. My mouth. Your pleasure. A simple service. Now, is that too much for a lonely woman to expect from a friend in this stark and godforsaken life?'

The first year Laszlo was in the sixth form, she'd allowed him to do it to her the other way. She remembered that it was a Sunday, like today. They had started by swallowing a dozen oysters, tippled a bottle of Liebfraumilch she'd won in a raffle and then he'd persuaded her to declaim Molly Bloom's soliloquy, calling her his Flower of the mountain. She managed it in a passable stage-Irish, Ada being a Purefoy by birth (a pretty resonance from the great book), though she herself was Forest Hill born and accented. The Purefoys, Patrick and Clare, were authentic Dublin stock, taking the boat across to Holyhead a year or so before Ada was conceived. Laszlo, who was a little lyrical and dream-headed at that age, boasted that he, by three glorious acts of serendipity, had discovered oysters, the music of Joyce's voice and buggery on the same afternoon. He was fond of shocking her like that in his new high-falutin voice, fancying himself as a sort of South London Dedalus, without of course the lost faith or cancerous mother driven to the grave, settling, or he declared to her, for the less exotic sins of deception, pride and excessive fornication.

'But of course, Dedalus never did it with Molly,' he pointed out to Ada.

'I don't believe a word of that,' she'd sniff.

'It's not in the book,' he'd protest.

'It was in her mind, which comes to the same thing, if the observations of the holy saints are anything to go by.'

'But not in his,' Laszlo observed.

'What do you know of the poor boy's unrecorded longings?' she'd say. 'If your Mr Joyce had any sense, he'd have let the lad get across her before he put his pen down.'

'I fear,' Laszlo used to sigh, 'that we have departed from the text.'

It was never an observation that disturbed her. She secretly imagined the author to be an enemy of poor Molly and cared little for the way he didn't give the woman what she needed.

'Not the kind of johnny I'd have gone dancing with,' was her final judgement.

What more was there to be said about the great Irish scribbler? They had his magical soliloquy, a celebration that encompassed all their needs, ringing bells where they should be rung. She was not above throwing a few crumbs the Dubliner's way.

'I suppose I prefer it to the other one,' she conceded.

'Which other one?'

'Hamlet's. Molly's is so much brighter. More life-enhancing, if you know what I mean.'

'A little higher,' he commanded her.

And in response to the urgency in his voice, she raised her pink rump to allow Ulysses to nose his vessel into uncharted parts.

Ada was seated on the pot, thinking about the alternatives of a quick shower or a more protracted bubble-bath, before getting dressed and catching a bus to Bromley to see the Brazilian clairvoyant at the Spiritualist Church, when she heard the front-door bell ring. She wondered whether it was Laszlo looking in on his way back from the Sunshine Home with a message about Aurora.

Outside, Selveratnam, detecting movements and noises in the Mulcahy flat, waited patiently. A cistern flushed. There were sounds of footsteps and a husky cough. Music filtered under the door. Inside, Ada slipped on her pink dragon dressing-gown and scuttled into the hall. She lit another cigarette and turned down the radio on her way to the door. It was opened cautiously. She was disappointed when she saw that it wasn't who she'd expected. Selveratnam noted that she was naked under her kimono, parted down to the swell of pale, freckled breasts.

'I was going to have a bath,' she murmured in a thick voice, staring hard at the little man.

'Hello, Mrs Mulcahy,' he whispered, scraping a step towards her.

She took a closer look. Had he been horizontal with his eyes closed, he might have passed for a corpse.

'Jesus Christ, it's Mr Selveratnam,' she breathed. 'Whatever have you been doing to yourself?'

'I've been extremely ill,' he whispered.

Ada was mesmerised by Selveratnam. He no longer looked like a lovable rabbit. He was toothless and his lips seemed strangely inflated. To think that Maya was once attracted to this squashed tomato of a man.

'I've lost my teeth,' he said, 'and some gum tissue as well.'

She emitted an involuntary squeak of distress, unprepared for horror of this magnitude. Life was tacky enough without having to contemplate such beastliness on a Sunday afternoon. She made an effort to escape from the unpleasant situation, pressing into service her remote and not unconvincing middle-class voice. The one she used for Jehovah's Witnesses and insurance salesmen. The go-away-quickly voice. Selveratnam eyed her with dull hopelessness as she tried to adjust to the revised geometry of his face. But it was the despair in his eyes that reflected the real damage.

'Mrs Gabor won't be back until fairly late tonight,' she declared. 'It's her day for a Tamil lesson.'

'It's Mudaliar, isn't it?' he mumbled, tears trickling down his cheeks.

'You're quite correct,' she said. 'I believe it is a Mr Mudaliar. The gentleman who owns the Thali of Boundless Light.'

She fiddled self-consciously with her kimono, drawing it across the cleavage that had been imprudently revealed, but noticing with sudden dismay a tear at thigh height, exposing a section of mottled haunch. Selveratnam, however, was beyond such matters. She looked down at him with genteel benevolence. The Tamilian swayed and held onto the wall.

'I'm about to die, Mrs Mulcahy,' he sighed; then lisped a valedictory few lines of devotional verse:

> 'When the dweller in the body,
> Has overcome the gunas
> That cause this body,
> Then he is made free
> From birth and death,
> From pain and decay;
> He becomes immortal.'

Ada Mulcahy eyed him with polite concern.

'Don't be so glum,' she advised cheerfully. 'There's time enough to think about dreary things like immortality. I expect you've picked up some foreign bug. The National Health Service will see that you don't come to grief. You mark my words, you'll be right as rain in a week or two.'

'I'm finished,' he said fatalistically.

My God, what an inconvenience, she thought, trying to exorcise him with a disinterested look. She was not in the mood to chew the fat over Hindu metaphysics, sensing that he was at the point of more tediously devout mumbles. She did not want to be diverted from her private concerns. And anyway, mantras and incantations made her want to yawn. Oh, what a bore the poor little bugger was.

'I'd ask you to come in,' she said, 'but I'm rushing to get out.'

Selveratnam appeared unconcerned.

'Don't worry. I'll sleep out here until Maya returns,' he said, promptly settling himself on the floor.

'I think it's against council regulations to sprawl around in public walkways,' she observed doubtfully. 'I've got Maya's key,' she said. 'Would you care to wait in her flat?'

He nodded gratefully, shivering slightly.

'That's very kind of you,' he whispered.

Ada returned inside. She came back with a key which she handed to Selveratnam.

He let himself into Maya's flat, dragging his bison-skin case across the threshold. Selveratnam was on the point of closing the door when Ada stopped him.

'Why don't you ring her at the restaurant? Give her a nice surprise, eh?'

He nodded blankly.

'I'll do that,' he promised.

Chapter 23

Subramanian Mudaliar, Mani for short, spoiled Maya. Not only did she eat most of her meals at the Thali of Boundless Light, but what meals she didn't consume on the premises she had delivered to her flat by Mani himself in his nearly new BMW. Although the Tamil lessons had not been as meaningful as either of them had hoped, their friendship had prospered. Mani was a paunchy forty-year-old with a kind of arboreal blackness that fascinated Maya. She had once imagined that he came from the heart of some remote Rousseauan jungle, camouflaged as he was for stealthy nocturnal activities. She was astonished to discover that he was an urban animal, raised beside the twinkling electric lights of Krishnaraja Sagara. Mani's blackness intoxicated her. 'It's velvet black,' she whispered to herself in wonder as she dreamed of stroking the satin smoothness. Mani was almost edible. He had introduced her to a South Indian halva made with puttoo rice. It was sweet and black. Whenever Maya put a piece in her mouth, she thought of Mani – sweet and black like the halva. Maya had known black men before. There was Earl, a rich walnut, and Bunny, who was a dark mahogany. But Mani was black. Like boot polish, or so she imagined. He was quite wonderful. And throughout those early lessons on Tamil verbs, she found it difficult to resist touching his skin from time to time, just to reassure herself of the miracle. One day she mustered enough resolution to ask him the impertinent question she hoped would lead in the direction she wanted. It was a contrived naïveté and he responded as playfully as she could have wished.

'Are you black all over?' she enquired with a shy smile.

'Well,' Mani grinned, 'as you can see, my palms are light teak and the inside of my mouth is pink. Now apart from another part of me that is deep purple, all the rest is what you call black. I am, in fact, a very dark brown.'

Maya's eyes sparkled.

'Do you want to see for yourself?' Mani asked cheerfully, for he considered that the exposure of his body to Maya was a normal courtesy which he as her host should not evade. But he solemnly pointed out that even-handedness was called for. And so that Maya should not feel unduly disadvantaged, he suggested that they both disrobe, for he was as much taken with her pinkness as she appeared to be with his near-blackness. And that is how they both came to be naked in Mani's study, halfway through the ninth Tamil lesson. She was experienced enough to perceive that Mani was aroused as she had seen few men aroused before. His purple-capped cudgel was one of the most beautiful objects she had ever examined. Being a generous man, he allowed her to play with it. That ludic act brought them closer together. Mani, on the other hand, was captivated by her butterflies and insisted on placing his appreciative lips on the Red Admiral and slowly kissing his way across her divide to the Purple Emperor. There was as much of the spirit of enquiry in his zetetic mouth and her exploring fingers as the agreeable sensuality of a primal encounter. And they both delighted in the simple rubbing together of their bodies, lost in the revelation of new tactile fantasies before their excitements could not be contained and regressed into a repertory of more brutish exercises.

'I'm sorry things have come to this,' reflected Maya, settling herself on his near-black shoulder and nibbling at his near-black ear.

'Don't worry, my dear,' he soothed. 'It should be just as difficult for you to learn Tamil under this sheet as it is sitting at that rather uncomfortable desk.'

'Will I never acquire the language?' she sighed in despair.

'Perhaps I may be able to inject it into you,' he mused mischievously.

'Oh, Mani,' she murmured, giving a shiver of nervous anticipation.

But although Maya persevered, it would not be extravagantly cynical to observe that during the ensuing years Tamil hardly occupied more than twenty minutes of the eight hours they spent each Sunday lolling about on Mr Mudaliar's bed. It was not that they were at it the moment Mani bolted the door. Far from it. First, the hand-spun coverlet (turmeric-coloured jigging cockerels on an ochre ground) had to be folded and placed in an armchair. And it was not unusual for half an hour to elapse before they yielded to their amatory inclinations. Maya liked to start the morning flicking through the Sunday papers as she sipped the sweet coffee he prepared for her in the silver samovar that rested on a gas-ring in a corner of the room. He never failed to be amused how easily the black ink of *The People* and *News of the World* transferred to her back and bottom, boasting how he was immune from such discolouration.

'I'm going to take a shower,' she'd exclaim, regarding her smeared body with disgust in the mirror.

'Not yet,' he'd protest, initiating another romp.

There were squeals, some dodging around the bed, token resistance and then submission. At eleven, they had a glass of iced buttermilk and an orpah, while Mani rehearsed the simple sentences he had taught her the previous Sunday. She frowned as she spoke the words.

'Nali ki var ar sare pal kundwa,' she'd say, adding, 'Remind me what that means.'

'Come tomorrow and bring half a seer of milk,' he explained with a smile. 'It's what you should tell the milk-girl when she calls with her buffalo.'

'At Crystal Palace?' she'd asked doubtfully.

'It would be more useful in Seringapatam, I suppose,' he agreed.

It was just four o'clock in the afternoon when they were disturbed. Mani picked up the phone.

'Yes,' he growled, 'yes. Just a minute.'

He placed his hand over the mouthpiece and looked at Maya wearily.

'It's Selveratnam. Our crazy waiter friend.'

'Where is he?' she asked anxiously.

'At your flat,' Mani explained. 'Ada let him in.'

'Bunny?'

'Maya my darling, my only love,' the mystic croaked.

'It's been a long time,' she complained a little irritably.

'I'm dying,' he whispered hoarsely.

For some inexplicable reason, he sounded funny. She turned a brief desire to giggle into a jokey warning.

'I hope you don't intend to snuff it in my flat.'

Although she did not seriously expect him to die, the thought of finding Bunny Selveratnam stiff on her new Astrakhan rug depressed her. She remembered a woman at work talking about the difficulty of cleaning the terminal fluids corpses expelled. Besides, she was expecting Laszlo that evening. He'd taken a fortnight's leave and they were setting off mid-week for a few days in Devon. She could do without a dying Selveratnam.

'I must see you at once,' he crackled.

'I haven't quite finished my Tamil lesson,' she snapped. She was certain now that the little man was sobbing. The sod was being tiresome.

'Let me speak to Mudaliar,' he whispered.

Maya handed Mani the receiver.

'Well?' demanded Mani. He had little use for the ex-waiter's snivelling.

'What are you doing with my fiancée?' Selveratnam demanded.

Mani laughed coarsely.

'What do you think I'm doing?'

He slid his hand between Maya's thighs and kissed her tenderly before he continued.

'Anyway, what are you concerned about? I haven't worn her away. She's about the same as she was when you buggered off on your mission to save the world. Twenty pounds heavier perhaps, otherwise almost the same woman.'

He handed the phone back to Maya.

'I'm sorry, Bunny,' she sighed, 'but things just happened. We didn't become lovers until after the ninth lesson, which I hope you'll agree shows a fair degree of restraint.'

'I forgive you,' he said, 'but hurry back here before I join the Universal Mind.'

Chapter 24

Maya was stunned at the sight of Selveratnam. The tiny man had shrunk. His eyes were red with weeping, his toothless mouth swollen and ulcerated. He appeared to be in considerable discomfort whenever he spoke and he could hardly walk ten paces unaided.

'You look dreadful,' she declared, hating him instantly.

She couldn't abide serious illness of any sort and wished he'd snuffed it before managing to crawl back to her flat. The cold and trembling hand he proffered was reluctantly accepted. It was damp with perspiration.

'Are you in pain?'

He shook his head and fished about in his waistcoat for a bottle of pills, rattling them at her with a weak smile.

'Pain-killers?' she asked.

He nodded and made a gesture indicating that he'd like a drink. Maya went out to the kitchen and returned with a tumbler of water. Selveratnam shook out a yellow pill and, placing it in his mouth, sipped cautiously.

'You're going to have to leave here. Crystal Palace, I mean,' he warned.

'Why?'

'Because when I fail to perform certain tasks, they'll be looking for me and, more than likely, you.'

'Your problems are none of my business, Bunny,' she said.

'Ah, but they will be. These bastards will make it their business. However, I can make it possible for you to build a wonderful new life for yourself.'

He tapped his bison-skin case. She frowned at him.

'I want nothing to do with your funny schemes, chum,' she snapped. 'All I want you to do is to vanish from my life forever.'

He lay back in the chair, watching her through defeated eyes.

Maya walked to the window to look out for Laszlo's car. She had been quite excited at the prospect of having Laszlo all to herself for a few days and now the arrival of bloody Selveratnam had complicated matters. She turned from the window and watched the Tamilian extract a manila envelope from his bison-skin case.

'Here,' he said, flapping the envelope at her. 'Hide this somewhere safe.'

'I want nothing to do with that,' Maya declared scornfully. 'Whatever is in there obviously doesn't belong to you.'

'Please take care of it. If only for tonight.'

She told him that Laszlo would have to be consulted first, he being the one who would understand what her legal position was. Selveratnam drew the envelope back. He looked frightened: she should speak to nobody about the envelope. Not even Laszlo. Maya frowned. She had no desire to be the repository of criminal secrets and insisted on knowing what the envelope contained.

'Bonds. They're to be delivered to a man at the First Nagasaki and Waikiki Trust.'

'That's where my Laszlo works.'

'My God.'

'You've stolen them,' she accused, her blue eyes filled with concern.

'I'm not due to deliver them for a few days. All I've stolen is time. Time to be with you.'

He offered her the package once again.

'Look after it until I leave here,' he pleaded.

Reluctantly, she took the envelope from his trembling hand and laid it on the table.

'Just for tonight. Understand?' she said and went into the kitchen.

'Where has our great love gone?' whispered Selveratnam from the doorway.

'A small part of it hung around like stale perfume for maybe a year or so. But five years is a very long time. When I heard your voice this afternoon, I knew there was nothing left. Everything I once felt for you had gone – poof.'

'Women are perfidious,' he lamented.

'Don't be pompous,' she reproved, adding, 'I'll tuck this envelope away beside my beluga. Not even Laszlo knows where I hide that.'

Maya opened a drawer and took out a small star screwdriver. Opening the refrigerator, she unscrewed a section of the door-panel. Behind the enamel baffle-plate was a shelf on which rested a jar of beluga. Selveratnam was curious about the contents of the jar. Maya unscrewed the top and allowed him a sniff. He made a face.

'It's dreadful,' he shuddered, 'like fish. I thought you were a vegetarian.'

'One of two weaknesses,' she confessed bleakly. 'Mani buys it for me.'

When they were back in the living-room, he fished about in his case until he found a dog-eared folder. He laid it on a chair before settling himself full-length on the sofa.

'I should have remembered what sort of woman you are,' he lamented.

Maya picked up the manuscript of her memoirs with a wry smile.

'But I never really suspected that you would betray my trust,' he cursed. 'You're just an "easy-meat" type of woman.'

It was intended as a barb but Maya was amused.

'You have an extremely poor memory,' she laughed. 'According to you, I was no better than a ring-tailed pariah bitch in my last incarnation. And as you know, I've been fairly easy in this one. I've been an "easy-meat" type of woman all my life. And if I fancy a guy, he'll find me easy. That's the way I expect to be until the end.'

'But not for me?' he whispered brokenly.

'Not for you. There's an old Hungarian saying: a vixen never returns to her vomit.'

She outstared him with proud defiance. She was still staring when the door opened and Laszlo ambled in. The sight of Selveratnam curled up on the couch cast a shadow on his holiday spirits. He darted a distasteful glance at the Indian, who had closed his eyes and was making a whistling noise.

'It's a snore,' Maya explained.

She informed Laszlo that Bunny was staying the night.

'I'll fix him up with a duvet. He shouldn't be any trouble where he is.'

She went into the bedroom, returning with a yellow duvet with blue florets which she threw over the tiny Hindu.

'Do you think we should take his boots off?' she suggested.

Laszlo pulled a face and grunted. Selveratnam was the last creature he wanted to see again. When he had first flown westward, Maya had never tired of boasting about the little mystic. His mission, she kept telling Laszlo, was messianic. She really believed in the charlatan's mumbo-jumbo. It really was quite ridiculous. And then there were the almost equally bizarre yarns about Selveratnam being an executive with a large multi-national. Who, Laszlo scoffed, would employ an ex-waiter from a curry restaurant as an executive?

Fortunately, Maya appeared gradually to have lost interest in the Hindu. She had scarcely mentioned him of late, and the Tamil postcards that dropped on the mat every week or so began to be slotted behind the mantelpiece clock with scarcely a glance. But here he was again, muddying the waters.

Laszlo switched on the television. Selveratnam did not stir. He lay still, breathing shallowly. The whistle was hardly audible now. There was a dull, greenish-grey hue to his damp skin. It seemed to Laszlo unlikely that he would survive the night.

'He's dying,' Laszlo declared coldly.

Maya frowned and motioned him to be quiet.

'He should be in the morgue.'

She shrugged, picking at the last of the grapes from a scalloped multi-coloured dish that had been a present from a former man-friend. Its red, yellow and grey Provençal twirls disgusted Laszlo, but he had never quite got around to breaking it.

'I've got the feeling that he's on the run from somebody rather ominous,' she said.

They sat for some time in uneasy silence, subdued by the Hindu's presence. It was an unpleasant situation. Maya refrained from disclosing the presence of the bonds. Perhaps tomorrow, she thought. And, having hidden the memoirs in her bedroom, she now wondered about the photographs, making a mental note to ask Bunny whether he still had them in his possession.

At eleven, Maya kissed Laszlo goodnight. He walked over to the sofa and had another look at the inert Selveratnam. Maya's light went out. He inspected the Tamilian again. There was no change. Hardly a flicker of life. He made his way to the kitchen. Slotting a couple of slices of bread in the toaster, he opened the refrigerator. Taking the star screwdriver from the drawer, he swiftly undid the panel in the door and reached for the jar of Maya's beluga. His secret raids on whatever Maya stored behind the panel had been taking place ever since he was a little boy, after he spied his mother tucking into a hitherto unrevealed pot of confit d'oie and discovered her practice of covertly indulging in delicacies which she concealed behind the panel. In time, Laszlo learned to unscrew the panel to ascertain what mouth-watering bonnes bouches Maya had hidden away for herself. It was a furtive but exciting game in which Maya had never caught or even suspected him. Over the years, he'd illicitly sampled her private caches of boutargue, foie gras, schwarzwurst, smoked salmon and, in the period when she was devoutly vegan, humble candied cherries and marrons glacés. Since her friendship with Mudaliar, however, she had regressed to caviar pressé, sevruga and beluga. And such an abundance of the fishy stuff did he provide for her that only the most immoderate of depredations would have been detected.

Laszlo noticed an envelope and picked it up. Undecided for a few moments whether to open and examine it before he replaced the panel, or to replace the panel and take the envelope to his bedroom for a protracted examination, he decided on the latter course. In his room, he munched at a square of caviar on toast as he undid the seal. He slid the contents onto his bed and carefully unfolded the rectangles of paper. There were twenty in number, each with a face value of three million Swiss francs. Sixty million Swiss francs. He stared at them, numbed, scarcely daring to draw breath. He examined them closely, smelled them and fanned his face with them. Sixty million Swiss francs in bearer bonds drawn on the First Nagasaki and Waikiki Trust at Geneva. His mind was exploding with excitement. How had Maya come by them? The answer followed instantly. Selveratnam. It proved the little bastard was on the run. He endeavoured to think clearly but was trembling at the magnitude of the possibilities that suddenly were available to him. On one point alone he reached ferocious certainty. These bonds were now his property.

Laszlo awoke with a light shining in his face. He opened his eyes and was surprised to discover the recently dying Selveratnam kneeling over him. A kitchen knife was pressed against his throat.

'You thieving devil,' the little man wheezed, 'give me back my property.'

Laszlo was unafraid. If anything, he was slightly amused. Even with a knife, Selveratnam did not alarm him. His response was expeditious and energetic. Jerking sideways away from the knife, he tossed the 'almost messiah' into the wall. Selveratam's skull struck the brickwork with a fearful crack. The knife disappeared in the bedclothes and whatever danger the Hindu's intrusion had posed was over in less than ten seconds. Laszlo retrieved the knife and laid it on his bedside table. Selveratnam did not move. He was dangling over the side of the bed, his neck wedged awkwardly against the wall. As Laszlo lifted him back onto the mattress, the head fell back slackly. There was no doubt. The little man's neck was broken. Laszlo searched for a heartbeat. He placed his face against Selveratnam's, trying to detect signs of breathing. There were none. Selveratnam had joined the Universal Mind.

It was three o'clock. Laszlo slipped on a pair of jeans, a pullover and trainers. Then he frisked the dead man, unbuckling a money-corset that encircled Bunny's torso and fitted around his thighs. He fished loose change and a cluster of credit cards from an inner pocket. In his wardrobe he found a large carpet-bag Maya had brought at a jumble sale some years ago, intending to use it on a summer holiday at a Rhyl holiday camp. Arrangements had been made to take Des, Ada and Aurora as well. In a Dormobile. And then Des had snuffed it.

Laszlo fitted Bunny Selveratnam into the carpet-bag. He heaved the bag into the living-room, where he picked up Selveratnam's bison-skin case from behind the sofa before letting himself out of the front door. He went down in the lift with his luggage and struggled to the blue Mazda parked in front of the entrance. There was nobody about. It was a cold, cloudless morning.

He felt a sense of mad exhilaration in the crisp matutinal silence as he returned to the flat. There was, however, something strange going on inside his head. He was aware at first of what sounded like a murmur just below the threshold of hearing. He listened. There was no doubt about it. It was the sing-song voice of Selveratnam. The noise annoyed more than alarmed him. It was irritating but could be drowned by a tuneless whistle or the humming of a song. And if he didn't take the trouble to listen carefully, it was no more troublesome than the buzz of a distant wasp.

Chapter 25

Laszlo felt that Selveratnam's body would be safe enough in the boot of the Mazda for the time being. It was the eventual disposal that would need careful thought. He let himself into the flat and moved silently to his room. Undressing, he climbed into bed. But he could not sleep and, sitting up with a start, fumbled for Selveratnam's elaborate money-corset. The buzzing in his head grew louder. Laszlo unzipped the six capacious pockets of the corset. In the first five, he found ten clips of one hundred fifty-pound notes. In the sixth, there were just six clips and a packet of photographs. They were of Maya, taken by Gaspar twenty years previously. Laszlo recalled Gaspar's tripods, time-exposure meters, assorted lenses, filters, studio-lights and wires that trailed through the rooms. Gaspar was the great photographer in their lives. Maya was naked in all the photographs. And although the style of the pictures had a kind of archaic cuteness, Laszlo found the images of Maya disturbing in their power. Maya with a bar of soap; Maya with a bicycle-pump; Maya with a black pudding; Maya with a vacuum-cleaner nozzle, and Maya under Gaspar, the last an arty celebration of two gleaming young bodies coupled in the act of love. Laszlo was so animated by these ikons of his mother that it was some time before he could return to the money. He counted the notes a second, third and fourth time, flicking through paper like an automaton as his eyes burned through the photograph of Maya below Gaspar, her fair hair fluffier and shorter and her thighs leaner than he could ever remember. But it was the optimism of a face, luminous with child-like rapture, fingers on the right hand tensed against a muscled buttock, that he could never erase from his mind. He imagined he heard Selveratnam chuckling demonically at this psychic branding. He was suddenly a prisoner of a moment twenty years distant, caught like a fly in amber.

Leaving aside the Swiss bearer bonds, Laszlo was now two hundred and eighty thousand pounds richer. Every time he trawled the figure through his consciousness, he hugged himself. His life was swerving away like a rogue missile into the darkness of an uncharted orbit. The tacky possibility that Selveratnam might still be alive crossed his mind several times. He visualised him tossing about in the carpet-bag, waiting to spring out like a genie.

Laszlo dozed for a while into a floating reverie that encompassed a pliant Maya lying against him in the dark, but opened his eyes to find himself alone. Dreams about the night's transactions now possessed him until he imagined that every nerve in his body was vibrating. He tingled, remembering that Selveratnam had been killed by him and as a consequence of that act he was rich. Buzzing. He listened intently as it shaped itself into the sing-song music of Selveratnam's voice. He imagined that he detected the word 'Escape'. He held his breath. Yes, there it was again. 'Escape.' And with an unmistakable South Indian emphasis on the first syllable.

In the morning light he pored over the photographs once again. He was elated when he identified the striped pantaloons of Gus his gollywog under the bed on which Gaspar and Maya were humping. The camera must have been propped against the window-sill. He thought of Gaspar setting it up, and the supine Maya watching him through half-closed eyes. Waiting for him on the bed. Had he snapped her before the act? A naked maja. And where was little Laszlo at the time? Probably across the hall with Aunty Ada, where he generally was. No more than thirty feet from the conjunction. Beyond the eglantine and vernal quatrefoils of the bedroom wall, a little blurred in the picture, but remembered with glossy clarity. He estimated that he must have been nearly three, and turned the picture to the window once more, enchanted by the projection of those naughty fingers drawing Gaspar towards her. The short, thin fingers of a young girl. Nail-bitten fingers that still vibrated with fervour. He listened for the creaking bed from across the arc of time, but there was nothing but velvet silence. Even the buzz in his head was lurking somewhere below the threshold of awareness.

He rose to make coffee and took a mug to Maya, sitting on the edge of her bed.

'Our little bird has flown,' he announced.

'Bunny?' she asked, her voice thick with sleep.

'He must have shot off before I got up. I didn't hear a thing.'

Maya was having difficulty trying to drink her coffee and occult her breasts at the same time. She put the mug down and climbed out of bed. She was naked and turned her back to Laszlo while she slipped on her dressing-gown. She went into the kitchen, holding the mug between her hands.

'Why don't you shower first?' she suggested, glancing at the refrigerator covertly.

He agreed, going off to the bathroom to provide her with an opportunity to check whether the envelope was still there. He ran the shower but listened by the door. He could hear her working on the panel and smiled when it fell with a clatter. After his shower, Laszlo found her sitting in the kitchen, her face clouded.

'Are you feeling all right?' he enquired.

She gave him a quick, troubled look, nodding her reassurance.

'I'm fine.'

But her voice lacked conviction, and Laszlo deduced that she was considering whether it would be an appropriate moment to confide in him. He was impressed when she chose to remain silent. Maya was a game-player as well and he loved her dearly for it.

It was a little after seven o'clock on that Monday evening. The 24th of March had been a cold but sunny day. Maya, a navy knitwear belted coat over her new blue and white striped dress, waited for a bus. A black patent-leather handbag was tucked under her left arm with an unread copy of the *Evening Standard* folded and slotted through the handbag's strap. Looped to her right wrist was an unfurled transparent umbrella. She was on her way to see Jenny Mikoajczyk. Jenny was the sort of friend she enjoyed visiting once every two years or so, this being the usual interval between Jenny's change of live-in boy-friends. Carl, the macho security guard, had departed and Paul, the sensitive timpanist, was in. Maya had spoken to her on the telephone earlier that day. Jenny liked to prepare Maya for any possibly unpleasant surprises. She had already confessed that Paul was a little shorter than she was and rather thin on top.

'But very droll, darling.'

'I love men with a sense of humour,' Maya declared.

'I'm so depressed about everything,' Jenny sighed.

'You suspect you've made a mistake,' Maya suggested.

'Not really. Paul is incredibly sweet. And, unlike that swine Carl, really thoughtful.'

Then there was a pause. Maya was patient, familiar with Jenny's brooding caesuras.

'Maya, have you ever had a shrimpy guy?'

Maya did not reply at once.

'Do you mean what I think you mean?' she enquired finally.

'Oh God, my life is so utterly stupid,' Jenny cursed. 'You see, the poor guy thinks he's OK in that department.'

Maya allowed herself a supportive murmur.

'You remember I told you that Carl was rather celebrated down there? Listen. I can't even feel Paul.'

Maya opened her mouth to comment but didn't. It was Jenny who closed the conversation abruptly.

'I can't speak now. He's at the front door with the shopping. See you at seven-thirty. We'll be on our own.'

Then she was gone.

Jenny, Maya reflected, invariably had crazy problems with her live-ins. Maya was pleased that she'd never succumbed to the temptation of living with a man. It was safer, she concluded, to keep the bastards outside the front door. The present arrangement she had with Mani was just about right. Sex on Sundays. And plenty of it. It gave her something to anticipate during the week. She realised that she was fortunate in having a man like Mani who appreciated her need for independence. True, she had once nearly got hitched to Bunny. That would have been a terrible mistake.

185

Poor Jenny. What on earth had induced her to allow this guy with a microscopic dick to move into her flat? Droll and sweet he might be, but a woman like Jenny obviously needed more. It must have been a mind-bending transition from a stud who allegedly humped her to orgasm with monotonous regularity to a partner who was hardly more functional than an overweight duvet. OK, so Carl was a womaniser. But he had his uses. She examined her watch, frowning irritably. She was going to be late.

A little Indian crossed the road by the corner. He stopped to light a cigarette near the news-stand. She imagined for a moment or two that he was Bunny, but the man was altogether more sprightly than the clairvoyant. Where on earth had Bunny gone? For a man who obviously wasn't much longer for this world, he'd slid away with astonishing stealth. However had he managed to unscrew and replace the refrigerator panel without either Laszlo or her hearing him? They had had some nice times together. And Bunny, despite his stature, was surprisingly well-endowed. She tried to remember Toulouse-Lautrec's assessment of himself. Was it, she wondered, 'a small coffee-pot with a large spout', or 'a little jug with a big handle'? Anyway, it was something like that. She had quoted it to Bunny after they'd made love for the first time. It made him laugh and pleased him no end. The 'nearly messiah' was not without a touch of vanity.

How she was looking forward to her holiday with Laszlo. He was growing more like Wolfgang every time she saw him, despite their colouring being so different. And despite herself, she thought wistfully about the sort of lives the legendary Ferraris were leading. She wondered what Polly would think about her handsome son. It would be pleasant, she supposed, to see her sister again. She half resolved to feel the way with a letter. And maybe it was time to tell Laszlo the truth. It was something that had to be done in the near future. Perhaps when they were on holiday together. Over a drink. She smiled to herself. The time, she decided, was ripe for revelations.

It was now dusk. A quick, fresh breeze had brought a patter of rain, scarcely sustained enough to put a sheen on the roads and pavements. Maya put up her umbrella. A young driver was suddenly aware of a wheel rolling slightly ahead of his vehicle towards a queue of people at the bus-stop. He realised with horror that the wheel belonged to his front near-side axle as the bread-van swerved, tilted, and hit the road, scraping to a halt in a tearing of metal and a shower of sparks. When he climbed out of the van he saw people gathered around a woman lying on the pavement. He ran towards the group, despair in his heart. There was a blue patent-leather shoe in the gutter. It was then that the young van-driver, numb with remorse, prayed silently for her recovery as they waited for the ambulance to arrive. And when they lifted her carefully onto the stretcher, he noticed that she had the most elegant and well-proportioned legs he'd ever seen.

Maya died shortly after Laszlo and Ada reached her bedside. She had never recovered consciousness. Laszlo left Ada at the hospital and walked quickly through the echoing corridors into the fine spring night. He walked around the streets of South London in the darkness, arriving back at Crystal Palace at first light. When he let himself into the flat, Ada was waiting for him. She told him that she had spent most of the night getting things straight.

'Straight?'

'I've done a week's wash and a spin-dry,' she said brightly.

She didn't tell him that she'd found Maya's memoirs under the bed when she was hoovering the place, spending some time tearing the offensive material into small pieces and flushing it down the john. Twenty flushes or more before the bits of paper were finally swirled into the metropolitan sewage system. All that dirty stuff about Maya fucking and sucking with so many guys would have hurt poor Laszlo. There was no need for dreadful memories of that sort about one's dearly beloved mother.

'She was on her way to see her friend Jenny Mikoajczyk,' Ada chattered. 'Jenny rang me just as I got back here.'

Laszlo stared at her dully. Although she did not apprehend it at the time, Laszlo now saw her as a stranger who had no part in his life.

'I was concerned about you,' she whispered, taking a step in his direction.

He suspected that she was trying to usurp Maya's place, and went into the next room without speaking.

'She dreamed of Saladin the Saracen on three consecutive nights,' brooded Ada, following him.

He stood with his back to the window, hands deep in his pockets, looking glumly at his hand-tooled boots.

'I'll make the necessary arrangements,' promised Ada, coming towards him. 'The Co-op did a first-class job for Des.'

She reached out to embrace him in consoling arms, but he evaded her with a deft sideways step.

After she had gone, Laszlo took a taxi to the hospital, where he'd left the Mazda. He drove back to the flat at Crystal Palace. As he switched the engine off, he heard the buzzing once more. He did not have to make an effort now to recognise the scarcely audible voice in his skull. It was like the whisper from a conch.

He opened the boot and lifted out the carpet-bag, detecting a sweet and not unpleasant odour that he recognised as Selveratnam's aftershave. Upstairs, he emptied the deep-freeze cabinet and stuffed the carpet-bag in, unzipping it to wedge a few frozen packages around the little Hindu. Laszlo thought that the tiny mystic looked better, more at peace, since their last meeting. He covered the corpse with cartons of peach melba (Maya's favourite ice-cream), peas, carrots, nutburgers, sweetcorn and green peppers. After he had jammed down the lid and locked the cabinet, he found he was sweating. The buzzing blurred into a hiss and then to a swishing of distant waves, sibilations that muffled a plaintive call that could have passed for the sound of a lost seagull. But he suspected it was not really that. 'Escape,' the bird seemed to cry.

Laszlo went to Maya's room and opened the deed-box she kept in her wardrobe. He tipped the contents of the box onto Maya's bed, slowly sorting the papers into two piles. The smaller pile included a number of official documents. There were three items to which he gave his particular attention. Two of them were contracts of insurance, and the third was Maya's last will and testament, in which he was named as the sole beneficiary of the estate. It bore the address of a local solicitor. He read the insurance contracts several times. It appeared that he would soon be five thousand pounds better off. Laszlo rang the two insurance companies involved and informed them that the contingency under which their obligations would presently be discharged had regrettably occurred, requesting them to send a representative to see his solicitor as soon as possible. Then he rang the solicitor. It was suggested that he would probably have a good action against the company that owned the bread-van.

'Father's Joy have always been sensitive to adverse publicity.'

He advised Laszlo that litigation was always inadvisable where matters could be arranged out of court.

'We should go for about fifty,' the solicitor said.

'What?'

'Fifty thousand.'

Laszlo replaced the receiver sadly. His dreams had centred around one person, and she was no longer there to share them. But now that Maya had gone, he felt an overwhelming need to escape as well. Because of Selveratnam, there was undeniably a fugitive aspect to his intended flight. He needed to distance himself from Crystal Palace. But he was resolved not to hide, rather to discard his identity and fashion a better one. It would be a sort of reincarnation. And one small thing was certain. He would never return to the First Nag and Waik again. The front-door bell rang. He opened it to find Ada outside.

'Would you like to visit Maya in the Chapel of Rest?' she asked. 'We could go down together.'

He shook his head.

'No thanks, Ada,' he said. 'I don't intend to go to that place at all.'

The night before Maya's cremation, Laszlo had a disturbing dream. He dreamed that he had visited the Chapel of Rest. As he walked towards his mother's body, he sensed that something was wrong. Maya's face was puffy and crinkled like a rubber mask that had sprung loose from the wearer. Her fine blond hair was drawn tightly against the side of her face in an unusual manner. He reached forward and moved the hair from Maya's right temple to reveal a black hole, large enough to accommodate a fat cigar. He was sure he had not seen that injury at the hospital. He remembered thinking how unblemished she was when Dr Levy advised him that his mother was dead. What had happened to Maya after he'd left the bedside? He moved closer to examine his mother and noticed with trepidation that her eyelids were twitching as though she was alive. Laszlo drew a lid back – then recoiled with horror. Instead of the bright blue eye he expected, the socket was filled with squirming white maggots. Who had robbed her eyes? And made the hole in her head? What did this mean? He started to weep uncontrollably in his sleep. A sense of outrage possessed him, but there was shame as well. He shook with impotence. How could he tell anyone about this ghoulish desecration? Nobody must know. Sympathy for such an obscenity would be unbearable. But what was he to do? Laszlo woke up screaming.

Chapter 26

It was time to run. Laszlo smelled danger in the air. Not only was there a corpse in his deep freeze but a fortune in misappropriated bonds and cash stuffed behind the refrigerator panel. Since Selveratnam's death his thoughts had revolved around the advisability of a sudden disappearance. But it was important to behave normally until his moment arrived. The prospect before him quickened his pulse, lifting the depression he had felt since Maya had left him.

He rang Harada to extend his leave, explaining that more time was needed to settle matters after his mother's funeral, then packed a travelling-bag with a few personal effects he kept at Maya's place, and left the flat while Ada was out shopping. He simplified her options by not leaving a telephone number or forwarding address. He found a room in a modest Bayswater hotel and plotted the next stage of the operation. He rinsed his hair a deep chestnut and planned to grow it longer. His eyebrows were dyed to match and he started a moustache, darkening the blond growth every morning.

Laszlo remembered that Serena Katz, a street-wise girl at the First Nag and Waik, had once mentioned a distant relative who not only ran a finance house but provided identities for people who had reason to disappear; like husbands, wives, mistresses boy-friends, debtors, the morbidly bored and those in fear of their sanity, happiness or lives. It was an innocuous comment that he had taken at the time as a light-hearted boast, no more than an entertaining exaggeration over a few drinks.

'And what about criminals?' he remembered asking her.

Serena shrugged.

'Everybody has their price,' she yawned.

'A dangerous business,' he'd commented.

'Our little Danny is not above a crooked turn,' she laughed. 'He

191

even charges seventy-five per cent over clearing banks' base rates for his legitimate loan business.'

'He must top the usury index,' he'd declared with an appreciative whistle.

Laszlo had no trouble in finding the number in the directory. Daniel Porter Brokerage Services Ltd was a Finchley concern with an address in the Bishop's Avenue. He rang and asked to talk to Daniel Porter. And that is how Laszlo found himself swishing along the gravelled drive of a residence in one of the more expensive habitats of North London. His maroon Daimler (an acquisition of hardly an hour earlier) nosed up to the Porter dwelling, an Ascot-Aztec frustum embarrassed by an arcade of Italianate arches. The tall leaded windows in blue stained-glass, basically Tandoori Romanesque, seemed to hint at a missing minaret. Somewhere, disturbed peacocks screamed. A snarling black chow hurled its thuggish body against an Eric Gill wrought-iron gate leading to the private garden.

Dr Porter was short and fat. He had, however, a touch of Levantine machismo about his smouldering eyes and grey shagger's moustache. He was the kind of herbert who swanned around after dark in a camel-hair coat, soft hat and reflecting glasses. Laszlo ambled through the door, casual in green cords, an orange wool tie and buckskin shoes with sponge soles. They squeezed hands genially. Dr Porter eyed his young visitor with a glint of friendly rapacity as they settled themselves in the study. Laszlo looked around attentively. The Wedgwood Room was furnished with several hundred leather volumes tastefully symmetrical in magenta morocco with gilt flourishes and gothic lettering on their spines.

'What can we do for you?' Dr Porter smiled, opening and shutting the drawer of his reproduction Sheraton desk continuously.

'I'd better put my cards on the table,' said Laszlo.

'Do that. Cards on the table is my favourite starting point.'

'I'm a criminal,' Laszlo announced slyly, 'and I want you to provide me with referees for a bank account and a passport. Also a nice, safe bio. I mean, a verifiable background.'

Dr Porter took a deep breath. He picked up a model Stuka bomber paperweight and flew it around between his forefinger and thumb.

'I don't know who you've been talking to, but I run a legitimate merchant bank here,' he claimed piously.

'At seventy-five over base?'

'Seventy-three point three per cent,' he corrected Laszlo peevishly. The reference to his interest rate had rattled him. It was clearly a sensitive issue.

'Look,' Dr Porter said, putting his Stuka down and wagging a finger at Laszlo. 'I take risks no other sonofabitch in the City is prepared to even look at. Seventy-three point three is peanuts. I'm a social service. I should come with the free orange juice and guide dogs for the blind. In any respectable country, they'd name streets after me.'

'Two thousand pounds in cash if you do the business,' Laszlo declared.

'I wouldn't consider getting involved with a real crim for less than five,' Dr Porter countered. 'I have my rep as a banker to consider.'

They haggled.

'It's five or nothing,' Dr Porter said, landing his bomber neatly on the *Financial Times* before getting up.

'I haven't got five thousand,' replied Laszlo.

Dr Porter regarded him contemptuously when Laszlo said that all he had was three thousand three hundred.

'I'll need four. K. That's my last price. Have you any collateral? I'll lend you the difference.'

Laszlo slipped Selveratnam's gold Rolex off his wrist. Dr Porter examined it carefully.

'Three three and this old timepiece perhaps,' he suggested, trying to look miserable.

'Three and the watch,' urged Laszlo.

'I'm not happy,' mused Dr Porter.

'Join the club,' said Laszlo. 'That's my father's watch. A death-bed gift. A memento from the cancer ward.'

They shook hands. Dr Porter informed him that he'd fix him

up with the directorship of a legitimate company of antique ivory artefact importers, established in 1896 at Pondicherry. Also a leaving certificate from a leading public school.

'What public school?'

'Hogg's Benches. At a place called Sheepwash.'

'I've never heard of it.'

Dr Porter smiled wearily. He raised his hands, mildly concerned at Laszlo's ignorance.

'It's far more exclusive than Eton or Harrow. I'm an old boy myself.'

Laszlo frowned. His face reflected his scepticism.

'Listen. It's the only school in the world that combines an intensive if unconventional academic training (Aramaic, tarocco, chess and yoga are compulsory subjects) with the market skills of medieval horse-traders. The founder, Billy Hogg, a defrocked Benedictine, blacksmith and presumed lover of Wat Tyler, was hanged at Faversham, cut down, resuscitated and smuggled out to Sheepwash in Devon. There he founded his famous school, where to this day only Romany is spoken in the breeding paddocks and sixth-formers trade horses at the great West Country fairs. Because of Hogg's near-miraculous reprieve from death, he was referred to as "The Phoenix", a nickname that inspired the school motto, "Accepto Robore Surgam".'

'OK, OK,' Laszlo protested.

Dr Porter unscrewed his gold-topped Sheaffer and poised it over a memo pad.

'I can fix you up at Brinkleys,' he said. 'That's my bank.'

'They'll do.'

'What's your name?' he enquired. 'Or at least, what name will you be using?'

'Thomas Flute.'

'As in the instrument?' the financier asked gravely.

'Just so.'

Dr Porter looked critically at Laszlo.

'You're using the wrong hair-dye,' he advised. 'I'll write you out a prescription for a terrific one.'

'Are you a medical doctor?'

Dr Porter smiled. 'No, but my cousin is. I scribble out a few in his name occasionally.' He paused and then added, 'And when will I pick up the geld?'

'It's here,' Laszlo replied, reaching down into the bison-skin case he had appropriated.

He counted out the necessaries, watched intently by the other man.

Laszlo procured Tom Flute's certificate from Somerset House, queued at Petty France for his passport, booked a flight to Nice, deposited two hundred and seventy-five thousand pounds in the current account he opened at Brinkleys and dropped in to see the manager about his fictitious business. The young manager was a cheerful, ex-public school boy, a Biggles-type character who exuded optimism. He had been warned by his boss that he shouldn't smile as much as he did, and had been practising business frowns when Laszlo was ushered in. It was no use. Arvie Stundish was a congenital smiler. A pleasant fellow.

'And what exactly will you be doing, Mr Flute?'

'Apart from my ivory interests in Pondicherry, I'm a free-lance diamond cutter.'

'Gosh. That must have required a great deal of training.'

'A fair amount, Mr Stundish. But it's hand, eyes and nerves that count. I suppose that I'm a sort of rock-doctor. My clientele is largely Swiss-based, but I'm employed quite a bit by Arabs, South Americans and the occasional Asian speculator.'

'Incredible,' murmured Stundish, slightly envious. He was quite taken by his new customer's youth, dash and contempt for the bank's investment facilities.

'Let's call this my petty-cash account,' Laszlo smiled, referring to his two hundred and seventy-five thousand pounds deposit.

He rented a security-box, allowing the young manager a sight of the sixty million Swissie bonds before he sealed the envelope and went off to lock them in the safe.

*

Stundish spent the best part of the evening telling his pretty but bored-looking oriental girl-friend, Thelma, about the remarkable rock-doctor. Three glasses of Monbousquet on, he still hadn't stopped talking.

'Aren't you going to kiss me?' Thelma complained, jabbing his shin under the bistro table.

'Oh, rather,' he snorted, bumping his lips against hers.

But his intrepid spirit appeared to be loitering about some Alpine defile with the charismatic fellow with nerveless hands.

Laszlo drove north to Bedfordshire, where he visited an estate agent in Woburn. With the minimum of fuss he acquired an eight-bedroomed Victorian ruin, a Gothic extravagance with an observatory tower and a respectable touch of dry rot. The original owner, Sjrogen Boote (1835–1920), was an astronomer of minor celebrity, the discoverer of a wispy comet that appeared every one hundred and seventy-five years (the next sighting will be in 2045), and a greenish star in the constellation of Cameleopardalis that he named Alpha Verdiboote. Its inexplicable disappearance in 1872 has been the subject of several learned papers. The house was located in the village of Mushington and was known as Boote's Folly, a xenophobic response to the decorative observatory tower, which was clearly more Siennese than English county in inspiration. The modest asking price of eighty thousand pounds, the agent explained, was due largely to malignant unsubstantiated rumours that a proposed motorway link would, if constructed, pass within three feet of the front door.

'The planning authority has denied any such proposal,' the estate agent assured Laszlo.

'And what do you think?' Laszlo asked.

'I'll stake my reputation as an estate agent that Mushington will be motorway-free for at least the next hundred years,' the man declared, bouncing his fist lightly off his desk.

'I'll buy that,' Laszlo said.

He paid instantly to demonstrate his good faith, slapping a

Brinkleys cheque-book on the table to produce the twirly Thomas Flute signature he'd been practising in magenta ink.

'But I must occupy the place immediately,' Laszlo observed, handing over the cheque.

'It's not customary before completion,' the agent declared, arching his brows most professionally.

'If anything goes amiss,' Laszlo pointed out, 'you've got my funds. And I'm prepared to indemnify the seller against any loss he may incur as a consequence of the sale. It's occupation or no deal, I'm afraid.'

'Well then,' beamed the agent, instantly subdued by the prospect of losing his profit on a property that had been on the market for more than two years. He reached behind a volume of Mawer and Stenton's *The Place Names of Bedfordshire* for a celebratory bottle of Palo Cortado, dribbling out a couple of schooners for Laszlo and himself.

The house, which Laszlo decided would be renamed Mushington Hall, needed considerable attention. But he found its possibilities stimulating. It had derelict stables, a stone barn, a ruined Victorian conservatory and four acres of stinging nettles. He found a red-faced Irish jobbing builder who agreed to restore, re-roof and de-infest the property for thirty thousand pounds, and he engaged a pleasant middle-aged couple, the Bagshawes, as gardener and housekeeper, and charged them with civilising the land and furnishing the building with expedition. As he stumped about his little estate, Laszlo remembered Selveratnam. He would, he reflected, compost well below a fruit tree. The prospect of enjoying fruit from a tree rooted in the tiny mystic touched a quirky element in his nature. A cherry tree, perhaps? There was a sort of poetry in the felicity that commended itself to him the more he considered it. He sought out the gardener.

'I'll need a cherry tree immediately,' he instructed Bagshawe. 'It's an old family tradition. Kindly prop the sapling against the conservatory. I'll stick it in myself.'

Bagshawe inclined his head respectfully.

'If you'll instruct me where to plant it, sir,' he murmured.

'I'm afraid I'll have to do it myself, Bagshawe,' said Laszlo. 'It's a light-of-the-moon job. But you may dig the hole. In the middle of the lawn might be a good idea.'

'On the lawn, sir?'

'On the lawn, Bagshawe,' Laszlo insisted, quelling the minion with a stiffish stare. 'And have it ready for me this evening.'

Laszlo drove back to the flat at Crystal Palace after midnight, arriving there at two in the morning. Letting himself in, he made for the deep-freeze. Selveratnam had now been there for nearly four weeks. He unlocked the freezer cabinet and prised the boxes of peach melba out of the carpet-bag. The diminutive Hindu, apart from a hoary crispiness of his hair and an icicle growing out of each nostril, looked in excellent condition. Laszlo slammed the freezer shut, drew the front door to, and lugged the frozen body down the rear stairway to the waiting Daimler. He got back to Mushington just before dawn. He inspected the hole. It was just right for a cherry tree, but Selveratnam, he felt, would be safer with at least another three feet. Laszlo applied himself vigorously with the shovel. At an estimated five feet or so, he dropped the carpet-bag to rest, filled in a covering of three feet, then planted the sapling. He beat the soil flat and went into the house to admire his handiwork through the patio doors. He was surprised to see Bagshawe about.

'Thank you for having arranged everything for me, Bagshawe,' called Laszlo in a seigneurial tone.

The gardner smiled. He was grateful that he was now employed by an English gentleman, having had to endure in his last job a crazy Iranian millionaire who would only allow orange flowers in the garden, arranged in horseshoe shaped beds, orange being the silly man's racing colours. It was, Bagshawe believed, a deliverance from the Almighty when Mr Pishavari slithered into the indoor swimming-pool with a terminal aneurysm. And both Bagshawes were enchanted by their new employer's voice. It was, they agreed, so very like that of the late Leslie Howard.

'I'd have done it for you,' Bagshawe said.

Laszlo nodded amiably.

'Planting the cherry tree is family trad,' he explained.

Chapter 27

When Laszlo got to St Tropez, he hired a caravan at Dunkelbaum's camp, Le Coq Hardi. He had chosen a naturist establishment because he imagined that it would be the quickest way to meet the right sort of people and to advertise his endowments without the more tiresome protocols usually encountered at exclusive hotels. Furthermore, he felt free at last. Great wealth, a pleasant house in the country and an identity that would in time express his flamboyant but gentlemanly inclinations, gave him a sense of exuberance and a certainty that he was finally shaping the kind of destiny he deserved. He was even learning to live with the intermittent buzzing in his head; if he didn't listen too intently, Bunny Selveratnam could be forgotten for days at a time. And he was strangely comforted whenever he thought of the cherry tree standing sentinel on the lawn at Mushington Hall.

He spent the days swimming and browning his well-muscled body on Pamplemousse Beach, and the evenings jigging to the monotonous thump of the 'Yé Yé' music much favoured by the trendy Varois young. During his third day on the beach, quite early on a cool sunny May morning, he noticed a woman of indeterminate age, not naked, as is the expected non-fashion of the area, but clad in a high-collared, flimsy black caftan, black pantaloons, a black scarf and a black straw hat. She wore saucer-size sunglasses, so that all that was visible of her was a large, blood-red mouth and areas of untropézienne, lizard-white skin. Laszlo, seduced by the aberrant, gave her a close view of his well-oiled cock which he bounced off one thigh as he sauntered past her stool. It was a trick he'd picked up from an Italian waiter. He was naked, except for his shades, gold Longines and the five-hundred-franc note under its strap.

'Hey,' she called out.

He stopped and smiled.

'Why don't you buy me another pastis?' she demanded.

He ordered two.

'My name,' he announced, offering her a hand, 'is Tom Flute.'

'How provocative,' she exclaimed, moistening her lips.

Laszlo raised his shades expectantly.

'And I,' she smiled, 'am Princess Lola d'Aoili of Esterel.'

Noticing the puzzled downward cast of his head (this despite a good-grade O-Level in Geography), she provided him with some supplementary information.

'Esterel is a tiny mountain kingdom appropriated by the French in corrupt boundary adjustments many centuries ago. Although the second-oldest kingdom in Europe, its very existence had always been disputed by the great powers and it has been the subject of secret annexations, counter-revolutions, restorations and coups d'état for well over a thousand years. Indeed, until the introduction of the Code Napoléon, the utterance of its name in France was an offence punishable by summary emasculation for males and mastectomy for females.'

'I'm sorry,' Laszlo murmured, offering to buy her another pastis.

'Are you renting a villa?' she enquired politely.

'A caravan.'

She did not answer immediately, gazing forlornly out to sea. After some time, she turned to Laszlo again.

'I've always had a soft spot for caravans,' she admitted nostalgically.

'Mine,' he said, 'is about four hundred metres or so up the beach.'

'I have,' she informed him sadly, 'sustained a damaged toe. I doubt whether I will be able to negotiate that sort of distance unaided.'

'I'll carry you,' he offered.

And before she could demur, he swept the princess off her bar-stool into his arms. He bore her like an exotic trophy through the naked and curious sunbathers, who appeared to adduce that this was a happening worthy of that domicile of the outré. At nine o'clock on a Monday morning in May, there was little to match the spectacle of Laszlo's progress along the Plage de Pamplemousse with Princess Lola d'Aoili in his arms, apart from an oblique political demonstration that took place throughout that month. This involved Baroness Geli von Kressenstein of Ludwigshafen, an obese German giantess of about ninety, a reputed friend of Leni Riefenstahl and former mistress of Joseph Goebbels. She stood as always, legs defiantly apart in the water, peeing imperiously on petit-bourgeois sensibilities as the plangent green shallows of the Mediterranean lapped her white, varicosed calves. If she was booed, the demonstration was repeated the moment she was able to refill her bladder. The police had been warned that it would be imprudent to arrest her, as Hengist Dunkelbaum, a substantial provider of local taxes, was a distant relative. *Nice-Matin* attempted to interview her, but the giantess's lips were sealed. An Austrian apologist suggested that the piddling was a stand against a Marxist-Moslem axis that had infiltrated the Côte d'Azur since the war and manifested itself by the proliferation of couscous restaurants in districts where there was significant Communist support. Yet another view, put about by the anti-vivisectionists, was that the pissing was an attack on domestic animals that had enjoyed the exclusive rights of urination and defecation along the beaches in the South of France for several hundred years. Some held that the giantess's public leakage was a gentle tilt against the municipality's practice of depositing untreated turds in the Bay of St Tropez in the middle of the night. But whatever the reason, the giantess's performance was an expected May event, listed in the better tourist-guides and a footnote in at least two histories of Var.

The moment she was in the caravan, the Princess Lola d'Aoili disrobed. She told Laszlo that she regarded a private viewing of her body as a modest payment for his hospitality. Laszlo noticed the princess was far older than he had imagined, although slim and wonderfully preserved. Her age could have been anything between sixty and, well, who knows? Her hennaed hair was cropped short and her breasts, no larger than moderately sized walnuts, were tipped with nipples that had been painted red.

There was a pink cicatrice below her heart, the scar of a knife-attack, she explained, by a mad mufti who was outraged by her friendship with a rabbi. She had no body-hair and her skin had an almost phosphorescent white pallor. Her eyes were her most alluring feature, dark violet below sweeping lashes and black, well-formed brows. Her teeth were large, strong and avocado in colour.

'You understand,' she confided as she uncoiled herself lasciviously on Laszlo's bed, parting her lean lily thighs before him, 'that I am no longer intacta.'

'I understand,' he nodded solemnly.

The princess held out her thin arms.

'Take me,' she invited graciously, red lips parted in a tired smile.

But before Laszlo could consider an appropriate response, she fainted. When he revived her, Princess Lola d'Aoili admitted that she had not eaten for four days. After a wedge of pissaladière, half a baguette dampened and resuscitated in the oven, a handful of figons, a portion of Auverne Bleu and five tumblers of Ricard, the princess confessed that she had slept with six thousand three hundred and nine lovers during the last fifty years or so, since her defloration in a boulangerie by a mentally retarded Bulgarian. She was, she recalled, eleven at the time. Among her lovers, she listed six members of European royalty, eleven heads or former heads of state, twenty-nine film-stars of international repute, sixty sports celebrities, one hundred and seventeen officers of the NATO armed forces, three from the Republic of China (members of a trade mission she encountered in Cannes), four hundred restaurateurs, seven with Michelin stars, and approximately five thousand partners to whom she had not been formally introduced. The rest, slightly under seven hundred, were close friends, among whom she numbered her late husband, Prince Django, who was killed by a novice windsurfer off the rocks at Famagusta the day the bloodthirsty Turks invaded Cyprus.

'What I need,' Laszlo said as he sucked thoughtfully at an olive stone, 'is a mother with social status.'

He hunted through his bison-skin case for a pen, paper and his book on European heraldry.

'Have you,' he enquired, 'a family crest?'

'Many,' Princess Lola replied, 'being related spermally to the Hohenzollerns, Bourbons, Romanovs, Saxe-Coburgs and Dracula families.'

'Splendid,' Laszlo enthused, flicking through the book on European heraldry and rapidly jotting down requirements for a composite crest.

They settled for tessellated battlements, un plage, le ciel azur, soleil et violet l'eau, not forgetting a cockatrice, and spent the rest of the morning devising the crest, sustaining themselves with a beaker of Bisquit apiece and a few olives. He told her that he had a small place at Mushington and raised the question of her becoming mistress of the establishment, assuming the role of his adoptive mother, widow of the late Major Agamemnon Flute of the Tibetan Mission at Lhasa. And he hoped that, as royalty, she would retain the title and dignity of a princess.

'Well, if I do consent to become your mother,' she mused impishly, 'we may have to consider the incestial implications, although it is a matter of historical fact that the greatest families have perpetuated themselves in this way. Incest is a potent and hallowed tradition. What is pedigree but incest? However, I must confess to an unaccustomed spasm of guilt at the thought of doing it with my son. It's quite delicious.'

'It might be expedient,' he suggested, 'to keep that aspect of our relationship secret.'

'You are a dreamy son,' she purred, 'magnificently equipped. What more could any mother desire?'

'Have I any brothers and sisters?' he enquired, joining her on the bed.

She told him the story of her first conception during the Vee-Sign War.

'In 1942,' she recalled, 'the exigencies of the great conflict separated me from my husband, Prince Django. As a consequence of my incredible beauty I was often mistaken for Garbo, although legwise I was more in the Dietrich class. Anyway, because of my mesmeric presence, the Archduchess Rosa felt that I would be safer living in a scabby district of Roma with my uncle, the Archduke Norbert, a retired papal lavatory attendant. Times were desperately hard. I disguised my attractiveness as best I could, shearing my hair, wearing clothes that were little better than rags and taking care never to venture too far from the decaying tenement where we lived. I was always hungry. We lived on stale pasta, haulm stew, and whatever squashed fruit we could cadge from the traders in a nearby market. Alas, despite my precautions, I was seen one morning from a passing Alfa Romeo. It stopped and reversed rapidly to where I was standing. Before I could comprehend what was happening, two smiling bastards in black bundled me into the back and I was carried off at a speed that made my stomach turn with terror. "Where are you taking me?" I whimpered. One of the men had his hands inside my knickers, while the other had ripped open my blouse to examine my breasts. "Fuck me and let me go," I pleaded. "I am a poor Catholic girl who lives with her club-footed uncle, a devout man whose life has been consumed servicing the needs of the holiest arseholes in Christendom, a man as familiar with the conformation of papal turds as you illustrious gentlemen are with the noses on your fathers' faces. Don't carry me too far from where I live," I begged, "or my uncle will die of anxiety. Please, great sirs, have your lewd ways with me while I mutter my beads and pray for your salvation." The bastards laughed. Loudly and ferociously. "You," one of them said, "will be scrubbed, polished and prepared for the most powerful cock in Italy." He was, of course, talking politically, while I was thinking physiologically.

'My God, I was terrified. The term "most powerful cock" filled my lower tubes with nervous wind. You must remember that the cocks I had seen until that time, being a respectably married woman, were run-of-the-mill affairs. Indeed, every time a lover slid his trousers down, I prayed to St Rita that his piston would not be too large to be accommodated in my modest cylinder. I was never disappointed. Indeed, some tools were so tiny that they slipped out if I coughed or asked the time of day. But in accordance with my more experienced cousin Gitana's advice, I always declared that they were monstrous and felt like oak trees inside me. This apparently was all my lovers wanted to hear.

They never cared a fig if I said that they had nice eyes, a pleasant smile or wise opinions. "Tell me," they would demand as they jockeyed away between my parted thighs like demented beasts, "have you ever experienced anything as glorious as this?" "Never," I would pant, jumping and writhing in a great display of uncontrollable passion, taking care of course not to be too energetic, for if they slipped out too often, some became so deflated that not even the most ingenious and diligent repacking could get them back in place. "I can't imagine what's become of me," was the post-coital cri de coeur I often heard. "Normally, I can keep it up for hours," they'd boast. "It must have been the dodgy calamari or the flat champagne or perhaps this lumpy mattress." I always took great care to reassure them. "It was simply fabulous anyway," I'd swear, nibbling at their ears. One or two of them would be sceptical. "Don't lie," they'd murmur forlornly. It was then that I put on the light and looked them in the eyes. "Darling," I'd say, "I never lie about something so central to my happiness as sexual satisfaction." "Really?" they'd croak hoarsely. "Really," I'd reply tenderly. But all this is no more than a conventional strategy for prudent fuckees. It should be taught at domestic science classes in every girls' school.

'Anyway, I was still speculating fearfully about the dimension of the most powerful cock in Italy, venting my fitful wind in a succession of discreet farts that I hoped would be stifled by the sibilance of a leaky gasket and the rasping bravura of a split silencer, when the Alfa Romeo stopped. I had scarcely time to make the sign of the cross before my brutal captors dragged me out. I was frogmarched across a cobbled courtyard to what looked like a museum. The place smelled of formaldehyde and yeasty bread. We passed under a baroque archway into a hall littered with marble statues of naked heroes in muscled poses and entered a brightly lit electric lift with mirrors and red plush seats. I remember being horrified at my reflection and wondered why on earth they had picked up a tramp like me. Holy Mary, I looked as interesting as steaming cow-dung. I learned later that the bald-headed pensioner ("Call me Uncle Pius") who had gifted me with bags of squashed aubergines and tomatoes for knee-tremblers behind the garbage-tip was a Fascist activist. My avuncular benefactor had boasted about my tightness (a vulgar male fantasy) to his bog-minded, black-shirted cronies. The thought of that betrayal still makes me rankle. I have never felt quite the same about bald-headed men since.

'We creaked up to the sixth floor, where I was consigned to Angelica, a plump monocular woman who prepared me for the occasion. I was first soaked in olive oil, then bathed in tepid goat's milk and finally rinsed in hot jasmine water. After I was towelled, my legs and arms were secured in four leather loops and I was suspended face downward, about four feet from the ground. Angelica inspected my orifices with diligence. She informed me that "the most powerful cock in Italy", apart from ruling the country with commendable panache, venerated female orifices, deriving much spiritual strength from feeling, sucking, smelling and filling them. It was almost sacramental with him, she explained. Angelica shone a pencil-torch into my most private parts. "You are definitely not a virgin," she laughed coarsely. "I am a married woman," I advised her proudly – well, as proudly as one could, dangling like a plucked turkey and having a one-eyed stranger rooting about in one's pussy. Angelica moved her torch a few centimetres higher. "And does your husband take his pleasure at the back door as well?" she asked. It was an impertinent question and I was profoundly offended. "He is not a tradesman," I sneered, repressing in time an almost reflexive declaration that he was a person of royal blood. "You will find," she said, "that Il Bandito is a truly heroic man in every way, and is quite prepared to take his chances in the narrowest and darkest of passages." Angelica lowered my harness and set me on my feet. I was kitted out in a red blouse, short slit skirt and a pair of six-inch wobblers. My lips were smeared with crimson paint and my eyes darkened with mascara. "Knickers," Angelica smiled, "will not be necessary. Il Bandito has precious little time to spare for romantic diversions." And before I was escorted down to the private rooms where I was to meet "the most powerful cock in Italy", Angelica squeezed me and licked my mouth. "I will be pleased to receive you whenever you need fresh bread and a pat or two of butter," she whispered, winking her residual eye rather suggestively.

'An hour later, in a room which I thought cluttered with dreary Renaissance rubbish, in a thoroughly uncivil display of sexist arrogance I was penetrated just as the Gorgonzola was being wheeled in, across a pearwood table that had once belonged to Savonarola, not ten paces from a balcony overlooking the Capitoline. It was after an orgy of Quaglietta di Vitello and Seppie in Zimino, the air drugged with Neapolitan love-songs and my young mind seduced by the glamour of black shirts, gleaming medals and squeaking, highly polished boots. Realising the constitutional impropriety of coupling with the head of a belligerent government (Esterel was neutral), I resolved not to return to the apartment of the Archduke Norbert. Ah, but what a night that was. Il Bandito dribbled Sengiovese between my thighs, nuzzling my winey cleft like a pig after truffles. It will always be a matter of regret that we never exchanged a single word. Strangely enough, I was quietly impressed by his masterful style, but he treated me with as much regard as one would a sweaty sock. There was no appreciative peck on the cheek, no cheerful handshake or even a polite nod of acknowledgement. I half expected some passing chatter about the unusual anti-cyclone around the city that had induced an epidemic of yokeless eggs, inexplicable menstrual floods and an infestation of drosophila. But nothing. I considered writing him a letter after the war to ask for the recipe for the excellent Seppie in Zimino, but by the time I had got around to purchasing some perfumed stationery, history had turned his page. They had strung the poor bugger up in Milano like a bag of dirty laundry.

'After he had finished with me, I managed to escape. I made my way across the country disguised as a Franciscan monk, through Ventimiglia into France. I was seven months gone before I got anywhere near my beloved Prince Django. It was a dreadful period of my life. Fondled and fumbled by carabinieri, fisherman, Wehrmacht soldiers, Resistance fighters, Carmelite nuns, gendarmes, journalists, hotel-keepers and a friendly venereologist, I made my way to St Tropez, where I heard Prince

Django was hiding. He was working on a yacht anchored two miles off this very plage. Although I was distressed to discover he had taken a job as a deck-steward with a Laval sympathiser (a shifty scumbag called Duclos-Duclos, who once bruised my arse with a misogynist bite while I was taking a shower), I was aching to see Prince Django once more. Plunging into the sea at night, I struck out in the direction of his yacht. There, in the cool waters of a May Mediterranean, I gave birth like a dolphin, a passing shoal of rascasse severing the umbilical cord. My child was borne back to the shore by the incoming tide and lost to me forever. If it had lived, the Esterel succession would have been secured.'

'But wasn't it technically a bastard?' Laszlo asked. He was up on bastards.

'Only God understands such matters,' Princess Lola replied gloomily.

'There are protocols such as gestation periods.'

'When a child is the only means of continuing a great line,' she observed, 'gestation periods are a technicality. If one had seriously to take account of the sleeping arrangements, there wouldn't be a single legitimate title in the world. Royalty is a wholly symbolic concept and has little to do with de facto fucking. Only two rules are generally relevant – and even these may be subject to exception. The first is that the embryo is by and large accepted to have been a resident of the putative royal womb; and the second, that a significant majority of people with a psychic interest in the birth should consciously acknowledge the authenticity of the ejaculation.'

Laszlo nodded at his adoptive mama's comments. He offered her a cheroot and, taking one himself, lit them.

'My second child,' she declared, 'was conceived miraculously. A straightforward job of parthenogenesis.'

'There was no father?'

'Not that I can recall,' she mused thoughtfully.

'You must have forgotten.'

Princess Lola d'Aoili shook her head sadly.

'It was in London. I had been shopping and decided to return to my lodgings across the park. And there, in the growing dusk, I was convulsed into sudden labour. I lay down beside a hawthorn bush and gave birth. It was a monster, not destined to live. So I slipped it into my shopping-bag, intending to convey the creature to a hospital when I found my strength. I must have dozed off, for when I awoke, the shopping-bag with my child had disappeared.'

'What sort of bag was it?' Laszlo asked.

'Just a plastic bag from Tesco. There wasn't much in it. A bottle of Guignolet, my purse, a baguette and the child.'

Laszlo's heart quickened with excitement. He took her hand in his.

'Let us pretend,' he said, 'that I am that child.'

'Don't be silly. It was grotesque, I tell you. I didn't even bother to report the birth. Why should I strive officiously to bring dishonour on the house of Esterel?'

'Look how I've prospered,' Laszlo smiled.

Princess Lola d'Aoili shook her head sadly.

'Tell me,' asked Laszlo, 'did you lose your son on the 7th of March, the feast day of St Thomas Aquinas?'

The princess's eyes closed. She stared at Laszlo for a long time, studying him carefully.

'It's impossible. The infant was hideously flawed.'

'Why don't you answer my question? Did all this occur on the 7th of March?'

'It was March certainly. Early March beyond doubt. But what you imply is impossible.'

'Why do you think they call me Tom?' demanded Laszlo. 'And my patronymic is no more than a reference to the French bread. The Guignolet and your purse, alas, were no longer there when I was found.'

'Your hypothesis is obviously nonsense,' Princess Lola murmured, 'but I am seduced by its felicity. You needn't tell me the truth. I have never been infatuated with facts.'

'We're two of a kind,' he said. 'Let us accept my explanation as a plausible dream.'

'My life is a plausible dream,' she said softly, 'and suddenly I feel that you are my own flesh and blood.'

He lay alongside her and stroked her cheek.

'I'm going to call you Mama,' he announced. 'I have never called anyone that before.'

The princess seemed strangely moved.

'And nobody has called me that either.'

She sat up, defending her hairless yoni with long, artistic fingers.

'We mustn't,' she whispered, tears in her eyes. 'It would be a mortal sin.'

Laszlo looked extremely disappointed, a gambit palm still on her tussock of venery.

'Please,' he pleaded.

Princess Lola suddenly scrambled away from him and out of bed as though she'd seen a ghost. Wrapping herself in a bathrobe, she relit her cheroot.

'I have received an admonitory vision,' she murmured, shivering at the thought.

'What do you mean?'

She indicated a point at the far end of the caravan.

'A tiny black angel with a blue, luminous halo materialised just behind the gas-cooker,' she said fearfully.

Laszlo emitted a snort of disgust.

'That,' he explained irritably, 'was only Bunny Selveratnam.'

It was a petulant and frustrated Laszlo who slipped into his jeans and escaped from the caravan. He ran out into the sunshine, barefoot across the fine sand to the sea, advancing sulkily into the water, his fists dug deep into his wet denims. He turned a little later than he should have, in response to a soprano shriek behind him, taking the glancing impact of a scudding windsurfer on his thigh. The topless surfer fell, dragging him down into the water with her. That was how he met Steffi Dunkelbaum.

Madame Dunkelbaum insisted on inspecting his contused thigh right away.

'You should sue my husband,' she drawled, running a finger lightly along the eight-inch weal.

Laszlo laughed. She was a tall, well-fleshed blonde in her late thirties with big grey eyes and an expensively tanned skin.

'It would do Hengist good to be prosecuted for my negligence,' she said. 'He's far too wealthy for his own good, and you are obviously a young man with more charm than money.'

'Does it show?' Laszlo asked.

'You have a hungry look. I have an instinct about such things. I saw you on the nude beach yesterday, posing beside some elderly women. And this morning you were carrying a very strange parcel. Are you a model? Looking for a part in a film? Or just waiting for a rich mistress to pick you up?'

Laszlo tried his shy, boyish grin. He knew from experience that this one worked best with older women. He attempted a blush, but found this more difficult to accomplish.

'You are cold on all counts, madam,' he said, running a finger slowly along the zip of his wet jeans.

'My name is Steffi Dunkelbaum,' she smiled, offering her hand in a vulgar but friendly manner. 'I have a fifteen-year-old daughter who is a clone of Brit Bidette, and my husband, Hengist, owns everything you can see.'

'And I,' he announced, 'am Tom Flute. I'm here for a few days with my mother.'

Steffi Dunkelbaum looked surprised.

'Your mother? How refreshing. That a young man should bring his mother to a nude beach. You are obviously the product of an extremely civilised upbringing.' She pursed her lips and rolled her eyes mischievously. 'You are sharing a caravan with your mama? No papa?'

'Colonel Agamemnon Flute, my father, is dead.'

'I'm sorry.'

'It was some time ago.'

'Well, Mr Flute, I would be delighted if you and your mama came to lunch. Perhaps a little hospitality can partially compensate for your injury.'

She pointed to a large white château that stood above a cluster of villas set among the wooded slopes of the Maures hills.

'We take aperitifs at eleven, and lunch at around twelve. But come as early as you please. Dress is informal.'

He glanced up at the château, to which there seemed to be no road.

'Have you got a helicopter?' she asked brightly.

'Not here,' Laszlo laughed.

Madame Dunkelbaum used a palm to steady herself on his bare shoulder as she pointed to a spot between a terracotta chapel and an outcrop of red rock. The nipple of her left breast brushed lightly against his chest as she turned to indicate the route. She lingered against him for a moment longer than necessary, enabling him to inhale the fragrance from her hair. Their eyes met. He was aware of the throbbing pulse in her throat, tiny ears as delicate as sea-shells and beads of sweat on an upper lip, while she was conscious of the possibilities of a louche mouth and the promise of strong, spatulate hands. A goatish awareness lit his eyes as he apprehended the moist heat of her subdued excitement.

'That is where the road begins,' she informed him, 'but it's inconveniently steep and unstable. You'll need a frisky car.'

'We have a Daimler Sovereign,' he said.

She shrugged and pouted. It was a slightly deprecatory gesture.

'An English car? Who knows? If you have any trouble, we'll arrange for somebody to come down to pick you up.'

Madame Dunkelbaum turned to go. He watched her walking up the beach. She gave Laszlo a cheerful wave before she was occulted by the wall of the beach restaurant. He noticed that, despite her size, Steffi Dunkelbaum moved with the fluency of a ballerina.

Chapter 28

Before lunch was taken at the Dunkelbaums', the guests assembled in the ballroom for drinks and a brief preview of the new studio symbol of Sham Shilverman Productions. It was projected onto a makeshift screen of four sheets stitched together and tacked over a wooden frame. Approving 'Ahs' greeted the flickering images of a beautiful, red-lipped Arab, a pair of harmonising zhivagos and a Rolls-Royce before the silhouetted skyline of minarets and domes. Then a festive swirl of Berlioz as the credits in a modish bastard rolled and the title 'LOVE IS THE END' loomed up in apocalyptic letters of fire that finally consumed the screen in flames. It was just a taster. There was applause and gushy enthusiasm.

Madame Dunkelbaum explained to Laszlo that the young Arab with the yowling zhivagos was one of the film's principal backers. A bell rang in his mind.

'Wasn't that the picture the National put on show recently?' he asked, remembering vaguely the recent controversy about the privatised wall on which it had been displayed.

'Yes, it's by *the* Wally Wazir. Some experts are hailing him as the Mohammedan Matisse.'

'Gosh.'

Laszlo was enchanted by the company. Everybody chattered genially across the Sole Meunière aux Poireaux and Plombière Marguerite. He was, at last, he reflected happily, among rich and famous people. For a while, his attention was engaged by the ghost of Izzy Dollar, a celebrated, recently dead poet, who was as large and as voluble as life to anyone with a soupçon of extrasensory perception. The mortified literary genius who had likened Laszlo's head to that of Achilles, now compared it to Wolfgang Ferrari's. The Italian movie-star sat at the other end of the table. Laszlo had the strange but not unpleasant sensation that he was in a wonderful dream. He suggested as much to a fussy little blonde whose throat was covered in pearls. She said that she believed that the Dunkelbaums had spiked the Bollinger.

'You even have Wolfie's eyes,' Dollar's amiable phantom cried with delight.

Laszlo studied the great Pisan actor as they ate. He seemed thicker and coarser than in the photograph Maya used to keep in her bedroom, his curls kinkier than Laszlo had imagined, indicating perhaps a not too distant Moorish ancestor. Laszlo had read somewhere that four generations of dilution uncrinkled the most tenacious frizz. A buzzing in his head. He suspected it was Selveratnam. A tingling premonition that he had the capacity to violate another dimension dissolved into a shot of Wolfgang's progenitor. He was with the living and the dead, among real people and clairvoyant images that had a sharp, cinematic reality. He panned towards a pale child with negroid lips, aux cheveux roux et crépus, fearful buffalo's eyes, carious teeth and a belly swollen with a fetal grandparent of Signor Ferrari. She floated protectively above Wolfgang's head, cradled in a spunky nimbus like a saint.

'Resurgam,' came a bitter cry as the film rolled to the leathery creak of angels' wings.

'Give us a few bars of Monteverdi, eh,' boomed a Chaliapinesque profondo.

The image faded. His eyes travelled down a passage, through an inner door to find her lying upon the familial milk-stained bed, vaulted and dark in an upper room of a crumbling terracotta building, looking past the ragged curtains of a window that overhung the slow, diarrhoeic Arno, a lonely tubercular creature, spiced by the crepuscular smells of frying garlic, chicken ordure, tethered goats, stale wine and fecal soup. He cut quickly to the cemetery gates, an unseasoned coffin and a modest wreath of Madonna lilies.

'Bastards,' cursed a hoarse voice of indeterminate sex. 'She was barely fifteen.'

Off camera, the sound of shuffling feet, twittering baroque

214

violins and the basso, more distant than before, concluding his sonorous direction with a barely audible 'Requiescat in pace.'

The volume of small-talk and laughter increased after lunch, the guests remaining bright-eyed and responsive as they trickled away from the table. Laszlo felt elevated with his new life, receiving and directing flirty glances at Madame Dunkelbaum, who looked radiant and Junoesque in an almost transparent white dress that emphasised her melon breasts and the fact that she was wearing nothing more than what appeared to be a G-string underneath. An ancient man in pink Bermuda shorts and a peaked commando cap was directing a camera crew, one with a dolly and boom, peeking in and out from the crescent-shaped terrace like a curious diplodocus, another on an overhead platform below a lunette in the gilt and rose ceiling, and at least two other hand-held jobs circulating among the guests. A profusion of cables snaked through the corridors of the château and there were black surveillance snouts everywhere, even in the john. Laszlo was slightly alarmed when he glimpsed a groin-level reprise of himself pissing being transmitted on a monitor in the hallway.

'What is happening?' he asked Madame Dunkelbaum, un-easily conscious that every whisper of their tête-à-tête was being recorded by ingeniously designed microphones incorporated into picture-frames, chandeliers, ornaments, book-shelves and flower-vases. His perception of these disguised spies was, he suspected, due to Selveratnam's presence in his skull. Madame Dunkelbaum was impressed by his unusual acuity.

'It's all going into *Love Is the End*,' she murmured. 'Sham calls it his volkslush, a kind of porridge through which the film will float.'

She pointed out an immense black statue of a supine female lower down the hill.

'That's Gaia, the Earth Goddess that Medusa is playing. Altogether, it will be a thirty-six-hour movie, screened over three days.'

'Have they started?'

'Not formally. But at a celebration on the Quai last night,

Medusa hinted that they were moving to the starting line. It was a party for the film's messiah, a very dishy Nicaraguan called Rama Ringaroo. Haven't you noticed the badges a number of people are wearing?'

She beckoned over a plump, swarthy man with a round face, an old-fashioned centre parting, a Gilbert Roland moustache, spotted bow-tie and co-respondent shoes.

'Basin darling, show Mr Flute your badge.'

Basin glided over to them, holding his pint of Bloody Mary at shoulder level. Laszlo peered at the lapel of his blue velvet jacket. On the disc was a well-muscled young man in a leopard-skin pouch, swinging from a tree.

'He's a sort of Tarzan,' Laszlo reflected.

'Right,' Madame Dunkelbaum said. 'Medusa O'Toole feels that the Edgar Rice Burroughs Tarzan books should be recognised as spiritual texts. His work is now prescribed reading at her L'Amauresque ashram.'

The buzzing that Laszlo hoped had gone away suddenly returned. It was as though he'd disturbed a bee-hive in his head. He started to tremble. When he opened his mouth, words that he had not intended were articulated in a clipped Tamilian accent that resonated around the room with the electric crackle of a tonny.

'The true messiah is Shri Bunny Selveratnam of Crystal Palace.'

Madame Dunkelbaum looked at him curiously. She managed an uncertain smile.

'How strange,' she said.

Laszlo rubbed his forehead with two fingers, then clenched and unclenched his jaw.

'It was meant to be a joke,' he smiled. 'I once knew a man who used to say that.'

'Quite a remarkable impression,' she said. 'You achieved the nuances of an Indian voice extremely well.'

Laszlo looked around self-consciously and noticed that he'd attracted the interest of the little man who looked like Benito Bandito.

216

'I must admit,' Laszlo said to Madame Dunkelbaum, uneasily aware that he was suddenly the centre of attention, 'I'd never considered the messianic implications of the Tarzan story.'

He turned his back on the sinister dwarf who looked like Bandito, unable to suffer the burning eyes a moment longer.

'You've been brainwashed by Judaeo-Christian stereotypes,' interrupted an imperious lady in purple sunglasses and a black Montez turban.

She spoke with a familiar metallic drawl. Laszlo, startled by the authority of her voice and the luminosity of her glacial, moon-white face, knew instinctively that she was a person of some significance. A woman with star quality. Where had he seen those plushy red lips before?

'Why the hell shouldn't the most important human incarnation,' she demanded, 'be a broad-shouldered, bisexual kid who can run, swim, fight and make love? A super life-enhancing hero with gleaming white teeth and a lot of balls.'

'I would have expected,' Laszlo said defensively, 'a messiah to be more pacific and spiritual.'

'That's coded language for a wimp,' the woman snapped. 'Who the shit needs a messiah incapable of strangling a lion or giving dames the ecstasy of multi-orgs? My contender is right out of the Ramayana.'

'But in the final analysis,' Laszlo argued, 'he's no more than a character in a Shilverman film.'

She looked at him with contempt.

'We're making a film about the final chapter of human history,' she said slowly, 'as it actually happens.'

Madame Dunkelbaum intervened as the woman turned away.

'That was Medusa O'Toole,' she told him.

Laszlo nodded glumly. He'd failed to recognise one of the ikons of the twentieth century.

'She vibrates with power,' Laszlo conceded.

'Pure goodness,' Madame Dunkelbaum reflected. 'It comes with living a blameless life.'

The buzzing intensified. Laszlo sensed it was being directed at the man who looked like Bandito and was now standing not far behind him.

'The short guy behind us,' he murmured, 'appears to be fascinated with me.'

She glanced around quickly.

'That's Sunburn Spillano,' she whispered. 'If he wasn't financially sterile, he'd be the President of the Spillano Garbage Corporation.'

The information chilled Laszlo's heart. He knew Spillano's name well from his investigations for the First Nag and Waik.

'Why is he staring at me?' Laszlo asked nervously.

'He's a homophile,' she replied with a reassuring smile.

Spillano was now beside them. He stared at Laszlo closely.

'I couldn't help hearing you mention the name of Bunny Selveratnam a moment ago,' Spillano rasped. 'Are you acquainted with this banana?'

'He was a waiter at the Thali of Boundless Light, an Indian restaurant in London.'

Spillano nodded. 'Crystal Palace.'

'Right,' replied Laszlo.

'And have you seen this guy recently?'

Laszlo shook his head, ignoring the screaming inside it.

'Not for many years,' he said.

Sunburn Spillano looked solemn.

'You know something, Steffi? They say it's a small world. The truth is, it's not much bigger than a fish's asshole.'

He considered Laszlo carefully. 'You from Crystal Palace?'

Laszlo moved his head vigorously from side to side. 'I once had a girl-friend who lived there. We used to eat at the Thali of Boundless Light.' He managed to squeeze out a relaxed grin.

'This dame you were horsing around with,' Spillano said. 'She wasn't called Maya Gabor, by any chance?'

Laszlo took a deep breath, dazed for a moment. But he managed to shake his head.

'I've never heard of her,' he muttered. 'The girl I knew was a Hindu.'

Selveratnam's babble now almost drowned his thoughts. Spillano did not hide his perplexity.

'Maya Gabor had a son,' Spillano mused, 'somebody called Laszlo. You ever run across a schmuck by that name?'

'It's hardly the sort of name one would forget,' Laszlo said, troubled by his lower bowel.

He was thankful that Princess Lola was by his side. He introduced her to Spillano.

'Did you say Princess Lola d'Aoili-Flute of Esterel and Lhasa?' Spillano asked, shaking her hand very slowly.

'That's right,' Laszlo replied. 'My father was Colonel Agamemnon Flute of the Tibetan Diplomatic Mission.'

Spillano appraised Laszlo and Lola with an enigmatic grin.

'Now if you guys had dreamed all those names up,' he said, 'they couldn't have been prettier.'

'We'll take that as a compliment,' Princess Lola laughed, gazing at Spillano with undiluted admiration. 'You remind me of somebody I once knew during the war,' she added, stricken by his resemblance to Benito Bandito.

But Sunburn Spillano, suddenly alarmed by her infatuated attention, seemed anxious to disengage himself from her threatened reminiscences. He moved off with the remark that he hoped his doppelganger was a good-looking banana.

'He was. He was,' Princess Lola called after him with emotion that Laszlo considered a little unseemly.

Madame Dunkelbaum reassured him with a smile, and the princess, her face touched by dreams, meandered into the park to hear the ghost poet's recital. When she had disappeared, Madame Dunkelbaum suggested to Laszlo that she'd seen Princess Lola somewhere in the past. He shrugged, reminding her that Esterel wasn't too far along the coast.

Madame Dunkelbaum led him to a large painting of the September 1938 Nuremberg Rally. It was a magnificent naturalistic piece of work, glittering with menace. Laszlo estimated that it was about thirty feet by twenty.

'Hengist's meditation piece,' she said. 'Medusa considers that it is important to have at least one dark artefact in the home as a reminder of our flawed natures and the possibility of a terrible destiny.'

'It certainly has an apocalyptic feel.'

'It hurts me if I stare at it for more than a minute. Some people

219

cannot breathe if they stay beside it too long. Medusa considers that the last fifty years or so have been a mistake. It would have been more appropriate if the Third Reich had immediately preceded the Final Conjunction.'

He raised his brows, abased by a crazy caprice to fuck her that instant, to take her on the floor before everyone, a need that was communicated by a wistful and vulnerable look. Her apprehension was immediate.

'The coupling of Uranus and Gaia,' she pattered on in a vague, confused sort of way. 'Heaven and Earth. Like in the nursery story, Chicken Licken, Chicken Licken, the sky is falling down. You see, filmically, the Nuremberg Rallies should march us towards a conclusion. Towards the end.'

She waved an elucidatory hand, murmuring that it made artistic sense. His desires slid urgently into hers, jigging between the ardour of bucking haunches. He was trembling slightly as he lit a cigarette, catching the odour of fresh oysters from the space between them.

'Medusa says that the last fifty years will probably finish up on the cutting-room floor. Banjo picks.'

'But how can one cut history?'

'History,' she said, pausing for a moment as she weighed the word in her mouth, 'history is only the story that one chooses to receive. The Machine is in here,' she said, tapping her head. 'It's a montage of dream-memory, film-memory, imperfectly remembered literature, personal reflections, newsreel fictions and the longueurs of real-time fillers. The history we teach our children is as much an invention as the most improbable Shilverman fantasy.'

She paused and raised her head, wiggling her fingers to acknowledge the dark, curly-headed Wolfgang.

'Ferrari is watching us,' she murmured. 'He has a sixth sense where I am concerned. I have to be cautious. He probably suspects that I've devoted too much time to you. For while my husband, Hengist, doesn't mind within reason who I spend my time with, my polysexual lover is outrageously jealous.'

'Is Wolfgang Ferrari your lover?' Laszlo asked, slightly dismayed.

'Not exclusively, of course,' Steffi Dunkelbaum smiled. 'But my present arrangements with him are fairly convenient, as Hengist appears to be interested in Wolfgang's wife, Polly. Incidentally, you look a bit like Wolfgang around the eyes.'

'I've already been told that,' Laszlo said sulkily. 'They're not my strong point.'

He was suddenly saddened that Maya was not there with him. She would have loved to meet the great Ferrari.

Steffi directed him with a guarded nod towards the balcony, glancing back into the crowded room before speaking.

'Poor Hengist,' she confided, 'is a little bruised by press comment about his financial support of a new political alliance of the right. He has always dreamed of a marching party with crisp uniforms, polished boots and well-constructed young men, strong enough to safeguard the fabric of human achievement. But the history of the mid-twentieth century has directed people's enthusiasms away from overt displays of patriotism and pride. Hengist fears we have become effete. "As squashy as the mildewed underclasses" was his memorable phrase.'

'But have we forgotten the terrible consequences of the Third Reich?' Laszlo asked softly, aroused once more by the ripeness of her red lips and the sunlight defining the contours of her large breasts.

'There were mistakes, of course,' she conceded, stroking his cock with her palm the moment they passed behind a column. 'Racism is clearly inefficient. We are all marchers now. Pinks, browns, yellows, blacks and all conceivable permutations of humanity. The new order will not be developed on the basis of race.'

'Oh?'

He rubbed a thumb against her dress, encircling a nipple. She looked around quickly and caught her breath as his hand lightly stroked her belly. They heard voices in the garden and drew apart.

'There is only one division that makes any sense,' she said rather loudly, more for those they could not see.

Laszlo eyed her with interest.

'Who then,' he asked, 'would be excluded from the new order?'

'The anarchic poor,' she declared with a glint of purpose in her eyes. 'Our snivelling have-nots will always be a problem until we've dealt with them. I mean the troublemakers who question the creation of personal wealth and the feckless rabble who would rather beg and rob than work.'

'And you really believe that?' he asked, sipping a ratafia he'd flighted off the server of a passing waitress.

She lowered her head.

'It's wrong to be so serious,' she said. 'We should be talking about more pleasant things.'

'Perhaps our destinies might overlap for a while,' he suggested, pressing himself gently against her when he was certain that they were unobserved.

They went down the steps into the garden as the other guests prepared to leave. He noticed that Princess Lola was walking arm in arm with Izzy Dollar's phantom, the eagle-faced old poet who was now showing off an enormous black hat. His white magisterial beard was shaped like a spear, and the scuffed brown cords and Brownwich Village cravat had a dated Bohemian charm. She was proud, the princess later informed Laszlo, to have walked with the spirit of the legendary Izzy Dollar, international genius, poet, maker of the infamous *Cuntos*, a work reviled, censored and burnt before the Vee-Sign War but which was now a standard Eng. Lit. text in most universities.

The histrionic Dollar's sepulchral tenor reached them as he declaimed to Princess Lola among the jacarandas.

> 'I have fucked women in three tongues,
> Sanscrit, Xhosa and Pali,
> Now I sing of the girls,
> Sweet as marachinos
> That I ate as a finale.'

'My mother and I,' Laszlo whispered to Steffi Dunkelbaum, 'have to leave St Tropez in three days.'

There was no equivocation in her reply.

'Tomorrow then,' she said. 'The restaurant Chez Guignard at Châteauneuf le Rosé. It's a longish drive, but I have to be careful. I should make it by noon.'

'I'll find it,' he assured her.

As they made their way to the car-park, Princess Lola apologised to Laszlo for leaving him with Madame Dunkelbaum.

'You looked so utterly bored. I suppose she was boasting about her daughter winning the junior windsurfing championship.'

'Oh no,' he replied, 'she was showing me her baguenadier arcade.'

Princess Lola laughed as they escaped from the Dunkelbaum fastness in a cloud of hot dust and Daimler fumes.

The next day, Steffi Dunkelbaum was pacing nervously about the car-park of Chez Guignard. She looked cool in a simple cream cotton dress and thong sandles that displayed her attractive feet and pink-enamelled toes to advantage. Laszlo was certain that her hair had been cut and rinsed a shade lighter since the previous afternoon. And to ensure he had not grotesquely misunderstood her signalled intentions, she ambushed him behind the privacy of an engrailed wall screened with red and white oleander blossoms. The moist succulence of her kiss on his surprised mouth provoked him. He had always found that the first meeting of mouths between new lovers had an intensity and promise that remained memorable when more intimate encounters had been forgotten. After lunch, they drove to a nearby motel and stayed for five hours.

'I have been waiting all my life for you,' she said as they lay in the long, coffin-like room, their bodies tacky and languid with love-making.

And if this observation was slightly flatulent, it was the sort of post-orgasmic effusion Steffi felt lovers expected.

After Laszlo's return to Mushington Hall, their meetings alternated between Paris and an apartment Steffi had inherited from her father in Martigues. Laszlo was never quite sure whether he looked forward more to the prospect of the amatory attentions Steffi expected or to the warm fishy smell of the Mediterranean and the marvellous Mulet à la Martégale they invariably enjoyed at a favourite restaurant on the front. In Paris, they patronised grander establishments, making do with Tendrons de Veau Marengo or boring Gigot à la Bretonne, washed down with the atrociously expensive château clarets on which Steffi doted. She always took good care to pay in cash. They were caught more than once passing a fistful of notes when the bill arrived. The waiters were inured to such practices and Laszlo was sanguine about the occasional scandalised look from those who lived more sheltered lives. The thought that Steffi treated him like a gigolo not only nourished his sense of drollery but invested their affair with a piquancy that sustained it well beyond what would have been his normal period of tolerance.

Chapter 29

Princess Lola adored Mushington. She advised Laszlo that it would be unwise to trust Bagshawe with much of the more simple landscaping she had in mind and felt that it would be prudent to enlist the services of a firm of garden architects from Fontainebleau.

'Simplicity, darling, is much too complex a matter to be entrusted to amateurs,' she said.

But Bagshawe, being a placid man and almost entirely untroubled by bright ideas, was the ideal candidate for maintaining the place. She was particularly concerned about reshaping the prospect from the long drawing-room and her bedroom suite directly above it. It was here that she wanted a two-tier medieval lawn, a gentle slope leading to a lower plateau. Stone steps were planned from the patio down to the level ground, with a path to the perimeter wall. She had, after much thought, decided against a bower, as dripping leaves reminded her of her sister's grave in the family wood near Tourettes-sur-Loup, the interment having taken place during a wet October when her black silk funeral blouse had been stained by the rust of the water shaken from the autumnal oaks. The Archduke Norbert, noticing the bespattered garment at a bar where the family later gathered for a valedictory eau-de-vie, said to her: 'Those are the tears of angels, my child.' In consequence, the blouse was never washed, but donated as a holy object to the gipsy church at Coqauvin, where it acquired a modest celebrity for the alleviation of herpes and mouth ulcers.

She spoke earnestly to Bagshawe.

'Do you understand the distinction between an authentic medieval lawn and the modern desecration of grass that passes for one?'

He eyed her wildly for a moment, managing a suitable deferential look before he cleared his throat. He seemed nervous.

'Perhaps madam would refresh my memory,' he murmured.

She frowned irritably at the vulgarity of the address.

'Officially,' she explained, 'I am Your Royal Highness, but as a dispensation not generally accorded to menials of your rank, you may address me as Princess. A madam, Bagshawe, is the female who manages the interests of hookers and their clients in a fuck-parlour. Comprenez?'

'Princess,' he breathed tremulously.

She smiled generously, adding that her comments were not intended to disparage what was after all an ancient profession, dignified by references in the holiest of books, but that since she could not escape the distinction of her birth, it was only equitable that those less fortunate than her should not avoid their obligations of respect. Bagshawe was abased by the facility of her logic.

'A medieval lawn,' she declared, 'is hand-sheared, ideally sickle-sheared. It has a coarse but even finish. Have you got a sickle?'

'A sickle, Princess?'

'That's right. One of those curved blades.'

He waved a hand across the two acres of proposed lawn behind the house.

'It's a vast area, Princess,' he murmured politely.

'Hire some village idiots. Half a dozen maybe to help you out. One shear a week should be dandy. I don't want to maintain too extravagant a finish.'

'In my opinion,' said Bagshawe, 'we could probably achieve the same coarse effect from a mower that has been specially adjusted.'

'You want to cheat?' she asked in horror.

'I have a sciatic condition,' he informed her in a low and piteous voice.

'Get the others to do the bending. You just walk around with a cattle-prod and supervise.'

On the lower lawn, Princess Lola planned to sink an oval shubunkin pond that would be graced by the crouching black marble Ondine she had persuaded Laszlo to buy in the Portobello

Road for twelve hundred pounds. From her hall-porter's chair (she was profoundly susceptible to English draughts) she hoped to enjoy the view of a seven-foot-high granite dolmen (actually a Shiva lingam from Trichinoply smuggled out in fifteen separate pieces) that she hoped to reconstitute and erect at the midway point of the boundary wall. Along this border, she proposed to have salvias, lupins and hollyhocks, with clumps of larkspur, lobelia and verbena arranged along the sides to the upper lawn. In the beds by the steps, she thought chrysanthemums, camomiles, zinnias and candytuft bordered with lavender-blue asters might work. But green, vast expanses of emerald-green plush, was dear to her heart.

'I am hot for a weeping willow or two,' she confessed to Laszlo, 'but I fear the effect would be grossly sentimental.'

Princess Lola was acutely aware of her native sentimentality and made virtuous efforts to subdue what Laszlo considered to be its more risible manifestations, like her passion for violets pressed behind glass, dreary paintings of bearded men in oilskin capes, and wide-eyed anaemic children touched by the damp promise of early graves. He mocked her tears when she described the raw, windbitten scrotums of young gipsies, donkeys coupling in a misty field, or recalled sleeping with some unseen lover in a dark, airless room that smelled of sour wine, cigarettes and squashed bugs. But he was amused by her stories of her paradise lost and was careful to spoil her with an affectionate squeeze if he suspected that he had gone too far with his gentle derision. She had persuaded him to have constructed at Mushington Hall an outdoor privy, no more than a simple Asiatic hole. Reluctantly conceding a flush, she insisted on a pail of water instead of toilet-paper for her post-excretory ablutions. And instead of a door, she favoured a myrtle hedge which gave her the glorious sensation of shitting in a beautiful valley of the Alpes-Maritimes. Princess Lola deplored the cultural consequences of toilet technology in Europe.

'There were times,' she declared, 'when doing one's job in the fields was obligatory, for what public toilets there were, were unapproachable for pyramids of turds and lakes of orange piss.

227

Indeed, one of the upper tributaries of the Loire has been almost wholly uric for two thousand years or more, resulting in a sub-species of carp so adapted to ammoniac liquid that a unique mutant has evolved called Truite de Pissoir, with three gold dorsal bars and a blue feathery tail. This almost boneless wonder is served in the more discriminating restaurants of the Ardèche.'

She reflected gloomily that efficient sanitary and sewage-disposal systems had driven the alfresco performers indoors, to the detriment of the great food and wine which human manuring produces. At least a dozen pre-1947 clarets owed their celebrity to the reservoirs of piddle to which their root systems had access. And of course there was the social cohesion that communal defecation inspired. While one could quarrel bitterly with a person whose acquaintance was restricted to café or salon, it was difficult to be acrimonious for long with someone whose intimacy was sustained by the daily contiguity necessary during the shared experience of bowel and bladder evacuation.

Chapter 30

Despite the preferred use of her maiden name, Thelma de Bereenbroeck was married. She was, in fact, Mrs Chancer, wife of Bevan Chancer, the Manager of Corporate Banking at the First Nagasaki and Waikiki Trust. Although this marriage had decayed significantly, it was still in the tenuous phase when the partners were careful not to be extravagantly venturesome or cruelly overt in their respective fornications.

The cycle of events that had brought the luminous Thelma into the equation, started with her Origami evenings on Fridays. Her Conversational Portuguese classes were already dedicated to Bricuse, the long-distance lorry-driver. But the Origami evenings provided the time and opportunity to expand her experience and to direct an innocuous workplace friendship with Arvie Stundish towards more sensual tributaries. For although the investments of the venerous Bricuse gave her great joy, Thelma had long lusted after a mate who shared her wider interests. The transition of her relationship with Stundish from one that involved strolling in the park, throwing bread at aquatic fowls, solving the *Guardian* crossword together and debating the crisis of Liberalism, to whispered confessions about her need to have expensive lingerie defiled, an admission that led rapidly to coupling on Stundish's narrow bed, below a pigeon-beshitten skylight, did not take overlong. Hardly two months. For when Thelma eventually presented herself at Stundish's Islington attic apartment at Origami time (seven p.m. on Fridays), there seemed little doubt in their minds as to how the next two hours should be employed. No sooner had the door been opened to admit Thelma than it was closed behind her; no sooner had the latch been drawn than they embraced; no sooner had they embraced than they undressed (in Thelma's case down to her mushroom panties); and no sooner had Arvie's impassioned teeth ripped away the vulnerable lace around her crotch than they set about fucking with febrile ferocity.

And if it was Stundish who talked a great deal about the remarkable Rock-Doctor, it was Thelma who first questioned his authenticity.

'I wouldn't be surprised if the young bugger was a crook,' she mused, reclining beside him in a tangle of damp sheets and entwined legs.

'Do you think I should speak to the police?' he asked anxiously.

'Don't be an absolute donkhead,' she sighed. 'This could be the chance both of us need. An opportunity to begin a new life.'

'It's risky,' he murmured.

'Well, if you haven't got the pendant bits to handle it,' she said, 'I think I know somebody who has.'

'Messing about with a client's funds is hardly the sort of thing a bank manager should undertake lightly.'

'There's a big-shot laundryman at Bevan's bank.'

'Jesus Christ, if that husband of yours even suspected that we were up to anything like this, he'd shop us. Me certainly.'

Thelma informed him that Bevan was the last person she'd take into her confidence. She suggested approaching Sam Yamaha, the Director of Non-Standard Funding at the First Nag and Waik, whom she'd met once or twice at bank dinners. The prospect of involving the director of a major bank in a shady deal alarmed Stundish. But Thelma was convinced that she could do a deal with the Japanese. She tried to cheer Stundish with the promise of a villa in the Algarve and the prospect of golf in the Iberian sun. But he was a timorous fellow, easily abased by the implications of such audacious villainy, taking a pessimistic view of his own capacity to see a project of such magnitude through to its dénouement.

Thelma reached for his pliant cock.

'What's the matter?' she asked irritably, tugging at the rubbery tube.

'I'm shit-scared,' he confessed.

*

Thelma found Sam Yamaha charming. He remembered her instantly. They arranged to meet for tea at the Ritz, squeezing hands inside the Piccadilly entrance. She was cheered by the profusion of mirrors, chandeliers, florid plasterwork and flowers. He escorted her past fuchsine velvet chairs and curtains, through to the showy Palm Court where he had booked their table under a life-size gilded statue of a vacuous, slack-mouthed nymph with a rapturous ascendant gaze. Thelma was quietly impressed by its vulgar vitality, despite her suspicion that the breasts had been machined on a capstan lathe.

The short, squarely built Japanese was agreeably attentive. She found his wistful stares flattering and quite unprovocative. There was an underlying subversive quality in his strong, broad face, and although his dignity was elegantly addressed by a suit of cinereous bespoke, an institutional tie (cerise and gentian diagonals), and girasol lapel-pin with matching cuff-links, the freshly cut Baccara in his buttonhole hinted at an antique raffishness. He was tolerably well-preserved for a man of sixty, the grey en brosse hair still luxuriant, the crinkled brown hands veinous, well-maintained and distinguished by a dappling of liver spots.

'Of course, there will be difficulties, Mrs Chancer,' he murmured.

'I would prefer to be called Miss de Bereenbroeck,' she said. 'Thelma, if you so wish.'

'Ah.'

Yamaha waited briefly for an explanation, smiling obliquely when none was forthcoming.

'Have either you or Mr Standish . . .' he continued.

'Stundish.'

'Have either of you been approached by a man, a diminutive Indian called Selveratnam?'

She shook her head.

'Just Flute, the young diamond-cutter, the man we call the Rock-Doctor. He was the one who deposited the Swiss bearer bonds.'

Yamaha looked interested.

'Did he deposit any diamonds? Perhaps a single stone?'

'There's nothing but bonds in the box,' she said.

'Are you aware that an extremely important stone called the Twinkle of Fatima has been taken from the Kulhanian Institute of Decorative Arts in Lisbon?'

'I've read about it in the papers.'

'There's a great deal of focus at present on the more mysterious members of the diamond profession.'

'Are you suggesting that Flute sold the Twinkle of Fatima for sixty million Swiss francs?'

'No, I'm not,' Yamaha smiled. 'You see, Thelma, I happen to know that the bonds were stolen while they were on their way to me.'

'You?' she gasped, shaken.

'Please, don't be disturbed. Your instincts were correct in the first place. This man Flute is a crook. He's probably an accomplice of Selveratnam, who's become a very hot property in certain quarters.'

'What do you suggest?' she asked.

'Replace the bonds with blanks. I'll arrange a tail for Flute after he discovers the bonds have gone. There's no hurry. We'll pick him up at his house and float around after him for a while.'

She thought Yamaha's plan of pursuit sounded rather vague and disingenuous. A suspicion that he was not madly interested in Flute, only the bonds, suggested itself to her. She looked at him expectantly.

'Let's come to the point of this meeting,' he said. 'The price for your co-operation is fifty thousand pounds.' He paused for several moments, waiting for her response.

'You can cut that which way you choose. Forty to you and ten to Stundish, or any other combination you fancy. I still have the option, of course, of going to the police.'

'Why the police? We've not committed a crime.'

'You've offered to sell me some hot bonds, darling.'

She looked concerned. Yamaha squeezed her hand. It was a gesture of complicity.

'Fifty thousand is a lot of money, Thelma,' he smiled.

'Okay,' she whispered.

'We'll drive to the First Nagasaki after we've finished tea. I'll pick up the cash and then we'll drive to Brinkleys and replace the bonds. You're a very lucky lady. Now, I suggest you phone Stundish and arrange access to Flute's box. There's a phone just outside.'

Thelma de Bereenbroeck rose and hurried out to the call-box. Stundish's voice sounded thin and nervous.

'Thelma? Where are you?'

'We're still at the Ritz. He's talking about calling the police.'

'Christ.'

'But I've talked him into giving you something to allow him to replace the bonds.'

'I don't want to get involved.'

'But you are involved, Stunny.'

'This is dreadful.'

'He's prepared to go to five thousand. Enough to enable you to get out of the way until things blow over. You can go to Portugal.'

'And what about you?'

'Mr Yamaha has asked me to hang around until Flute makes a reappearance. Besides, darling, how far will five thousand go between the two of us? He tells me that there is a possibility the cache is the property of a dangerous thug called Selveratnam, a guy who will stop at nothing.'

'Thelma, this is crazy. Suddenly I can hardly breathe for worry. I haven't had an asthma attack since I was a boy and all this trouble is bringing one on. Why the hell should I screw myself up like this?'

'Drop out for a while, like I said. Crash a few balls down the fairway. Sod around in the sun. By next week you could be a thousand miles away.'

'Let's call this nonsense off, Thelma.'

'You know we can't, darling.'

'Thelma?'

Icy despair gripped his heart as she put the phone down on him.

She joined Yamaha, who was just polishing off his third

frangipane tartlet. He brushed the crumbs from his lips with a serviette.

'He's terribly nervous, Mr Yamaha,' she admitted ruefully.

He gave her a smoky, cinematic look, his fingers reaching out to touch hers. It was sneakily done, between the silver cake-stand and the Minton teapot.

'Are you happy with your side of the deal, my dear?' he asked, the solicitous murmur surprising her with its darker register. It was, she learned later, his mating voice.

She gave him a reassuring smile.

'Everything seems fine, Mr Yamaha.'

'Good,' he growled, 'good.'

He looked at his watch and frowned.

'We'd better get started. There's money to pick up before we call at Brinkleys.'

Yamaha was a fast worker. Thelma waited for him in the taxi while he shot into the First Nagasaki. Barely ten minutes later he handed her a treasury pouch and a manila envelope.

'The envelope is for Stundish's cut,' he smiled. 'I suggest you do the split before we get to Brinkleys. Incidentally, it's in Scottish hundreds for convenience.'

She counted out fifty hundreds and slid them into the envelope. Yamaha watched her with admiration. She gave him a quick smile as she stuffed the balance from the treasury pouch into her capacious shoulder-bag.

'I've always liked ladies who know what they are worth,' he observed.

'I hope Stunny doesn't give any trouble.'

'It should go like clockwork, Thelma,' he declared, extracting an envelope from his pocket. 'The blanks,' he explained.

Yamaha placed a hand lightly on her knee. 'I must admit to envying Bevan Chancer when we first met at Toshiro Harada's silver jubilee.'

'The Hyde Park Hotel, wasn't it?'

He nodded, gently exploring the underside of her thigh.

234

'You took my breath away. Somebody told me that Chancer had married a Japanese girl. I've never been too keen on my own countrywomen. But when I saw you, I knew you weren't Japanese. You're Eurasian, aren't you?'

'Yes. My mother is Chinese and my father is Dutch. I'm rather less exotic. I grew up in Balham.'

'A wonderful cocktail. Chancer must be incredibly jealous of you,' he suggested, massaging her flesh lightly.

'We're almost at the stage of going our own ways. It was never a successful marriage.'

'Why don't you call me Sam, eh?'

'Sam?'

'Sure. We could have a nice time together.'

Thelma lifted her leg slightly, wondering how far his emprise would lead him. The first tentative explorations of men always amused her. She caught the driver's eye in the mirror. A plump Semitic guy with dark, heavy-lidded eyes and a Maxim Gorky moustache. He had a sad humour in his soft, pampered face. Yamaha's hand moved up to her yoke. She felt warm.

'There's a lot more where that fifty K came from,' he whispered. 'After we've sorted out Stundish and the bonds, I'll take you to see my collection of inflatables. Real life-size dolls.' He grinned. A twisted, sideways one.

'Are they what I think they are?' she asked, giving him a sly, lascivious look.

He nodded.

'They're masterpieces. They've got everything a lonely man needs.'

'Not tonight,' she said, remembering Bricuse. 'I've got my class in Conversational Portuguese.'

She drew his hand away as the taxi stopped. The driver turned around. He gave them a lugubrious look. He had seen most of the action through the mirror, but knew instinctively that flippancy would not be a good idea. Old guy. Young girl. Besides, he had more important fish to fry. He gave Yamaha a pliant, submissive look, smelling the bonus. A big tip. He was right. Yamaha peeled him a tenner for a three-pound fare.

235

'Keep the change,' the Japanese grunted.

The driver watched them jinx up the steps to Brinkley's. He slid down the cab windows and wafted a copy of the *Daily Mirror* around. The air was doped with perfume and aftershave. He turned up the ventilator fan, then got out and opened the rear doors. That kind of stink gave him hay-fever. After he'd scrambled back into his seat, he made a telephone call. It was answered instantly.

'Sheik Yusuf?' the driver asked quietly.

When Yamaha got back to his place with the bonds, Sunburn Spillano telephoned again. He was in a restless and dangerous mood. For some weeks now, Yamaha had had to endure Spillano's malefic brooding.

'Has that son of a fucking whore Selveratnam shown up yet?'

'It's a mystery, Sunburn. Selveratnam is not the kind of rabbit to go down a hole.'

'He was with your man Laszlo Gabor. Those bastards are running together. I'm putting tails on every rat-faced sonofabitch involved.'

'Maybe they'll turn up, Sunburn.'

'That's a very unwise observation to make, Sam. And out of kilter with your usual sharp predictive insights.'

'I was whistling, Sunburn.'

'Maybe,' Spillano snapped. 'And how was tea at the Ritz?'

Yamaha paused just an instant before answering the unexpected question.

'It's always very special there, Sunburn. I had three frangipane tartlets.'

'At the Ritz?'

'I ordered them for the occasion.'

After their conversation, Yamaha reflected that he could be at the start of an extremely tedious phase. He suspected that Sunburn would not relax until he'd nailed Selveratnam and Gabor. Most of the time Yamaha did not feel unduly threatened. He was not given to needless apprehension. He did worry just a little, though, about Spillano's unexpected reference to the Ritz. He recalled the plump taxi-driver with the heavy-lidded eyes and Maxim Gorky moustache, remembering that he appeared to be waiting for them in his car outside the hotel. He wondered whether he was Spillano's man, deciding, however, after some thought, that the idea was improbable. But he would have given the contents of a fat wallet to have been able to see the face that asked the question. And he sincerely hoped that Mr Spillano wasn't smiling when he did so.

Chapter 31

Laszlo's mind had been strongly exercised by the prospect of converting the Swiss franc bonds into sterling as soon as possible. Until this step had been taken, his worth was no more than an abstraction – pieces of paper without the easy convertibility of a domestic bank balance.

He dropped into Brinkleys to see his friendly bank manager. Since his first visit, they'd established quite a rapport on the phone and had even made tentative arrangements to play squash together. The manager enjoyed Laszlo's stories about the diamond market as much as Laszlo relished telling them. Laszlo was therefore surprised to find the manager's office occupied by a substantial gentleman with an ominously red face, pulpy nose, close-cropped grey hair and bulbous blue eyes, magnified by the thick lenses of his spectacles. He held the card an inch or two from his eyes with the uncertainty of someone who was partially sighted. He half rose as Laszlo came through the door.

'Mr Flute?' he checked in a gravelly voice bruised by nicotine and undiluted spirits. He thrust out the brutish paw of a front-row forward and announced himself. 'Jesperson.'

'I was expecting to see Mr Standish,' Laszlo mumbled, forgetting then incorrectly remembering his young friend's name.

'You mean Stundish,' Jesperson corrected. 'Went off to foreign parts last week to skive for a firm of port-shippers, I understand. Lucky sod.' He managed a phlegmy laugh. 'What can we do for you?'

'I have some Swiss bonds in my deposit box,' Laszlo explained, crossing his legs to exhibit the yellow and red spangled socks the princess had bought him for his birthday.

Jesperson tried to focus on the unexpected blur of colour, sensing vaguely that there was an indecorous dimension to his visitor's apparel.

'Deposit boxes, or at least the contents therein, are not our concern, old chap,' he crackled, sticking a fag in his mouth and jabbing the packet towards Laszlo.

Jesperson lit them both with a trembling hand.

'Your key, your loot. We're not interested, not unless some charlie tries to jemmy one open during office hours. I'm here to help you with the other bits. The giving and taking of funds, so to speak. Do you need an overdraft or a loan?'

Laszlo shook his head.

'That's the spirit,' Jesperson wheezed.

He slid the data-card closer, angling it away from the reflected light of his desk-lamp.

'And how long have you been in the ballast business?'

Stundish, the previous manager, a young man who temperamentally perhaps was a shade frivolous for a major clearing bank, had inscribed 'Rock-Doctor' on the card, doodling a chain of rectangles with sparkle dashes around each one.

'Rocks, is it?' Jesperson enquired finally with a crushed look in his eyes.

'Diamonds.'

Jesperson's jowls wobbled. He scratched his pulpy nose.

'Wrong end of the what-have-you, old chap. Sorry.'

'Not at all.'

'Hardly got my corns under the table. Only took over from, er, the other fellow last week. Used to be in Singapore. Ten years. Know the place? No?'

Laszlo shook his head.

'Hot. Very hot, but devilishly clean. They run a helluva tight ship out there.'

Jesperson glanced at his watch three times. Laszlo smiled amiably.

'Is there anything else we can er . . .'

'I'd like to cash some foreign bonds.'

'Bonds? Oh? How much are we talking about?'

'Sixty million Swiss francs.'

Jesperson jerked his head back, trying to zero in on his visitor's face. He was surprised to find that, from one projection, Laszlo's features were those of a famous film-star.

239

He changed the perspective, lowering his head and moving it slowly over the desk. Jesperson had been despondent for months about his deteriorating sight, but the thought of an ophthalmist's verdict gave him the shakes. Strangely enough, after three double scotches his vision seemed to improve dramatically. The problem, his live-in friend Peggy suggested, could be his nerves, like his impotence and facial neuralgia. He crushed out one cigarette and lit another.

'Sixty million. Tidy sum that.'

'Yes.'

'You want it on sterling deposit?'

'I suppose so.'

'Well, if you bring them from your box, we'll take things from there. Couldn't do it today, of course. A week all right?'

'Fine.'

Jesperson stood, stumbling as he trapped his thighs against the desk. He rang a bell. A lissom, almond-eyed girl in a grey costume appeared.

'Miss de Bereenbroeck,' Jesperson said, 'will you please show Mr Flute to the safe-deposit room.'

He waved a hand affably in Laszlo's direction.

'Pop back with them when you're ready.'

Laszlo followed the girl down the corridor.

'Do you have your number?' she lisped, looking at him.

'I'll be OK,' he assured her with a low smile, his appreciative gaze lingering on her longer than was really necessary. Miss de Bereenbroeck had a silky fall to her straight black hair, full lips touched with pink and eyes of liquid amber. He withdrew the envelope and, slitting it open, took out the twenty pieces of paper. As he glanced at them, he suddenly went cold. In the first place, the paper had a pinkish tinge to the edges that he didn't remember. In the second place, there was no reference to Swiss francs anywhere. They were blank. He went through the sheets carefully several times, lifting them one by one to the light. Miss de Bereenbroeck watched him intently. The sixty million Swiss francs had been replaced by twenty blank pieces of paper. He thought instantly of Stundish, sunning his thieving arse somewhere on the Iberian peninsula. The paper fell from his nerveless fingers across the floor.

'Is anything the matter?' Miss de Bereenbroeck asked.

'I've been robbed,' Laszlo muttered pensively.

'You'd better see Mr Jesperson,' she suggested anxiously.

Laszlo did not answer for some time. He stood motionless, deep in thought. Then, very slowly, he retrieved the scattered pieces of paper. He slid them back in the envelope. He suspected that Fate, or somebody acting on Fate's behalf, had dealt him a retributive blow for which an immediate remedy seemed improbable. He could hardly go to the police, or advertise too publicly his misfortune, without attracting the attention of people who could be interested in the whereabouts of Bunny Selveratnam. He replaced the envelope in the box and locked it.

'Do you want to see Mr Jesperson?' she enquired.

Laszlo shook his head.

Miss de Bereenbroeck accompanied Laszlo to the foyer and allowed herself a sly smile as she watched the confused young man venture out into the bright autumn morning. She waited until his introspective figure walked slowly through a flutter of sunlit pigeons to merge with the progress of scurrying commuters. It was time, she reflected, to make a phone-call. A simple message was left on Sam Yamaha's answering-machine. 'The Rock-Doctor called,' she enunciated carefully. Unfortunately, only minutes before Thelma de Bereenbroeck had transmitted this intelligence, the intended recipient was being wheeled into a morgue.

Chapter 32

The loss of the Swiss bearer bonds had disturbed Laszlo rather less than he imagined it would. He sometimes half believed that they had not been there in the first place and were merely one of Selveratnam's feats of legerdemain. Certainly matters could have been worse. He was hardly destitute and had begun to lead the gentleman's life to which he'd once aspired, alternating between Mushington with Princess Lola and his trips to France to visit Steffi Dunkelbaum. Unsurprisingly, after rather more than two years of this undemanding existence, he grew morbidly restless. While Princess Lola thrived, more than content to run the show at Mushington, Laszlo suspected that he needed something more. A business perhaps. It was a thought that preoccupied his mind a great deal.

It was Steffi who eventually warned Laszlo about Princess Lola's disreputable past. She raised the indelicate matter while she nestled on his shoulder below the blue silken tester and baroque immensity of her globe-trotting mama's bed.

'Is the princess really your mother?' she asked.

'Sure.'

'Hengist is certain that Lola was the woman who operated as a street-walker in Coqauvin twenty-five years ago.'

'He could be mistaken,' Laszlo protested.

'He could,' she agreed, 'but Hengist rarely forgets a woman's face once he has had sex with her.'

'And he did that with Princess Lola d'Aoili? My mother?'

She told Laszlo that when she disclosed that the princess was his mother, Hengist had laughed.

'I'm afraid,' she confided, 'that your alleged relationship with Lola excited his curiosity about you.'

Laszlo ran his fingers over the amplitude of Steffi Dunkelbaum's well-fleshed arse.

'I told him that you worked in Amsterdam as a diamond-cutter and that we were thinking of going into business together.'

Laszlo smiled.

'When can we start?' he enthused. 'It sounds like a wonderful idea.'

Steffi, owlishly solemn, chewed her lip. There appeared to be something else on her mind.

'Listen,' she murmured after a while, 'would you mind if I made a film of us making love? Something to play back when I'm on my own. I want a close-up of you entering me.' She sat up and pointed to the foot of the bed. 'I've got a camera there.'

'Christ!'

She giggled and indicated two other positions, one above the bed and the other on the wall closest to them, disclosing that the cameras should be activated by a bedside switch. When questioned, Steffi admitted that she had done it all before and confessed that, for her, the film of the act was of more importance than the act itself.

'It's closer to the kind of reality I crave,' she reflected.

'You needn't have told me,' he fussed.

She suggested that what was required was a pornographic effect and that could only be achieved if he was conscious of what he was doing. The pornography lay in the acting. He regarded her thoughtfully.

'I really don't mind, you know. I've always been a sort of actor manqué.'

She bit his ear joyfully and reproached him for being as soft as a snail. They embraced. Then she disengaged herself, leaning out of bed rather self-consciously, to press the switch. Laszlo found himself listening for the cameras. They were remarkably silent. Steffi lay back and made herself comfortable. Was she parting her thighs a shade wider than usual? he wondered. It was a thought he couldn't subdue. She offered him her mouth. He covered her lips with his, pushing his tongue against hers and sliding his inflated cock against her side. The realisation that they were being filmed provoked an erethistic threat that he struggled to contain by turning his mind to matters unrelated to their present

243

activity. He half-slitted his eyes as he mounted her, Steffi drawing his buttocks downwards and closer. He worked slowly inside her, contemplating the grotesque arabesques of the marquetry fashioned below the swags of the semi-lunar head-board. He was in the process of furnishing Mushington Hall with reproduction furniture, but this was the real thing. He had coveted Steffi's mother's bed from the moment he first saw it. Twelve generations of Malraux (Steffi's maiden name) had copulated, conceived and given birth in it. The idea had a simple grandeur that pleased him. He was captivated by continuity.

'Didn't you say,' he whispered, his mind quite taken with the felicity of the design, 'that this bed was the work of Boulle?'

Steffi shut her eyes and bucked wildly below him.

'What?'

'Seventeenth-century?'

She bit her lip and dug crimson nails into Laszlo's back as she jigged away urgently now, closing her dreams to his ruminations on French antique furniture.

'Merde,' she panted fiercely, convulsing to a final spasm.

Afterwards they lay, she in his arms, still and silent for several minutes.

'What are you thinking about?' Steffi asked eventually, dabbing at his damp hair with her fingertips.

'About how pleasant it's been these last three days,' he replied, demonstrating his tenderness by licking the dimple at the point of her nose.

It was perhaps a greyish lie, for at the moment Steffi had asked him the question, he had his mind on furniture, wondering how much the Louis Treize would make at auction. He had also made up his mind quite suddenly that three days was as much as he could take of her at a time. Steffi Dunkelbaum was beginning to bore him.

His affair with Steffi came to a sort of conclusion at Le Défi. They fucked again after that, a couple of times perhaps, but that's where it really ended. At Le Défi. They had just settled down to examine the carte when Steffi spotted Hengist, a second later than he had spotted her. He came towards them with his blonde companion, beaming affably.

'My God, he's with Polly,' Steffi whispered.

Laszlo turned his head quickly, following Steffi's gaze – and was dazed with unbelief when he caught sight of Polly Ferrari. She was a reincarnation of his beloved Maya. He could hardly breathe with excitement as she approached.

'Steffi, my darling,' she bubbled, 'how marvellous to bump into you like this.'

She leaned forward to kiss Steffi, nodding politely at Laszlo.

'It's been a day of the drollest coincidences. I discovered poor Hengist looking utterly miserable in the George Cinq bar this afternoon and absolutely insisted he brought me to Le Défi for dinner. I had come up to town to do some shopping and Hengist was involved in some dreary horse-trading.'

'I was arranging a nomination to a stallion,' he laughed. He looked quickly at Laszlo, shrewdly appraising the situation.

'I have a mare in season that requires covering,' he explained with a glint in his eye.

'Won't you join us?' Steffi invited.

It was an offer they couldn't refuse. Steffi laid her hand over Laszlo's. An audacious gesture.

'Tom has been helping me with some diamonds. He's an expert, you know. We may even go into business together. So, I thought it would be pleasant if we could round off our rather hectic day with a meal.'

Appearances having been managed to everybody's satisfaction, protocol now demanded that Hengist pay particular attention to his wife – something that he hadn't done for some time. Laszlo and Polly were obliged to make the most of the unusual circumstances. He sensed that she did not think a great deal of him, but was determined to change her mind. And Laszlo knew, the moment he held her in his arms on the dance-floor, that his life had been touched with a kind of magic. She moved a centimetre or two from his loins as they shuffled around. He squeezed her hand apologetically, chastened by the slight recoil of her body as he pressed against her.

245

'I'm sorry,' he murmured.

She changed the subject, getting down to what she saw was the business of the evening.

'Are you staying with Steffi at St Cloud? That's where she used to take Wolfgang.'

'And you didn't mind?' he asked, hardly taking his eyes off her for a moment.

She appeared to find his attention tiresome.

'You haven't answered my question,' she said, frowning.

'Why do you ask?'

'Because if you are,' she said, 'it might be a good idea if we left before the Dunkelbaums. It would give you an opportunity to collect your more intimate accoutrements before Hengist found them. Steffi is a good friend of mine.'

'I had no idea he was jealous of Steffi.'

Polly regarded him curiously.

'It's bad form to trip over another man's slippers in your wife's bedroom.'

'Like a wife finding another woman's diaphragm in the bathroom,' Laszlo suggested brightly.

Polly Ferrari did not appear to be entirely comfortable with his more provocative analogy.

'That sort of thing,' she murmured gravely.

'And us?' he asked, coming closer once again.

'Just drop me off at my hotel,' she said. 'I can take care of Hengist's things. The Dunkelbaums will understand what we are about and I'm sure will be grateful.'

'You wouldn't care for my help at the hotel?'

'No,' she said firmly.

'Perhaps we could have a drink somewhere?'

'It's not really that sort of occasion,' she observed.

'I'm sure you must be Hungarian,' Laszlo murmured as the music stopped.

'It's all in *Bottin Mondain*,' she said, half-stifling a yawn as they left the floor to join the lugubrious Dunkelbaums.

*

So it was at Le Défi that Laszlo found himself taken with the madness of loving a woman as much as he had Maya. The notion that Maya had returned to him in the shape of Polly Ferrari sent his mind into unconsidered orbits. He was haunted by the possibilities of her body, certain of its geography, the Mickey Mouse nipples, the soft swell of her belly, the golden vee of flocculence and the camber of strong thighs – everything except butterflies on her dimpled arse. Strange, it was the memory of butterflies that surprised his eyes with tears, his loss suddenly redefined in the memory of reality and the substance of shadow. He knew that there was no escape from the chains his imaginings had contrived and was fearful of the certainty that this woman would never need him as much as he now needed her. What was he to do? He sent her a dozen red roses every day. There was no response for several weeks. And then, a curt acknowledgement from a secretary informing him that the flowers were being redirected to the Hospice of the Holy Innocents at Menton. He temporised for a few days before cancelling the order.

Chapter 33

When Bevan Chancer, recently returned from a damp fortnight in Pau, heard that Sam Yamaha, Director of Non-Standard Funding at the First Nag and Waik, had barely twenty-four hours previously fallen mysteriously to his death, he poured himself a large Laphroaig. He swirled the malt indulgently around his mouth before swallowing it at an injudicious but practised speed. He lusted after Yamaha's job. After several minutes of sustained lusting, he decanted another measure of Laphroaig into his empty glass. Then he rang Froline Nablus.

Froline Nablus heard the buzz of her telephone as she unlocked the front door, her slim body moist and twitchy with exertion having employed the previous sixty minutes in search of twenty pieces of paper that were now tucked safely in her iguana shoulder-bag. The quest had taken her from Hampstead to Knightsbridge and back, revving her battered cerise Lamborghini through the evening traffic. She had let herself into Sam Yamaha's flat, found the foam-rubber replica of La Belle Otero, rummaged feverishly under the celebrated courtesan's ruched skirt and the tiered passementerie of her pearl satin pantalettes, before extracting a scrolled manila envelope wrapped in a red, white and blue capote anglaise secreted in Señora Otero's lubricious holster. Contemplation of the sixty million Swiss franc bearer bonds induced in Mrs Nablus a shiver of almost orgiastic exhilaration. The phone was allowed to trill until she had recovered her composure. But before she could lift the receiver, the ringing had stopped.

When Chancer rang again a few minutes later the phone was picked up almost instantly. He suspected that she sounded disappointed when she recognised his voice. He had always admired the silkily musical quality of Froline's voice. He waited for an elegiac commentary on the deceased Yamaha. She had worked rather more closely with the Japanese than he had. But she had other information.

'Have you heard,' she hissed, 'that Laszlo Gabor has disappeared?'

'What do you mean?'

'Well,' Froline said, 'Harada gave him a month off because of his mother's death. That was six weeks ago. One of his neighbours, a Mrs Mulcahy, has told the bank that she is concerned for his safety. Finding a note in his flat with Yamaha's name and address, she went to see him, hoping Sam would be able to throw some light on Laszlo's whereabouts.'

'It's unusual for a neighbour to show that degree of interest.'

'She's an aunt or something. Anyway, Mrs Mulcahy was actually outside Sam Yamaha's apartment when he fell, narrowly missing her but killing her dog.'

'I did hear something about him falling on a dog.'

'A white miniature Samoyed bitch called Goulash. Apparently it was very valuable. She phoned Harada this morning demanding compensation. We're giving her three hundred just to shut her up.'

'Do you think Gabor's disappearance is linked to Sam's death?'

'Who knows? But it's curious that he's vanished at such a promising point of his career. I understand that Harada was promoting him again.'

'It's a bloody scandal,' brooded Chancer.

'I shall wear black tomorrow,' Froline decided, gliding off on a different tack, 'and drop into St Mary Woolnoth after lunch for a few minutes' meditation.'

'I had no idea you were a Christian.'

'I'm not,' she laughed, 'but I do tend to appropriate other people's holy places. I have even spent time in the occasional synagogue.'

'I'm an atheist,' Chancer confessed. 'Do you mind if I join you?'

'I didn't think you cared much for Sam,' she remarked.

'Hated the bastard,' he admitted, 'so a little contrition for my ill-will may do no harm.'

'An atheist and a Moslem kneeling side by side in a Christian church to remember a Buddhist is rather a surreal situation,' she reflected.

Froline Nablus had scarcely put the phone down on Chancer when chimes ('Oranges and Lemons') summoned her to the door. The visitor, a tall man in Arab costume, was not un-expected. It was her brother, Sheik Yusuf Hamami. She latched the door and regarded him with tearful happiness. He embraced her, tilting her face back and kissing her gently on the mouth.

'We must leave as soon as possible,' he said. 'It will not take Spillano long to discover who fixed Yamaha.'

'But wouldn't that arouse suspicion?' she asked anxiously. 'Since nobody knows you are my brother, it might be prudent if I carried on with my job at the bank.'

'I daren't take that risk with you, my dove,' whispered the Sheik, closing her lustrous eyes with quick kisses.

'But this place is filled with Wally Wazir paintings and sketches,' she said. 'Several of them are unfinished. I'd be happier if we crated them all up and took them with us. If anybody got into the flat, they'd put two and two together.'

'We haven't the time,' the Sheik replied. 'You see, I've got a contract out on Spillano so things might get very difficult. Our best hope is to drive down to my little sanctuary in the Albigeois. We'll be safe there. Should the affair go our way, we could be back in London within the week.'

Froline gave him a look of playful glumness. She was within two months or so of a Wally Wazir retrospective at the Hayward Gallery and her Cairo agent had just sold the idea of a zhivago comic-strip to *Al Shaab*. But the promise of a holiday with her Sheik quickly displaced other considerations. Filaments of hair rose along her spine and she grew spicy and uncomfortably receptive.

They had secretly lusted after each other since her pubescence, but this sneaky interest was only advertised, albeit in excessively restrained and decorous ways, after a lonely Froline Nablus had set up house in London. For although their romance had simmered for many years with nothing more audacious than occasionally clasped hands, breathy sighs and the covert exchange of moony glances, the first yoking of their flesh had taken place barely forty-eight hours earlier.

Two nights previously, events had moved to a sudden conclusion. After dinner together, following a late business meeting with Harada and Natalie Tolstoy, Yusuf had driven her home. This was not unusual. But on this occasion the conversation had taken an uncommonly subversive course, elliptically sensuous with expressions of muted regret that the needs of the flesh were unjustly subject to social convention and theological firman. They spoke with feeling of the beginning of creation, a golden and happy age when incest was the only way the human race could be perpetuated. When Froline concluded rather wistfully that it would have been wonderful to have lived at that time, the Sheik murmured his concurrence, covertly acknowledging her bare knee with the straying fingers of his gear hand. The remainder of the journey was travelled in brooding silence; Froline moist and submissive as a doe awaiting service, while the Sheik contemplated darkly the imminent violation of a frontier he had only dared cross in his more implausible dreams.

Froline's phone-call from her husband was not expected until one a.m. London time. This gave her an hour to change, shower and review Yusuf's merger prospectus which involved the buyout of the First Nag and Waik's commercial paper operation. She left him in the drawing-room, playing a Mantovani tape, sipping a bowl of black mocha and pencilling through the new Ethical Paper's presentation he would be mailing to Natalie Tolstoy in a few hours' time. Froline hurried to the bathroom. She brushed her teeth, shrouded in steam from the prodigal gush of hot water, listening to the sugary swirls of 'Charmaine'. Later, as she was completing her shower, a familiar shadow fell across the frosted glass of the cabinet door. And despite her lubricious expectations, she palpitated with alarm.

'Yusuf?' she called in trepidation, an arm hastily occulting her nipples and a palm cupping her glossy black pubes with reflexive pudicity.

The door opened and there he was. Without a word, he lifted her out of the cabinet and licked her wet face.

'I'm still soapy,' she protested weakly.

He muttered something about her being a slippery sort of girl anyway, before depositing her on the dressing-room's peacock-blue Cossack rug. She would have preferred him to have carried her to the bed. 'The bed, Yusuf,' she screamed in her mind, but so intense was her excitement that she was unable to articulate anything more substantive than incoherent grunts of bewilderment. The vigour of his entry astonished her.

'Ah,' she cried in wide-eyed response, then 'ah' again, biting her lip as she tried to capture his shuttling flesh with pulsing contractions until she fluttered and melted into him.

When they eventually got to bed, the Sheik chewing happily on her earlobe, she petulantly complained that no man had the right to remain so indecently huge and hard. And if that was intended to be modest exaggeration, Yusuf elected to take the comment seriously.

'Do I hurt you, my dove?' he enquired solicitously.

Froline shook her head and giggled, reminding him of the old saying that a very tight fit was the right fit.

When Joe buzzed her at two a.m. Tripoline time, Yusuf chivalrously unsheathed himself and rolled away, settling beside her like a faithful hound.

'You sound breathless,' Joe remarked.

The husky voice, all the way from Libya, sounded reassuringly cheerful. It made her feel less guilty.

'I've run in from the kitchen,' she panted.

'The kitchen?'

'I was poaching an egg,' Froline bubbled, appeasing the expectant Yusuf by curling sideways and skittishly treading his springy cock with restless feet.

Now, quite unexpectedly, Yusuf and she were going away

together, It was, despite all the ominous shadows in their lives, a delicious prospect. She felt uncontrollably wanton. Yusuf told Froline that he would expect her outside the apartment in half an hour. Within that time she grabbed an overnight case and skipped down the stairs to join her brother in his white Rolls-Royce.

'A concession to convention,' she explained laughingly as she adjusted her veil and folded her black galabia into the car.

'I think you're overdoing it,' Yusuf smiled.

'It serves as a sort of disguise,' she remarked, wriggling feverishly in her seat. 'Look,' she called joyfully, lifting the voluminous garment and lying back.

Sheik Yusuf swerved to avoid an elderly pedestrian as he glimpsed the luxuriant raven thatch between her slim, nut-brown thighs. Froline was not wearing her briefs.

Chapter 34

Sham Shilverman's ninety-fifth birthday (a psychic number, being the square of his penile length, 9.7467943 inches approximately, measured before an invited audience in a crystal cylinder at 95° Fahrenheit in the Persian Steam Room of the Eusapia Palladino Foundation, Honkeyville, on the ninety-fifth anniversary of Madame Blavatsky's birth, 31 July 1926, Julian calendar) was to be celebrated at Medusa O'Toole's-L'Amauresque ashram. But the first tentative rehearsals commenced two years earlier.

A wooden stage with a white curtain as the backdrop was constructed within an arc of tiered seating in a forest glade. Spotlight platforms were improvised on strategic trees and a projection tower erected at the appropriate focal length from the screen. Branches were lit with winking coloured lights, and a shimmering silver sphere suspended in the flies shone smiling images of Shilverman that appeared and disappeared with the coruscations of the globe. At some distance from the woodland theatre was a pavilion hidden among the shrubbery in which the Vanity Springs Philharmonic Orchestra (with an expanded string section) played music from the Shilverman films.

Shilverman, whose papa had been a blind violinist from Odessa, although not averse to gushy melodic swells, could not bear the sight of musicians at work. They reminded him of poverty, the old country, stale borsch, black suits with shiny arses and elbows, evoking disagreeable nightmares of mortality. Any mention of death, or even illness, now made him weep piteously. It was, his friends hoped, a passing phase. Medusa O'Toole had arranged for the entire Shilverman canon (those produced, directed and written by him) from *Hello, Golgotha, Hello* (1916) to *The French Kissers of Fleurie* (1959), seventeen high-kicking blockbusters in which the O'Toole magic was visible in no less than twelve, to be projected continuously over the period of the celebrations and relayed by satellite to ancillary festivities throughout the civilised world. The party was scheduled to last ten days.

The rehearsals were extravagantly ambitious. Stand-ins for celebrities due to appear, and the lesser characters in Shilverman's life who elected to appear as themselves at the rehearsals, were presented on stage and applauded with enthusiasm. There was an aberrant convention in these preliminary appreciations that ensured that the more obscure the person introduced, the more manic the reception. Sometimes, the audience of film-buffs demanded speeches or performances from these shadows of the great life. A lavatory attendant from Gonad Gulch sang 'Some of These Days', and an octogenarian hooker who claimed that she once blew Shilverman at a health ranch in Dysentery City, was not allowed to escape from the stage until she had stripped and tossed her G-string to the baying wolves clustered around the proscenium. Happy times.

Shilverman was not at first persuaded that the near-cosmic scale of the proposed celebrations was a sound idea. It had valedictory resonances that depressed him.

'Think of your ninety-fifth as a dress rehearsal for the centenary,' Medusa coaxed.

'And then what?' he brooded. 'Nothing but cold earth and maggots.'

'But you're coming back, sweetheart. We've got a resurrection in the script.'

'When?' he fussed, looking at her fearfully.

'After the final credits. Remember, you've got to pick up the Best Film award.'

Shilverman looked miserable. He cursed the Creator for allowing him to wither. Now, at ninety-three, he felt as weak as shit, his memory let him down, he dribbled piss if he was not obsessively scrupulous when shaking himself dry, and he could hardly get it to twenty degrees.

'Do you really think I'll make a hundred?' he asked wistfully.

'If we look after you,' said Medusa. 'Not too much bourbon, too many sheegars or naughty chickadees.'

A nostalgic look welled into Shilverman's eyes.

'If I go, I want to be embalmed, tricked out in a tuxedo and dancing-pumps, than laid out under a glass cover in a room with the lights on,' he reflected. 'And I'd like a packet of rubbers in my jacket pocket, just in case. Sunburn was telling me about a physician in Geneva who performs miracles with anaconda tissue. There's this Indian guy who works for him, the little regurgitator. Apparently Dr Zeiss fixed him up like new with an anaconda transplant. I could use some of that material myself. All I need is a new liver, kidneys, testicles, and maybe a strip or two of muscle fibre around the base of my cock.'

'I'll call Sunburn tomorrow,' she promised.

Shilverman's thin lips split apart. He reached out a brown mottled claw and gripped Medusa's hand.

'Do you remember my cock in 1926?' he breathed, a lubricious glint in his pale green eyes.

She nodded. 'You were a superman. Sure spoiled me for other guys.'

'Did I?' he laughed, coughing as he tried to catch his breath.

'Amandine Kennedy once told me how you made love to the entire chorus of *Yankee Pankee* on two consecutive days and nights.'

Shilverman waved a hand in protest.

'Naw. She was thinking of *Give My Regards to Irkutsk*. Eighteen girls in fifty-two hours. It's all on film. Pancho Villa bought the only copy from me in 1920.'

'One helluva stud,' Medusa laughed.

'Do you know,' Sham wheezed, 'I can remember all those little sweethearts' names. And I never fail to include them in my prayers when I kneel down every night.'

'Three of them should be at your party. Amandine Kennedy, Mavis Schultz and Berenice Huberman.'

'Only three?' he muttered, suddenly saddened by the realisation that so many of those glorious, squirming, giggling girlies were probably dead.

'A lot of them might not be able to travel,' she explained quietly.

'There was such a lot of softness there. And innocence. Making love was fun in those days.'

'And these days as well,' Medusa assured him.

'Is it, Medusa? Is it still fun?'

She kissed his cadaverous cheek.

'You mustn't tax your wonderful brain with those sorts of metaphysical questions, darling. I'm going to fix you a bourbon-spearmint before lunch.'

Sham cheered up a little at the prospect of a bourbon-spearmint but called Medusa when she got to the door.

'You won't forget to talk to Sunburn about the anaconda skin.'

'I'll try and reach him after I've seen to your drink.'

She smiled at him and winked the old O'Toole smile. He narrowed his eyes as he stared at her.

'You've got new eyes,' he said. 'Beautiful new eyes.'

'I thought you'd never notice,' she mocked.

'Green, aren't they?' he asked, squinting.

'Blue, baby. Danube blue.'

Chapter 35

Laszlo, like his Maya, was an inveterate dreamer. He had, of course, Gaspar's steamy photographs to start him off, but she was always respectably covered in her nocturnal appearances. And now she was mixed up with Polly. The composite chimera came to him most nights, her mouth painted red, attired in a white, lace-trimmed déshabillé he remembered from his childhood. He could never induce her to look directly at him. At best, she appeared three-quarter face, her anxious gaze somewhere above his shoulder. Generally she materialised in profile, like an Egyptian tomb painting or the monarch's head on a coin. On rare occasions, she was discovered prone on deserted beaches from precarious Daliesque perspectives. There was no laughter in these reprises, only a comforting sense of union. She had the quiet dignity of an angel in their transits through fragrant gardens, perhaps sitting with him in woodland restaurants at tables dappled in sunlight, just a chink of china and the whisper of friendly voices as the wind rustled through deciduous trees.

Sometimes he found her, still in a white, lace-trimmed déshabillé, barefoot on the mountains. Ah, she had such beautiful feet, sensibly formed, a little on the broad side but with a peasant's symmetry and strength; feet designed for springy grass and fertile earth rather than the constraints of nylon and modish footwear. The mountain dreams were rarely happy. She would hear his voice and come to him, leaping and bounding down impossible slopes, the warning to take care frozen in his throat as he watched her descent. He would turn away before she had overreached herself and plummeted like a rag doll, striking the snow-covered teeth of hidden rock, vanishing into the powdery whiteness of a glacier or the treacherous jaws of a bergschrund.

And there was the intrusive Selveratnam, of course. For some time he had been trying to release himself from the shackles of the little Tamilian who, he suspected, had seduced Maya into another incarnation. He felt little remorse for Selveratnam's death, which he saw as self-defence, but was disturbed by the purgatorial reflection that the price for the Hindu's life had been Maya's. That thought was a shadow in his life. An implication he did not want to contemplate. But Laszlo was relentlessly pursued in his night flutterings by the little man. And whatever diversions his subconscious devised, Selveratnam evaded them.

Many of Laszlo's fantasies were concerned with the pursuit of females with whom he had not coupled during his waking hours. Wet-lipped Cynthia, her pale, solemn face rising like a cantaloup from the crinkled nest of Miss Proby's beaver, blue, hairless phosphorescent Kirsty, labial, loamy Thelma and hungry-mouthed Lola. But most of all he wanted Polly, whose mushroomy cleft he savoured like a foraging boar. But even as he moved between raised and compliant thighs, losing himself in appreciative softness, Selveratnam, his insidious black demon, would appear. He poked into the corner of Laszlo's mind, peering, sniffing and at times boldly appropriating a dangling leg of Laszlo's partner to hump for himself, slithering around the limb like a horny dog. His staccato sing-song voice rattled around Laszlo's skull.

'Piss off,' Laszlo would snarl, grinding his teeth and willing the intruder off his subconscious screen. But Selveratnam persisted, loafing about, fingering everything, and so usurping the private fucklands of Laszlo's dreams that he would be compelled to rise, switch on the bedside light, pad fretfully to the bathroom, scrub his teeth, gargle with an aromatic bdellium solution and dunk his face in cold water, drying it ferociously with a rough towel.

Laszlo's toilet literature (he retained a few books and magazines in a wall-cupboard) ranged from Edward VII's autographed copy of *The Memoirs of Dolly Morton*, which had some 'curious anthropological observations on the radical diversities in the conformation of the female posterior and the way different women endure chastisement' (Carrington, Paris, 1894), to *The Complete Onanist*, an international compendium of genitalia, with of course their proud and happy owners, the seventy-five nationalities arranged to suit most androgynous palates, the hetero- and homosexual illustrations arranged on alternate pages to pleasantly confound complacent libidos lost in the arcane jungle of self-love. The handsome book (1,500 pages of glossy colour photographs, Feltschrift Press, Frankfurt, 1978, 975 DM) had coffee-table pretensions, for it included cosmopolitan recipes, butterflies, flowers and automobiles in subtexts below the pulsating porn. Only after the relief of a leisurely hand-job, lingering generally on pages 173 and 985, Myfanwy and Isabella, did Laszlo feel disposed to return to bed.

Strangely enough, it was Mrs Bagshawe who helped him to survive Selveratnam's hauntings. She gave him a supply of Tedium, hallucinatory sleeping-pills that ensured the dreariest of dreams. Within seconds of his head touching the pillow, he was whirled away into a grainy silent film where the grey characters appeared to be composed of ectoplasmic mist from the navel down and communicated in barely legible, flickering captions about matters like 'The Gulf Stream', 'Cathedral Architecture', 'Contract Bridge', 'Dental Hygiene', and 'The Gold Standard'. It was a sort of deliverance.

Steffi's reference to Princess Lola's trade in Coqauvin had disappointed Laszlo. While he did not expect his new mother to be an authentically royal body, and knew from her own report that she was not unfamiliar with the attentions of friendly strangers, the fact that she did twenty-franc knee-tremblers behind the church at Coqauvin was not happy news. He led her towards the subject of her past with a reference to the Dunkelbaums over breakfast.

'Had you ever,' he asked quietly, 'met Hengist Dunkelbaum before that lunch at his chateau?'

She nodded, spooning away at a melon.

'About half a dozen times,' she admitted, 'behind the Church of St Lazarus at Coqauvin.' She could see that he looked displeased but could not repress a grin and a mischievous wink.

'He was a customer. I used to charge fifty francs a time in those days. They were generally twenty-second jobs, so it was good money. It worked out at nine thousand francs an hour or three hundred and sixty thousand francs for a forty-hour week. If the flow of work could have been guaranteed, I'd have been a millionaire several times over.'

'Are you telling me that you were a whore?'

She looked at him with wry amusement.

'You needn't turn up your snout like that. Most people on this earth have to do their share of whoring and a great deal of it is much less morally sound than straightforward fucking. Am I any the less of a princess because I allowed men in need to tuck their guns in my holster for a few seconds? In those days, fifty francs could buy an excellent five-course meal with wine at one of the nicer restaurants along the Quai at St Tropez. Twenty seconds was all I needed to fill my belly. Even your princes of industry have to do more to earn a crust.'

'He recognised you,' Laszlo informed her gravely.

'I'm flattered,' she smiled. 'I was an extremely handsome woman in those days. Even Medusa O'Toole was envious of my poise. Sham Shilverman wanted to whip me off to Vanity Springs to make me a movie-star, but I decided that whoring suited my anarchic nature. And as I said, the money wasn't bad, particularly when Shilverman allowed me to work L'Amauresque.'

'I thought,' he reflected, 'it was a spiritual place; an ashram.'

'L'Amauresque had a strange and stormy beginning. It started as an exclusive girlie club in the Maures hills, managed by a subsidiary of Sham Shilverman Enterprises, though the land and buildings belonged to Hengist Dunkelbaum. A former chorus-girl from Lyons called Gaby La Mulatière was the principal hostess in those days. She organised the parties for the club and supervised the hiring of freelancers like myself. Demand for girls far outstripped supply on saints' days, public holidays and week-ends. Nudity while dancing was part of the house style and the thés dansants were wildly popular among successful businessmen. They would lunch at the restaurant and then linger around in the bar until the naked dancing started at three.

'It was Medusa O'Toole who changed everything. She had for some years been nibbling away at various fringe religions, being herself a former Russellite who drifted into Spiritualism, Theosophy and Hinduism. The Eusapia Palladino Foundation which she founded in those days was just a log-cabin near the club sauna. It was basically a planchette-palour and healing centre. One afternoon, legend has it, during a multi-orgasmic seizure, Medusa had a vision in which she saw the statue of Gaia lying on the seabed not far from St Tropez. She persuaded Shilverman to search for and retrieve the gigantic stone effigy from the Mediterranean sludge. They chartered a salvage-boat and steamed into the bay. A large object was located exactly where Medusa had predicted. It was secured in a cradle of steel hawsers and winched onto the deck of the vessel. It was indeed the black Gaia that Medusa had seen in her vision, scabbed with crustacea, sea flora and dried globigerina ooze, and it was installed at the gates of L'Amauresque. Medusa had little trouble in procuring Shilverman's approval for a change of use and L'Amauresque was advertised in the fashionable glossies as a retreat for the better class of pietist. It was then that we heard about the Final Conjunction, a cataclysmic coming together of Uranus the sky and Gaia the earth.'

'Foreshadowed in the parable "Chicken Licken, Chicken Licken . . . the sky is falling down",' Laszlo commented.

Princess Lola looked impressed.

'I see you've got the theology right,' she smiled.

She told him that Shilverman very naturally had the exclusive world-rights to produce a film of the Final Conjunction. There was a great celebration. Everybody, even the rank-and-file whores, linked arms to sing 'Ave Medusa', a hymn that L'Amauresque adopted as its signature tune. Happiness vibrated through the air. The one ill-mannered exception to the general concord was Gaby La Mulatière.

'Medusa O'Toole wouldn't be allowed to get away with this garbage,' she screamed, 'if the no-talent cunt wasn't getting it from Shilverman.'

Medusa was outraged.

262

'You must be some kind of pig's arsehole,' she snarled, 'to talk about a saint-like person in that unladylike manner. Don't you know that I am one of the most mesmeric presences ever seen in technicolored movies? My smile will never be forgotten, that's for sure.'

'What's a smile?' Gaby sneered. 'Teeth, gums, mouth mucus and a pair of labial suckers. It's no heavy business.'

A sudden and furious fist-fight followed. Medusa took a couple of cracking right chops to the left cheekbone before sliding in with a sapping womb-shot followed by a demon forehead that splintered Gaby La Mulatière's elegant nose. It was a decisive and bloody conclusion. The triumph of good over evil.

Princess Lola claimed that following the claret, agave root and hypnotic mantras, the evening seemed to dissolve. She recalled a humming, purring and wailing ebony choir, aggressively ecstatic, rejoicing in being taken up into the heavens over the wooded slopes of the Maures hills, whirled around above the Bay of St Tropez in a magic mistral, then set down in a shower of driftwood, mussel-shells, seaweed, rusty hypodermics, used condoms, plastic suntan-oil containers and lager bottles on the Plage de Pamplemousse.

'We were really floating that night,' the princess laughed.

She had wandered along the beach in the dark with men plucking lutes like figures from a Piero della Francesca fresco, white-shrouded, sporting turquoise nimbuses and pulsing out songs about a death-defying happiness. And men she believed to be the sons of the great Earth Mother Gaia arrived in St Tropez, cunningly disguised as magnificent Senegalese beach-vendors, bearing ivory-coloured woollen blankets, belts, safari hats, bangles, necklaces, plastic elephants and ornamental brass trays. The black men picked their way among the prawn-pink bodies on the sand, past cold and hostile eyes, fearful of the power and beauty of negritude. She said that one only had to consider the kind of people who hated blackness and patronised women to be reasonably certain that Medusa O'Toole was right. God was probably the black mother of the universe. A black Gaia, creaming with love. It was a psychic deduction that resonated with mystical truth.

263

'I'm sorry,' Laszlo murmured, 'about being priggish about your whoring.'

'You're still only a little boy,' she teased. 'The acquisition of wisdom is a long and painful process.'

'Tell me about Coqauvin,' he insisted, reaching across the table and squeezing her hand affectionately.

'I lived with three Senegalese in the backstreets,' she recalled wistfully.

She told him that she had cooked, stitched and cleaned for them, sharing their food and the mattresses placed side by side in the tiny room.

'My friends,' she boasted, 'were deep purple and smelled of almonds, sour cream, strange spices and the decaying vegetation of distant forests. They were gentle, wise and full of laughter, sharing me without jealousy or conceits of precedence. And they never took me against my will.'

Chapter 36

Laszlo's return to Crystal Palace to visit the Mulcahys was not something he undertook with any degree of enthusiasm. It had been occasioned by the sight of Ada and Aurora, shabby and wild-haired, wheeling a pram along a pavement in Lewisham. His Sovereign was idling at the traffic-lights when he caught sight of them. He glanced back, squinting in his mirror, feeling helpless and unable to stop or attract their attention. He calculated as he turned the corner and drove on, trapped by the traffic, that he had not seen Ada for nearly two years. He was troubled by a number of questions. Whose child was it? Why was Aurora not at Purley? Why did they look so tattered and down-at-heel? Were they in any trouble? So he returned reluctantly. And he went bearing gifts. There was a red and white spotted parasol for Aurora, a litre of Napoleon Fine Champagne for Ada, a jaunty *Nice-Matin* cap he'd found in the sea off the Plage de Pamplemousse and a box of Turkish delight which he hoped Ada would give to Tom when she next visted the Sunshine Home.

He approached the flat in trepidation. It was Aurora who opened the door. She threw herself into his arms instantly, squeezing him breathless. Ada was behind her, more than a little scruffy and tired in appearance. She smelled vaguely of onions and warm stew.

'Laszlo,' she whispered, her voice cracked with weariness.

He explained how he'd seen them in Lewisham earlier that day.

'I saw Aurora pushing a pram,' he murmured.

Ada's eyes filled with tears. Laszlo went quickly to his bag of presents. He placed the Turkish delight and *Nice-Matin* cap on the table, handling Aurora the red and white spotted parasol.

'And that's for Tom,' he said, indicating the gifts.

Ada came to him. She held him close to her and stroked his hair as though he needed comforting. Like the old days.

'Tom's dead, Laszlo,' she said quickly. 'He died six months ago.'

'My God,' he muttered, 'what happened?'

'He just pined away.'

'Pined?'

'He used to sit near the gate, waiting for you. When you didn't come, he stopped eating. One morning they found him dead. He'd gone in his sleep.'

Aurora laughed. It was as shrill as a scream. She was happy to see Laszlo and Ada together. She pushed against him, sucking her thumb and laying her head on his chest.

'There's a bottle of cognac for you,' he said to Ada, lost in dismal thoughts.

Ada picked up a packet of cigarettes. She offered Laszlo one and took one herself. She lit up, containing the news he had really come to hear in her knowing eyes.

'There's a little man in the next room who you'll be proud to meet.'

'A boy?' he asked. 'Is he yours?'

'And yours,' she informed him. 'You're a father, Laszlo.'

Although the news was clearly ridiculous, he felt unreal.

'There must be some mistake,' he sighed bleakly.

'I've called him Laszlo, after his daddy.'

She seemed grey all the way through. Defeated and dead-eyed. He followed her into the bedroom. The furniture had been rearranged. The bed was now under the window with a cot at its head. He noticed that the David Shepherd elephant was back and that the blue flying ducks were now pink flying geese. A black papier-maché giraffe-necked cat stood at the side of her cluttered dressing-table. He remembered the chipped Horace Horsecollar money-box and the imitation tortoiseshell pin-tray with cigarette burns.

Ada lowered herself over the side of the cot and bore the bundle wrapped in blue to Laszlo.

'You can hold him,' she said, placing the swaddled object in his arms.

He looked down at it, then glanced at Ada in surprise. Her face was contemplative and maternally beatific. Laszlo examined his charge again. It was a dark-haired plastic doll.

'I suppose,' Ada said, 'he takes after my side of the family. They're on the dark side. Not the Purefoys mind, but the Gilhooleys. My grandmother always claimed that they were tinkers.'

'He's not much of a Gabor,' Laszlo admitted, eyeing her carefully.

'He's got your voluptuous lips,' she declared.

He smiled sadly.

'Well, I don't expect that you've been playing around with anybody else.'

'No, indeed,' she said, 'it's your spunk that made him all right. Father Meredith wouldn't christen him in the church, so I did it myself in the kitchen, using genuine holy water. He's Laszlo Dedalus Gabor. What do you think of that?'

Laszlo swung the doll in his cradled arms. It had the lightness of a dream.

'He's a wonderful little creature,' he said, making the blue eyes open and close as he swung it about. 'How old is he?'

'Three months,' Ada replied. 'He's small for his age, but beautiful beyond words.'

Laszlo carried the doll into the next room where Aurora was watching television. She looked up and laughed. He sat down, still with the doll, beside Ada on the settee. She had not looked after herself but had submitted to a despair that held no solution.

'Do you need any money?' he asked quietly.

She shook her head.

'I just want you, Laszlo,' she said.

He did not speak. He realised that he had returned to a terrible place, the air filled with pain and madness.

'Why did you run off?' she asked 'You had such a wonderful job with Mr Harada.'

'I was a pimp,' he said flatly, looking at the plastic doll.

'But you were an important man in the bank. They told me how much they missed you.'

267

He shook his head glumly, subdued by his repugnance for her. Even poor laughing Aurora he now found tiresome and vaguely threatening.

'I had to take Aurora away from the Sunshine Home,' Ada said, 'after Miss Egremont left and Tom died. She didn't like it there anymore. Not the way things had been going. But she's a good girl and helps me quite a lot. She peels the potatoes, washes the dishes and pushes little Laszlo's pram around the park every morning, don't you, Aurora?'

Aurora grinned, her face shining with vacuous happiness. She got up and squeezed in between them.

'You mentioned that Miss Egremont had left the Home,' he observed, turning his head towards her behind Aurora's back.

'Given the bullet,' Ada sneered. 'She and the matron. It appears that Father Loyola and Mrs Mercury caught them at it in the lounge.'

'What do you mean?'

'Do you know Daisy Mercury?'

'No.'

'She's the cook there. Well, Daisy Mercury compained to Father Loyola, who is the Chairman of the Sunshine Trust, that Miss Egremont and the matron used to cavort in the lounge every night. After work, Daisy often pretended to go off, but sneaked back to watch what was going on. She peeked at them through the rhododendrons by a side-window. It was always after lights-out, mind you. At least, past the time the lights were supposed to be out. They were shameless, those two. They didn't mind doing it with the lights on. One never knew what effect it would have on poor Aurora. Daisy Mercury tells me that they used huge dildoes. Candy-striped ones with red luminous ends.'

Laszlo handed the doll to Ada.

'I must be off,' he announced.

She looked at him reproachfully.

'But you've only just come. Not even a cup of tea.'

'I'll send you some money,' he promised, looking around restlessly.

The flat stank of hopelessness. He wondered about Cynthia

Egremont, hating the unknown Mrs Mercury, despising himself for not visiting Tom sooner and loathing poor, dirty Ada for relishing the prurient story. Aurora screamed. It was a shrill sound of exhilaration. She lifted her cambric dress to reveal white cotton knickers.

'Bobby Shafto went to sea,
Silver buckles on his knee'.

'Pull your skirt down,' shouted her mother.

Ada sidled up to Laszlo, giving a discreet nod in Aurora's direction.

'I've had her tubes knotted,' she advised him softly, 'and not before time. One of the men in there had interfered with her. And that bitch of a matron didn't seem to care. This bastard, a man of fifty or more, used to slip into Aurora's room at night. Poor kid didn't know what was happening. The doctor confirmed that she had. Well, we knew it was this fellow for sure. But were there others?' She shrugged. 'Listen,' she urged, 'let me put the kettle on.'

'I can't stay,' he smiled, slipping on his coat.

'I still read Molly Bloom's Soliloquy,' she murmured, holding his arm.

He turned to give her a perfunctory kiss on the forehead. Aurora bounded forward and into his arms. She cuddled him affectionately. He kissed her on the cheek. She pursed her wet lips in his direction and he allowed her to slobber over his chin.

'I'd like an address,' Ada pleaded. 'Sometimes I get so utterly down in the dumps. If I could only see you, now and again. Or even hear your voice.'

She was crying now, making a miserable snuffling noise as she tried to wipe her eyes with the back of her hand.

'Give me a phone-number, Laszlo,' she sighed.

'I promise I'll keep in touch,' he replied.

'Laszlo,' she said, 'I still love you. Always remember that.'

He nodded, touching the hand she held out to him in farewell.

Turning away, he left the Mulcahys. He strode across the hall and down the stairs.

She remembered as the door closed that she hadn't told Laszlo about poor Goulash being crushed by that Japanese man who worked at the bank, and about the nice Mrs Nablus who gave her three hundred pounds in compensation. Imagine forgetting to tell him that. The next time perhaps. The next time, she resolved, she would tidy up. And even fix a ham and cress tea for him if she only knew when he would be calling.

Chapter 37

The circumstances that had led Laszlo Gabor to be indulging in brittle conversation over Poulpe à la Provençale at the dining-table in the sleekly panelled saloon of a floating Bacardi-palace called the *Voracité* had an obliquity that was not entirely exceptional in his chameleonic existence.

Hardly a week earlier, he had been positioned near a lounge window of the Waldorf, cursing the stinking Aldwych traffic and dreaming of the lunch companion he awaited, who was already more than one hour late. He was beginning to suspect that the woman he loved had stood him up once again. Idling over a Bloody Batory, an outrageously large vase of Polish spirit and tomato juice in pulverised ice, enlivened by tabasco, tamarind, a pinch of nutmeg and spearmint leaf, with a sly rub of shaddock zest around the rim of the frosted glass, he brooded about his obsessive passion.

About the same time as Laszlo had swallowed his third Batory, his absent lunch date, Polly Ferrari, was taking a Byrrh with Sunburn Spillano at a café on the Promenade des Anglais. Separated from the young man who lusted after her by a crow-flying distance of about seven hundred miles, she knew that she was unlikely to manage lunch at the Waldorf, a circumstance she mildly regretted and for which she had tried to apologise by phone. Finding the lines engaged, Polly did not persist in trying to reach Mr Flute. Anyway, Sunburn Spillano represented serious business. And she had found the flattering attentions of even the prettiest young men tedious, ever since her discovery of Wolfgang's polysexual instincts. For although she occasionally allowed herself to be invested by the opposite sex for reasons of expediency, Polly's inclinations lay elsewhere. Young girls as sweet as Cavaillon melons were now her bag.

However, she did, being a woman of conscience, consider that the persistent Flute was entitled to some hospitality after a breathless two-year pursuit that had seldom strayed beyond the bounds of propriety. If she was not seriously persuaded by his flowers, amorous verses, jewelled valentines, canaries in gilded cages and tiresome invitations to dine in boring restaurants, his stamina amused her sufficiently to make her believe it might be time to mitigate the numerous disappointments she had caused him.

The receipt of an invitation from Polly Ferrari to join the *Voracité* for a ten-day cruise in the Adriatic was as wildly welcome to Laszlo as it was unexpected. However, the names of at least three of the other guests gave him cause for reflection. Of these, he suspected that the least sinister but most intrusive might be Wolfgang, the husband of the woman he wanted for himself; the most sinister but hopefully least intrusive, the secretive Sunburn Spillano; while the most dangerous appeared to be Thelma de Bereenbroeck, a person who he feared had the capacity to establish inconvenient links between his two lives.

Recognising signs of an instinctive funk (intermittent diuresis and cold sweats) he decided on audacity, calling Thelma at Brinkley's before nervousness had wholly assimilated his reason. He was informed that she had left the bank and was now running her own boutique (sports, sun and swimwear) somewhere along the Bromley shopping strip. Thelma was surprised to hear from him but sufficiently intrigued by his re-emergence in her life to accept an offer to eat with him the following day. It had been a long time since she had last seen the 'Rock-Doctor'. He picked her up at the boutique and drove her out to Osculata's.

Thelma was attired in a pink pyjama-suit of crushed silk and a pair of knee-high patent-leather red boots. She had destroyed her luxuriant hair with severe, uneven cropping, the glossy sheen he had much admired defaced by crusted gold and ochre streaks.

Over lunch, she told Laszlo that it had been Yamaha and Stundish that had taken his bonds, Stundish having done the caper for twenty K, and all she had got out of the deal was a short lease on a shop property in Bromley and a medium-term credit facility from the First Nagasaki to enable her to stock the garments necessary to kick-start Flash Fash into commercial life. Laszlo's scepticism was restrained enough not to be provocative.

'And this,' she murmured, flashing a ruby ring in a horseshoe diamond cluster on her right middle finger.

He nodded appreciatively. It seemed a tasty incentive to keep quiet.

'It was Yamaha's mother's,' she explained, adding, 'We had only slept together once before he fell out of the window, so it's all I was left with.'

Laszlo suggested that if they were to go on the proposed cruise, it might be expedient not to mention the nature of their past association. He admitted that he had been holding the bonds for a man called Selveratnam, who had mysteriously disappeared. It was necessary in the circumstances to secure the bonds until the legitimate owner returned. Thelma nodded politely. Her credulity was almost as equally measured as his and calculated to cause the minimum of offence. It was not until they got to the liqueurs that he essayed a direct question.

'What exactly,' he asked, 'is your interest in the cruise?'

'You mean apart from the sea air and the pleasure of bobbing around the Adriatic?'

'Apart from those delights,' Laszlo murmured.

'I'm doing a physical thing with Wolfgang Ferrari,' she confessed. 'Although it would be more than presumptuous to term what we have going for us "love", I have a current obsession to reserve my body for his almost exclusive use. He sends me flowers and expensive gifts, we phone each other twice a week and couple like crazy beasts whenever we meet. I even dream about the guy.'

'You appear to be heading towards a love-type situation,' Laszlo agreed.

'It's not been going all that long,' she said. 'We only met three months ago at the Cannes Film Festival.'

'You were there on. . . ?'

'Business,' she replied quickly. 'Swimwear and marine casuals.' She smiled a smile of sunny candour. 'And there's also the opportunity to meet Sunburn Spillano. Wolfie is fixing that.

You see, I'm thinking of expanding my business. I'd like to dive into the manufacturing and wholesaling areas. Perhaps develop a retail franchising network. And Spillano Garbage could help with those ambitions.'

She took a cigarette from Laszlo, allowing him to light it. They both puffed away reflectively for a while. It had been an excellent lunch.

'And you,' she murmured, 'are you still in the diamond business?'

He nodded, fishing a card out of his wallet.

'I've recently acquired a place in Hatton Garden,' he said. 'I'm in partnership with a woman called Steffi Dunkelbaum.'

Thelma's eyes lit up.

'I know her. Wolfie introduced us at Cannes. We were having lunch together when Madame Dunkelbaum walked in with her daughter.'

'The girl who's a ringer for Brit Bidette?'

'That's right. Madame Dunkelbaum was OK, but a bit on the sniffy side.' Thelma lay back in her chair. 'Fancy you being in cahoots with the Dunkelbaums.'

'A smallish world,' he agreed, sipping his Strega. 'I'm surprised,' he added, 'that they're not on the cruise.'

'Wolfie doesn't like her,' Thelma informed him.

'Is that so?' he enquired solemnly, picking a piece of tobacco off his tongue.

She bent down below the table to scratch her calf inside the right boot, and reappeared with a question ready-made in her mind.

'And have you any particular reason for going on the trip? Apart from the sea air and the excitement of sailing to Venice?'

'I'm in love with Polly Ferrari,' he said simply.

Thelma de Bereenbroeck laughed with delight.

'That's fantastic,' she said. 'Wolfie hinted that she was basically a dike. I had no idea that there was a guy involved. We could work for each other. I'll try and keep Wolfie out of your way.'

Laszlo frowned.

'It's not as simple as that. My passion is, I regret, unrequited.'
'How incredibly romantic,' she enthused.
'I'm cautiously optimistic,' he brooded.

They were on their way to the car when Thelma shot a casual question in his direction.

'Did you ever run into a character called Laszlo Gabor? I understand Sunburn Spillano thinks he's the man who's hiding Selveratnam.'

Laszlo managed a negative mumble, but his mind was troubled by the approach of a dark cloud or two on the not-so-distant horizon.

It had been a good week for Sunburn Spillano. Fortune had dealt him some very tasty cards. Not only was the Security Squad of the Spillano Garbage Corporation hot on the trail of Sheik Yusuf Hamami and his sister Froline Nablus, alias Wally Wazir, but Natalie Tolstoy had taken over the First Nag and Waik and Polly Ferrari had got her hands on L'Amauresque. Furthermore, Claudine Zola of Spermtrek had successfully addressed the question that had been teasing him all his life.

He had often wondered how he, a guy whose brain-waves occasionally registered on seismometers, could possibly be the offspring of Joe and Mitzi Spillano who, had they been any brighter, might have scored a point or two for vacuity. Now the problem was solved. He was, in fact, the son of Benito Bandito, who apart from being a philosopher and man of action had once been 'the most powerful cock in Italy'. Even his mother was a princess. OK, so she had a touch of spicy form and was known around the bars of the Côte d'Azur variously as Esterel Evie, Leaky Lola and Senegal Sue. But three names were often an indication of class and sometimes, when used in a bitter and dismissive manner, corrosive envy. Not being an emotional sort of individual, Sunburn restricted his filial enthusiasm for his long-lost parent to the delivery of a dozen yellow roses every day. They arrived at Mushington Hall with a card that read simply, 'Primogenitally Yours, S.' A shade enigmatic, perhaps, but informative enough to give the princess a few maternal flushes pending his visit to receive her benediction after he'd returned from the *Voracité* cruise.

And what was almost as exciting as finding a mother was the prospect of being on board with two half-brothers, one on either side of the equation. He felt like an 'equal' sign. Wolfie was halved on his father's side, and Tom Flute on his mother's. Also it was comforting for Wolfie to discover that his beautiful mother, Sylvana Spillano, hadn't been frisking around with some macassar-marinated no-goodnik, but had managed to get her belly filled by 'the most powerful cock in Italy'. Furthermore, she'd been paid the pretty compliment of having Bandito's blackshirts murder her. Such a romantic termination as well. What more could a dame want? There was undeniable status in a political snuff-job. Jesus, it was barely a nudge or two below being a historical footnote.

When Sunburn found out that Tom was family, he'd nudged Polly into inviting him along, which she was happy to do since she owed the guy a favour anyway. Everything was slotting into place. Life felt as good as a straight shot of sulph. But there were two pieces of shit on the ceiling. The first was that sonofabitch Selveratnam. And the second was the Houdini who called himself Laszlo Gabor. Laszlo, Sunburn reflected, had at present a rather tenuous purchase on the family tree, being Wolfie's secret melt. But if Mr Gabor had anything to do with the dematerialisation of the Twinkle of Fatima, then the only way the schmuck could stay there would be suspended by his collar from a fairly inaccessible branch. Seriously.

Chapter 38

'Are you going to read the tarot for me?' Claudine Zola asked as she licked the lobe of Hasheena's ear.

They lay naked together on Claudine's black and orange coverlet, an extravagance of chinoiserie that Hasheena loved. The bedroom led onto a shuttered balcony that looked down over the higgledy-piggledy rooftops of Vence, the tiered eminence of the Alps to the left, receding from the broken rock of the nearest red hills to the misty blue peaks on the horizon, blurred by cloud and tipped with snow. To the right was the perched town of St Paul. Far below its medieval assurance, earth-removers ravaged the hill's underbelly and grinding bull-dozers scraped raw trails in preparation (the hoarding said) for soi-disant traditional dwellings. A desecration; hardly more than the speculative pargeting of drab breeze with pink roughcast for strangers who would come to buy pretty dreams.

Claudine loved Hasheena's breasts, which were hard and curved with nipples the size of black olives. She gently smoothed the bulge of Hasheena's belly with the palm of her hand, sliding tenderly into the abundance of her pubic growth; hair that curled up almost to her navel and down in feathery wisps along her firm brown thighs. When Hasheena put on her briefs, Claudine used to playfully tweak any tuft that remained uncontained.

'Oh, it's all right for old women who are bald down there,' Hasheena joked, making a grab for Claudine's furrow.

Hasheena could never resist threatening Claudine with her middle finger. This was always done when they were in a hurry, dressing or about to part. Claudine would become helpless with laughter when the finger came towards her. She would run around the furniture for a few moments, allowing Hasheena to finally catch her, holding her hand and imploring mercy. Then they would kiss, just brushing lips at first, but eventually embracing fiercely, moving their tongues deep into each other's mouths. At parting, it was always Claudine who cried. Life had been marvellous since she had found Hasheena. Before her, there had been Nirjis, a Lebanese girl who worked as an actuary in Monaco. That had lasted for four years and overlapped her crumbling relationship with Claude, a charming racing-driver who she suspected was more in love with his hard body and biggish cock than he was with her. He would exult at the fact that he could sustain an erection for forty minutes, and was a great man for weightlifting and jogging. He was convinced that he was a magnificent lover and had almost persuaded Claudine that he was, until Nirjis kissed her after she dropped her home one night. A simple kiss – it was a revelation. They spent the night together at Nirjis's flat in the Croisette. And that was that. After Nirjis was transferred to London, she allowed, for some inexplicable reason, Marbuk, a cheerful Algerian who worked for the estate agents in the same building, to fuck her. She clenched her mind in repugnance as he moved in and out of her, realising in horror that it was a mistake. Poor handsome Marbuk didn't apprehend how she hated what he had done to her when he kissed her goodnight.

It was at Biot that she first saw Hasheena. She was taken by the way she swung as she walked along. It was so natural. Like a lioness. And the glittering blackness of her big eyes. Claudine actually followed her around the street-market for a while, listening to the hoarse voice as she haggled with the stall-holders. She caught Claudine smiling at her and smiled back.

'It's hot,' she said, for want of something better to say.

'Will you join me for a coffee?' Claudine asked.

Hasheena looked surprised.

'Me?'

Claudine nodded happily. The moment a person falls in love approaches without warning and seizes one like a murderer by the throat. Hasheena came towards her.

'OK,' she laughed, as though she sensed that although there was something preposterous in a chic Frenchwoman wanting to make friends with an Arab girl, there was an indefinable joy in their meeting. They sat together before a small café in a modest square that looked down an alley of crumbling tenements festooned with washing. It was the first place they found. They giggled like school-children at the flies that defied their flapping hands and the friendly old dog that rubbed itself against their bare legs.

'What a terrible place,' complained Hasheena.

'Who cares?'

The heat lurked even in the shaded narrow streets of the town. It burned Claudine's eyes and funnelled up her moist, perspiring thighs. She drew her skirt back, almost above her knees, and discreetly jiggled her legs to move the hot air. After the coffee they had gazpacho and a pistachio cornetto apiece. Hasheena told her that she was twenty and had been married for two years to a man who had been a market-trader in leathergoods but now owned a pottery shop in Vallauris.

'How old are you?' asked Hasheena.

'Twenty-nine.'

'That's old,' she said, blowing out her chubby cheeks in surprise.

'Old,' agreed Claudine, reaching out and touching her hand for the first time.

It was at that point that Hasheena averted her eyes and looked anxious, as though she was working out a problem in her own mind.

'Have you ever had a woman friend?' Claudine asked quietly.

She was aware of her inner turmoil, hoping that Hasheena would want to be close to her. Perhaps if they only met occasionally for coffee, she thought. She was almost breathless with a deep need to be with Hasheena and never lose her.

'Do you like Arabs?' Hasheena asked after a while.

'I don't see people like that,' Claudine confessed. 'I mean, I don't see differences in that way. I see nice people and the other kind.'

'You're a nice person,' Hasheena smiled.

'Thank you.'

'I think we're going to be friends,' Hasheena said, giving Claudine an owlish look.

279

Claudine's amethystine eyes twinkled with delight.

'Would you care to come to my apartment in Vence?' she asked quickly.

'Now?'

'Why not?'

It was mid-afternoon when they arrived at Claudine's place. Hasheena looked around in wonder at the Turkish wall-hangings, a life-size white porcelain Buddha in one corner, two giant blue Japanese vases filled with jasmine, muguet des bois, a poster of the gamine Caron, a mirror advertising the 1929 Hupmobile, and tinkling black and white bead curtains.

'How beautiful,' Hasheena declared.

They came together passing between two rooms. Claudine stopped Hasheena and kissed her on the mouth. Hasheena did not seem surprised.

'Do you mind?' Claudine murmured.

Hasheena shook her head.

'No.'

And the next time Claudine kissed her, Hasheena responded with wild and hungry affection.

'We haven't got much time,' Hasheena grumbled as she set the tarot cards in a horseshoe spread. They leaned over a long coffee-table decorated with tiles of butterflies ringed with wild flowers.

'We really ought to cover our bodies when addressing the tarot,' Hasheena observed. 'Respect is due to the cards.'

Claudine pouted and, stretching a hand across the table, cupped Hasheena's left breast in her palm.

'Claudine, you're quite shameless. We will probably be struck blind for insulting the Qabalah. Anyhow, what's so urgent about a reading?'

'You see,' Claudine explained, 'an unusual man has entered my life.'

Hasheena looked at her in mock horror.

'A man? Faugh. How disgusting.'

'It's not like that. It's to do with work. And quite honestly, my darling, I fear him.'

'How can I be sure that he's not your secret lover?'

'Oh? You're not in one of those crazy moods, are you?'

'Look at all those silly cards. The Moon reversed. A failure of nerve. Are you frightened to act out any situation facing you?'

'I'm not sure.'

Hasheena turned up a succession of reversed cards.

'It's indecision all the way, Claudine. Very boring.'

Hasheena played out the cards a second and then a third time.

'I have something here. One who rides roughshod over others. A ruthless man.'

'That could be him.'

'And do you know his story?' a wide-eyed Hasheena demanded.

Claudine nodded.

'Is it really terrible?'

'Pretty bad.'

'Tell me,' Hasheena insisted.

'I could do with a coffee.'

'I'll make it,' Hasheena said, jumping up.

They went into the kitchen, arm in arm.

'His father,' Claudine related, 'was the most powerful cock in Italy.'

'I've never liked Italians,' Hasheena sniffed.

'And his mother was a princess, albeit one whose credentials were not entirely satisfactory.'

'Was she or wasn't she?'

'It's a complicated matter.'

'Where did the Spermtrek lead you?'

'To the most surprising places and conclusions. Would you care for a coucou?'

Hasheena shook her head. 'Darling, I'm as fat as a milch-goat.'

Claudine drew Hasheena to her. They kissed.

'What about my story?' Hasheena fussed.

'This scion of the most powerful cock in Italy was found as a newborn baby on the Plage de Pamplemousse by what is now Le Coq Hardi Caravan Camp. As I said, his mother was a princess. At least, that is what she called herself. One of the Esterels. They used to work with the circuses around here. Acrobats, fire-eaters, jugglers, fortune-tellers and tight-rope walkers. One of them can still be seen playing his fiddle around the bistros of St Tropez.'

'Gipsies,' sneered Hasheena.

'Ah, there's more to the princess than that.'

They sipped their coffee thoughtfully.

'Tell me about the baby that was found on the beach,' said Hasheena, taking a modest bite out of Claudine's brioche.

'The baby, found lying on the waterline, was barely a few hours old, it was severely sunburned and near to the point of death when Helmut, an alsatian that belonged to Baroness Geli von Kressenstein of Ludwigshafen, seized the infant by its head and carried it off to the shade of an umbrella pine for a quick snack. The baroness, who was paddling in the Mediterranean, shocked by what she saw, lost control of her bladder and piddled in the sea, so diverting Helmut, who fortunately had been conditioned to respond positively to his mistress's urolagnian stimuli.'

'May Allah strike her dead,' Hasheena cried.

'It's a happyish ending,' Claudine promised. 'Helmut abandoned the child. He joined his mistress in the water, splashing up to her joyously and ramming his sensual snout up her piss-sodden culottes for a rapturous sniff. The baby was hooked into the tatter-bag of a beachcombing beggar-woman and taken to St Tropez. There it prospered until the Great Liberation, when it was bartered to a Captain Joe Spillano for five hundred Luckies and a dozen Hershey bars.'

'What about the German pervert?' Hasheena asked.

Claudine gave her a measured look of reproof.

'The baroness was basically a dog-lover. Poor Helmut was taken out of action by an Audi taxi in Russelsheim in 1951. She returns to the Plage de Pamplemousse every year for a solemn uric requiem that until now has defied rational interpretation. The investigation has cost the man who was nearly Helmut's petit déjeuner the best part of a million dollars.'

'That seems a lot of money,' Hasheena mused. 'And the mysterious princess? The baby's real mother?'

'Ah. The search for *her* identity has taken us almost twenty years. It started well before I joined Spermtrek. And now it is over at last. I have just posted a confidential report to my client. Our fees will be more than five million dollars.'

'Five million dollars?' gasped Hasheena.

'That's nearly what it cost us, darling,' laughed Claudine.

'Who would pay five million dollars just to discover what the sleeping arrangements were?'

'Have you heard of Sham Shilverman?'

Hasheena shook her head. She snuggled up to Claudine.

'We only have ten minutes left,' she said huskily. 'And even so, you'll have to put your foot down. The tarot reading will have to wait until tomorrow, I'm afraid.'

Claudine's hand moved down inside Hasheena's briefs. Hasheena laid her head on Claudine's shoulder, making herself accessible to caressing fingers. She gyrated slowly as her garment was drawn down.

'I swear to drive like Ascari himself,' Claudine pleaded before finding Hasheena's mouth with hers.

Their underwear made a splash of blue and pink on the kitchen floor as they returned to the bedroom. They moved awkwardly, enbracing each other all the way.

'You French,' grumbled Hasheena, half-closing her eyes as she positioned herself on the bed, 'are essentially a depraved race.'

Chapter 39

One of the things that make novels less
plausible than history, I find, is the way they shrink
from coincidence.

— Tom Stoppard.

Laszlo was agreeably surprised at his reception on board the *Voracité*. Polly was more attentive than he imagined she would be; Wolfgang treated him with the easy familiarity of an intimate friend; and Sunburn Spillano, although preoccupied for most of the time with Basin Sorel, was not averse to making a fourth at bridge or playing a little ping-pong, a game at which he was surprisingly adept, using a demon pen-grip and demonstrating a talent for spin that Laszlo found virtually impossible.

On the first morning, Basin and Sunburn positioned their deck-chairs on the port side. They lounged around in dark glasses, yachting-caps, floral shirts and Bermuda shorts, playing chequers most of the time with intermissions at the ping-pong table. Polly had her nose in a Colette novel, Wolfgang whirled fish-lines over the taffrail, trawling for star-gazers and shad, while Laszlo sat not too far from Polly, leafing with little interest through a biography of Proust that he'd found on his cabin table.

He was besotted with Polly. He closely observed her most trivial movements, delighting in the way her mouth turned up puckishly when she smiled, the curves of her sorcerous legs, the silken fall of the yellow hair and the pout of those full lips when she disapproved of anything. He detected the trace of a lisp when she spoke too fast, and longed to grasp and lick her small, Maya-like fingers. He was entranced by her ears, the arch of her neck, the way she masticated her food, sipped her wine and the manner in which she held her head to one side when listening intently. He was provoked by the perfume of her body and itched with desire when his salacious eyes traced the outline of briefs below her light summer skirt. The previous night, alone in his cabin, he had lain brooding and priapic, only accepting sleep when he could meld himself into her dreamy flesh, awaking in the morning scrotum-plump and desperate to catch a glimpse of her once again.

'Do you like Proust?' Polly murmured when she caught him sneaking a hungry look at her.

'I haven't read him,' he admitted, biting his lower lip in mock guilt.

'But you must,' she urged, 'he's an indispensable furnishing for a modern mind.'

She put her copy of *La Maison de Claudine* aside and talked quickly and easily about her bookish inclinations.

'Good writers,' she reflected, 'like Proust, Joyce, and Nabokov, must be re-read many times.'

'I like Joyce,' he said, 'but I find Nabokov heartless.'

She nodded.

'He's as cerebral as Bach,' she smiled. 'All three, however, have at least one common element. They combine high art with comedy. They are the great comic writers of this century.'

'Do you like the Claudine books?' he asked.

'I adore them,' she declared with passion. 'I'm refreshed by them. For me, they're about the innocence I have lost and yearn for. But I suspect that one's literary predilections have little to do with one's personality. Butchers probably read sentimental novels.'

'I'm not too sure about that,' he said.

Later he told her that he liked Hungarian women, and she asked him quickly how many he'd known.

'Two,' he confessed sheepishly. 'One of them I knew very well and loved, and the other I didn't care much for at all.'

Polly laughed at what she perceived as his disingenuousness.

'Fifty per cent on a sample of two doesn't say much for your empiricism or, for that matter, Hungarian women.'

'I hadn't included you,' he said, flirting a little. 'When I do, the average will improve quite dramatically.'

Meanwhile, things did not appear to be going well for Thelma. She complained to Wolfgang that not only had she started a troublesome period on the very day they embarked, but she had developed a problem for which there was a need for clinical attention. She was not comforted when Wolfgang suggested a brief consultation with Cabral, the paunchy Portuguese cook, after he'd finished his big sizzle for the English breakfasts. Apart from a fairly basic first-aid box that housed the simpler palliatives like clove oil, asprin, Nembutal and sloe gin, Santan Cabral took care of the more complex medical problems. His skills encompassed the treatment of abrasions, burns and cuts, the administration of injections, general massage and the stitching of cloven flesh.

'I wouldn't allow that smirky bugger to finger me,' she fussed.

'This is not going to screw up our arrangements, is it?' Wolfgang enquired anxiously.

'I'm in pain, Wolfie,' she sniffed. 'I think it's my kidneys.'

'We're putting in to Cagliari in a day or so. Maybe you can see a doctor there.'

Thelma nodded.

'Life's an absolute bastard,' she reflected, her eyes welling up with tears.

'Do you want me to rub you down there?' he murmured.

'Where?' she snapped.

'You know,' he whispered.

Thelma shook her head. Then, biting her lip to contain her disappointment, she scuttled down the gangway to her cabin.

Just before they docked at Cagliari, Sunburn received the message he'd been waiting for. It was a cable with the information that the unclothed corpses of Sheik Yusuf Hamami and Madame Froline Nablus had been discovered in a chateau near Albi (·38 calibre close-range head wounds). Although there were no traces of the Swiss bearer bonds, the Spillano Garbage agents had recovered dollar bills, drafts and jewellery to their approximate value. They had also appropriated four years' interest compounded at 15 per cent plus pursuit and exchange adjustment expenses. The loot had been taken from a wall-safe behind a painting of Adam and Eve posed between two pensive zhivagos. This was, for Sunburn, extremely cheerful news.

When they disembarked, Thelma went off alone and the other five hired a six-seater Fiat that Wolfgang drove, making for his friend Pietro Casanova's place at Nuoro, where lunch had been arranged. When they arrived at the white palazzo, it was shuttered. They rattled the gates for several minutes, and eventually an ancient woman approached cautiously, peering through the bars with suspicion. Her obese son followed with a shotgun and a black Doberman on a chain. There was much shouting and snarling. Signor Casanova, it appeared, was possibly in Sumatra, maybe Taiwan or even New Zealand. He was not expected back in Nuoro for six months. There was obviously some unfortunate mistake with the month or even the year. There was no food and the house was closed until September, when Signor Casanova's daughter would be arriving. The obese servant held up two stubby fingers.

'In two months,' he shouted.

'In two months,' the toothless mother repeated, also demonstrating this fact with her fingers and smiling for the first time.

The party climbed back into the bus and rumbled along the dusty road, finding in due course a trattoria where they endured a less than perfect meal. They returned to Cagliari in the afternoon, having agreed to meet Thelma at a tavola calda adjacent to the garage from where they'd hired the Fiat. She looked despondent.

'I have to fly to London as soon as possible,' she sighed. 'I've got a serious kidney infection and need specialised treatment.'

Earlier that day, she had been examined by a physician in Cagliari. The news was as dismal as she'd expected.

'You have a chancre on your labia minora, signora,' he murmured. 'It is almost certainly evidence of syphilis.'

He gave her a large shot of procaine penicillin immediately, instructing her to visit a clinic on her return to London.

'It's quite a simple problem to treat,' he said, 'and should not in any way inconvenience your day-to-day existence, but it would be inadvisable for you to fornicate until you have been cleared by your doctor. If you know the source of infection, it would be prudent to inform him so that he should have treatment as well. Also any other partners you may have enjoyed . . .' He stopped, and shrugged his shoulders

She nodded, then paid him. Wandering out into the hot sunlight, Thelma meditated on the dark and sinister transits of the Treponema Pallidum sailing under the skull and crossbones from beyond the lost horizons of time. Perhaps, she brooded, there might be another opportunity, but on further reflection she suspected that there would not. Wolfgang had appeared almost disappointed to see her. Was it the ochre-tinted cropped hair, she wondered, or the fishnet poncho that didn't quite seem to work with her sailor outfit? She dismissed the strange thought that somehow he had intuitively sensed the presence of danger when they first kissed formally on deck. He had, she recalled, seemed unusually withdrawn and hesitant. Men, Thelma concluded, were bastards; she regretted that she'd not allowed the Italian to fuck her, so gifting him with her chaplets of love. That now not being possible, she wished him dead.

The *Voracité* set off for Venice. Their course lay through the straits of Messina, and northwards. Wolfgang did not appear to be unduly diminished by Thelma's absence. Indeed, Laszlo found him in particularly high spirits. They were partners in jokey games of bridge, Sunburn and Basin making up the four. Polly sat a little apart, rumpling through a tired copy of The *Wall Street Journal*. Laszlo caught her eye from time to time. The drinking started with some Monica de Cagliari and progressed to cognac.

The mood became celebratory and a shade adventurous. Polly went to her cabin just before midnight and the four men took a turn on deck, Laszlo noticing Sunburn and Basin kissing ardently in the shadows beside the inflatable tender that had been secured to the aft starboard rail. And when Wolfgang slid his arm around his shoulders as they stood watching the blazing lights of a splendid liner that passed hardly a mile away, Laszlo did not feel threatened or uneasy; only extremely happy. He wondered what Maya would have said had she seen him now, an intimate of Wolfgang Ferrari. Long before he returned to his cabin, Laszlo suspected that he was far more intoxicated than he had ever been in his life.

He undressed and lay on the bed, subsiding into reveries of Polly, recalling as he drifted what he had asked her (was it after the third rubber?), no more than a whispered precative over coffee when the others were out of earshot.

'Come to me tonight,' he'd hissed intemperately.

She did not appear surprised by the existential bleakness of his request, and responded with a murmured 'Ah' or some such monosyllable, turning away abstractedly to address Basin. He sensed Selveratnam shuffling about in a corner somewhere, corrupting his lust for Polly by his devilish presence. And then fell quickly into the violet chasm of a profound alcoholic sleep, supine and naked in the warm, airless night.

It was not unpleasant at first. A slow friction against his cock as he emerged from the depths. And he was not sure whether his shock was triggered by the thought of Selveratnam holding a knife against his throat on that fateful night or a nervous response in finding a real person poking him. He struck out with his hands and raised his knees, levering the intruder away, suspecting, as he awoke to the smell of a familiar aftershave and the crash of broken glass, who it was. He switched on the light. Across the debris of a drinks cabinet lay the naked form of Wolfgang. Apart from a small cut across his upper left arm, there was no blood. As Laszlo knelt over the body, it momentarily dissolved into the corpse of Selveratnam. The buzzing in his head returned. He panicked, unable to evaluate Wolfgang's condition. He thought bleakly of death as he slipped on a coat and ran down the gangway to knock at Polly's door.

'It's Wolfgang,' he muttered when she finally appeared. 'He's had an accident.'

She put on a dressing-gown and, opening a drawer, extracted a black medical box. Back in Laszlo's cabin, she dropped to her knees beside her husband, feeling for his pulse, then laying her face against his chest. Laszlo watched her in trepidation.

'Well?'

Polly shrugged. She opened the box, taking out a hypodermic and ampoule.

'What's that?' Laszlo asked. 'Are you sure it's OK to pump it into him?'

'I think it's magnesium sulphate. Cabral uses it on him in an emergency.' She located the vein in Wolfgang's arm and injected him. 'It's the stuff he needs for his heart condition.'

Laszlo thought of the fat Portuguese cook with some distaste. 'He was probably knocked unconscious when he struck his head on the radiator,' he suggested

Polly listened for Wolfgang's heart once more. They waited, Polly on her knees and Laszlo standing behind her, looking on hopelessly. He listened to the muffled sound of the engine and the swish of the boat through the water. Just a gentle creaking and swaying. Finally, Polly rose to her feet and shrugged.

'He's gone,' she announced in a flat, unemotional voice.

'Jesus Christ.'

'The sonofabitch drank too much,' she said bitterly.

She asked what had happened. Laszlo gave an account of how he'd found Wolfgang on top of him.

'I knew he had a buzz for you,' she said. 'In a way he was relieved that Thelma wasn't in the frame anymore.'

Laszlo turned away with a sigh.

'I was just getting to know the guy,' he murmured.

She rummaged in her dressing-gown pocket.

'Cigarettes?' she asked.

Laszlo found a packet by his bed. He gave her one, lighting that and another for himself.

'Don't you think we should tell the others?' he asked.

Polly was deep in thought.

'We should be in Brindisi in the morning,' she reflected.

Laszlo settled beside her on the bed, a reassuring palm on her knee.

'Of course,' she mused, 'we must expect an explosion of publicity, a great deal of morbid interest and some investigative journalism of the more sensational kind. Wolfgang is a household name in Italy. Furthermore, an autopsy could reveal damage of which we are unaware. It could complicate matters.'

'Like what?'

'Like insurance, the suspected involvement of third parties, and an immoderate degree of police attention. Not an ideal state of affairs.'

'Shall we ask Sunburn's advice?' Laszlo asked.

The idea did not commend itself to her.

'He's an extremely vengeful man. You've only seen the sunnier side of him. I'm afraid he'll not forgive you for what has happened.'

'It was hardly my fault,' Laszlo protested.

'Listen, Tom,' she warned, 'Sunburn is a very private character. It would not be untrue to say that he's paranoid about publicity. Indeed, theoretically, as a Financially Sterile Entity, he hardly exists in what people imagine to be the real world. In a way, I consider it's my duty to protect him from any provocation of this sort.'

'Do you work for him?' Laszlo asked.

She nodded. 'Let's say we work for one another.'

She got up and considered Wolfgang's body dispassionately.

'I've got a reasonable idea,' she said.

Laszlo stared at her. Despite the warmth of the cabin, he succumbed to an involuntary shiver. Polly appeared remote and detached from the reality of the night's horror. She nodded towards the port-hole.

'Shove him through that,' she ordered starkly.

'Overboard?'

'In the long run it might be simpler.'

She looked at Laszlo. He was conscious of her seductive magic. He stood up, fearful, uncertain of what she'd suggested. But he knew there was nothing he could refuse this woman. Polly sucked on her cigarette and met his bewildered gaze.

'We'd better hurry,' she suggested, glancing at her watch. 'It'll be light in an hour or so.'

Laszlo made up his mind suddenly. Bending over the body, he hoisted Wolfgang to his chest and then heaved him over one shoulder. He recoiled at the pliant dampness of the male body, imagining for a moment that Wolfgang's pendant arm had moved of its own volition. Polly had already unbolted the port-hole window. She helped him position and then push the body through. They hardly heard the splash as Wolfgang fell from their hands. Then, unexpectedly, Polly slung the medical box after her husband.

'What's that for?' Laszlo demanded.

'A simple precaution,' she replied. 'One never knows where an interrogation of Cabral, for example, might lead.'

Laszlo was silent as he cleared up the glass and moved the damaged furniture against the bulkhead.

'You didn't like him much, did you?' he asked later.

'Not much.' He noticed that she was trembling.

'Have a brandy,' he suggested.

They downed a couple of stiffish drinks. He checked his watch. Half-past three. Somebody down the passage flushed a lavatory cistern. Polly stubbed out her cigarette and lay back along the bed.

'Perhaps we shouldn't have done it,' she reflected.

'What do you mean by that?' Laszlo asked in alarm.

Polly shrugged. 'It's too late now, anyway.'

Laszlo heard the awful buzzing in his skull once again. And Selveratnam, a leporine grin on his face, suddenly materialised at the foot of the bed like a black garden gnome. Laszlo rubbed his eyes, swallowed another large brandy and turned his back on the intrusive apparition.

'What's the matter?' Polly asked.

'Nothing,' Laszlo replied. 'Nothing at all.'

Laszlo found that the angle of Polly's head on the pillow was such an extraordinary evocation of Maya that it was difficult not to believe that she had returned to him by some trick of Fate. He remembered Maya's heavy breasts, rounded belly and honey-coloured fuzz. Leaning over the bed, he kissed Polly's mouth, suddenly aware of the warmth and sharp bouquet of her perspiring flesh. She half-raised herself, eyeing him warily.

'We've both had more than enough to drink,' she observed glumly.

Laszlo drew her dressing-gown apart. She was wearing a blue nightdress, through which he could apprehend the weight and contours of her breasts. He kissed first one and then the other over the silk.

'I love you,' he pleaded, knowing it was an inadequate profession of his cunt-crazy fever for the woman he'd fucked so many times in his dreams.

Yet he'd have loved her even if she'd dematerialised in his arms, leaving nothing but ectoplasmic mist. He was, without any doubt, Polly-possessed. She now accepted the inevitable. Her fingers caressed his hair.

'This has to be a big mistake,' she warned quietly.

He found her mouth again. She neither repelled nor encouraged his soft lips.

'Put the light out,' she instructed.

She smiled quietly at his grotesquely priapic silhouette in the semi-darkness – but allowed him to help her shuck off her garment. He devoured her; kissing, licking, groping and whispering insane endearments that she received in silence. He rubbed his lips against her floss, the furrow-probing tongue and fingers taking her like a ripe melon, shaking as she astonished him and herself by assuaging his tumidity in her fervent mouth. Later, when he entered and flooded into her, he cried. He cried like someone who had lost and found everything of value in his life in the same climacteric spasm of time. Polly, who knew that this young stranger could never be part of her dreams, wondered bleakly at his sadness, cradling him on her shoulder. He was still there when first light illuminated the cabin. And as she turned into him, he saw a Purple Emperor on her left buttock.

'It's on the wrong side,' he murmured drowsily.

'What?'

'Your Purple Emperor,' he smiled, still smudged by sleep.

Polly pushed him away and jumped out of bed. A premonition

293

that had troubled her from the moment she had first seen him suddenly shaped itself into sinister fact. Laszlo stared at her dimpled arse in disbelief. She had a Red Admiral as well. What did it mean? His heart quickened.

'Polly,' he called, reaching for her in his confusion.

She slipped on her dressing-gown and stared at him as though she'd seen a ghost. Polly had no doubts now about his identity but waited for him to speak.

'My mother,' he explained, 'had the same two butterflies on her bottom as you. The positions, however, were reversed.'

'Who are you?' she demanded, knowing but fearful of the answer.

'My name,' he confessed, 'is Laszlo Gabor.'

She regarded him in sorrow.

'It is not,' she mumbled brokenly. 'Your name is Laszlo Horvath and I'm your mother, Maya. Wolfgang was your papa.'

The story, the whole convoluted story, followed over cups of hot black coffee. As Polly spoke, Laszlo ached for her more than ever before, but sensed that she'd already begun the retreat from his unwanted love. The warning was in her blue eyes. For a few hours, fantasy had been made flesh and now was fantasy again. All that remained was despair and less hope than he had ever known.

The *Voracité* was just outside Brindisi harbour having entered the Strait of Otranto on her northward course to Venice. It was a misty morning but the sea was relatively calm. The alarm was raised, a whooping siren that excited everybody out of bed.

'Wolfie has disappeared,' proclaimed Basin in anguish.

The six crew members and four passengers hung over the rails looking blankly around at the green scummy water.

'He sometimes goes for a swim,' Saldhana the captain said with a cognisant wink.

'He could have had a heart attack in the water,' Laszlo suggested.

'Why should he?' Saldhana snorted. 'Signor Ferrari is as strong as a horse.'

'He doesn't have a bad heart?' Laszlo enquired limply.

'What? A man who'd think nothing of swimming fifteen miles? He's a sort of superman,' boasted Santan Cabral, the cook.

Laszlo shot a dark look at Polly, who'd started to weep with cinematic bravura. Sunburn was masterful in the emergency despite his obvious grief. He had, after all, only recently promoted Wolfgang from cousin to half-brother. He volunteered to take two of the crew with him in the tender to search the area to the south. Saldhana said that they would radio Brindisi and ask for an air search to be conducted.

'He's nowhere to be seen,' Basin Sorel declared, sweeping the waters around them with his racing binoculars.

Cabral pointed to an object about half a mile to the south-east. The tender was lowered and sped off in this direction. It was an hour or so before a coast boat appeared. Two members of the local carabinieri came aboard, followed in a fishing-boat by a photographer, reporter and priest, who commenced an un-solicited mass in the galley. Two of the crew accepted the offered sacrament and the reporter tried to tape-record interviews with everyone. Polly sobbed. The carabinieri insisted that Saldhana make for Brindisi. Everybody would be required for further questioning. After about an hour, the tender returned. An empty barrel, a decaying lamprey, the case of an old piano and a truck tyre was all that they had found. Sunburn Spillano declined to make a statement, pointing out that he was a Financially Sterile Entity and did not want to cast a tax shadow of any kind.

The *Voracité* remained in port for three days. They decided it would not be appropriate for them to continue up the Adriatic to Venice. Polly gave the definitive interview.

'I'm inconsolable,' she sniffed, raising her hand to her fore-head.

Fortunately, three photographers captured her anguish for posterity. It made a nice front-page shot in the *Messaggero*, edging out a picture of Mount Etna and the exclusive that the greatest deposit of diamonds on earth was located below its molten core.

Chapter 40

'Do you think,' asked Sunburn Spillano, 'that you could goose up the search for Selveratnam and Gabor?'

Claudine Zola shrugged.

'As you know, Mr Spillano, Spermtrek specialises in determining the sleeping arrangements, a complex, time-consuming and often tedious business. What you require could be quite as easily accomplished by many other investigative agencies.'

Spillano eyed her carefully.

'I'm putting my marbles in your pocket,' he grunted.

She opened one of the folders on her desk.

'While we have no problem with the picture you've given me of Selveratnam, I'm afraid that the one of Gabor leaves much to be desired.'

'It's the only one we've got,' snarled Spillano. 'Possibly the only one in existence. Even his ID shot has vanished from the employment files of the First Nag and Waik.'

Claudine Zola frowned.

'A fuzzy snapshot of a boy in short pants, eight or nine maybe, posed between his Aunt Moura and a Mrs Ada Mulcahy is hardly good enough, Mr Spillano. We've had our visualiser produce dozens of sketches of what she thinks the adult Laszlo Gabor should look like. We've tried the face with a beard, a moustache, a beard and moustache, a half-set, balding, bald and bushy. We've furnished him with spectacles, shades, eye-patches, carious teeth and nasty facial scars. We've played around with combinations of these projections, doing right and left profiles, full-frontals, left and right three-quarters, gazes ascendant, descendant, horrified, horny, happy and hungry. And so far, Mr Spillano, the results have not been too encouraging.'

Sunburn Spillano made a sour face.

'I wouldn't be wildly surprised,' he observed, 'if Mr

Selveratnam were no longer on this planet. He was not a very robust specimen anyway. Which makes my interest in Gabor a little more intense than it is healthy or reasonable for a guy to have in a total stranger. His disappearance is what is known in certain circles as a provocative vamoose. Apart from a possible homicide, an extremely unkind act even among us more competitive entrepreneurs, there is the vexing question of some property Mr Selveratnam had on his person. Now we're talking about a pensionable employee of the Spillano Garbage Corporation, madame. And Spillano Garbage never walks away from its obligations.'

Claudine Zola blew out her cheeks, shaking her head from side to side.

'We have one possible sighting,' she said. 'Do you remember the Baroness Geli von Kressenstein of Ludwigshafen?'

'You mean Joseph Goebbels's ex-mistress, the friend of Leni Riefenstahl, the dame who pisses in the sea?'

'That's right. The lady who saved you from Helmut.'

Spillano's face darkened with a spasm of guilt.

'Fuck. And I didn't even send her flowers. The Baroness, I mean.'

Claudine Zola smiled.

'She thinks she met a man who approximates to one of our visualisations in 1980. It was on the Plage de Pamplemousse.'

'Nineteen-eighty? That was four years ago.'

Claudine Zola nodded.

'Let us not forget that she's ninety-seven and her memory could be impaired. The young man's name, she suggests, might be Piccolo or Oboe; Horn maybe. Humbert Horn, she feels, has a ring of authenticity.'

Spillano scowled.

'So the sonofabitch could have changed his name?'

'Why not?'

A distant bell started ringing in Spillano's head. The solution hadn't come, but he was certain that it was on its way, fizzing around the circuitry of the Spillano cerebral mush. He blinked as unformed questions queued at the margins of his awareness.

Something told him that he'd seen the sonofabitch recently. He decanted himself a tumbler of Célestins and, taking a mouthful, brooded about Laszlo Gabor, alias Humbert Horn. He had never felt more like totalling a human being than he did this guy. But first things first. The bastard had to be lifted, then nailed to the floor.

'Perhaps we could try an additional strategy,' Claudine Zola suggested, 'which although fairly marginal might produce results.'

Sunburn's eyes flickered thoughtfully.

'It's just possible that Gabor summers in the St Tropez area. We could trawl Mrs Mulcahy around the cafés, restaurants, bars and beaches for a month or two. If he was around, she just might be fortunate enough to spot him.'

'Needle-in-a-haystack stuff,' Spillano brooded.

'Provided she was willing to help, it would add another fifty thousand francs to the bill. That would include a chauffeur-escort, of course.'

'Good money after bad,' he mused.

'More than likely,' Claudine Zola agreed.

'Do it,' he snapped suddenly.

'Fine,' she said, 'we'll try to persuade Mrs Mulcahy to have a sunshine holiday.'

Spillano rose. Something was troubling him. He sensed that sonofabitch Laszlo was lurking around a not-too-distant corner.

Chapter 41

The news of Wolfgang Ferrari's presumed drowning was a tedious setback to the production of *Love Is the End*. Even Medusa O'Toole showed signs of irritation about the project, while Shilverman brooded with Schopenhauerian weltschmerz on the futility of hope. As they had many miles of film showing Wolfgang doing the business as Uranus, and as the prospect of finding a credible lookalike was unrealistic, there was a red figure of twenty-five million dollars to rub away before they could jog back to the starting-blocks. Even a preliminary meeting of Shilverman, Joe Spillano and Harada (representing the First Nag and Waik) ended in turmoil when Harada, after taking a private call from Natalie Tolstoy, disclosed that his bank was not prepared to toss any more yen into the pot and Joe Spillano suggested, in an injudicious aside, that maybe they should consider replacing Medusa O'Toole and go for younger players.

'You goddam shithead,' snarled Shilverman, shaking a fist at him. 'It's Medusa or nobody.'

There was much shrugging, cursing and threatening before they reluctantly agreed to convene a further meeting. But Sunburn Spillano had also been reported as going lukewarm on the project, and Sheik Yusuf was no longer around to issue his buoyant clichés of continuing faith in Shilverman's genius.

The confusion and lack of direction that Medusa had confidently predicted would be submerged by the celebration of Sham's ninety-fifth anniversary persisted to confound those happy expectations.

Although the great event was scheduled to encompass ten glittering days, the pattern of the projected schedule was nudged into unforeseen chaos for the first seventy-two hours, when the Bloemfontein organisation, Djambokov, to whom Hengist Dunkelbaum had awarded the contract for streaming the guests, encountered problems with the lexical sort, due to their dedicated asteroid being unexpectedly smothered in the detritus of transiting meteorites. This resulted in the corruption of the identity-recognition module, treating VIPs as VAPs (Vandals and Parasites) and vice versa. VITs (Very Important Tourists) and VATs (Vagrants and Transients) were, however, treated with the punctiliousness their status suggested.

VITs were kissed ardently by curvaceous cuntkins or bronzed bumbeaux, creatures chosen for their dazzling smiles, flawless skins and bodily protuberances that could best advertise Medusa O'Toole's sponsored line of shimmering leotards.

VATs were glad-handed by perspiring matrons and perceptibly seedier males (facial erysipelas, indifferent dental work, slack abdominals and armpit fuzz were not automatic disqualifications), tricked out in slightly soiled chariot-chitons that were first used in a Swiss watch-manufacturer's abortive remake (1960) of *Bien Heure*.

The VITs were invited into the Hospitality Salon, allowed an aperitif or two, an assiette of assorted canapés and a dip into bowls of stoned olives, pickled walnuts, crystallised cherries, anchovies and chunks of rubbery mimolette.

The VATs were corralled into Beer Pavilions where crisps and Dalmatian lager were available for those with the right combination of slot silver.

But the trouble occurred when the VAPs (mainly beach-sleepers, shaggy bikers with their pillion-pokes, bored surfies, sunburnt freeloaders, displaced hooligans, friendly playgirls in search of play, wealthy recidivists, and drunken Anglo-Saxon football supporters) soaked up the resources reserved for VIPs. The Béchamel String Quartet were bullied through a programme of pop music until their bowing hands seized up. Their original programme of Monteverdi, Mozart and Brahms had to be abandoned after the viola player was debagged and fellated by a ferocious Australian wearing nothing more than a baggy Test cap and a green jockstrap. Magnums of chilled Veuve Clicquot (La Grande Dame '79) were decanted down coarse gullets trained on indifferent bitter. Beluga, smoked salmon, lobster, grilled quail, elver vol-au-vents, roast widgeons, fin de claires and appetising displays of Selle de Chevreuil Briand were devoured at the moment of sighting; companions (male and female) thoughtfully provided by Miss O'Toole to dine and dance with, were gang-banged in toilets, while the sloe-eyed, plump-arsed menials (specially flown in from South East Asia) were grossly abused before the twilit shadows fell across the brooding statue of Gaia and pre-dinner cocktails tinkled over small-talk on the leafy verandahs of L'Amauresque. And still the VAPs came. It was as though the promise of bestiality had been conveyed to their nostrils on the musky Mediterranean breezes. By the second day, the pressure of space meant that bowels and bladders were vented in the most unlikely places. Harlequin-hued membranes of protein-rich vomit floated beside wine-dark turds bobbing about in the Hockneyesque azure of the pool. Scatological versions of folk-songs and national anthems were screamed until voices were reduced to hoarse whispers. Bruised yobbery fought to challenge and defend concepts of Lebensraum through the wreckage of furniture, while others sobbed with drunken remorse and sadness. The VIP area rapidly deteriorated into a miasmic tip. Duckboards criss-crossed the billiards-room and cocktail-lounge to avoid the festering bog of fecal porridge, seething with bluebottles, wasps, mosquitoes, maggots and albino tapeworms. Indeed, an Irish entomologist, Bertie Hayes, later sighted a cloud of tsetse flies and (what luck) a Congolese fritillary, a rarity seldom seen far from hippopotami wallows. The sloe-eyed, plump-arsed menials continued to submit themselves to scandalous misuse. Those who were locked in bedrooms prayed silently and devoutly for insensibility or death. A few of their more fortunate companions had managed to hook it into the safety of the Maures woodland during the second night.

In the meanwhile, the VIPs, being in general persons of sound character and high motivation, behaved in an exemplary manner. They demonstrated a commendable stoicism, even rejoiced at the unexpected bounty of the harsh arrangements. To some of them, it evoked their salad days in the armed forces, a golden age of spartan living, esprit-de-corps and enemies that they could instantly recognise and kill. They sat around camp-fires, talking with nostalgic animation about rubbing sticks together, cold showers, the glory of hard tack and the supreme importance of honour.

News of the horrendous cock-up reached Medusa O'Toole on the third morning. Rising from her recuperative bath of warm bullsperm and yogurt, she acted with expedition. A company of ex-legionnaires (recommended by her French agent), accompanied by razor-toothed hyena-hounds, were flown in by helicopter. The VIP environment was purged of intruders within half an hour. Before two hours had passed, the area was cleaned, fumigated, repaired and ready for use.

New companions were recruited from a Niçois model-agency, while the depleted ranks of the sloe-eyed, plump-arsed menials were augmented by procuring children with an obvious talent for well-mannered deference from the lycées of Coqauvin and St Tropez. Barely four hours after the first VAP had screamed in dismay as the ivory fangs of a razor-toothed hyena-hound sank into pliant flesh, a red carpet was in place, the tormented Béchamel String Quartet replaced by the Hollandaise Hot Shots, an ebony choir eager to hum Gershwin at the wave of a sepia palm occulted in a cockloft above the Valentino Bar, and the first celebratory Cirrholette rattled into a frosted glass by Scintillating (one hundred and seven authentic white teeth) Siggy, the Cocktail Commanchero.

Sham Shilverman, wearing a grey and beige tux, rode into the ballroom on his platinum scooter. He rose on tremulous pins, backing slowly out of the saddle to the polite applause of the assembled VIPs. Medusa O'Toole, soignée in a black velvet backless gown, long gloves and two ropes of pearls, approached, allowing Sham to take her in his arms as the Hot Shots (screened from view) trundled their way through the first few bars of 'Destiny'. Sham, still lissom at ninety-five, shuffled bravely. Here and there, traces of the Kennedy Two-step, Pig-Trot and Cock-Flutter obtruded slightly into his waltzing. Medusa was as terrific as ever. Each swirl evoked gasps of admiration, and while envious women spectators bitched about her age (eighty-five), men in whom the incandescence of passion had long cooled to no more than modestly warm clinker lusted to catch a glimpse of her legendary thighs. A septuagenarian ambassador from a hot-blooded Latin country, unable to bear the provocation of her crimson, wet mouth for more than five minutes at a time, kept scurrying to the lads' room to adjust his Y-fronts until eventually the dam burst, forcing him to retire disconsolately to his Cabane des Rêves.

By the time the ebony choir had replaced the Hollandaise Hot Shots, who retired briefly to the Emerald Room for their contractual break (a discreet fart, piss and scandalised yak about the injuries sustained by their fellow musicians of the Béchamel String Quartet), serenity had settled once more over L'Amauresque.

The VAPs had their footwear, bikes, money and credit-cards confiscated by the gendarmerie, were conveyed sixty kilometres north of L'Amauresque and abandoned halfway up a minor mountain (1,350 metres), from where they were ordered to make their way home. This was viewed by many sensitive people as a vindictive response to what several European papers reported as mere pony-play. Anguished parents (many of the VAPs were minors) organised petitions, politicians made speeches, poison-pen letters were addressed to Miss O'Toole and a bomb-threat originating from a call-box in Essen was taken seriously for several days.

Adjustments were made. The VATs were upgraded, given a courtesy visit from the ebony choir (two choruses of 'Ibe Seen De Glory Ob De Lawd Somewhere . . . Oh Yeah Somewhere' from Medusa O'Toole's *Cotton Pickin' Capers* of 1931), served Mateus Rosé with the fish course and allowed bone serviette-rings at all meals. The VITs were also given unexpected benefits. They were permitted to visit the VIP lounge after dinner and put their names down to have a Cirrholette rattled by Scintillating Siggy. They were also promised one sloe-eyed, plump-arsed menial (re-inforcements awaited from Tenerife), to every three VITs as an alternative to the post-prandial Castro de Luxe.

On the fourth day, the Shilverman retrospective began to be

screened on a continuous basis. Men in dark glasses and cream stetsons strolled in accompanied by tall, breastless women sheathed in silk with sheeny Eton cuts, pivoting intemperately on their pelvises as they slid along, hollow-cheeked, slack-mouthed and dazed with ennui. They arrived in chauffeur-driven stretched Hispanos and elongated Dusenbergs driven straight off the pages of a pre-war *Dernier Cri*. (That was the Paris glossy edited by Sophie Erhardt and her gifted philosopher brother Isaac, who was sent to his death by a collaborator for half a kilo of coffee and a slightly-used six-volt automobile accumulator.)

Sham was unsure whether it was all part of a film or a remembered dream. A film or a what ... He watched the cavalcade through the fronds of an Aleppo palm, drawing meditatively on his mini Guevara. The figures flashed up to him when he least expected them, refracting into beams of light before he could wave a hand or say hello.

'Can you see all those dead kids coming back to see my pix, honey?' he murmured to his octoroon companion, who had settled beside him in her cherry-pink floral shimmy. They sat thigh to thigh.

'Dead what?' she giggled.

Her skin had a warm amber sheen, and she had slanted cinnamon eyes, long lashes, plump red lips and just a trace of pretty crinkle in her honey-tinted hair. It was her job to relight the Guevara that kept going out. She had done it four times already. Sham just didn't suck too well these days.

'It's all wet and soggy,' he complained.

'You're funny,' she giggled, allowing him her best faked smile and a discreet palm run of her chubby knee.

'You're not dead, are you?' he whispered, savouring the heat of his flesh with exploratory fingers.

'You wanna make love to me?' she enquired with a polite, child-like slurring of her words.'

'Jesus, honey, I'm ninety-five,' he cursed as she lit what was no more than a stump once again.

'I don't mind,' she said earnestly.

'Perhaps we'll fuck in Heaven,' he brooded hopefully.

'I'm not going there yet,' she pouted. 'I'm only nineteen.'

'I'll be ready and waiting for you in seventy years or so.'

'Do you think they fuck in Heaven?'

Sham Shilverman leaned over and kissed her ear.

'I sure hope so. It's been the joy of my life from the age of twelve until I got to eighty-nine. After that, what I did didn't deserve to be called fucking. Tucking would be a more accurate description. A man's cock has no right to pass away before he does. It's against the law of moral equity.'

'Have you forgotten how to do it?' she chided him, kissing his ear in reciprocation.

'Shit no, honey. I screw myself stupid every night in my dreams. Those shuttered chambers of remembered desire where the living fornicate with the dead. It's the only place Medusa can't follow me.'

'Do you know Medusa O'Toole?' she asked with big eyes.

'We're the best of friends,' he said.

'Is that all?' she asked sceptically.

'There's nothing sweeter than friendship, honey,' Shilverman declared. 'Nothing. Not even a two-hour fuck in a rubber dinghy.'

'Did you ever sleep with her?'

'Sure. And I even slept with little girlies that I didn't care too much about at all. But it's very special when you get to sleep with a friend.'

'You probably exploited women,' she said reproachfully.

'Exactly right. Bang on,' Shilverman agreed.

He slung away his mini Guevara and shaped a Castro de Luxe for his trembling lips before continuing. 'In mitigation, honey, I suppose I showed a lot of dames what they thought was a good time. You know, eating, drinking, getting presents. In return, they joined me in my dream. They were all part of the big film. We just rolled and rolled.'

'It must have been a terrible thing to have loved a man like you.'

Shilverman almost chuckled. His thin lips parted a little.

305

'I guess I spread my ass around some. You know, honey,' he said, slitting his eyes, 'I used to be one helluva dancer. Good enough to be a professional. Making love was just an extension of that. Most good dancers make good lovers. The music is somewhere in their bodies. Now, when two people making love hear the same music, well, that's really something.'

'Did you ever have a girl like me?'

Sham Shilverman nodded. His eyes misted over as he remembered a sticky afternoon in Caracas. He found her hand, held it and squeezed it again and again.

'There was a kid called Trixie. She looked like a beanpole when dressed. "Narrow" I suppose would be the appropriate adjective. But when she took her clothes off, the geography altered quite dramatically. Surprising girl. Unexpectedly fleshy around the hips, with solid thighs, a bottom that was low, rounded and wonderfully muscled. A pair of hard melons. Just a vestigial hint of steatopyga, I suppose. Quite delicious.'

She giggled. 'You're describing me.'

Sham sucked more aggressively on his cigar than he had all night.

'Now this kid's business was a good half-inch lower than one would expect,' he whispered.

'Holy Mary. It's quite uncanny. You must have second sight,' the girl squealed.

They clasped hands and put their heads together. He pressed his dry lips against the epicanthus of her left eye. A shadow moved above them. Shilverman looked up in irritation at an amused Hengist Dunkelbaum.

'What do you think you're doing with this beautiful child?' Hengist reproved.

Sham Shilverman puffed blue smoke up at Dunkelbaum. He gripped his companion tighter.

'We're talking dirty together, Hengist, and I'm really enjoying myself. At ninety-five I'm entitled to be indiscreet. So why don't you fuck off?'

Dunkelbaum frowned. Shilverman hadn't improved with age.

'Medusa,' Hengist informed him, 'has requested me to ask you

306

whether you'd be willing to say a few words at dinner tonight. Presumably something sanitised. An English Cabinet Minister who's led a rather sheltered life will be present.'

'OK, OK. That'll be fine,' Shilverman replied, wagging his cigar impatiently at Dunkelbaum.

'Thanks,' Dunkelbaum smiled, turning away.

Shilverman took another robust suck and, shaking the ash from his Castro de Luxe, put it down. His sucking had improved miraculously. For a moment, he felt energised and young again. He turned his attention to his companion once more, moving the back of his hand slowly against the firmness of her belly.

'You haven't told me your name,' he complained, elevated by the enjoyment of her freshness.

'Trixie,' she giggled, her eyes sparkling at the joke.

It is probable that he did not catch what she said. If he did, it was certainly the last word he ever heard. For, quite suddenly and without warning, Shamuel Shankey Shilverman had stopped breathing.

The unexpected demise of Sham Shilverman had a profound effect on Medusa O'Toole. At first sceptical that such an inexplicable event had indeed occurred, she derided those who reported him dead and instructed the Hollandaise Hot Shots to scratch their way through the first sinuous bars of 'Matrosen' (it was their tango) as she sang huskily into his ear:

'Ja, das Meer ist blau, so blau – und das geht alles seinen Gang
Und wenn die Chose aus ist – dann fängts von vorne an
Ja, das Meer ist blau, so blau – und das geht ja auch noch lang
Ja, das Meer ist blau, so blau, ja, das Meer ist blau, so blau
Ja, das Meer ist blau, so blau, das Meer ist blau.'

Sham did not flicker. She continued to sing to him. There was no response. It was then that she suspected that all was not well. His body was raced to the clinic at St Tropez where that establishment's most specialised resources were dedicated to his revivescence. Shocks, stimulations and injections were administered. Every effort was made to induce Shilverman to throb again. Even Sanskrit mantras were chanted to trick the great film-maker into consciousness. Finally, at six o'clock the following morning, when all else had failed (he had been unofficially dead for ten hours), a tape of selected music from his films was vibrated through anal electrodes along his cortex to the Shilverman skull. For six hours, the magical music haunted the cold landscape of his cerebral chamber. At noon, the physicians reluctantly reported to Medusa O'Toole that there was no perceptible change in his condition. She was outraged. Somewhere, somebody important had goofed. A balls-up of cosmic proportions. While a team of embalmers kicked their heels outside his private suite of rooms, waiting restlessly to eviscerate and preserve him, Medusa railed against the injustice of fate. She cursed Gaia, threatening to chuck the effigy of the Earth Mother back into the sea. She badmouthed every god, prophet and religion she could remember. Blear-eyed and sobbing, she adjusted to the grey reality of the situation by laying into Sham's corpse for fucking off midway through a film. A thoroughly unprofessional thing to do.

'Sham, you unfeeling bastard,' she screamed with the resonant despair of star-quality sadness.

It was Joe Spillano, in his role of oldest friend, who eventually persuaded her to leave the clinic, giving a discreet nod to the doctors to throw the support machinery switches. The embalmers moved in with their gutting-knives and pickling fluids.

Shilverman, spotlit in his beige tux and polished dancing-pumps, pink, blond and glitter-eyed, looking fifty years younger than he did when the end came, was back in the L'Amauresque ballroom before the celebrations for his ninety-fifth birthday had ended. He was propped up in a white satin armchair, an unlit Castro de Luxe between the index and second fingers of his right hand, the left tucked in his jacket pocket. He was protected from dirt and destruction by a membrane of insect-repellent and curiosity-proof plastic. A slot-machine designed to dispense instant Shilverman eyelid and mouth movements had been planned. It was ambitiously hoped that this would combine the science of modern mummification with a state-of-the-art display of electronic animation techniques.

If Wolfgang Ferrari's disappearance into the Adriatic had generated problems for the proposed production of *Love Is the End*, Sham Shilverman's death effectively sidelined Medusa as a movie-star for the first time since she had made her debut in Sham's *The Waltzing Werewolves* (1918). Her faith in a Supreme Being that she could roll dice with had evaporated into a Pyrrhonic mist.

'I reckon,' she remarked to Sunburn during a long-distance call to Venice, 'that we could turn L'Amauresque into a very classy whore-pit again.'

He made sympathetic noises.

'It's a funny thing you said that, Grandma.'

Chapter 42

The funeral was a modest and dignified affair. The walnut casket was no more than three feet long. It contained the Shilverman brain, organs, entrails, osseous fragments, and appendages it would have been vaguely improper to preserve. Bimbo Braganza squeezed credible Bach-like fugues out of the electric organ, the ebony choir hummed with valedictory restraint, and Pablo Fecundo de Laprida, alias Rama Ringaroo, the Nicaraguan messiah (who had decided to go into business on his own account), read from the *Mahabharata* in Spanish. Medusa was subdued but not bitter. She had at last accepted that an irreversible mistake had been made but wished that she could get her hands around the Creator's throat.

Yet, just a week after Shilverman's incineration, Medusa O'Toole's life took an unexpected and exhilarating turn. She opened the unread report that Sham had been sent by Spermtrek. Sham, ignorant of Medusa's earlier live birth, had been driven by a torment of jealousy to dicover the true begetter of the foetal Gertrude. Claudine Zola's document disclosed that the father of Gertrude was Joe Spillano. Medusa, aware of the cyclical arithmetic, had suspected this all along. There was confirmation of Sham's infertility, a condition embarrassingly well-evidenced by over five hundred sperm tests to which he had submitted himself over fifty years. The conclusions were all the same. Dud spunk. But that stark and simple fact Sham had not been able to accept. He deluded himself that, given enough vibrant spurts in the right direction, he could, deo volente, confound the clinicians and generate a rogue spermatozoon that would not only complete the fallopian voyage with the pizzazz of a Humboldt but *PING* an unsuspecting egg. And that improbable expectation nourished Sham's dreams until he drew his final breath.

It was, however, the details of Medusa's *live* birth in the same report that set her tingling with excitement. The infant had survived. The adult it had become was alive and well. The news raced around her head, again and again. She gave an irritated frown at Clay McHutchinson's deathbed deposition. The unspeakable shit had claimed fatherhood. A picture of a white-haired Clay, blind, deformed by arthritis and demented by GPI was included. She suspected the icy hand of the Terrastricken Intelligence Agency. Clay was probably part of a conspiracy to protect Tusker Ruseveldt. It amused her to realise that Spermtrek had got this one wrong. Five million dollars and they had cocked up the seeding arrangements. It was a warm and heartening thought. She took her copy of *Shining Hours* off the shelf and opened it at the bookmark that had been there for longer than she cared to remember. A postcard of a thick-set man with a walrus moustache, gold spectacles and a white stetson. He sat imperiously astride a prancing palomino. Tusker Ruseveldt, the President of Terrastricken. The guy she knew as Uncle Moose. She closed her eyes and seventy years were sucked up the scuthole of time.

Strong cigars, sweet-smelling pomade and creaky leather. Wheezy Uncle Moose. He unslotted his brass belt-knuckle, shimmied his trousers down to his knees, unlaced grey flannelette long johns and came at her with his fat pink salami. Stubby fingers of his right hand curled around it protectively.

'Up those legs a mite, girly. Ah ha. Let Uncle Moose have a squint at the gate of life. Oh my, you pretty little cuntypoo.'

And then he was there, wheezing and pushing. Just the ticking of the clock. More wheezing. Samson barking. Chickens clucking. A minute, maybe two. Rubbing away on the sighing bed. Squishy squish. There. A little more patience. A cough. Off the bed and buckling up. She sat up, closing her parted legs with a sweet, modest movement (part of a remembered dance shuffle), managing to catch a glimpse of him scuttling out of the door, stetson askew. On the chair lay the presents. A box of peppermints, lingerie and the pouch with a hundred silver dollars. No sooner had Uncle Moose cantered away than Clay loitered in. He was invariably a little laconic and sheepish after one of the visits.

'He's left the stuff, then?'

'Yuh. On the rocking-chair there.'

'You want to?'

'Now?'

'Why ever not? For Jeez sakes. I am yer regular beau, ain't I?'

'Oh shit, Clay. Pass me a peppermint cream first.'

'I don't want you munching that stuff when I'm French-kissing you.'

'I really want a peppermint cream, Clay.'

'Spoiled l'il bitch.'

'Wha?'

'You heard me. Spoiled l'il bitch. Spoiled l'il bitch.'

Medusa had relived the birth a thousand times. The red, crinkled, black-haired girl that had slithered out of her. She examined a yellowed newspaper cutting with the story that five of the Estrelitas, daring gipsy acrobats, had died in a caravan-fire near Rodez. But the child, Lola, had survived. In her reveries, she had always thought of the baby as Annushka-Marie. That was her make-believe name. The name she shared with nobody. She bought a doll and gave her that name, uttering it in the dark when her door was locked. But she guessed that Lola would have to do. She repeated the name to herself several times. The statement from Spermtrek was unambiguous. Lola was living in England. An address and telephone number were provided. This was worth every cent of Sham's five million dollars. He could not have bequeathed her a more magical present. She poured herself a large cognac. It was not her usual style to crank herself up with booze, but the experience she now faced made her shake with excitement. It had been seventy years since that red, crinkled, black-haired girl had slithered out of her. What she was doing now was madness. But she dialled Mushington Hall anyway. It rang just four times. Mrs Bagshawe answered. She had to think for a moment before she realised who Lola was.

'You mean Princess Lola d'Aoili-Flute of Esterel and Lhasa?'

Medusa O'Toole trembled.

'I think so.'

While she waited anxiously for her daughter, who was completing her business in the outside privy, a police mug-shot of Leaky Lola, accidentally caught up in the summary of expenses, fell at Medusa's feet. She picked it up, recognising the face instantly. Her feelings were wild and complicated. Yet, despite the shock of discovering Lola's unsavoury identity, the intoxication of finding her daughter persisted.

'It's Momma,' Medusa croaked, constricted with emotion.

Their conversation was prolix, arcane, convoluted, tearful, hysterical and tender, shot through with the magic of discovery, surprise, demency and extraordinary challenge to their expectations. They quickly established that they were acquainted with one another by reputation and sight. In a nutshell, Lola had slept with several of Medusa's friends, including the late Sham Shilverman. Medusa, of course, had the visibility of celebrity. Lola had whored around L'Amauresque in the days of Gaby La Mulatière and was gradually marginalised when Medusa began her promotion of an upmarket religious dimension. But street-walker or no street-walker, authentic children are difficult to come by for an eighty-five-year-old with a womb as unproductive as a petrified walnut. As their respective stories unfolded, Medusa resolved to be a good mother, and Lola a dutiful daughter. The revelation of her real papa's name suffused Lola with an immoderate pride. She was the natural daughter of a former President of Terrastricken, no less. The thought made her purr, and instantly relinquish her psychic rights in the obscure gipsy dispensation that only dreamers, poets and lunatics recognised.

'I'm sorry Papa's dead,' she sighed.

'I never knew him that well,' Medusa admitted.

'It would have been glorious being able to reside in the Grey House, if only for a miserable presidential term,' Lola observed wistfully.

'His good lady might have objected to our presence, sweetheart.'

'Oh, how I detest stuffy people,' Lola sniffed.

'I have a nice postcard of your papa. A well-set-up sort of fellow with a walrus moustache, gold spectacles and white stetson, riding a prancing palomino.'

'I'll use that to commission a painting of him to hang over the mantelpiece. Pictures of men on horseback give a room a touch of dignity.'

Lola reflected sentimentally on her genesis. Somewhere in the whoosh of a particular Tusker Ruseveldt ejaculation (was the sky blue, were the birds singing, the clock ticking and the smell of home baking percolating through the house?) swam her wonderful progenitor, a miniature Buster Crabbe splashing up a crocodile-infested Limpopo. The sudden certainty of her fatherhood made her see sperm in a new light. It was sad that she'd never treated that primal fluid with the respect it merited. What she hadn't accepted passively into the labyrinthine lacunae of her body, she had ingested as a neo-dietary substance, according the metaphysical stuff no more importance than a slurp of yogurt or a gobful of cottage cheese. Not to speak of those lost tribes that were soaked up by nightgowns, peignoirs, pyjamas, handkerchiefs, knickers, Y-fronts, sheets, counterpanes, socks, shirts, towels, mattresses, Kleenexes and even the shag of household and hotel carpets. It would be salutary for those who took spermal streams for granted, to have access to a microscope. To meditate on those millions of heart-rending wigglies. A universe of abortive endeavour. They were dark and pensive thoughts.

As they spoke, Medusa O'Toole's grandson, sipping his matutinal goat's milk in a suite of the Excelsior Palace Hotel on the Lungomare Marconi in Venice, was sharing three decisions he had made with his friend Basin Sorel, who was having a morning tub.

The first was that Sunburn was going to phone his mama that morning and confess that he was the sender of the yellow roses every day.

'Isn't life wonderful?' called Basin. 'I feel as though she was my mama as well.'

314

The second decision was that he planned to set up house in Honkeyville with his mama, grandma and Basin.

'What about L'Amauresque?' asked Basin, soaping his hunkers.

'Polly Ferrari is quite capable of handling that,' Sunburn declared.

Finally, he planned to hunt down and total Laszlo Gabor himself.

'Wouldn't that prejudice your status as a Financially Sterile Entity, darling?' asked Basin.

'Not if I eliminated any witnesses at the same time,' Sunburn reflected, wagging his head to the barely audible strains of a Gagliano motet.

'Isn't it incredible,' said Medusa to her daughter, 'that my grandson, your eldest boy, happens to be a dear friend of mine. I have known him since he was an infant, without realising that he was my flesh and blood. The world, my dear, is no larger than a creaking bed.'

Lola's heart missed a beat.

'I have only one son. A young man who I adopted called Tom.'

'But were you not impregnated by the most powerful cock in Italy?'

Lola shivered with apprehension.

'I lost that child swimming in the Mediterranean years ago.'

'But he was found on the Plage de Pamplemousse. Your boy. My grandson.'

Tears welled up in Lola's eyes.

'Could it be the person who sends me yellow roses? The card appeared to be vaguely indecent. I imagined it was some guy coming on strong.'

'That's your son,' Medusa laughed.

'I can hardly believe this wonderful news,' Lola murmured.

'His name,' Medusa announced, 'is Sunburn Spillano.'

'My God.'

'What's the matter?'

'Ah,' Lola breathed in wonder. 'He's the beautiful guy I met at the Dunkelbaums.'

'I've been trying to ring him all morning, but I understand he's not back from Venice where he went with his lover, Basin Sorel,' Medusa informed her.

'Is my boy gay?' asked Lola with interest.

'It is hardly an appropriate way to describe Sunburn. Taciturn would be more accurate. Even morose. But he's militantly homophilic, if that's what you mean.'

'I was not entirely certain whether I'd screwed with him or not. Not that I disapprove of incest, but it's rather pointless breaking the rules if you're unaware when you're doing it. Sin should always be a conscious act. Otherwise how can you appreciate the guilt?'

'Lola darling,' Medusa interrupted, fearful that her daughter was becoming too theological for comfort, 'I insist you fly out to your momma immediately; or at least in time for lunch tomorrow. I'll arrange for little Sunburn to be here as well.'

Lola nodded happily, feeling more important than she ever had before. The family, she reflected, was a sort of sacrament.

'OK, Momma.'

She replaced the receiver. The phone rang immediately.

'Is that the Princess Lola d'Aoili-Flute of Esterel and Lhasa?' came a Venetian, female voice.

'That is correct.'

'I have a personal call for you from a Signor Sunburn Spillano.'

She waited, almost faint with joy.

'Mama?' came a rich baritone.

'Sunburn,' she whispered, her face drenched in tears.

Chapter 43

Ever since the voyage of the *Voracité*, Laszlo had begun to experience hazy withdrawals from reality. His doctor had suggested psychiatric counselling, prescribed tranquillisers and recommended exercise. Swimming, squash, that sort of thing, the physician urged, regarding him through unperceptive eyes. He appeared to be talking horseshit. Laszlo chatted to a Catholic priest, who gave him a booklet on doctrinal matters and sold him a rosary. And that seemed to be more horseshit. Then in a pub near Leicester Square he met a young man called Ferdie, who was helpful. Ferdie was lanky, fair-haired and nervously restless. He had blue owlish eyes and drummed the table a great deal with his fingers. He promised Laszlo that he could fix him up with some rather special medication. Laszlo listened.

'Are you a doctor?' Laszlo asked.

'The best,' Ferdie replied with assurance.

He informed Laszlo that what he had was a despair management problem and that all he needed was to find a reality with which he was more comfortable. Laszlo nodded. The pills he provided didn't come cheap, but Ferdie declared that they were only slightly hallucinatory and reasonably non-addictive.

'The accepted wisdom,' Ferdie told him, 'is that you shouldn't combine the stuff with alcohol. But that is, in my opinion, the most effective way to use them.'

'Isn't that dangerous?' Laszlo asked, realising that it was a foolish question when he saw the scorn in Ferdie's big eyes.

'What's danger?' Ferdie laughed. 'I'm afraid you're going to have to rush a few fences if you want to get away. Crash through the big bastards. Scratch yourself.'

Ferdie was right. Only the forbidden combination of the green and white pills and alcohol seemed to lift him. He placed two of the mind-benders in his mouth and washed them down with a gulp of Glenfiddich. Sanity leeched through his brain like cleansing acid. He grabbed his brief-case and set off towards Bond Street station.

He had wasted a day at the shop waiting for Polly's promised phone-call and tried to reach her himself without success. He decided he would have just enough time to pick up his car from the garage, phone Princess Lola, visit the Ataxerxes Cellar at Finchley for a Psito Octopodi and pitta, and drive down for the ten o'clock ferry crossing at Dover. He had to see Polly as soon as possible. There were many questions to be answered. He bought an *Evening Standard* and hurried in the direction of the escalator, settling behind a fat, bearded man trying to read the *Herald Tribune*. From the step above him came a mellifluous chirruping from two girls with almond eyes and baggy black trousers, using an avian tongue he regretted he could not comprehend. He referred to the share-listings and checked three of his recent punts that seemed to have stuck in the shallows. Up a point. Down a point. He yawned, feeling light-headed, and then as though he was being energised by the movement of the escalator. The step vibrated below his feet as the belt rumbled around. 'It's like the wheel of life,' Maya had once joked. She hated the end of the escalator where she feared her shoes might be trapped in the steel teeth. She called it the point where the day of human existence passed into the night of waiting for the soul, never failing to give a little squeak of alarm as she jumped to safety. He remembered an illustration in a Victorian boys' encyclopaedia Maya had picked up for him at a jumble sale when he was ten. In the section 'The Miracle of Modern Transport' were several drawings of the London Underground system, one of which depicted the construction of the revolutionary moving staircase. A gush of air laden with warm oil, perspiration and paint thinners ruffled his hair as he reached the bottom.

He was uncertain whether it was the ikons set along the walls at intervals of ten spaces or so, of a slender, white-lipped blonde, mahogany-brown and expensive, advertising hair-spray, or the snub-nosed, ash-haired gamin in torn jeans playing Fauré's 'Papillon' on an echoing fipple-flute, that had disinterred a

318

buried memory of being with Maya in that very spot as a child. The texture of that perception was so powerful that it evoked the smell of her woollen cardigan and the pressure of her hand on his child-head. Why hadn't she told him the truth? he brooded, picturing her as an astonished face, Gaspar caught in the act of unbuttoning her white, swan-skin pyjamas, perched on the bed and leaning across her. The tenderness in those blue eyes and the gentlest reproof on her lips.

'Laszlo, my love. You should knock before rushing in.'

One breast with its brown Mickey Mouse nose revealed, her hand moving up to draw the jacket together. Gaspar's knowing smile when Laszlo came in. He estimated that he must have been three. No more than that. Of course, Maya was not in any way like Polly, who not only had abandoned him as an infant but had betrayed him as a man. And he recognised the dark nature of his own complicity in what had been done on the *Voracité*. Quite simply, he had lusted after her body, using it for making love to a dream. A dangerous pursuit of an improbable idea. The confusion of shadow for reality. He was suddenly conscious of his revulsion for Polly, but it was the purgative power of that feeling that astonished him. He felt exhilarated, then just as quickly subdued by the bizarre thought of submitting himself to judgement. Judgement? He had always regarded judgement as the ultimate joke. However, the uncomfortable thought persisted.

Laszlo had never enjoyed travelling under the ground. As a boy, when he was in between stations, he imagined that he was in a time-capsule, locked forever with the strangers who shared his compartment. Fortunately, forever didn't last too long. He liked to memorise the stations and closed his eyes as the train rattled along, opening them to check whether he was where he thought he was, when the train stopped. It was bad luck to peep in between stops, which he nevertheless did at times; when he felt particularly reckless or had a compulsion to defy fate. Now he found himself playing the game again. Would there be time, he wondered, for an interrogation before Baker Street?

'I tossed my father in the Adriatic, Inspector.'

'Oh yes, sir?'

'And then I fucked my mother.'

'Dear, dear. You really appear to have got yourself in a little deep, sir.'

'Of course, Inspector, at the time I didn't know the gentleman I threw overboard was my father, or the lady I was giving it to was my mum.'

'A traditional Oedipal defence, is it, sir?'

'I'd like to think that they were extenuating circumstances, Inspector.'

'Ah. As that jolly little gent on *The Brains Trust* used to say, it all depends what you mean by extenuating.'

'Well, even Oedipus wasn't fellated during his formative years in Corinth, was he, Inspector?'

'I don't believe Sophocles alluded to it, sir.'

'I was, Inspector. When I was no more than eleven.'

'Child abuse is extremely common in the Home Counties, sir.'

'But this was SE19, Inspector.'

'Goodness gracious. I would have hoped that our metropolitan standards South of the River were slightly more elevated than that.'

'Were you ever fellated as a boy, Inspector?'

'No, sir. I was an adult when I came to that particular dispensation. Twenty-eight. Twenty-nine. Perhaps even thirty. And I'm sorry to confess that the lady-person who did the job wasn't my good wife. Maud, you see, is a vegan and so is at a disadvantage taking meat in any form, sir.'

The compartment filled up at Baker Street. He resisted a feeling of claustrophobia by sneaking another couple of pills into his mouth. He was comforted, though, by the sound of angels using a German-accented English as the train rattled out of Swiss Cottage. He peeped. The two angels hung over him. They had no wings. One was a tall, heavy-lidded creature with a gingery Sweet Adeline moustache and Dundrearies, and the other a pretty cherubim with rose-pink lips and dark curves of pre-razored fluff across his upper lip. He was about sixteen. They were both in three-piece brown suits with soft hats to match.

'It's my conviction, Papa,' the sixteen-year-old angel said, 'that our people cornered the market in tricky genes five thousand years ago.'

320

'Those kind of generalisations make me nauseous, Max.'

'Look, Papa, there could be a commercial niche sometime in the next century for a gene wholesaling enterprise. Maybe gene retail outlets too, in our more important conurbations. A whole new industry could evolve. Gene counsellors, gene designers, gene compatibility specialists, gene brokers and even gene security agents.'

'As Momma said, you're a chronic neophiliac. Why can't you live in the here-and-now, Max?'

'Because I want to get to the then-and-there before the competition, Papa.'

'We're all prisoners of time, Max. Like the galley-slaves in *Les Misérables*. Keep pulling on the oars and we'll all make it together.'

'I'm going to escape, Papa.'

'You were always a troublemaker, Max.'

'This one is Finchley, Papa.'

'Already?'

Laszlo found a phone-box and rang Princess Lola. There was no reply. Where the hell had she gone, he wondered, remembering they had given the Bagshawes the week off. He went into a pub and ordered a large malt, swallowing two more capsules before returning to the phone-box. He tried Polly again. This time she answered. He knew now that he had the secret of dealing with all the shit. Ferdie was right. Strength and certainty surged through his body. He told her that he had been thinking of going to the police. There was silence for about a minute. He laughed to himself, enjoying the beauty of the traffic on the Finchley Road as he scratched his balls. He looked around, smiling at everyone, thinking about the wonderful angels who had got on at Swiss Cottage. God, how he adored those angels.

'Polly?'

'I'm still here,' she said. Her voice was icy.

'Well, what about it, Polly darling?' he called, winking at an Indian girl waiting for a bus.

His pubes felt on fire. He scratched away, slipping a hand down the front of his trousers. The girl turned away. Polly was saying something. She seemed to be talking too slowly. Like a gramophone record playing at the wrong speed. He needed to quicken everything up.

'Talk faster,' he shouted.

'What?'

Dumb bitch, he thought, momentarily angry, then suddenly easy in his mind. He felt relaxed. A red omnibus filled with people stopped. It was the most beautiful thing he'd seen in his life.

'I think going to the police would be needlessly provocative,' she said.

Jesus, she sounded cold. Why hadn't he realised before that she was the Snow Queen?

'There was another guy apart from Papa,' he giggled.

'What?'

'It was a funny. I said Papa instead of Wolfgang. Joke, OK?'

'You've been drinking.'

'Not too much,' he laughed. 'It really is very nice in London right now. As I said, there was another man. A harmless little fellow called Selveratnam.'

'Selveratnam?'

'Yes, he was Maya's fiancé.'

'What happened?'

'I killed him as well.'

Laszlo told Polly the story, informing her that he'd buried the Tamilian's body under a cherry tree at Mushington Hall.

'I think,' she said, 'that it would do no harm for us to discuss your options before your next move is made.'

'I don't give a fuck about options, Polly,' he said gaily.

'Tom darling,' she said, 'there's no harm in waiting another day, is there?'

'Listen,' he said, 'my name is Laszlo. Laszlo Gabor. OK?'

As he listened to her pleading voice, he knew that he never wanted to see Polly again.

'Goodbye, Polly darling,' he sneered.

'Tom? Laszlo?'

There was a fear, almost panic, in the manner in which she articulated his names.

Laszlo collected his Mercedes and drove to the Ataxerxes Cellar for a meal. He sat by himself near the window, at peace and warmed by his new contentment. He considered many things. How he'd defiled the name of the man whose name he'd appropriated. Lah lah. Lah lah. The beautiful man with a broken face who had pined for him. He decided to visit Ada and Aurora before he gave himself up.

After the meal, he drove to Ada's place. A West Indian woman answered the door. She told him that her family had been living in the flat for three months and that she had no idea where Mrs Mulcahy was. He went downstairs to his vehicle, sitting for a while in the dark, smoking and listening to the sounds of children playing.

When he got back to an empty Mushington Hall, it was already nine o'clock. He made several phone-calls to acquaintances of Ada's. Daisy Mercury from the Sunshine Home informed him that they had been seen tramping around London with a pram filled with old clothes.

'I believe,' she sniffed, 'that they're begging and sleeping rough.'

Laszlo took two more green and white pills and poured himself a stiff malt. When he went upstairs, he fell across his bed. He desperately wanted to see Maya, but she didn't appear. Then he saw Selveratnam coming through the door, the bison-skin case in his hand.

'They've come for you, Laszlo,' the little man warned.

'Who?'

'The men out there in the night,' Selveratnam said.

Laszlo went to the window. The garden was flooded with light. He detected figures of men moving from visibility in the penumbra into the blackness of the shrubbery and back again. Sunburn Spillano in a long dark coat and a big hat walked into the light.

'Hi, Sunburn,' Laszlo shouted cheerfully.

Spillano did not look up. A mechanical digger moved into place, biting a chunk out of the lawn. The cherry tree was plucked out by its roots. Men now walked around the hole where the cherry tree once had been. He thought he could see what appeared to be fragments of Maya's carpet-bag. And then he saw something blue sparkling in a mound of upturned clay that he suspected was the remains of Selveratnam's body. The blue stone had an astonishing glitter. Spillano stepped forward and picked it up, holding it before him for all to see. Its refracted light twinkled through the night.

'Well done, Sunburn,' Laszlo called.

Once again, Spillano did not acknowledge his presence. The son of the most powerful cock in Italy strutted towards the building, giving orders. Laszlo saw a petrol-tanker drive into the light. A hose was connected and unfurled towards the house. Laszlo watched with calm and without fear. He could hear the swish of liquid on carpets and furniture. The smell of petrol vapour filled the bedroom. He could, he decided, climb down the observatory tower at the other end of the building. He felt an audacious certainty about his ability to escape from Spillano.

Laszlo ran out of the bedroom and along the corridor to the door that led to the tower stairway. He climbed quickly to the top. Unlatching a window-light, he broke the glass around it to contrive an aperture large enough to pass through. He stepped out into the cold night air and made his way around the narrow parapet, cutting his hand on the jagged glass as he steadied himself. He felt sharp and crazily happy, sensing Selveratnam's presence behind him. He looked around, but there was nobody there.

'It won't be too bad, Laszlo,' the little man appeared to be saying, although there was no voice, just a gusting wind that lifted his shirt.

A searchlight blinded him at the moment he found some purchase on a ledge below the overhang of the parapet and his hand secured his descent on a granite fleur-de-lys. They had set the house alight. He felt the heat of the fireball through the broken observatory window as he worked himself to the dark side of the tower for his progress downward. A crackling of burning wood. Showers of sparks streamed across the garden over the perimeter escarpment into a nearby wood. He had always been good at climbing. Scraping his face against the brickwork as he slid around a corner, Laszlo half-turned when he heard a woman call his name. He peered down into the darkness, clutching for his next support. But the gargoyle that he gripped crumbled in his hand. He fell sideways. A woman stepped into the red light from the fire, her arms outstretched and her wild face raised towards him. It was Laszlo Gabor's final vision before he broke Ada Mulcahy's neck.

CUT ......

YOU GODFORSAKEN MOTHERFUCKER ......

CUT ......

Chapter 44

He was never quite persuaded whether he was where he was supposed to be. There were, for sure, some subliminal aspects in his remembrance of other times. The mushy path beneath bare feet, mucilage squelching between apprehensive toes, whiskery filaments brushing his questing snout as he savoured the truffle-scented vapours of secret places. A rodentine homunculus, palpitant, receptor of conchyliated whispers from inner lagoons, swelling like a blowfish to exquisite vibrations that set his spine tingling like a dulcimer.

Yet he was fearfully aware of what he imagined were unpleasant alternatives: the slurp of oars across water, heart-beats, sucking, breathy moans, a tinny alarm-clock, kisses, doors opening and closing, children crying, voices from other rooms, metallic coughs, a woman singing, creaking springs, dogs barking and the distant crowing of an uncertain cock, a mosaic of sounds that menaced him with a reality he found difficult to confront.

He slid, then slid again, confounded by sunlight, yellow and hot, streaming across the architecture of marmoreal thighs. He tensed quickly back, reflexing like a snail into the cleft, only to slither finally downward, articulating in his pith screams of despair that would never be heard. And falling again, inexorably towards an unknown beginning.

Luton
October 1990

The Seeding Arrangements

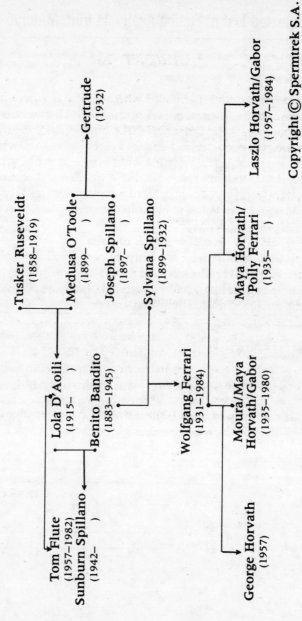

Tusker Ruseveldt
(1858–1919)

Medusa O'Toole
(1899–)

→ Gertrude
(1932)

Joseph Spillano
(1897–)

Sylvana Spillano
(1899–1932)

Lola D'Aoili
(1915–)

Benito Bandito
(1883–1945)

Tom Flute
(1957–1982)

Sunburn Spillano
(1942–)

Wolfgang Ferrari
(1931–1984)

Maya Horvath/
Polly Ferrari
(1935–)

Laszlo Horvath/Gabor
(1957–1984)

Moura/Maya
Horvath/Gabor
(1935–1980)

George Horvath
(1957)

A Selected List of Fiction Available from Minerva

While every effort is made to keep prices low, it is sometimes necessary to increase prices at short notice. Mandarin Paperbacks reserves the right to show new retail prices on covers which may differ from those previously advertised in the text or elsewhere.

The prices shown below were correct at the time of going to press.

☐	7493 9145 6	**Love and Death on Long Island**	Gilbert Adair	£4.99
☐	7493 9130 8	**The War of Don Emmanuel's Nether Parts**	Louis de Bernieres	£5.99
☐	7493 9903 1	**Dirty Faxes**	Andrew Davies	£4.99
☐	7493 9056 5	**Nothing Natural**	Jenny Diski	£4.99
☐	7493 9173 1	**The Trick is to Keep Breathing**	Janice Galloway	£4.99
☐	7493 9124 3	**Honour Thy Father**	Lesley Glaister	£4.99
☐	7493 9918 X	**Richard's Feet**	Carey Harrison	£6.99
☐	7493 9028 X	**Not Not While the Giro**	James Kelman	£4.99
☐	7493 9112 X	**Hopeful Monsters**	Nicholas Mosley	£6.99
☐	7493 9029 8	**Head to Toe**	Joe Orton	£4.99
☐	7493 9117 0	**The Good Republic**	William Palmer	£5.99
☐	7493 9162 6	**Four Bare Legs in a Bed**	Helen Simpson	£4.99
☐	7493 9134 0	**Rebuilding Coventry**	Sue Townsend	£4.99
☐	7493 9151 0	**Boating for Beginners**	Jeanette Winterson	£4.99
☐	7493 9915 5	**Cyrus Cyrus**	Adam Zameenzad	£7.99

All these books are available at your bookshop or newsagent, or can be ordered direct from the publisher. Just tick the titles you want and fill in the form below.

Mandarin Paperbacks, Cash Sales Department, PO Box 11, Falmouth, Cornwall TR10 9EN.

Please send cheque or postal order, no currency, for purchase price quoted and allow the following for postage and packing:

UK including BFPO
£1.00 for the first book, 50p for the second and 30p for each additional book ordered to a maximum charge of £3.00.

Overseas including Eire
£2 for the first book, £1.00 for the second and 50p for each additional book thereafter.

NAME (Block letters) ....

ADDRESS ....

....

☐ I enclose my remittance for ....

☐ I wish to pay by Access/Visa Card Number

Expiry Date